I wish to thank John Baugh, assistant professor of linguistics, the University of Texas, for his time and help.

I also wish to thank the patient librarians at the Temple Public Library who have helped me so much through the years.

Most of all, I wish to thank my mother and father, without whose memories about East Texas and rural life in the early 1900's, I would never have been able to write this book.

* Chapter 1 *

Luke Turner's hands gripped the wooden handles of the plow, his arm muscles bulging with the effort of keeping the plow in place as he followed the two-mule team. The plow's half shovel attachment bit into the ground, peeling back the black earth, breaking it up for him to return with the plowshare and make furrows.

The sun lay warm on his back, and the fresh smell of newly cut earth filled his nostrils. Luke loved the land, loved it more than anything except Sarah and their child. He found a deep, primitive pleasure in feeling the earth in his hands and beneath his feet and a welling pride as he imagined the green shoots coming up in the spring and the tall corn and the thick white cotton bursting its hard bolls at harvest time. He even loved the sweat and the backbreaking work that stretched his body to the limit.

The land was good anytime—in the heat of summer, in the winter lying fallow, at harvest—but the best of all was now: spring, when everything was beginning, when he sank his plow into the fertile earth and started the growing process all over again. The days were warm, not yet mercilessly hot as they would be in summer. The trees were flowering and turning green with buds. In the pasture and along the rise behind the house, the spring flowers were thrusting up from the earth—deep purplish blue bluebonnets and blazing orange red Indian paintbrush, yellow buttercups, wild daisies, and pale pink evening primroses. The world seemed new and sweet, and anything was possible. Luke was filled with the strength and promise of the land, as full of rising life as the trees and plants.

He reached the end of a row and turned the team. He paused, wiping back his hair from his forehead. His hair was damp with sweat and clung to his forehead and neck. Even though the day was mild, he was hot from the daylong effort of holding the plow in place. The muscles of his arms and back ached. He glanced at the sun. It was getting late, and soon Sarah would start worrying. He would finish this row and go home, or else Sarah might take it into her head to come looking for him. He didn't want her putting herself out in her condition.

Luke clucked to the team, and they cut another row, then started for home. When they reached the barn, he unharnessed the team and turned them loose in the corral. He started toward the house, then stopped and gazed at it for a moment, truly looking at it instead of merely accepting it as part of his life and routine. He saw afresh the old house, two stories tall, repainted white just last fall, with green shutters at the windows. A small porch and three steps led down from the side door into the yard, and, only partially visible from this angle, another porch ran the length of the front, with a swing for sitting in and a trellis of honeysuckle sheltering one end.

Sarah's grape arbor stood in the back; soon it would be leafed out and cool inside. Not far beyond it was a huge oak tree, still bare of leaves. Its massive trunk split into two about four feet from the ground, and one trunk curved down and out, spreading across the yard. In the summer its deep shade was the coolest place on the farm. There was a pear tree, already showered with white blossoms, and two small peach trees that he'd planted three years ago. A bright yellow forsythia bush and Sarah's jonquils bloomed along the side of the house. More fruit trees grew in front, and down close to the road was the chinaberry tree where he'd stood that morning he first came to work here, shivering and coatless, watching the lit-up windows. Then Sarah had come out and called him inside.

A child sat on the bottom step of the side porch, digging

in the dirt with a stick, her hair a spot of bright gold, glinting in the dying sun.

Luke's throat clogged with a pleasure so sweet and intense it was painful. This was his home. He hadn't ever thought to have a home, certainly not one like this. He had grown up in a sharecropper's shack, with no mother and a father who was worse than none at all. After that he had known only the harsh confines of prison. The first place that had ever been his, that he had really wanted to be, was here on the McGowan farm in the small room in the barn.

This house was a place out of his dreams, and it never ceased to amaze Luke that it was also his reality. It had taken over a year for him to stop thinking of it as the McGowan place, but as *his* home.

The child raised her head and saw him, and a grin burst across her face. "Daddy! Daddy!"

She ran toward him, her short legs pumping. As usual, there was mud on her white stockings, one shoe had come unbuttoned, and the ribbon in her hair was loose and flapping.

"Sweetcake!" Luke met her halfway and lifted her into the air, tossing her high over his head and setting her squealing with delight and laughter.

The side door opened and Sarah came out, shielding her eyes with her hands. "Luke." She smiled and started down the steps.

Luke settled Emily on his hip and went to the porch. "No. Don't come down."

Sarah shook her head, amused. "I'm not an invalid. I'm only six months along, you know."

"Still, no point in your going up and down any extra stairs."

Luke looked up at his wife from the foot of the stairs. She wore an old blue dress, faded by many washings and hours on the line, and the waist was loosened to accommodate her swelling body. Her thick brown hair was braided and coiled at the base of her neck severely, but around her face, soft strands had come loose and clung to her skin. She wasn't a beautiful woman, more pretty than anything else. But her translucent skin had the glow of pregnancy, and her cheeks were flushed with color from the heat of the kitchen. Her expressive hazel eyes shone, and she appeared to Luke to be the most breathtaking woman in the world.

Some said that Luke Turner worshiped the ground his wife walked on, and he guessed that was true. She was more than his wife, more than the woman he loved. She was the center of his existence, the bedrock on which everything else was founded. His life had been hard. He had known poverty and neglect. He had known the contempt of others, the humiliation of trial, and the awful helplessness of conviction for a crime he hadn't committed. But the one thing he had never known was love. Until Sarah.

She had given him trust, understanding, and compassion. She had given him free-flowing love and the sweet treasure of her heart, body, and mind. Luke knew he would love her until the day he died—and after, if that were possible.

Luke set Emily down and went up two steps, so that his head was on a level with Sarah's. He spread out his hand on her belly, as he often did, eager to feel the life within her. "How are you?"

"Fine." Sarah brushed back a lock of his damp hair. "How about you? Tired?"

"No. I'm fine." Trust Sarah, carrying a child and with all her work and a lively two-year-old to take care of, to be worrying about whether *he* was tired. "All I did was break some dirt."

He kissed her on the lips, meaning to give her only a peck, but her lips were so soft and inviting his mouth lingered. He thought about sliding his tongue across her lips, opening them, but decided he'd better not. Emily was right there, after all. He had the evening chores to do. And it would only make him want more what he couldn't have.

A small foot scraped across the wall of Sarah's abdomen beneath Luke's hand. Luke jumped, then grinned. "No need to ask how *he*'s doing." He tilted his head toward her stomach.

"No. He's doing very well."

Luke leaned forward to whisper in her ear, "And well he should be. He's living in the sweetest place on earth."

"Luke!" Sarah gave him a playful push, her cheeks burning even more brightly; but there was pleasure in her eyes, and her hand lingered for a moment against his chest.

Luke stepped back reluctantly, knowing that he ought to avoid temptation and not wanting to. "I have to do the chores."

Sarah nodded. "Supper'll be ready in a few minutes."

Luke turned and walked to the barn. Sarah remained on the porch, watching him. She liked to look at him walk. He moved with a loose, lean-hipped stride, his hands thrust into his back pockets. Below his rolled-up sleeves, the musculature of his arms was rock hard. Sarah knew well how he looked beneath the flannel shirt and worn denim, smooth and sleek and tough, without an ounce of extra flesh. She knew, too, the strength of his arms and legs and the tenderness of his hands. Sarah shivered. It always surprised her a little how much she wanted him, how easily desire for him came to her. Just the sight of him, just his whispered suggestive comment, just the feel of his breath against her ear, and she was as soft as putty, eager for his touch.

Sarah suspected that the hunger she had for her husband would shock most people. She was that nice Sarah McGowan, whose only reprehensible act had been to marry Luke Turner, from the trashy Turner family, a man who'd spent five years in Huntsville prison for rape.

Sarah's lips thinned. It still made her angry to think of what had been done to Luke—of the way he had been accused by a woman almost any man could have with no need for rape and then railroaded by indifference and life-long prejudice into a prison sentence. Neither Sarah nor her father had believed Tessa Jackson's story that Luke had raped her. She had been obviously pregnant at the trial; but Sarah was sure Tessa had claimed Luke raped her simply to escape the beatings of her wild-eyed fanatic of a father. People had believed (or chosen not to disbelieve) her story simply because Luke had had a bad reputation. He had drunk too much and had run with a bad crowd. He had beaten up Jimmy Banks at the Fourth of July dance one year. He had been constantly in trouble at school. He had spent his time with loose women, and there had been an aura of sexuality about him, a look of knowledge and experience far beyond his eighteen years. It had been easy to believe that Luke was a seducer of women—and how far was it from that to rape? He had bad blood, anyway; everybody had known that.

Only Sarah had seen the goodness in Luke. She hadn't believed that he had raped Tessa, and when he had been released from prison almost four years ago and her father had hired him on as a field hand, she had discovered Luke's kindness, loyalty, and hard-working nature. Gradually, layer after layer of the defiance and anger covering him had been stripped away, and Sarah had come to know the man inside, the essential core of goodness that had been twisted and tarnished by the years of scorn and defeat. When Sarah's parents had died, she had married Luke because it seemed the only way to remain on the farm she loved; but as the months passed, she had realized that she loved Luke. With each day for three years she had grown to love him more. Sarah could not imagine a life without Luke's love and strength. Without the sizzling desire he awakened in her.

"Mommy, Mommy." Emily tugged at her skirts, and Sarah pulled herself from her contemplation of her husband. "Wanna eat."

"Yes, dear. I know. Let's finish supper."

Sarah went inside, Emily at her heels. The kitchen smelled deliciously of apricots, which she had stewed this afternoon and made into fried tarts. She glanced at the half-moon tarts cooling on the counter and smiled to herself. Luke loved her apricot tarts, and she could guess how he would greet the tangy-sweet smell of the kitchen.

Sarah stirred the pots of black-eyed peas and turnips on the stove, then pulled open the oven door and peered inside. The sweet potatoes were browned and oozed trickles of syrup when she pierced them with a fork. Sarah removed them and pressed a finger against the baked cornbread. She shoved it back in to bake a little longer. After stirring the pots again, she began to set the table. Emily carried the utensils for her and laid half of them out in a haphazard fashion before she caught sight of the cat and was lured away. Sarah finished laying the places and added a dish of butter, the milk pitcher, and a jar of strawberry perserves. She pulled the pan of cornbread from the oven, sliced it into squares, and set them on a plate. She dished up the peas, turnips, and reheated remains of yesterday's pork roast and carried them all into the dining room.

Luke entered the kitchen and stopped, sniffing the air. A cat-that-ate-the-canary smile spread across his face. "I must have died and gone to Heaven. Apricot tarts."

He reached out toward the counter, and Sarah playfully swatted his hand. "Not until after supper."

"Yes," Emily piped up. "Mommy told me."

Luke chuckled. "I'm sure. Well, if you're going to be tough..." He went to the washstand and poured water from the large pitcher into the bowl to wash his hands and face. He joined Sarah and Emily in the dining room, where Sarah was filling Emily's plate and spreading her food out to cool. Luke slipped an arm around Sarah's waist and squeezed her. "You're the best wife in the world."

Sarah smiled and leaned into him. She wasn't, she knew, but she loved to hear him say it. And if she wasn't the best, she knew for sure that she was the happiest.

They sat down and bowed their heads, and Sarah said a quick grace. Then they dug into their food, eating with the simple hunger of people who had worked hard. They talked little at first except to request that something be passed, but as the first pangs of hunger were assuaged, Luke and Sarah began to chat about the day's events—small, ordinary things, nothing earth-shattering, but the essence of their world.

When the meal was over, Sarah brought out the plate of tarts and poured coffee for herself and Luke. She sat back and watched happily as Luke and Emily devoured the sweet fried pies.

"Mmmm, still warm."

"Enjoy them. That's the last of the dried apricots. No more until the new crop comes in."

"Then maybe I'll eat only two. Save the others for later."

Luke speared another one with his fork. "What's the matter? Aren't you having one?"

Sarah grimaced, one hand going to her stomach. "I've been eating too much. I've gained weight."

"You're supposed to."

"No. I mean, in other places." Sarah's fingers went to her cheeks, poking at the new fullness there.

"Nonsense." Luke cupped her face with his hands, his fingers caressing her cheeks. "You're beautiful."

Sarah's cheeks warmed with pleasure at the compliment. "You really think so? I look so awful and big . . ."

Luke's hand slid down her throat to the tender hollow above the collar of her dress. "You look perfect."

Sarah smiled. "Thank you."

Reluctantly Luke's hand left her skin. "I wish I could show how beautiful I think you are."

Sarah's breath came a little faster, and she glanced down at her lap. Luke's mere touch had sent a flush of desire through her body. It had been three weeks since they had made love, and she was hungry for him. She had always been thoroughly immodest and unladylike in her passion for her husband. One would think that when she was pregnant her body would be kind enough to lose its desire, but it seemed, perversely, that she felt it even more then. Nor did it help to know that Luke suffered as much as she. The flash of hunger in his eyes, the faint tremor of his fingers on her skin, the set of his full mouth that spoke of repressed desire—all called forth an answering passion in herself.

There were times when Sarah wondered if they really had to abstain; maybe their lovemaking wouldn't harm the baby. But last time, when she was carrying Emily, old Dr. Banks had expressly forbidden any congress between them, warning that it might hurt both Sarah and the baby. Sarah was willing to risk some hurt to herself, but she had to protect the baby. The farther along she was, the more danger there was to the child; so they had to be more careful now than they had been the first few months.

They had made it through the final three months last time without any lovemaking, Sarah reminded herself. Surely they could do it again. But somehow she didn't remember it being quite this difficult.

"I better get Emily cleaned up and into bed." That would help her avoid temptation. Sarah stood and held out her hand to her daughter. "Come on, sweetheart."

Luke watched them go, unable to keep his eyes off the gentle sway of his wife's skirts. He reached for a third tart and ate it. The taste was a poor substitute for Sarah's lips.

He carried the dishes in and stacked them in the sink for

Sarah, then poured himself another cup of coffee and stood at the side door, sipping it and looking out at the night. He could hear the murmur of Sarah's and the child's voices upstairs and occasionally a squeal of laughter from Emily. Luke smiled to himself. Life was a constant delight to Emily.

He set the half-finished coffee down on the counter and climbed the stairs to Emily's room. His daughter sat on the side of her bed, face freshly scrubbed, dressed in a long white nightgown, her hair neatly plaited into two short braids. Sarah was beside her, a large, colorfully illustrated book of Grimms' fairy tales open on her lap. She was reading, and Emily's eyes were wide with wonder. Luke lounged against the frame of the door. He had never heard the story; he had never heard any of the stories Sarah read and told to Emily. No one had ever read to him. But it made his chest swell with love to listen to Sarah reading the tales to their child. His daughter would know them, and she would know the love that lay behind the reading of them. She would never know the hunger, pain, and shame that he had grown up with, even if it killed him to keep them from her.

Sarah finished the story and glanced up at Luke. She smiled. She had heard him come to the door. He often stood there, watching their bedtime ritual, and she knew that it soothed him, that it somehow made up for what had been missing in his own childhood.

"Daddy!" Emily darted across the room and flung herself into Luke's arms. "Hug and kiss. Hug and kiss."

"Hug and kiss." He bussed her loudly on each cheek and on the mouth, then squeezed her to his chest. Emily wrapped her arms around his neck and hugged him tightly. "Break my neck," he growled, and she giggled and clung even harder.

Luke carried her to the bed and tossed her onto its feathery softness. Emily laughed uproariously. "Again. Again."

He shook his head, smiling. They both knew she would wheedle him into it, and she did. He tossed her onto the bed a second time, then she slipped out of bed to kneel beside Sarah and say a brief bedtime prayer. Sarah tucked her in, kissed her, and turned down the wick of the kerosene lamp until it went out. The pale white light of the full moon streamed through the window.

"Mr. Moon's big." Emily turned her head to gaze out the window at the night sky.

"Yes. He'll keep you company."

Emily nodded and pulled her rag doll tightly against her chest. Her eyelids were already wavering when they left the room. When they reached the kitchen and Sarah saw the dishes Luke had stacked in the sink, she smiled. "Thank you."

He shrugged. "You wash and I'll dry them."

"You don't need to do that. You've had a hard day in the fields."

"If I help, they'll be done sooner, and we can sit on the porch and look at Mr. Moon."

Sarah giggled. "All right."

They did the dishes in easy companionship, talking and joking as they worked. The love in Sarah's chest was enormous. Luke was one of a kind. There weren't many men who would help with "women's work" even when their wife was pregnant. But for all the toughness of Luke's reputation (sometimes deserved, Sarah admitted), with Sarah he was always considerate and gentle. Luke said that gentleness was something she had given him, but she knew that it had always been inside him.

Even with Luke helping, it wasn't quick or easy work, particularly scrubbing the large cast-iron pots and pans, and by the time they finished, Sarah's back ached. It was a relief to sit down in the swing on the front porch, and Sarah leaned back with a sigh.

"Tired?" Luke asked, and Sarah nodded. He put his arm around her shoulders, and she snuggled against him. His flannel shirt was soft beneath her cheek, and he smelled of earth, sweat, and skin, a familiar scent that never failed to stir her. Heat snaked through her abdomen.

Luke kissed the top of her head. She was warm and pliant against him. The air was thick with the scent of honeysuckle that adorned the trellis at the end of the porch, a sweet, heady odor that wrapped around Luke seductively. He wanted her.

He knew it was pure temptation to sit out here with Sarah

and look at the moon-washed yard, the scent of honeysuckle teasing at his nostrils, Sarah's body soft in his arms. But he loved it too much to avoid the temptation. There was nothing as sweet as holding his wife in his arms, nothing as bone-deep satisfying.

His right hand went down to her stomach and smoothed over its roundness. It never failed to fill him with awe to think of his seed resting inside her, growing to life. He felt the familiar surge of power in his loins. "Are you feeling all right?"

"Yes. A little tired, sometimes, but . . ." Sarah shrugged. Tiredness was a fact of farm life, especially in the spring and summer.

"When do you go to see Dr. Banks again?"

"A week from Saturday."

His hand curved around her belly again, protectively. He hated to think of Sarah's seeing that bastard Banks, hated to think of him touching her. He had despised Jimmy Banks for eleven years, ever since that rich kid from town had gotten Luke's sister Julia pregnant.

Luke hadn't even known Jimmy had been sneaking out to the Turner shack to see Julia until she had announced one day late in June that she was marrying Will Dobson. Dobson was a brutish sort, not nearly good enough for his sister, and he and Luke had disliked each other cordially. Dobson had been hanging around Julia for nearly a year, but she had clearly not welcomed his suit. It had been a shock when Julia decided to marry him, and Luke had questioned her about it until finally she had broken down and admitted that she was marrying Dobson only because she carried Jimmy Banks's child and had to give it a name.

Three days later, at the annual Fourth of July dance, Luke had found Jimmy Banks dancing with one of the "good girls" from town. He had charged up on the platform and started slamming his fists into Banks, and it was only because several men had seized Luke's arms and held him back that Luke hadn't beaten him up much worse than he did.

Of course, it hadn't changed anything. Luke had spent the night in jail. The town had gossiped about it for a few weeks. At the end of the summer, Jimmy had gone back to Tulane to school. And Julia was married to Will Dobson.

Julia lived near Gideon, in the next county, but Luke never saw her. Dobson had gotten his revenge by not allowing her to visit Luke or even attend his wedding. Luke had missed Julia. She had been his only real family. She had mothered him, and he had protected her from their father's worst rages. They had clung together for the only love and support either of them had known. Not being able to see her had added to his hatred of Jimmy Banks.

Banks, of course, was still to all appearances an exemplary person. He had graduated from Tulane, then from the Tulane medical school. He had lived for a long time in New Orleans, but a couple of years ago old Dr. Banks had died, and Jimmy, now Dr. James Banks, had returned to take over his father's practice.

Luke had managed to avoid Banks until a couple of months ago when Sarah had gone to him about her pregnancy. Luke didn't like the man being Sarah's doctor. Every time he saw Banks, the old bitterness curled in his stomach, eating at him. Luke was a different man now, however, not a hotheaded boy anymore, but a man in control of himself. No longer did the wildness take him; no longer did the pain and anger build up in him until he thought he had to hit somebody or burst from the force of it. Sarah needed a doctor; Luke wouldn't let her be attended by only a midwife. Because James Banks was the only doctor around for miles, she would see James Banks—no matter how much he disliked the man.

"Luke!" Sarah said in mild protest, and Luke glanced down at her, surprised at her tone.

He realized that his fingers were digging into her shoulder, and he relaxed them. "I'm sorry."

Sarah smiled. "It's all right. What were you thinking about? For a moment there, you looked all coiled up inside, like you used to."

Luke shook his head. "It was nothing. Just thinking . . ."

"About Dr. Banks?"

"I guess so."

"And your sister?"

"Yes."

"You miss her, don't you?"

"Yes." For a moment Luke's face was stern and sad, then he smiled down at her. "But I have you, and you're all the family I need. You and Emily." He patted her stomach gently. "And Bud, here."

"Bud?"

"Or do you think Sonny'd be a better name? Bubba, maybe?"

"No! Most definitely not." Playfully Sarah swatted his arm. "No son of mine is going to be Sonny or Buddy or any of those things!"

"No?" He grinned, his eyes devilishly alight.

"No."

"Well, what do you think, then? Daniel?"

Sarah tilted her head to one side. "Maybe." Her face grew serious. "You want a boy, don't you?"

"I'd like one." He put his hand under her chin and tilted her face up. "But don't you go thinking I wouldn't be happy with another girl. I would love a daughter. And there's always another time."

"Good." Sarah stretched up and kissed him lightly. It was the merest taste of her lips, and it left him wanting more.

Luke's hand moved to her throat, spreading out to caress the soft skin there. How fragile she was, how delicate. It seemed crazy that her very delicacy would make him want to crush her to him, to consume her, even as he wanted to protect her. Yet that was exactly how he felt.

He nuzzled her neck. She smelled faintly of the apricots she had stewed this afternoon, a tart, sweet scent that stirred him. Her flesh was soft against his lips. He opened his mouth on her skin and tasted it with his tongue.

Sarah made a soft moan, and her hands went to Luke's arms, digging into his shirt. "Oh, Luke. Do you think—do you think it would be so bad if we ignored what the doctor said, just this once?"

Startled, Luke lifted his head. Sarah's eyes were closed, her head lolling back against his arm, and her face was soft and slack with desire. Wrapped up in his own longings, it hadn't even occurred to him that Sarah might miss their lovemaking as much as he. "Oh, sweetheart." His hand slid down her throat and across her chest. He covered one of her breasts, and she made a noise deep in her throat and stirred. Her nipple was a hard point against his palm. "I never thought . . ."

He circled the nipple with his thumb, dreamily watching it thrust against the thin material of her dress. Sarah's hands moved to his hair, sinking into its thickness. His blood ran thick and hot in his veins. He wanted her desperately; it was madness to continue. But he couldn't resist pleasing her, satisfying her, at whatever cost to himself.

His hands went to the front of her dress, trembling a little as they unfastened her buttons. Sarah's eyes flew open in surprise, and a smile crept across her mouth. "Luke."

He smiled back, his mouth full and sensuous, heavy in the way she knew so well. He bent, and his mouth touched hers lightly, hovering over her for a moment. Their breath intermingled, hot and moist. Then his lips sank into hers so deeply she felt the hardness of his teeth. His tongue thrust into her mouth, moving slowly, firmly, savoring her hot, honeyed taste.

Sarah's arms wrapped around his neck, and she pressed up into him. His chest was hard against her breasts, and she moved against him, abrading her nipples with the cloth between their bodies. Luke sucked in his breath at her movement, and his kiss deepened. His teeth scraped her lips. Desire pulsated through him.

He pulled her across him so that she sat in his lap. Her bottom pressed against his already turgid manhood, further heightening the fierce pleasure building in his loins. With one arm Luke supported her back while he kissed her, and his other hand went to the opening of her dress, spreading the sides apart and sliding beneath the dress to the cool, sheer cloth of her chemise. He cupped her breast through her underclothes. It was heavy, fuller now that she was pregnant. He could see the dark circle of her aureole and the thick, pointed nipple. He thought of their son suckling her breast, his little fingers kneading the soft white flesh, and he wanted her with a desire that went far deeper than just sex.

"Sarah." Luke's voice was rough with yearning. He pulled down the chemise to expose her breast. He had seen her naked time after time, yet the sight of her never failed to excite him. He wanted to take her in every way a man could have a woman, wanted to fill her completely. His control hung by threads.

Luke leaned back his head and closed his eyes, sucking in air. His arm was clenched tight as iron behind her back. Sarah opened her eyes, puzzled. She looked at his taut face and neck, harsh and beautiful in the pale moonlight. She reached up and caressed his cheek lightly. Luke opened his eyes and gazed down at her. Sarah saw his hunger and she saw his control, and she knew with disappointment that Luke would not make love to her tonight.

But then he bent and took her nipple into his mouth, and Sarah wondered if she was wrong. His tongue moved gently over the hard button of flesh, circling and caressing. No one would have guessed the leashed hunger within him, so soft was his mouth on her breast. But he caressed her now for her, not himself, and he took great care not to hurt her tender breasts, sensitized by her pregnancy.

Luke pulled down the cloth from her other breast, and his mouth made its lazy way to it. Sarah felt the slight scratch of his chin and cheek, unshaven since early this morning, a counterpoint to the softness of his mouth. The air was cool against her nipple, damp from his tongue, and it pebbled even more. Her loins were heavy and liquid with desire. She ached to feel his hardness inside her, and she moved her hips a little, beckoning him.

The shifting of her body rubbed his engorged shaft, and instinctively Luke shoved her hips down, moving her against him, aching to reach fulfillment and loving the ache. His teeth sank into his lower lip as he struggled for, and found, control. His hand went under her skirt, pushing it up, sliding along her legs to their juncture. Sarah made a choked sound and arched her back, pressing up against his hand. He slid between her legs, caressing the hardness of bone beneath the cloth, touching the dampness of her desire.

His hand moved up and untied the drawstring of her undergarment. He caressed the mound of her abdomen, sliding downward to the prickle of hair. Sarah drew in her breath sharply. His fingers moved into the hot, moist crevice of her femininity, exploring the slick folds of flesh. He stared down at Sarah's face, watching the play of emotions across her face, the restlessness and longing, the pleasure, the almost unbearable buildup of passion within her. He loved seeing what he did to her, loved watching the pleasure take her.

His finger slid over the tiny button of pleasure between her nether lips, stroking and pressing. Sarah moved beneath his touch, circling her hips, squeezing her thighs together as though to entrap the pleasure. The waves of pleasure were growing in her, building, climbing until they were so intense she thought she must die from not reaching the end. Then his finger moved quickly, and the gathered force exploded within her.

She groaned, digging her heels into the wooden slats of the swing and arching back, shaking all over with the intensity of her satisfaction. Pleasure coursed out through her body, flooding her with heat and sharp, prickling tingles of enjoyment. She stayed taut for a moment, pulsing with the afterwaves of passion, then slowly, panting, she relaxed. Her breath came out in a broken sigh.

Sarah opened her eyes and smiled up at her husband. Her face was flushed and loose with contentment, her eyes glowing. "Oh, Luke." She brushed her hand across his face and down the column of his neck. His skin was searing. "Thank you."

"My pleasure."

She started to get up, but he held her tightly against him. She glanced at him, puzzled. "Don't you want to go up to bed so we can—"

"No." He shook his head. His voice was hoarse. "No. You remember what Doc Banks said."

"But—"

He laid his cheek against her hair, enveloping her with his unspent heat. "That was for you, sweetheart. Just for you."

"Oh, Luke!" Sarah flung her arms around him, burying her face in his chest, love flooding her at his generosity. "You're so good, so kind."

He chuckled. "Hardly. I just love you."

She clung to him, and he rocked gently, holding her. It seemed to him that he held the world in his arms.

* * *

James Banks walked his last patient to the door and opened it politely for the gray-haired woman. She smiled at him. "Thank you, Dr. Jim."

He forced himself to smile back despite the fact that it was seven o'clock, he was tired and hungry, and this was the fourth time in two months that Mrs. Singleton had come in for an imaginary illness. Her husband had died six months ago, and her only son lived in Greenville. She came because she was lonely more than anything else. "It's no trouble, Mrs. Singleton."

She patted his arm. "You always were a good boy. Your mother must be very proud of you."

"I hope so." James watched Mrs. Singleton navigate the four shallow steps to the walk, then closed the door and pulled down the shade over the glass upper half of the door. He leaned back against it and closed his eyes, sighing. He was a handsome man, with thick black hair, warm, chocolate brown eyes, and even features; but tonight weariness blurred his looks, and he appeared older than his thirty-one years.

It had been a long day, one that had begun at five o'clock this morning when he'd been called to the depot where a railroad worker had had his leg crushed uncoupling a car. James had managed to save the man's life, but not the leg.

James opened his eyes and pushed away from the door. He walked down the hall past the examination rooms and through the door leading into the house.

It was a large, elegant house. James had grown up here, and he knew every inch of it, just as he knew every nook and cranny of his father's office. He smiled to himself. He'd been here two years, and he still thought of it as his father's office; old habits died hard. He shrugged out of his suit jacket and hung it over the newel post of the staircase as he passed by, then continued into the kitchen, untying his string tie and unbuttoning his collar and cuffs as he went.

Lurleen sat at the kitchen table with her daughter Dovie, chatting, and she rose to her feet when she saw James. "Well, I declare, it's about time, Dr. Jimmy."

"I'm sorry, Lurleen. You shouldn't have waited for me. Hello, Dovie."

"Hello, Dr. Jim." Dovie stood up, too, to help her mother serve the food she had kept warm in the oven. Dovie was a tall, slender woman, handsome to look at, with large dark eyes, well-modeled features, and smooth skin the color of coffee and cream. James wondered why a nice-looking woman like Dovie hadn't married by now, instead of living with her mother in the servants' quarters above the carriage house. But there was something very contained and controlled about Dovie that he guessed kept men at bay. She wore her thick, curly black hair pulled back from her face and subdued into a tight knot. Her dark skirt and white high-necked blouse were plain to the point of severity. Dovie carried herself ramrod straight, and her face was stern. She looked the epitome of a schoolmarm, which was what she was at the small schoolhouse for the town's black children.

The two women set a platter and bowls of food on the table in front of James. "Mmm." He began to fill his plate. "Why don't you join me?"

Lurleen snorted. "We done ate already, Dr. Jim."

"Then have a cup of coffee and keep me company."

Dovie was quick to accept. She clasped her hands in her lap and leaned forward, eager to talk. "I heard you treated a man down by the tracks this morning."

"Yes." James smiled slowly. He knew Dovie; she wanted to hear every last detail. Ever since he could remember, Dovie had been at his heels, wanting to know something— pestering him to teach her to read and write and figure numbers, asking to read his books, interrogating him about his college courses. She was the most intellectually curious human being he had ever met. One day James's father had found her struggling through one of his thick medical tomes when she was about sixteen, and he had given Lurleen the money to send Dovie to the college at Tuskegee.

Dovie shot James a fulminating glance. "Now, don't you tease me, James Banks. I remember you when you were still in short pants."

"Dovie! That ain't no way to talk to the doctor!"

James chuckled. "Don't get on her, Lurleen. She's right;

I was teasing. Okay. One of the railroad crew got his leg crushed this morning.''

"What did you do? Were you able to set it?"

He shook his head. "No. It was too severe. I had to amputate." He began to describe the operation.

Lurleen threw up her hands and rose quickly. "Lord, Dr. Jim, you drive me right outta this house." She glared at her daughter. "Girl, you crazy, sittin' there listenin' to that without turnin' a hair."

Dovie's lips quirked into a smile. "Sorry, Mama."

"I promise we'll talk about something else," James put in, and Lurleen sat back down.

Dovie hesitated, then said, "There's a boy at my school who worries me."

"What's the matter?"

"He has a long cut on his arm, says he got it from barbed wire, and it's not healing. His arm's starting to puff up and look a funny color."

"Bring him in to see me tomorrow."

"His parents don't have any money."

James shrugged. "That doesn't make his arm any better, does it?"

"No." Dovie smiled. "Thank you."

"Don't mention it."

James finished eating and went upstairs to his mother's sitting room. She was reading when he came into the room, but she set aside the leather-bound book with a smile. At fifty-two, Anthea Banks was still a lovely woman, and she carried herself regally. She came from one of the best families in Willow Springs; her ancestors had been among the first to settle in Farr County. Her sister was married to a judge, and her cousin was the bank president.

"James, dear." She held out both her hands to him.

"Hello, Mother." He clasped her hands and sat down on a hassock near her chair.

"Working late tonight, dear?"

"You know how it is."

Anthea gave a wry grin. "I'm afraid I do."

She squeezed his hands. Anthea wasn't an expressive woman; but she loved her son deeply, and she was very proud of him. He was all one could hope for in a son:

handsome, intelligent, and kind. But he was a lonely man. His whole life was his work, and though now and then he called on an eligible girl, he hadn't been serious about anyone since he'd moved back to Willow Springs. It bothered Anthea to think of James living without the love of a wife and children. She suspected, from a look he got in his eyes sometimes, that there had been heartbreak somewhere in his past; but she was not the sort of mother to pry, so she didn't bring up the subject.

For a few minutes, they chatted about their days. Anthea told him about the Baptist Women's meeting that afternoon in Rachel Corbell's house, and James related a few amusing anecdotes from his work, carefully expurgating anything that might be ugly or harsh. When Anthea began to look tired, James kissed her on the cheek and went back downstairs.

The kitchen was dark, and Lurleen and Dovie were gone. James went into the dining room and took out a bottle of Kentucky bourbon from the sideboard. He poured himself two fingers, and, glass in hand, strolled out onto the front porch. He stood for a moment sipping his drink and gazing out at the dark, silent street. The honeysuckle bush along the side fence was in bloom, and the air was heavy with its sweet, heady scent.

James closed his eyes, a wistful sadness creeping through him. Honeysuckle had grown wild behind the Turner house, and all that sweet, short June while he and Julia lay in the shelter of the trees there, he had smelled it. He had never been able to smell honeysuckle since without thinking of Julia.

He took another swallow of bourbon. It was pointless to think about it after all this time. Eleven years. Yet he could still see her as she had looked that day in Harper's store, when he was home for Christmas. It had been years since he'd seen her, and he had had trouble placing her for a moment. She had looked so much like a woman at seventeen, so little like the child he had seen at school. She had worn a faded pink dress and a shawl, and a saucy red knitted cap had sat on her pale golden hair, hanging loose and silken around her face. Her eyes had been a clear, startling blue. Her face was delicate, her eyes huge, and she had a sweet, vulnerable air. He had thought she was the most beautiful woman he'd ever seen.

James wondered where Julia was now and what she was doing. Probably had a passel of kids and looked twice her age. He didn't know why he still thought about her sometimes after all these years. He guessed it was because she had been his first, and you didn't forget your first woman, your first real love. Your first heartbreak.

James tossed down the rest of the drink. It was a smooth fire in his throat and stomach.

He could never forget Julia—the softness of her body beneath him, the sweet taste of her mouth. He would always carry the memory of their lovemaking inside him—just as he would always carry the pain he had felt when he had learned she'd married Will Dobson.

At first he hadn't believed it. She had lain with him, and James knew he had been her first man. She had told him she loved him. He had loved her desperately, had wanted to marry her. Then, suddenly, she had married Will Dobson— without even telling him. He had had to hear it from her father.

He hadn't understood it. He had thought about it a million times, and he never had understood it. Julia had said she loved him. How could she turn around and marry another man? But she had, and all he could think it meant was that she hadn't really loved him. She must have deceived him, used him for some hidden reason of her own.

At first he had been angry and bitter. He had drunk too much and spent too much time in New Orleans's Storyville. But eventually the pain had eased, and he had gone back to his studies and qualified for medical school. Over the years, his life had returned to normal. He had become a doctor. He enjoyed his work. He rarely thought of those few, brief months when he had been in love with Julia Turner.

Just sometimes . . . like tonight . . . when he smelled the strong scent of honeysuckle in the air.

James sighed and turned away. It was time to stop mooning about on the porch and go to bed. His days started early. He turned and went back into the house, shutting the door on the evening air.

* * *

Julia Dobson glanced over at the bed in the corner of the room. Vance and Bonnie lay curled up together, their eyes wide open and fixed on their mother. Bonnie's thumb was firmly planted in her mouth. They were too frightened to go to sleep. They had been scared of their father in life. Now they were scared of him in death. Julia wished she could have put them in another room where they wouldn't have to see Will's dead body stretched out on the table, but their house consisted of only one large room, and there was no other place for the children to sleep.

Julia sighed and turned her attention back to the table where her husband lay. Will's death had stunned her. He was only thirty-seven years old; she had expected to live out most of the rest of her life with him. But Vance had come running to the house this morning, screaming that Daddy was sick, and she had found Will stretched out on the ground beside his plow, the team waiting patiently. He had been unconscious. She had sent for the doctor, but Will was dead by the time he came. The doctor had said it was probably a heart attack, uncommon in a man Will's age.

With her neighbor's help, Julia had washed the body and dressed it, folded his hands across his chest and weighted his eyelids with coins. Now all that was left was the long night of sitting up with the body. She supposed she ought to pray for Will, or recall pleasant memories of him. But there had been precious few pleasant memories, and at the moment she couldn't summon up a prayer, except maybe one of gratitude.

She was glad he was dead. Well, not glad, really; she didn't wish harm to anyone. But she was relieved. Yes, certainly she was relieved. She would no longer have to be afraid that he might hit her. She would no longer have to worry about protecting the children from him if he was mad or drunk. She wouldn't have to listen to him curse her or be reminded of the favor he had done her by marrying her. Nor would she have to lie quiescent under him, enduring his clumsy hands and the violation of his entering her.

He hadn't been a terrible husband, Julia guessed. He hadn't hit her as often as some men hit their wives, and he'd never taken his belt to her. He had kept a roof over their heads and food in their mouths, even if it had never been fancy. And he had given her child a name.

The trouble between them hadn't been all his fault. She didn't love him, had married him not loving him, just so the baby she carried would not be illegitimate. Will had wanted her so much that he had been willing to marry her, knowing that she carried another man's child, but the knowledge had always been a bitterness within him. Julia had cried on their wedding night, loving Jimmy, aching for his tender caresses instead of Will's rough fondling. Though she had cried into her pillow, trying to muffle the sound, Will had heard it. If Will hadn't been very good to her, neither had she been fair to him.

Even now when he was dead, she couldn't feel anything for him.

All she could feel was relief that he was dead and fear because she didn't know what she and the children would do. Will was sharecropping this land, so the house didn't belong to them. The owner of the property would want to put someone else here to work the land. Where would she go? How would she take care of two children all by herself?

She tried not to think about that. She folded her hands together, closed her eyes, and tried to pray for the repose of Will's soul. But Julia knew that deep inside, she was really praying for herself.

* Chapter 2 *

Julia buried Will Dobson in the cemetery beside the Antioch Baptist Church, three miles down the road from their house. Only Julia, her children, and their neighbor, Lula Braswell, and her two sons were there. The preacher said a few words over the grave, and Mrs. Braswell's sons lowered the pine casket into the open hole. Julia stood for a moment, staring down at the grave. Bonnie and Vance were on either side of her, dressed in their best clothes, holding Julia's hands.

"Is Daddy down there?" Bonnie asked.

"Yes, sweetheart."

"How will he get out?"

"He won't." Julia smoothed her hand over her daughter's hair, neatly captured in braids. "When you die, you don't get up anymore. You lie in the earth."

"How will he meet Jesus, then?"

"It's not his body that goes to Heaven." If, in fact, that was where Will was headed; Julia had her doubts. "It's his soul, and that's already left his body. When he died, his soul flew away to meet Jesus."

"I don't think Daddy—" Vance began, but Julia squeezed his shoulder sharply, casting a significant look at his younger sister, and the boy subsided.

Lula Braswell came up to them and hugged Julia affectionately. "Why don't I take the children on over to our place? You could have some time here to yourself, then you all could eat dinner with us. How about it, Bonnie? Would you like some of my gingerbread cookies? Vance?"

"Yes, ma'am," Vance answered, casting an uncertain look at his mother.

"Thank you." Julia smiled at the older woman. "But you've done too much for us already. I don't know what I'd have done without you." Mrs. Braswell had been more than kind. She had helped Julia lay Will out, and her two sons had built the casket. Julia couldn't have afforded to buy a coffin. Just paying for the pine slats for the box and giving the minister a stipend for the service had taken almost all of the money she had saved.

"It's no more than what you'd have done for me. Than what you *have* done for me." The Braswells' youngest girl had come down with a terrible fever the year before, and Mrs. Braswell herself had been so sick she hadn't been able to care for her, so Julia had nursed both of them until Lula was back on her feet. Mrs. Braswell had been Julia's fast friend since then, despite Will's obvious disapproval.

Julia smiled. "Thank you. I would appreciate it."

Lula led the children to her wagon while the Braswell

boys lowered the coffin into the ground and shoveled the dirt back in on top of it. They patted the black earth down into a mound, and Lee, the youngest, stuck a crude wooden cross into the ground and held it while the other boy hammered it in with the back of the shovel. They shouldered their tools and tipped their hats to Julia.

"Sorry, ma'am."

"Sorry, Mrs. Dobson."

"Thank you."

They joined their mother and Julia's children in the wagon and drove off. The preacher took Julia's hand and offered his final condolences before he, too, left. Julia turned back to the fresh grave. She was alone. She stared down at the mounded grave. Now was when she should make her peace with Will. Now was when she should cry.

No tears came. Julia leaned over and placed half of the handful of wildflowers she had gathered at the base of Will's marker. She turned to the grave beside his. It was short, only half the length of Will's, and the earth had settled so much it was flat. It had, after all, been almost nine years. It, too, bore a simple cross of two small lengths of wood hammered together, so weatherbeaten that the words scratched into it were almost unreadable now: Pamela Dobson, b. January 3, 1895, d. Nov. 8, 1896.

Weeds had sprung up on it, as they did every year. Julia yanked up each shoot and tossed it away. She knelt beside the marker and laid down the rest of the wildflowers. She took off her gloves and slid her hand over the ground in a kind of caress, as though it were the baby she touched.

"Pammy." She had been Jimmy's daughter, the child for whom Julia had married Will Dobson, and Julia had loved her to distraction. She had looked like Jimmy, with his thick, dark hair and chocolate brown eyes, and she had had a smile like sunshine. A thousand times over the past nine years, Julia had longed to see that smile again.

But she had died of scarlet fever when she was less than two years old. Only the fact that Julia had just had Vance, who depended on her utterly, had kept her going after Pamela's death.

Julia touched the rough cross. She wished she had the money for a granite marker. Before many more years passed, no one would know that a sweet child lay here beside the man who was not her father but the man who had given her his name.

The tears that would not come for her newly dead husband gathered now in Julia's eyes and rolled down her cheeks. She had lived with Will for almost eleven years, cooked his meals, nursed him through sickness, borne his children because it was her duty, because she owed him. But she had loved Pamela.

Julia leaned her head against the faded marker and cried.

The next day Mr. Harrington came to see her. The children were out in back playing and Julia was at the stove, stirring a mess of poke salad greens flavored with pork middlings, when she heard the sound of a vehicle pulling up in front of the house. She looked out the front window and saw Harrington, and her heart sank. He was the owner of the property they lived on, and she knew what he had come to say. She had hoped for more time to make up her mind about what she was going to do.

Julia lowered the fire under the greens and the pot of pinto beans and went out onto the front porch, nervously wiping her hands on her apron. "Morning, Mr. Harrington."

"Morning, Mrs. Dobson." He got out of the buggy and looped the reins around the porch post. "Mind if I come in?"

"Of course not. You're welcome."

She stepped back, clasping her hands together to hide her nervousness, and watched Harrington climb the steps and go into the house. He went to Will's chair, but remained politely standing. Julia caught her error and hurried to sit down. "Please, have a seat."

"Thank you. I was real sorry to hear about Will," Harrington began heavily. He was a portly man with thinning hair and a large, Teddy Roosevelt mustache of which he was inordinately proud. He owned half the land around Gideon, and Will had farmed for him for the past four years.

"Thank you."

He glanced around the room. Julia realized with astonishment that he was nervous, too. He sighed. "I reckon you know why I'm here."

"Yes."

"If it was winter, I wouldn't hurry you none. I let the Widow Hall stay in their place all winter, you know, after Arthur died."

"Yes, I know."

"But with it being spring and all—well, I have to get this land planted soon, or there won't be a crop this spring. I have to give it to another tenant."

"I know."

He cleared his throat. "I talked to Gerald Miller about it this morning, and he and his family are going to move in here." Julia nodded. She didn't know what to say. "He—I'd like him to start as soon as possible. So I'm going to have to ask you to leave the house by day after tomorrow. That's when I told Miller he could move in."

Julia's eyes widened. She hadn't expected it to be quite this soon. She had thought she'd have a week, at least, to pack their things and decide where they would go.

Harrington's eyes darted around nervously. "The thing is, ma'am, your husband owed me some money. I loaned him the cash to get through that winter three years ago after the drought wiped out all the crops."

"Yes, I remember." Julia smoothed her hand across her forehead, pushing back the wisps of fine hair that had come loose and clung there. "I—how much did he owe you?"

"Well, I also loaned him the money to buy the new team and the wagon last month. Of course, he thought he'd have plenty of time to pay it back."

Of course. No one ever thought about a thirty-seven-year-old man dropping dead.

"The fact of the matter is, ma'am, Will owed me two hundred and forty-three dollars."

"Two hundred and forty-three dollars!" Julia's stomach plummeted. "But I—we don't—"

"Now, don't fret. I know you don't have the money. I've been thinking about it. You won't be needing Will's tools or the mule team and wagon. Why don't I just take those things in full payment of the debt?"

Julia frantically tried to calculate how much the animals and tools were worth. But what choice did she have? She owed Harrington two hundred forty-three dollars, and she couldn't get the money except by selling those very things. It would be easier to swap them. It was just that she had been hoping she could sell the team and tools for a little money to pay for room and board in town until she could get some sort of work. But now she would have nothing. Nothing!

She looked away to hide the tears in her eyes. "All right."

"Good. Then that settles it." Harrington looked relieved at having it done with so easily. "You're a reasonable woman, Mrs. Dobson."

He rose and started toward the door. "I'm real sorry about Will." He opened the door and paused. "I'll send one of the boys over this afternoon to pick up those things."

Julia nodded.

"Good day, ma'am."

"Good day."

Julia stared sightlessly at the closed door. She was more scared than she had been at any time since she'd been pregnant with Pamela, knowing Jimmy would never marry her and not knowing where to turn. Then she had had a baby inside her that she had to take care of. Now she had two children. That was what made it so frightening—being responsible for someone else's life. If it had just been her, it wouldn't have been so hard to face. Somehow she would make her way, and if she starved, well, dying wasn't the worst thing that could happen to a person. But when there were children involved, she had to make the right decision. She couldn't let them starve or be cold or sick.

Mechanically, Julia went to the stove and stirred the contents of each pot, working out of habit, with little idea of what she was doing. Where was she to go?

She didn't have much choice. She had hoped that with a little money she would be able to manage on her own. But without it, she couldn't rent a room or even feed Bonnie and Vance until she found a way to make a living. There weren't many opportunities for a woman to make money. She could sew, take in laundry, or cook and clean house for someone else. It would take time to find a position in someone's house or to bring in enough sewing or laundry to live on. What she had planned to do now seemed impossible.

That left only one thing: She would have to throw herself on someone's mercy until she could find employment. Mrs. Braswell would be kind enough to take her in, but Julia couldn't ask it of her. Mr. Braswell sharecropped Harrington's land, just like Will had done, and they were barely able to keep their own family fed. Julia couldn't add three more mouths to their dinner table. Julia's grandmother had died two years ago, and after that her father had left the area. No one knew where he had gone. She had no other relatives to turn to, except Luke.

She thought Luke would take her in. They had been close when they were young. But it had been so long since they'd seen each other. His feelings might have changed. Will hadn't let her visit him, even when Luke had been on trial or when he had gotten married. Luke might think she'd snubbed him; he might be angry with her. Even if he was willing to take her in, she hated to ask it of him. He had a new life now. He was married to Sarah McGowan, who came from a "good" family. Sarah wouldn't want to have her around. Julia was afraid she would be an embarrassment to her brother, even a burden.

Julia looked down at her red, rough fingers and her faded, much-mended dress. She was as common as dirt; Sarah McGowan would be appalled. She might give her shelter out of pity or from love of Luke, but Julia knew that inside Sarah would be mortified at having her for a sister-in-law. Julia knew she didn't talk as nice as Sarah; she would do and say the wrong things. Sarah would think Julia was plain and cheap. There had been talk, she was sure, when she had married Will; folks would have said she had had to get married. Sarah would remember that. No. Sarah wouldn't want to have her around, and that would cause Luke trouble. She couldn't hurt Luke.

But what else could she do? She had to go to Luke's for the sake of the children. She would start looking for a job as soon as she got there; she'd take her family off Luke's hands quickly.

Julia called the children inside and dished up the greens,

cornbread, and beans. She poured buttermilk into glasses.
The children dug into their food with gusto, but Julia
couldn't work up an appetite. She sat and stared at her plate,
crumbling her piece of cornbread into it.

"Bonnie, Vance, I have something to tell you."

The two children looked up at her as they continued to
fork the food into their mouths.

"We have to leave this house. We've got to pack everything up."

"We're gonna go?" Bonnie asked, her face falling.
"Forever?"

Julia nodded.

"Where are we going?" Vance asked.

Julia tried to smile. "Someplace you'll like, I bet. We're
going to visit your Uncle Luke."

Julia couldn't move her furniture without the wagon and
mules. They would have to walk all the way to Willow
Springs and could take only what little they could carry. The
Braswells agreed to keep Julia's chickens and the milch cow
and let her store most of her possessions in the shed behind
their house until Julia could get a place of her own. Julia
packed a small suitcase with a set of clothes for herself and
each of the children. They hadn't many, so it wasn't difficult
to limit the number. She looked at her children's worn,
mended clothes and scuffed shoes, and shame swept her for
what Sarah would think of them. But, she reminded herself,
she had no choice.

By the end of the following day, the house was cleaned
and empty. Julia killed one of their hens, fried it, and
packed it in a small sack along with some cornbread, sweet
potatoes, and half a loaf of white bread. They spent the
night with the Braswells, and the next morning Mrs. Braswell
fed them a solid breakfast of biscuits, bacon, and eggs. Julia
and the children set off, with Julia carrying the suitcase and
Vance, the sack of food. Bonnie held the simple rag doll
that Julia had made her for Christmas last year. Luke's farm
was in a different county, at least thirty miles away; Julia
wasn't sure exactly how to get there; and she carried only

two silver dollars in her pocket. She was scared to death, but she knew she had to do it.

They had walked less than a mile when a farmer they knew came by in a wagon and offered them a ride. He took them into Gideon and gave them directions to Willow Springs. The road out of Gideon was larger and better traveled than the first one they'd been on, and two wagons, a surrey, and three men on horseback passed them as they trudged along. One of the wagons stopped and gave them a ride for a few miles. The day grew warm, and the children were soon thirsty. Julia was thinking she would have to go up to the next farmhouse and ask for a drink from their cistern, when they came to a stream.

They knelt beside the stream and, cupping their hands, drank from it. Julia wet her handkerchief in the water and wiped the dust from their faces. Then they removed their shoes and dabbled their tired feet in the water. Julia brought out the cornbread and fried chicken, and they ate in the shade of a cottonwood tree. Afterward, Julia leaned back against the tree trunk, and Bonnie curled up with her head in Julia's lap, and all three of them napped. But Julia didn't let them sleep long. They needed to reach Luke's farm before their food ran out. Besides, Julia didn't relish the idea of spending many nights on the road.

They continued walking. The glories of spring were all around them—bright wildflowers, the green of new grass and budding trees, a gentle sun and cool breezes—but Julia didn't notice any of those things. She just concentrated on walking. The suitcase in her hand grew heavier by the minute, and she wished that she had left behind some of its contents. The children began to drag, especially little Bonnie. Finally Bonnie sat down in the road and cried. Julia picked her up and carried her, and Vance dragged the suitcase along. Julia knew she had to stop soon. They were all exhausted, and it was growing dark. But she pressed on, looking for some form of shelter.

They came upon a small, obviously abandoned shack. The floor was dirt, one wall had collapsed, and the roof had gaping holes, but at least it was dry and somewhat protected from the elements—and from the eyes of passersby. Julia built a small fire, and they roasted sweet potatoes over it.

They were so hungry they ate the potatoes as soon as they were done, even though they burned their mouths.

Julia pulled off Bonnie's shoes and stockings and found that her shoes had worn blisters on her little feet. Tearing off a strip of her own petticoat, Julia wrapped up Bonnie's feet. Tomorrow she would have to let the children go barefoot, despite the bad impression it might give Luke's wife.

Julia had the children put on their coats, and she wrapped her shawl around herself. She spread out her cloak close to the coals of the fire, and they lay down together on it, huddled together for warmth with Bonnie in the middle. Though the April days were warm, the nights were still cool. Julia lay awake for a long time, cold and scared. She kept thinking about a snake sliding into the hut, seeking warmth, or a pack of wild dogs who smelled their food. Or maybe a passing stranger.

She turned onto her back and stared up at the stars through the hole in the roof. She hadn't lived a privileged life, but she had never had to sleep outdoors before. She had cooked on an open fire only a few times in her life, when she and Will had moved somewhere, and then Will had been there to lay the fire and to protect them. They had slept inside the wagon those times, with a tarpaulin over their heads, a mattress beneath them, and warm blankets all around. Julia shivered. She was in charge of two children, and she didn't feel adequate to the task.

Silently, almost unconsciously, she prayed: *Please let us get to Luke's safely. And, please, please, don't let Luke turn us away.*

When at last Julia fell asleep, she slept fitfully, chilled and unused to sleeping on the hard ground. She awoke the next morning as soon as the sun shone in through the collapsed east wall and sat up gingerly, her muscles screaming and her body bruised and sore. She thought with longing of her feather bed. She let the children continue to sleep while she built up the fire. She unfastened her hair and did her best to brush it out and coil it tightly atop her head without the benefit of a mirror. She shook and brushed at her dress to remove some of the dust of the road and floor. Julia had always hated to be untidy, and she was chagrined to think how disheveled and dirty she must appear now. Poor white trash, she thought, and felt like crying.

When the children awoke, they ate a quick, cold breakfast of cornbread and set out on the road. At first Bonnie and Vance skipped along, glad to be out of their shoes and rather enjoying the adventure. They'd never been this far away from home before or gotten to camp out like pioneers. But by noon they were beginning to droop.

When they came to a town, Julia bought beef jerky with a little of her precious supply of money and even splurged for two sticks of peppermint candy for Bonnie and Vance. They ate the last of the chicken and drank water from a stream for lunch, then doggedly plodded on throughout the afternoon. Before long Julia had to carry Bonnie. Then Vance gave out, and she had to carry the suitcase as well. By the time they stopped for the evening, Julia was dead tired.

They roasted potatoes for supper again, and Julia divided the beef jerky between the children. Bonnie and Vance needed their strength far more than she did, and she had given them most of the meat at lunch as well. Julia was unable to find an abandoned shack this night, so they slept in the open, huddled against a board fence a short distance from the road. Julia slept little, and she awakened the next morning feeling as weary as when she had lain down.

Her stomach rumbled with hunger, but their food supply was almost gone. She gave Bonnie and Vance the last of it, two squares of cornbread. She hoped they would reach Luke's soon. They were almost to Willow Springs, she thought, and surely it wasn't too far from town to the McGowan farm.

It was almost noon when the family reached the town of Willow Springs. There was a house beside the road that advertised that its owner took in boarders and served meals. Julia stopped at its back door, embarrassed to come inside because of their dusty, ragtag appearance. She bought plates of beans and bread for the children, which they ate sitting on the back porch. Julia took only a cup of strong black coffee for herself. They would reach Luke's today, and surely she could stand a little hunger until then. She didn't want to spend any more of her money than she had to. If

Luke should have moved or not want her there, this bit of money was all she had between her family and starvation.

Julia asked directions to the McGowan farm from the cook, and the woman smiled. "The McGowan place? I haven't heard that in a couple of years. It's the Turner place now. Go on out the Greenville road. After three or four miles, you'll come to a yellow house—that's the Sweeney farm—and there's a road off to the right. You take it and just keep walking for, oh, another mile or so, and you'll see the Turners' house. Nice white house with green shutters, real pretty."

"Thank you." Julia was surprised to hear it called the Turner place. Despite her brother's presence there, she had assumed that the local people would still call it by Sarah's parents' name. A Turner wouldn't be important enough to call it by his name.

Bonnie and Vance liked the food and the shaded backyard and didn't want to leave the boardinghouse. They protested when Julia said it was time to go but obediently fell in behind her. They trudged through town and out the Greenville road. It seemed as though with every step they went more slowly. Vance sagged, and Bonnie began to whimper. Julia picked up the little girl and carried her. Her burden felt heavy as lead. Julia's head began to swim, and abruptly she set down both Bonnie and the suitcase. Julia sat down on the case, her head lowered, fighting her sudden dizziness.

Perhaps she should have eaten something, after all. She was so tired. She wondered how they'd ever make it. Julia squinted down the road. Was that the yellow house where they should turn? She couldn't make herself get up yet.

The children were glad for a rest and plopped down beside her on the edge of the road. A man on horseback trotted past, tipping his hat to them. Julia told herself she must get up. The momentary weak spell was gone. But she couldn't make herself rise.

A large man came around the curve, walking in the opposite direction from them. He wore denim coveralls and a plaid flannel shirt, and a large felt hat drooped down over his face. His skin was black, with a coppery tint. His nose was flat, his mouth straight, and his eyes were shadowed by the wide brim of the hat. A chill of unease ran through

Julia. She was unused to black people, and this man was a little scary. He was big, and there was something bold about the way he carried himself.

"Ma'am," he said as he drew near, and tipped his hat to her.

Julia swallowed and gave him a brief nod. She stood and picked up her suitcase, the prick of fear giving her fresh impetus. She took Bonnie by the hand and started toward the distant house, moving briskly. Suddenly, the house wavered in her vision. Julia became sickeningly unsure of her footing. She dropped the suitcase, one hand going to her head. "Vance . . ."

"Mama?" Bonnie looked up at her questioningly.

Black spots danced before Julia's eyes. The horizon tilted and turned dark.

"Mama!" Vance turned and lunged toward Julia, grabbing her arm. But he wasn't strong enough to hold her up, and Julia crumpled into a heap on the road.

"Mama! Mama!" Bonnie set up a high-pitched shriek.

Vance fell onto his knees beside his mother. Her eyes were closed. She looked as if she were asleep. His father had looked the same way when he died. "Mama!" He shook her arm. "Mama!"

Vance glanced around him frantically. The large man who had passed them had stopped and was looking back at them. Vance jumped to his feet, waving frantically. "Mister! Mister!"

The man loped toward them, his sack bouncing on his back. He dropped the sack and knelt beside Julia, feeling for her pulse. "What happened?"

"I don't know!" Tears gathered in Vance's eyes. Bonnie was sobbing unrestrainedly. "Is she dead?"

The man shook his head. "No. She ain't dead. She jus' pass out. Where your home? Where you headed?"

For a moment Vance couldn't think. He stared at the man.

"Boy? You all right?"

"I—uh. Uncle Luke's house. We're going to Luke, uh, Turner's house."

"I don't know it. I ain't from around here."

"It's down there." Vance pointed. "The lady said, turn

right at the yellow house, and it's a couple of miles down the road.''

The man nodded. ''I jus' pick your mama up and carry her there.''

''All right.'' Vance grabbed his sister's hand and the handle of the suitcase, and they set out.

The big black man walked easily, even carrying Julia like a baby in his arms, and Vance was hard-pressed to keep up. As they walked, Julia's eyelids fluttered open, then widened, and she gasped, staring at the strange dark face above hers.

''There now. You awake. You all right, ma'am?''

''I—yes. What h-happened? What are you doing?''

''I be carrying you to the house your boy told me about. You done fainted in the road.''

''Oh. I'm sorry.''

He smiled faintly. ''Nothing to be sorry about. You feelin' sickly?''

''No.'' Julia shook her head. ''I'm healthy as a horse. I—you can put me down now. I'm all right.''

''I don't know 'bout that. But I set you down.''

He put her on her feet. Julia wavered and had to grab the man's arm to keep from stumbling.

''Mama!'' Still crying, Bonnie launched herself at her mother and wrapped her arms around Julia's legs.

''Mama? You all right?'' Vance came to stand beside her, his small face worried.

''Yes. I'm fine now. Really. I was just a little weak. I'm tired, and I didn't have lunch.''

Vance reached out and took her hand. He didn't want to act like a scared little boy, but he had to touch her, just to make sure the world was back in its normal place. ''I didn't—know what to do. The man came and helped. He said you wasn't dead, and he picked you up and carried you. He carried you a long way.''

Julia squeezed her son's hand and sat down on the suitcase to rest. She put an arm around each of her children and leaned her head against Bonnie's. ''Let me catch my breath, and we'll go.'' She looked up at the man looming before her. ''Thank you, uh . . . I'm sorry. I don't know your name.''

''Micah, ma'am. Micah Harrison.''

"Micah. I'm Julia Dobson, and these are my children, Vance and Bonnie. I appreciate very much what you did. It was kind of you."

Micah shrugged. His face was impassive, impossible to read. "Wasn't nothin'."

"Well, it was quite a bit to me." Julia stood up. "I feel like such a fool, fainting in the middle of the road. I'm glad you didn't leave me lying there." Julia felt a little guilty for having been scared of this man earlier. "Well, we better be on our way."

Julia reached for the handle of the suitcase, and the world wobbled around her. Micah's hand shot out and grabbed her arm. "I better help you." He picked up the suitcase as if it were light as a feather. "I'll carry this thing for you. It be too heavy for a lady and two little ones."

"I ain't little!" Vance protested vigorously.

"No, guess you ain't. But you need to be lookin' after your little sis. She sure looks tired."

"Oh." Mollified, Vance turned to Bonnie and took her hand. "Come on, Bon, it ain't far."

They started down the road, Julia leaning against Micah's supporting hand. They made a slow, halting procession. Soon Bonnie sat down in the road and began to cry, so Micah swung her up to ride atop his shoulders. He picked up the suitcase, and they started off again. Julia leaned more and more heavily upon his arm.

Finally Micah said, "I better carry you."

"No. I can make it. I'm too heavy for you to carry."

A grin touched his face, dazzlingly white. "You don't weigh nothin'. It'd save us time. I have you there in nothin' flat."

"Mama! Look! There it is! Is that it?" Vance cried, pointing excitedly. He was a little in front of them, past a clump of trees. They caught up with him and looked where he pointed.

Less than fifty yards away, a narrow dirt track turned off the main road and led to a two-story frame house. Julia gazed at the house, entranced.

A porch stretched across the front of it, and bright flowers and bushes bloomed around the foundation. A chinaberry tree stood near the gate, and closer to the house were

smaller, blossoming fruit trees. To one side were a barn and
a corral, where two horses stood dozing in the sun. In
another section of the corral were a cow and calf. Hens
picked their way across the narrow road and yard, heads
bobbing, feathers gleaming in the sun.

It was the picture of tranquillity and prosperity, and Julia
was filled with happiness for Luke and such longing that she
thought her heart must burst. "Yes. You're right, Vance.
I'm sure that's it." She gave Micah a smile and started
forward.

* Chapter 3 *

Sarah opened the oven door, letting out a blast of heat, and
reached in to pull out two loaves of bread. She set them on
the rack to cool next to the cherry and pecan pies. She
looked across the room at Emily—if she didn't check on her
every few minutes, there was no telling what she would get
into. Emily was on the floor, happily mixing a pasty
concoction of flour and water while her rag doll leaned
against the wall, watching. Emily's dress was splashed with
water and decorated with white blobs. Not too bad,
considering . . .

The baking was done for three days. All she had to do
was clean up the pans and start supper. Sarah glanced out
the window over the sink to see how much of the afternoon
was left, and her eye was drawn to a movement by the gate.
There were people standing there.

She leaned over the sink to see better. "What in the
world?" Sarah washed off her hands and dried them on her
apron, her eyes on the strange little group walking up the
path to her house. A young boy led the group, and behind
him came a large man carrying another child on his shoulders. In one hand he held a sack and a suitcase, and his

other hand supported the small woman who walked beside him. The man was black, and the woman and children were white. All of them looked dusty, tired, and thoroughly bedraggled.

Sarah stepped out onto the side porch and shaded her eyes with her hand. They were almost to the house now, coming around to the side door, as almost everyone did except on Sundays. "Hello!" Sarah called.

The man set down his bags and removed his hat. "Afternoon, ma'am."

The boy's steps slowed, and he turned back to walk next to the woman. The group stopped a few feet away from the porch. Sarah gazed at them. She had never seen the man or the children before, but there was something familiar about the woman. Her hair looked to be blond, though dimmed by dust, and her eyes were light colored, blue or gray, and rather sad. She was too thin, and her triangular face was delicate. Sarah felt a wave of pity for her. She seemed so tired and careworn. Who was she?

Julia stared back at Sarah. Sarah was pregnant and blooming with health and just looking at her made Julia feel old and worn out. She didn't know what to say, or even what to call Sarah. She had called her Sarah when they were children in school together, but now it didn't seem right that she would address someone like Sarah so informally. Yet it seemed equally wrong to call her own brother's wife "Mrs. Turner."

"I'm sorry to come like this, with no warning," Julia began finally.

Sarah frowned. She knew this woman; she should recognize her. Sarah went down a step, drawn toward her. The woman offered a weak smile, and suddenly it came to her. "Julia? Are you Julia?"

Julia nodded.

Sarah hurried down the remaining steps, holding out her hands. "I can't believe it!" She took Julia's hands and squeezed them. "I'm so happy to see you. Luke will be thrilled. Oh, this is wonderful. Are these your children?"

Relief swept Julia. Sarah was still kind, as she had been when Julia knew her at school. She wouldn't turn them away. Julia nodded. "Yes. Bonnie and Vance. Children, this is your Aunt Sarah."

"I'm pleased to meet you." Sarah smiled at the children. "My little girl will be so happy she won't know what to do. Emily?" She turned her head to call Emily from the kitchen, but naturally, she was already there, watching the scene curiously. "Emily, these are your cousins. Why don't you take them inside? They might like some of those cookies we baked a while ago."

Sarah turned back to Julia, and her glance went curiously to the man beside her. "This is Micah Harrison," Julia said, answering Sarah's unspoken question. "He, uh, helped me and, uh, carried my case for me. He's been very kind."

"She done fainted on the road," Micah explained bluntly.

"What! Oh, my goodness! Here I am, making you stand out in the sun, talking. Come inside and sit down." Sarah took Julia's arm and propelled her up the stairs and into the house. At the door, she paused and turned to Micah. "Would you like something to eat?"

"That'd be real nice."

"Let me get Julia settled, and I'll bring you something."

The children were sitting on the floor of the kitchen, a cookie in each hand. Sarah grinned. "Well, you all look as if you're doing fine."

She steered Julia to the table and pulled out one of the chairs for her to sit in. "Now, what's the matter? Why'd you faint? Are you sick?"

"Oh, no. Please, don't worry." It warmed Julia to have Sarah express concern about her; it hadn't happened often in her life. "I didn't eat lunch, that's all, and I guess I was a little tired from walking."

"You walked out here from town?"

Julia shook her head. "From home, just the other side of Gideon."

"Gideon! You *walked* all that way!" Sarah stared in astonishment. "It must have taken you days."

Julia nodded. "We left Wednesday."

"My goodness." Sarah could think of nothing to say that would adequately express her dismay at the thought of this frail woman and two small children walking for three days.

"Well, what am I doing? You must be starved. I'll fetch you something to eat."

She brought the children to the table and poured them glasses of milk. She put on a pot of beans to heat while she sliced a loaf of bread and spread several slices with pale yellow butter, which melted instantly on the hot bread. Sarah laid the plate of bread and a pot of preserves on the table and set the table with plates and eating utensils. She added a platter of cold sausage and bacon left over from breakfast and a bowl of the warmed-up butter beans.

Seeing how hungrily Julia and her children gulped down the food, Sarah suspected that it had been more than just lunch today that they had missed. How had they managed on the road three days?

Sarah heaped another large plate with food and gave it to Micah. He took it gratefully and sat down on the porch steps to eat it. Sarah thought that he, too, had been awhile without food. It had been good of him to stop and help Julia. "Are you from around here?" she asked him.

"No, ma'am, sure ain't. Jus' passin' through."

"Are you looking for work?"

"I be steady lookin' for that."

"My husband will be in from the fields soon, if you'd like to talk to him about work."

Micah looked up at her, and Sarah found his face as blank and unreadable as Julia had. "Thank you. I 'preciate that."

"No trouble." Sarah stepped back inside. There was something different about that man. She couldn't put her finger on it, but it was something about the way he carried himself, the way he looked at her. Even his accent was a little odd. He didn't need to say it for her to know he wasn't from around here.

Julia ate until she was stuffed, but it was all so good and plentiful that she wished she could have eaten even more. Sarah bustled about the kitchen while the others ate, preparing supper and cleaning up the pans she had used for baking. Julia knew she should get up and help Sarah, but she couldn't raise the energy. The kitchen was overly warm from using the oven all afternoon, and the air was sweet with the mingled smells of pies, bread, and cookies. Julia leaned back against her chair drowsily.

"Julia." Julia jerked out of her doze at the sound of Sarah's voice. She looked up to see Sarah standing over her.

"I'm sorry. I must have slipped off." Julia straightened, glancing around her. The children were no longer there, and the table was cleared. When had Sarah done that? "You should have awakened me earlier. I should have helped you . . ."

"Don't be silly. You're dead on your feet."

Now the questions would start, Julia thought. Sarah would want to know why Julia was here, what had happened to make her walk all the way from Gideon, and how long they would stay. It was perfectly reasonable to have questions when a sister-in-law you hardly knew dropped in on you out of the blue. But Julia dreaded revealing her whole pitiful, embarrassing story, especially to a woman like Sarah McGowan, who had never known hunger or want. Julia wet her lips and tried to prepare herself to answer Sarah's questions.

But Sarah didn't ask one. She said only, "I fixed up a room for you and another one for Vance. I'm putting Bonnie in with Emily. I sent the kids upstairs to wash up and take a nap. I thought you might like to do the same."

Julia stared at her, surprised, then slowly a smile of breathtaking sweetness crept across her face, transforming it from careworn to almost pretty. "Thank you. Yes, I'd like that."

Julia followed Sarah up the stairs, her hand sliding over the smooth walnut banister. The wood gleamed. The whole house gleamed. Julia had never been inside a house this spacious and pleasant. They walked down the hall past a room where the girls were already curled up in a four-poster bed. White eyelet-embroidered curtains hung at the windows, matching the duster and coverlet of the bed. The door of the next room also stood open, revealing a sturdy pine bed, chest, and washstand. Vance sat on the bed, just looking around him. Julia understood how he felt. When Sarah opened the door to what was to be Julia's room, her reaction was much the same.

Julia walked into the guest room and looked around her. When Sarah quietly left, closing the door behind her, Julia moved to the windows and looked out. Her room faced the front of the house. For a long moment, she gazed at the white and pink blossoms of the fruit trees moving a little in the breeze. Then she turned back to the room. The bed was oak, and it was covered with a colorful quilt in a Texas star design. A braided rug lay on the floor beside the bed.

Julia went to the washstand. A white stoneware pitcher and bowl stood on it, with a plain white towel and wash-cloth hanging on the rack. Julia poured water into the bowl and washed her face and hands. It felt so good and the soap smelled so delicious that she skinned out of her clothes to wash all over. It was glorious to be rid of the dust. She only wished she could have taken down her hair and washed it, too, but there wasn't enough water in the pitcher. Besides, she was far too tired.

Sarah had laid out one of her own white cotton night-gowns on the bed. Julia put it on and slipped into bed. It was unbelievably soft after two nights of sleeping on the ground, and it smelled faintly of lavender. Julia snuggled down into the feathery comfort. How lovely it was here. How kind Sarah was. Tears gathered in her eyes and seeped out beneath her lids even as she drifted off to sleep.

Downstairs, Sarah hummed softly to herself as she scrubbed the Irish potatoes and rubbed them with bacon drippings, then stuck them into the hot oven to bake. She grinned a small, secret smile, thinking of how Luke's face would look when he saw Julia. He would be so happy! Sarah knew how much Luke loved his sister and how much he had regretted her marriage to Will Dobson and the separation between them.

Sarah thought about running out to the fields to tell him immediately. But then she wouldn't get to see the joy on his face when he walked in on Julia, unknowing.

She occupied herself by making supper and speculating about Julia. Sarah wouldn't have been so rude as to ask Julia point blank why she was here, but that didn't mean her curiosity wasn't aroused. Obviously Julia hadn't trudged all the way from Gideon just for a visit with her brother. She must be in some sort of trouble. Had her husband left her?

Or, more likely, it was the other way around. Luke said that Will Dobson was a crude, even mean, man. Perhaps he had hit her, or worse.

Sarah put on a pot of corn and another of collard greens and took out the pieces of round steak she had tenderized earlier this afternoon and left to soak in milk and eggs. She set the big black skillet on the largest eye of the stove and plopped a huge spoonful of lard into it. When the fat was sizzling hot, Sarah dipped each piece of meat into a mixture of flour, salt, and pepper, and laid it into the pan. The grease popped and hissed with each new addition. She kept a watchful eye on the frying meat, turning it with long tongs to avoid being burned by the hot grease. When it was brown and crisp, she set it out to drain and poured the old grease into an old pot kept for that purpose.

While she was working, Micah came to the back door and asked if she would like any chores done, so she had him do the evening chores of feeding the animals and bringing in a fresh supply of wood for her stove the next day. She glanced at him out the window now and then while she cooked. He seemed a hard worker.

The children soon arose from their nap and went to play outside. Sarah kept an occasional eye on them, too. It was nice knowing that Vance and Bonnie were with little Emily, so that she didn't have to watch her continuously. Preparations for supper went much more smoothly without Emily's presence in the kitchen, too.

The sun was getting low. It was almost time for Luke to come in from the fields. The food was done. Sarah set the table, continuing to look out the window for him. When she spotted Luke coming in from the fields, Sarah ran to the stairs and called up, "Julia! Luke's home."

A muffled voice answered her, and assured that Julia was awake, Sarah hurried out the kitchen door and into the side yard. Bonnie and Vance stood at the foot of the porch, looking across the yard toward Luke. Emily had run to him, and he had picked her up and was now hugging her and nuzzling her soft neck. He looked up at Sarah and waved, then started across the yard toward her.

"Bonnie. Vance. Why don't you run inside and clean up now?"

Sarah didn't want to have to introduce them to Luke and spoil the surprise. The children scurried back into the house. They had had enough experience of a man's uneven temper to be glad to get out of one's way when he returned from a hard day's work.

"Sarah." Luke kissed her lightly in greeting. "Who is that man in the barn? He said he'd take care of the mules. Did you hire somebody?" It wouldn't be like Sarah to do that.

"He asked if he could trade some chores for supper, so I said yes," Sarah replied. "I told him he'd have to talk to you about a job, though."

It wasn't an unusual occurrence to have a drifter be given a plateful of food by his kindhearted wife and let him pay it off with a little work. Luke frowned, saying automatically, "I don't like you talking to those drifters when you're here alone." It scared him to think of someone being around Sarah when he was out in the fields. The most frightening thing in the world, the only thing he could think of, really, that scared him, was something bad happening to Sarah or Emily.

"I can't turn them away." It was Sarah's usual response in their long-running argument over the subject. "Besides, I didn't let him in the house, like you told me."

"Good." But there was something else going on here besides a drifter seeking work. Sarah's cheeks glowed with color, and her eyes danced. She practically vibrated with suppressed excitement. He started to smile. "What is it?"

"What?" Sarah returned innocently.

The smile gained a definite hold on Luke's mouth. He enjoyed looking at Sarah like this, all pink and bubbling. "Something's afoot. What is it?"

"I don't know why you'd think that."

"Those children you just hid inside the house, for one thing. They obviously don't belong to the man in the barn. Who are they? Why are they here?"

Sarah chuckled. "I'm not going to tell you yet. You have another visitor, too. Why don't you come inside?"

Luke couldn't imagine who could engender such eagerness in Sarah, but he followed her into the house without another

word. When she smiled at him like that, he would have
followed her anywhere.

When they stepped inside, Sarah took his hand and
whisked him through the dining room into the front hall,
where he had a full view of the staircase. A woman was
coming down the stairs, and she froze in mid-motion when
she saw him. She said nothing, simply looked at him, and it
was a moment before Luke could say anything, either—or
even move.

"Julie?" The word came out softly, wonderingly. It
couldn't really be her. It had been so long.

She nodded. She looked almost scared. Luke was so
different from the sixteen-year-old boy Julia remembered.
His frame was still wiry, but he had fleshed out. He was a
man now. Still handsome enough to sing birds out of the
trees—maybe even better looking—but not the same. His
face was older, with lines of experience that hadn't been
there before, but, curiously, it was not harder. The old
pugnacious look and the wary, defiant air were gone. His
stance was open and at ease, and his face was almost
peaceful. *I don't know you.* Tears formed in Julia's eyes,
and she wasn't sure whether she was happy for Luke or sad
for herself.

Luke moved, breaking the tableau. "Julie!" He broke
into a grin and hurried toward her, his arms extended. There
was no mistaking the elation in his voice, the intermingled
joy and amazement. "Julie!"

Julia giggled and flung herself into his arms. He squeezed
her to him and whirled around, lifting her up off the floor.
Julia held on tightly, closing her eyes, shutting out the rest
of the world for that brief instant of love and safety. "Oh,
Luke."

Julia's tears started in earnest then. Luke set her down
and stepped back, holding her at arm's length to look at her.
"I can't believe it! It's really you! I never thought I'd—"
He pulled her back for another hug, laughing. "Oh, Julie!"

She could do nothing but laugh and cry and hold him and
try to look at him, all at once. He hugged her so hard it
hurt. He looked over her head at Sarah. "Did you know
about this?"

Sarah, smiling mistily, shook her head. "Not until this afternoon."

"Julie, what's happened? What are you doing here? Oh, hell! Forget that. Just let me look at you. Are you all right? Are you sick or anything?"

"No. I'm fine, really. Just a little tired."

"I can't believe—it's been so long."

"Eleven years."

"Eleven years. You're still beautiful."

"Then you're still a liar." Julia smiled up at him, wiping the tears from her cheeks. But, Sarah thought, with that glow on Julia's face as she gazed at Luke, she did look beautiful, despite her tiredness and lack of care.

"God, I'm glad you're here."

"My children are with me." She turned to where Bonnie and Vance stood, staring wide-eyed at the scene before them. "Bonnie, Vance, come here. Meet your Uncle Luke."

"Your children." Luke stared at them. Of course, he'd known she had children, had to have had since she'd been pregnant when she left home. But somehow the idea had never had much reality. "Hello, there." Luke squatted down on their level. "I'm your uncle." They nodded silently, not sure what to say to this man. "I'm pleased to meet you."

"Children," their mother said meaningfully.

"Pleased to meet you," they chorused, and Luke grinned.

"I see she's got you better trained than she ever did me."

"I learned my lessons with you," Julia retorted.

Luke stood up and ruffled the children's hair, aching to touch them, yet not wanting to force them or frighten them. "I'm glad you're here. Emily been showing you everything?"

They nodded, and the boy said, "Yes, sir."

"I—I'm sure you wonder what I'm doing here," Julia began, lacing her hands together in front of her. Sarah thought she looked like a child bracing herself to confess a prank to the school principal. There was something fragile about Julia, something that made a person want to hug her and assure her that you'd keep the bad things away. Sarah suspected that no one had ever kept the bad things from her, though.

"I just want to look at you," Luke interjected. He knew

that whatever Julia had to say was hard for her, and doubly so in front of Sarah and the children. "We can talk after supper. I bet these little ones are starving. I know I am."

"That's right," Sarah added. "Let's eat first."

The family sat down around the table, and, much to Julia's astonishment, Luke folded his hands and lowered his head along with Sarah and Emily, and Sarah said grace. Julia stared. Luke looked up and caught her staring at him, and he winked. "Sure got respectable, didn't I?"

Julia nodded. He was her old Luke, yet he wasn't. The changes in him seemed only to the better, but it left her unsure what to make of him.

Luke glanced toward Sarah, his gaze soft and loving. Julia had never seen him look like that, and it made her heart hurt with love and happiness for him and a little regret for herself. "Sarah's done it to me." His hand covered Sarah's where it rested on the edge of the table. "Didn't you, sweetheart?"

She smiled back at him, the love in her eyes equally strong. "Somebody had to, I reckon."

"I want 'tato," Emily piped up, and the tender moment was gone. They began to dish up the food and eat.

Julia and the children thought what they had eaten a few hours earlier was plentiful, but it was a mere snack compared to this meal. They rarely had chicken-fried steak, and when they did, it was a very special occasion. Their meals ran to beans and greens and rice; and if there was meat, it was usually pork middlings cooked in the vegetables. They dived into the meal with gusto; and when they finished, their plates were as clean as if they had wiped them. There was peach cobbler for dessert, with cream poured on top, and that was the best of all.

Julia, Sarah, and the girls cleaned up afterward, and Sarah took the children upstairs to put them to bed, leaving Luke and Julia alone to talk. Julia told her brother the story of Will's death, their financial straits and of her decision to come to him. She was grateful for Sarah's tactful departure. It was far easier to talk alone with Luke. It was still embarrassing, but she knew that Luke understood; he had once lived the same kind of life she had.

"I'm sorry," Julia finished softly, gazing down at her

hands. "I didn't want to burden you with my family, but I didn't know where else to go. And the children . . ."

"What are you talking about?" Luke sounded indignant. "Where else should you go, except to your own family? You're no burden to me. I want you here. Julie, I'm so happy. I've missed you for years."

"Oh, Luke!" Julia's head came up, and she looked at him, tears shining in her eyes. "I've missed you, too! I felt so bad that I never came to see you, that I didn't see you get married. That I wasn't there when you were on trial."

"There was no reason you should have been there," he replied gruffly. "It was no place for a lady."

"I'm no lady; I'm just a Turner."

"Don't say that!" Luke looked fierce. "You're as good as any woman. I won't let you talk that way about yourself. If Sarah hears you, she'll give you a real earful." He grinned ruefully. "She always does me if I say something like that. She's a wonderful woman." His smile turned dreamy. "Sarah believes that you can be whatever you want, that it doesn't matter how you started out or what your name is. She's made me believe it, too. She's given me so much—I don't mean the farm, but inside. She showed me what I can do. She gave me a chance when there wasn't another soul on earth who would have."

"She sees who you really are, like I do."

"Yeah." Luke grinned. "And she doesn't even hold that against me."

"Oh, Luke." Julia made an expression of mock exasperation. "She must be a saint to put up with your teasing."

"She probably is."

"But even a saint couldn't be happy about having a strange woman suddenly living in her house. I don't want to make trouble between you and Sarah."

Luke smiled and touched Julia's cheek. "I can't imagine a woman less likely to make trouble than you."

"But it's hard to have a stranger in your house, especially one with two children. Sarah won't like that."

"You don't know Sarah. She's happy that you're here. She came out to meet me tonight, glowing all over, like she had a wonderful secret. She loves me, Julie." Luke's voice roughened, and he glanced away. "She loves me so much I can't believe it. She wants me to be happy, and she knows how happy it makes me to have you here. Sarah's good; she's generous." He paused and shrugged. "There's no way to tell you. You'll just have to see it for yourself. But for now, take my word for it. You won't be a burden. You won't create trouble. Sarah and I want you here."

"Thank you."

"Besides, Sarah's six months along; she could use a helping hand. The housework is a lot for her to do by herself, even when she's feeling good. But with her getting heavier and tireder and with summer coming on—well, it'd be impossible. The Crowleys, our neighbors, were going to send their oldest girl over to help starting next month, but you being here will be better."

"That's true. I could do a lot of things for her." Julia's spirits brightened. This house and all the extra work that went with summertime would be too much for a pregnant woman. Julia realized that she would be useful, not a burden. If Sarah really was as nice as she seemed, maybe she wouldn't look down on Julia and think she was ignorant and low class. Maybe they could even be friends. And by the time Sarah was able to handle all the housework and the new baby by herself, Julia would have had plenty of time to look around for some kind of work. Perhaps she could even build up a little nest egg by taking in sewing in her spare time.

"There. See? You're a blessing, not a problem. Now, tell me how you got here. Who is this Micah fellow?"

"I walked," Julia replied simply.

"You what? All the way from Gideon?"

"Yes. How else could I come?"

"Why didn't you telegraph me? I would have come and gotten you."

"I didn't think of it. It would have cost money, and I—I didn't think of it."

Luke grimaced. He guessed a few years ago he wouldn't have thought of it either. "I'm sorry."

Julia shrugged. "It wasn't that bad. But it was tiring, and we didn't bring enough food. A mile or two from your house, I—well, it was silly, but I fainted. Micah happened along, and he helped me. He carried me part of the way, until I came to, and after that, he carried the suitcase and let me lean on him; my knees were watery.''

Luke sighed. "I'm sorry this happened to you. Things will be better for you now. I promise." Luke rose from his chair. "I'm going out to talk to this fellow who helped you. And you better go on up to bed. You need the rest."

"All right." Julia stood up, too, and reached out to take Luke's hand. "Thank you."

"No need to thank me. I'm glad you're home."

"So am I."

When Luke returned to the house, Sarah was already upstairs getting ready for bed. She sat in a chair, bending down to unlace her high-topped shoes and slip them off. She smiled up at Luke, and he brushed his hand against her cheek.

"Julie's husband's dead."

"What?" Sarah had thought of other reasons for Julia to be here, but not of that. "But he's not very old, is—was he?"

Luke shook his head. "Thirty-six or so, I guess. He dropped dead in the fields. A heart attack."

"Oh, my goodness. How awful for her."

"He's no loss."

"Luke!"

"What? His being dead doesn't make him any nicer."

"No, but . . . well, I'm glad she came to us."

"She didn't have much choice." Luke sat down and began to pull off his work boots. "Will was sharecropping forty acres for a man named Harrington, and the man wanted to put a new tenant in the house."

"You mean, he made Julia leave her house right after her husband died!"

"Yeah. That's why she set out on foot with the kids. She doesn't have any money. Will was in debt to Harrington, so Harrington took the tools, wagon, and team in payment of the debt."

"Luke! How terrible! Poor Julia."

Luke smiled. He had been certain of Sarah's sympathy,

but it pleased him to hear her confirm it. "I told her she could stay with us."

"Of course." Sarah smiled. It would be nice having another woman in the house, not just for a hand with the chores (although that would be a pleasant relief, too, especially as she got heavier with child), but mostly for conversation and companionship. It was often a lonely life on the farm, not seeing neighbors or family except on Sundays, with only a two-year-old to keep her company during the day.

It would be fun to chat with Julia while they washed and hung out the clothes or cooked supper. They could laugh over the things Emily did. Maybe Julia would tell Sarah stories about Luke's childhood, the sort of sweet things Luke wished she knew about her husband—the way he had looked, his first word, the games he had played.

"She was afraid she might cause problems here," Luke told her.

"Why?"

He shrugged. "I guess because she doesn't know you very well."

"Well, with some women it might be a problem. I mean, every woman has her own way of running a house. But I can't see Julia and me fussing over things like that, can you?" Luke shook his head. "Anyway, even if she were cantankerous or lazy, she's your sister. I couldn't turn her away."

Luke unbuttoned his shirt. "I told her you would be fine with it."

Sarah finished undressing and slid a white cotton nightgown over her head. Luke watched her, his fingers growing still on his buttons. Sarah's stomach was swollen with the child she carried and the gown was plain and voluminous, but, even so, the sight of her putting it on stirred his loins.

"I hired Micah." Luke slumped down in his chair, stretching out his legs, to watch Sarah unbraid her hair.

"Did you? Good. You need a hand." The thick strands of her hair loosened when Sarah unfastened her braid, but didn't fall apart. She pushed her fingers through her hair like a comb, separating the strands. Her hair clung and curled around her fingers.

Luke wet his lips. "Yeah. Well, he did a good job on the chores this afternoon, and he helped Julia. He's staying in the room in the barn. I gave him sheets and towels."

Sarah picked up her brush and began to pull it through her hair. It fell in thick, brown, silky waves down her back, clear to her hips.

Luke went to stand behind her. He took the brush from her hand and began to brush her hair himself. He loved the feel of it in his hands, warm and soft, catching on his calluses. "Being in that room made me think about when I first came here. When I lived there."

"I remember."

He smiled faintly. "I used to lie awake in my bed every night, thinking about you."

"Oh, Luke."

"It's true."

"You acted like you didn't know I was alive."

He gathered her hair in one hand and twisted it lazily around his hand and arm, watching it catch the light. He bent and kissed the top of her head. "I was scared to death of you, afraid I'd frighten or disgust you. I wanted so badly for you not to fear me."

Sarah rose and took his face between her hands. "I never feared you."

"I know. You're an amazing woman."

"No. I just know you."

Luke bent and kissed her, releasing her hair and letting it slide through his hand. He wanted her, as he always did, but he refrained, as he always did. "I love you."

"I love you, too."

They climbed into bed, and Sarah snuggled into his arms. She fell asleep quickly, as she did nowadays, but Luke lay awake for a long time, listening to her soft, even breathing and feeling the soft warmth of her body. He knew there wasn't a man alive happier than he was.

* Chapter 4 *

Julia was amazed at how easily she and the children fit into Luke and Sarah's life. All the fears she had held about her sister-in-law proved to be wrong. Sarah was pleasant and easy to talk to. She never demanded or told Julia what to do, but always asked. There was nothing in her tone or manner to indicate that she thought herself better than Julia. She treated Julia simply as her husband's beloved sister, a woman whom she wanted to know and like—and by whom she wished to be liked! That amazed Julia more than anything else, that Sarah McGowan should be concerned over whether Julia Dobson liked her and was happy in her home.

They worked well together, both of them hard workers and neat to a fault. They fell into a natural division of labor, with Julia taking on the heavier tasks that were difficult for Sarah in her condition. At first Sarah protested that Julia was working too hard and would hurt herself, but Julia simply laughed. "Haven't you got that backwards? You're the one who should take it easy."

"But you—are you sure you're up to it?"

Julia shook her head, smiling. She knew that her small size and pale coloring often deceived people into thinking she was fragile. "Don't worry. I may not be big, but I'm strong as an ox. Just let me worry about the heavy things."

Before the day was out, Sarah had to admit that Julia was right—she might look as though a hard wind would blow her away; but she was strong and loaded with stamina.

Sarah was glad for the help. She had forgotten how much more quickly the chores went when there were two women to do them, especially with Vance and Bonnie to take care of small chores and keep Emily occupied. They were done each day with time to spare, so Sarah suggested that they use their free time to make the children some new clothes, pointing out tactfully that Julia must have had to leave most of their clothes when they moved.

Julia supposed that she ought to be too proud to accept Sarah's charity, no matter how kindly Sarah phrased it. But she couldn't bring herself to refuse the offer. She longed to see her children in something new and pretty, just once.

Sarah brought down several lengths of material from a trunk in the attic, and throughout the next few days, they worked on the children's clothes every moment their hands were idle. With two of them sewing, the work went quickly and by Saturday they had finished a simple outfit for each of the children. Then Sarah brought out two of her own dresses and insisted on altering them to fit Julia's smaller frame.

Julia protested, but when she tried them on, she couldn't bear to refuse them. One dress was blue and the other, a dusky rose, and they did magical things for her coloring. The sleeves of the rose-colored one were tight, with long, buttoned cuffs, and puffed out at the shoulders. A narrow row of ivory lace decorated its cuffs and collar.

Julia looked at herself in the mirror, wanting the rose dress so much she could taste it. "It's awfully fancy."

"Fancy! What do you mean? It'll be perfect for church or company."

"Well, yes, you're right." Julia turned before the mirror, craning her neck to see the back. No doubt it didn't seem fancy to Sarah, but Julia had never had a dress with lace on it, even the one she had worn on her wedding day. "I just meant, it's maybe too fancy for me. I don't know if I look right in it."

Sarah gave an inelegant snort. "Don't be silly. Luke!"

He came up the stairs and smiled at the sight of his sister in the dress.

"Tell her that she looks right in that dress," Sarah ordered.

"You look beautiful."

"See?" Sarah said around the pins in her mouth and continued pinning up the hem. "If I hurry, we can get this ready for you to wear to church tomorrow.'' She glanced up. ''That is, I mean, if you want to go.''

Julia thought of going to church in Sarah's pretty dress, with her children in brand new clothes and Sarah there to smooth her way. It was vanity and pride, of course, not good reasons to go to church, but still . . . she wanted to go. ''Yes, I'd like that.''

The next morning after chores, Julia was surprised to see Luke come down dressed in a black suit and white shirt with stiff celluloid cuffs and collar. Julia realized that he was going to church with them. Julia had never known Luke to step foot inside a church before. She sneaked a glance at Sarah, but Sarah, struggling to get Emily's feet encased in her little black boots, seemed to find nothing unusual in Luke's going to church.

And when they arrived at the New Hope Methodist Church, no one there seemed surprised to see Luke, either. People did turn to look at them when they walked in, but then they just smiled and nodded to Luke and Sarah. No one looked surprised. No one turned away and began to whisper furiously to his neighbor. No one seemed offended.

Julia felt self-conscious. She often did. She had learned as a child that she didn't fit in most places—not at church or school or the other places where ''good'' people belonged. Because she had been quiet and well behaved, Julia had been tolerated (as Luke and her older brother had not been), but she had always been aware that she was there on sufferance. She knew that people looked at her and waited for her to do something that would reveal her as a true Turner.

She knew that they were looking at her here, wondering who she was and what she was doing here. She was very aware of Sarah's borrowed straw hat on her head and Sarah's pink dress on her body and Sarah's white gloves on her hands. Did everyone realize that none of these things were her own? Did they think she was like a pig dressed up in finery? Julia raised her eyes timidly from her hands and met the interested gaze of a bearded man sitting in the next pew beside three stair-step children.

Sarah leaned over and whispered in her ear, ''I think you've caught Bill Langley's attention.'' Sarah's voice was light and amused. "Tread carefully; I've heard his boy is a terror."

Julia felt a flush spreading over her cheeks, and she glanced at Sarah. "You can't mean that he's—"

"Interested in you? Oh, can't I?"

Julia turned her attention back to her primly folded hands. Sarah must be mistaken. No man would be interested in her. She'd lost whatever looks she'd had long ago. Why, she was twenty-eight years old and had two children! The years and the work showed on her. She had seen the fine lines around her mouth and eyes and the dulling of her burnished hair and blue eyes. It wasn't possible that a man might still desire her. Certainly not in church!

She looked up again, but the man was no longer looking at her. Relief spread through her. Sarah had to be wrong.

The sermon was long. Julia glanced over now and then at Luke and more than once caught a glazed look in his eyes. She knew he was bored, but he sat patiently. They sang a few hymns, but Julia didn't know many of them. Will hadn't liked for her to go to church; he had never wanted her to socialize. And, of course, when she had lived at home with her father and brothers, she had never gone to church. But she followed along in the hymnal, enjoying the sound of the music. This was a peaceful, simple church, and she liked sitting here, listening to the preacher's mellow voice and the solemn songs.

After the service, the congregation moved down the center aisle and out onto the steps of the church, gathering in little groups on the steps and in the yard. A middle-aged man and woman with several children of all ages came over to greet Luke and Sarah, and it was obvious from their smiles and enthusiastic greetings that they were special friends. Sarah introduced them to Julia as Jake and Mary Etta Crowley. The Crowleys seemed genuinely happy to meet her.

Julia liked Mary Etta Crowley on sight. She was a large woman with traces of her youthful good looks still on her face. There were laugh lines around her mouth and eyes, and her brown eyes were sharp and alight with interest. "So you're Luke's sister, are you? I've heard him talk about you often. Such a pretty little thing you are, too. And such nice children. I'm sorry to hear about your husband. It must be quite a loss to you."

"Thank you."

"But it's an ill wind, I always say, 'cause here you are to help Sarah when she needs it. I know she's grateful."

"Oh, no, I'm the one who's grateful."

"Hush," Sarah interjected pleasantly. "I don't want to hear any more talk like that from you. I need you. You've already been a tremendous help."

"How have you been feeling?" Mary Etta asked Sarah, and they launched on a long, thoroughly engrossing discussion of pregnancy and its problems.

Julia glanced over at Luke. He stood talking to Jake and the Crowleys' oldest boy, Burt, both of whom listened to Luke with great interest. Julia could see the respect in Burt's eyes.

Other people joined them, some pausing only to say hello, others to chat. Sarah introduced Julia to everyone, and they returned her greetings politely. She was accepted, Julia thought, because of Sarah—and Luke. Nearly all the men stopped by to say hello, and some of them lingered to talk. There were no askance glances, no hesitations in greeting Luke. Some clapped him on the back or shook his hand with affection. Others simply nodded or said a word or two. But no one treated him as an outsider. And Luke— Julia was amazed to see his expression so open, sometimes smiling, sometimes serious, but never hard and bitter. He didn't stand with his arms crossed over his chest and his eyes narrowed and suspicious, as if he were waiting for someone to say the wrong thing, as he once would have. Over the past few days Julia had become accustomed to the changes in her brother, but now, seeing him with other people, she noticed them all anew. Luke Turner no longer looked for trouble.

The Crowleys joined the Turners for Sunday dinner and wound up staying most of the afternoon. Hearing Luke talk to Jake, Julia sensed the strong bond between them, and she realized that the older man was almost a father to Luke, the kind of father he had never found in his own flesh and blood. A lump of pain crystallized in Julia's chest, but she wasn't sure if it was sadness for what Luke had missed all his life or happiness for what he had now.

Later, when the Crowleys had gone and Luke was outside doing the evening chores, Julia and Sarah sat alone in the parlor, their hands busy with the mending.

"Luke's changed a lot," Julia commented, glancing at her sister-in-law. "He's happy, and I never thought he would be. It's because of you."

Sarah smiled. "He hasn't changed. He just let out all the good stuff inside him that he never allowed people to see before. It's not me that's done anything. It's Luke."

"Then you saw in him what no one else did, except me."

"That's because I loved him," Sarah responded simply. "He's given me every bit as much as I've given him." She turned to Julia, her sewing dropping unnoticed into her lap. "He made me happier than I'd ever been in my life. I was never loved as Luke loves me, heart and soul. I love him the same way. Sometimes I lie awake at night, scared to death, thinking what if something happened to him? I don't know what I'd do without Luke. I wouldn't want to live."

Julia's heart squeezed inside her chest, and she thought, suddenly, of Jimmy. She had felt that way about him, long ago, when they had been in love. She had thought that she couldn't live without him. But she had. "That kind of love is precious. I'm very happy for Luke."

Sarah thought she caught the glimmer of tears in Julia's eyes. She reached out and took Julia's hand and squeezed it. Julia returned the pressure. Then they smiled a little shyly and moved back and the moment slid away.

As the days passed, Julia's looks changed, though she was unaware of it. Part of the reason was the new dresses she wore, some made over from Sarah's clothes and one a brand new dress from a piece of sky blue cotton that Sarah had insisted on making. Part of it was the fact that she was eating three good meals a day, and she had lost her earlier gauntness. But the change was more than either of those. The lines of stress and care had melted from her face. No longer was there a narrow groove perpetually between her eyes. Her mouth wasn't grim anymore, the lips held tight and straight.

She felt safe now. She didn't have to fear her husband's volatile temper nor endure his invasion of her body at night. There was no need to worry about the lack of food or whether the crops would be enough to pay back Mr. Harrington or how she would get together the money to clothe and shoe her children.

She looked younger, her hair shinier, her eyes bluer. The delicate color was back in her face, and her mouth was once again soft and full. She had lost the beaten-down look, and she was pretty, even beautiful when the sweet smile touched her face.

Luke and Sarah saw the change, and it pleased them. Sarah began to think happily of matchmaking, turning over in her mind the eligible bachelors available and wondering which of them would be right for Julia. She deserved somebody special.

The next Saturday they went into Willow Springs to get the mail and buy supplies. It was a treat to go to town, and the whole family was excited. Julia wore her new blue dress and proudly put her children in their new clothes. They climbed into the wagon and drove off, Micah and the children in the back and Julia sitting up on the high seat next to Luke and Sarah.

They went first to the seed store, where Luke made his purchases. Micah helped Luke load the heavy sacks into the wagon, then went his own way.

Micah had the rest of the weekend free, and had two weeks' pay in his pocket. He was feeling good. He'd worn his best shirt and trousers, as well as his father's Mexican-tooled leather belt. He pushed his hat back at a jauntier angle. He planned to enjoy himself today. First he would look around the town a little, find out what was what. He would learn where moonshine could be bought, and he'd buy a jug. There would be dancing someplace, and he'd find that, too. And at the dance, he would find a willing woman.

Micah smiled to himself at the thought. Women, that was what he liked best back here, maybe the only thing. There weren't many women out farther west, particularly not his own kind—if there was such a thing. He had discovered a long time ago that he wasn't like anyone else. He had his feet half in one world, half in the other, and though he could survive in either, he really didn't belong anywhere. His father, a freed slave from Georgia, had been a "buffalo soldier," one of the famed black cavalry. His mother had been a Navajo Indian. When he was little, he hadn't known he was odd, hadn't realized that he was neither fish nor fowl. Around the fort he had fit in. The other men had been like his father: tough, proud, independent black men. There had been several women like his mother, Indians who lived with soldiers. Later, when his father had left the army, they had moved to a small town in the New Mexico Territory, and there his father had plied the trade of blacksmith, to which he'd been trained long ago when he was still a boy and a slave. There had been no one else like Micah's family in that town, no other squaw, no other black man, and Micah had begun to realize how different he was.

He had known that he had no place with the Navajos, but, listening to his father talk about Georgia and his family there, he had decided that his people lay back east. He hadn't been able to understand why his father never wanted to return. When he had asked, all his father said was that here in the West he was free and a man, which made little sense to Micah. He hadn't understood until his father's death when Micah was fifteen and had packed his bag and ridden to Georgia. He hadn't understood until he'd been thrown in jail in Texas because he carried no bill of sale for his horse—and though he was released, he never saw the horse again—and been beaten up in Louisiana for being uppity because he carried his head too high and looked people in the face when he talked to them.

When he had reached Georgia, his relatives had welcomed him. They had listened to his tales of his father with great interest, but they had chuckled and shaken their heads over the stories, and Micah had realized that they thought his father had been touched in the head to go so far from home and live so odd a life. He had seen the doubt in their eyes when they looked at him, taking in the different sheen of his skin, the different texture of his hair, the different molding of his bones. He looked like Sam, too, only not quite. He was their race, and he was family, but he wasn't quite that, either. He talked differently and walked differently. He could ride a horse better than any of the whites in the county, whereas his family had walked all their lives and held themselves lucky to own a mule for their plow. His ma had been a wild Indian, and there was something a little wild about him, too.

Micah had felt the pull of kinship, the comfort and companionship of being with others whose skin was like his, but he hadn't been able to stay there. He had gone back west and worked on a ranch in New Mexico. Ever since then, he'd been a drifter, going from one place to another, never staying long, never fitting in wherever he went. Sometimes the pull of his own kind was too much, the loneliness too great, and then he would go to East Texas or Louisiana. Eventually, the lure of freedom would bring him back west. He had traveled all over the West, and he had traveled throughout the South, rolling back and forth. He was a drifter, out of place wherever he lived; but he was thirty-five years old now, and he'd been doing it for twenty years. He'd gotten used to it.

Micah walked unerringly to the black section of town and strolled around it, looking over the people and watching them look him over. He'd gone through that process a lot of times, too. There was always one particular street corner where the young men gathered to talk. Micah soon discovered it and paused to chat with them. He could see them sizing him up, but they answered his questions without hesitation. The best liquor to be had was purchased a mile out of town at Two-toe Jim's (so known because all his other toes had been blown off when his still exploded ten years ago). There was dancing every Saturday at Opal's, where certain types of women also were to be found.

Micah wasn't much for talking, another product, perhaps, of the way he'd been raised, and he soon left the young men. He ate lunch at a rooming house on Ninth Street, and afterward he sat on a low rock wall in front of the house and watched the occasional passersby. That was where he saw the woman.

She was dressed in a prim black skirt with a high-necked white cotton blouse, pinned at the collar with a small cameo brooch. Her hair was slicked back into a tight bun, and on top of her head she wore a flat straw boater hat. She walked in a tight, no-nonsense sort of way. In fact, everything about her was tight and no-nonsense. But Micah could tell that beneath that skirt her legs must be wickedly long, and her waist was so small he could circle it with his hands. The idea of doing just that appealed to him. He liked tall women, and this one's face beneath the hat was classically lovely, her brown skin smooth and soft. She was a contradiction, feminine loveliness reined in tight. A challenge.

He pushed himself up off the wall and followed her, catching up with her in front of the next house. She turned and glanced at him when she heard his footsteps. No expression touched her face, and she turned her head right back, stepping all the way to the side so that he could pass her. Micah smiled and pulled even with her. The sight of her face up close did nothing to discourage his interest. Her skin was as lovely as it had looked from a distance; her eyes were large and luminous under thin, arched brows; and her mouth was full and sensual.

"Afternoon," he remarked pleasantly.

Dovie Mitchell kept her face turned straight ahead and said nothing. She wasn't about to let that man start a conversation with her. She had seen him as soon as she turned the corner, sitting on the low stone fence, a tall man with wide shoulders and well-developed arms. She had guessed immediately that this was the stranger in town, about whom she'd heard everyone talking at her aunt's earlier this afternoon. Not much went on that wasn't all over the black community in a matter of hours.

Dovie had watched him covertly as she'd walked up the block, and she had been fully aware when he stood up and began to follow her. There was a funny little catch of excitement in her stomach when he drew close; and she couldn't stop herself from glancing at him, even though she knew that she shouldn't give a stranger, a drifter, even a look. He was handsome; the gossips hadn't been wrong about that. His features were strong, his face wide, and his cheekbones high. His eyes were pure black, without the least trace of brown, and his skin had a copper tint to its darkness. There was something different about him, something almost foreign, and that made him intriguing.

But Dovie Mitchell was not about to be intrigued by a drifter.

"Nice day," Micah went on when she didn't respond to his greeting.

Dovie kept her mouth shut and her eyes firmly ahead. She wasn't the type to be picked up by a masher on Ninth Street. If the man hadn't been a stranger, he would have known it.

But, then, if Dovie had known Micah, she would have known that he wasn't easily put off. He strolled along beside her, watching her elegant profile and wondering if her icy manner would melt in bed. He would like to find out. "My name's Micah Harrison. I work at the Turner place."

The fact that he had a job didn't change Dovie's opinion of him. He was still a drifter, just working for a week or two until he had the money to go on. She turned and gave him her coolest, blankest stare. He smiled back. She could feel the charm of his smile all the way down to her toes. She doubted that he usually had any trouble finding a woman.

"I hear there be dancin' at Opal's Saturdays. Maybe we—"

"No." Dovie stopped and faced him. "We could *not*. I have tried to let you know that I am not interested in talking, walking, or doing anything else with you. But apparently I have to tell you flat out. I do not wish to go dancing with you tonight. Nor do I have any desire to speak to you. So, please, stop following me and trying to strike up a conversation."

Micah's smile broadened. "Girl, you sure can talk. I never heard so many fancy words come out of a mouth at one time in my life."

"I hope you understood their meaning, too."

"Oh yes, ma'am." He continued to look at her. He liked looking at her. And he liked her voice, crisp, clean, and educated. "Where you learn to talk that way?"

Dovie's mouth twisted in exasperation. "Leave me alone." She enunciated each word separately and distinctly. "I walk right past the sheriff's office on my way home."

Amusement lit his eyes, and that irritated her further. "And you so important, he gonna run out to protect you?"

Her eyes flashed. "He knows me. He knows that what I say is the truth. Now, if you'd like to put it to the test, we can go see him right now..."

He grinned. "Oh, no, ma'am, you done put the fear of God into me." He tipped his hat with exaggerated politeness. "Good day, ma'am." He started off, but couldn't resist throwing back over his shoulder, "I be seein' you."

Dovie grimaced. "Not if I see you first," she muttered. She started once again for home, walking even faster now in her irritation. She didn't have time for lowlifes like that. She didn't have any interest in them, either. Not even if he did have a good-looking face. Not even if there was something about him that pulled at her.

Behind her Micah sauntered back in the direction from which he had come. It looked like he would have to find someone else to dance with, at least for tonight. He smiled, remembering the fine flash of her eyes. There'd be other nights.

If Julia had been amazed by the way Luke had been accepted at church last Sunday, she was doubly so in town today. He was greeted at the seed store like a valued customer. No one turned away from him; no one called him "Digger"; no one looked at him warily, as if wondering what he might do next. They called him "Mr. Turner" or "Luke," and they nodded or shook his hand. She even heard one of the men asking Luke's advice about purchasing some cattle.

After they left the seed store, they strolled through town, looking in the shop windows and enjoying the day. Eventually they wound up in Harper's store, where the children rushed immediately to the candy jars. Stu Harper, standing behind the counter, laughed, and leaned over the counter to talk to them. "Why, hey there, Emily, who are your friends?"

"Cousins," Emily informed him proudly.

"Cousins?" Stu straightened and looked at Sarah. "Hello, Sarah. Luke."

"Stu." Luke nodded.

"Hi, Stu." Sarah smiled, taking Julia by the arm. "This

is Luke's sister, Julia Dobson, and her children, Bonnie and Vance. Julia, this is my brother-in-law, Stu Harper. He's married to my sister, Jennifer.''

"It's a pleasure to meet you, Mrs. Dobson." Harper smiled at her.

Julia returned his smile shyly. "Mr. Harper."

Stu reached into one of the glass jars on the counter and pulled out three peppermint sticks. "Think you kids can eat these without getting sticky?"

"Oh yes!" they chorused. Bonnie gazed, wide-eyed, at the candy.

"Here you go, then." He handed them the sticks and came around the counter, ruffling Emily's hair as he passed. "Say, Luke, I got in that wire you've been wanting."

"Good." Luke followed him into the hardware section.

"I hear you've bought another twenty acres from the Widners," Stu commented as they walked away.

"Yeah, I'm going to run a few more cattle on it."

Sarah watched them go, a smile playing about her lips. Luke and Stu would never be real friends; but their relationship was a far cry from the day that Stu had accused Luke of marrying Sarah for her farm, and Luke had hit him. They had achieved a certain grudging respect for each other, and Sarah and Jennifer no longer had to smooth the waters between them at every family gathering.

Looking at the two men, Sarah found it hard to believe that she had once thought she was in love with Stu. He was a nice-looking man, handsome and broad-shouldered, but compared to Luke, he was bland. He had none of Luke's spark, none of his sense of fun or his smoldering sexuality. Sarah watched Luke bend and pick up a bucket of nails, his supple fingers curling around the handle, the muscles and tendons of his arm standing out. His hair, the color and texture of corn silk, fell down over his eyes, and he impatiently tossed it back from his face. He glanced up, and his eyes, startlingly blue in his tanned face, met Sarah's across the room. He smiled at her in a slow, sensual way that spoke of the nights they had spent together. A familiar heat curled in Sarah's abdomen. No, there was no comparing Luke with any man.

Luke winked at her, then turned back to his business.

Sarah tried to collect her thoughts. "Let's see now, where's my list? Oh yes, first of all, we need some material for clothes."

"What?" Julia looked horrified. "Oh, no, not for the children and me!"

"Yes, for the children and you. Bonnie and Vance need more everyday clothes and nice little Sunday outfits—a lacy white dress for Bonnie and a suit and shirt for Vance. You ought to have a few blouses and skirts, as well as something special for parties."

"Parties! I don't go to parties."

"You will this summer. In a couple of months it'll be time for the Fourth of July dance."

"I wouldn't be going to that."

"You will, too. I'll be big as a cow by then, and Luke will need someone to dance with. Who better than his sister? I won't have to feel jealous."

"Sarah, I can't accept such generosity."

To Julia's amazement, Sarah looked hurt. "But I want to. It's so much fun—I mean, I can't look good in anything nowadays. Whatever I make for myself will look like a bag, no matter what. I wanted to sew something pretty and have it look nice on you." She paused, gazing sad-eyed at Julia, and Julia was stabbed by guilt.

"I'm sorry. I didn't realize. I hate for you to spend so much money on us, but if you want to . . . if it makes you happy . . ."

Sarah smiled. Three years of living with Luke had taught her how to handle the prickly Turner pride. "Yes, it will make me very happy. Come on, let's look at the material."

They sent the children outside to sit on the steps and eat their candy, and Sarah and Julia moved down to the cloth counter. They were soon engrossed in materials and colors, and they hardly noticed the other people who entered and left the store.

"Good afternoon, Mrs. Turner," a male voice said behind them.

Julia froze. She knew that voice. Sarah turned.

"Dr. Banks! How nice to see you." Sarah's smile was stiff. Now, this was an awkward situation if ever there was one—Julia having to meet the man who had seduced and

abandoned her years ago. Everything Sarah could think of
to say seemed wrong.

"You look as if you're feeling well," James went on
politely.

"Yes, I am, thank you."

His gaze flickered to Julia, half turned away from them,
then back to Sarah. Almost immediately his eyes snapped
back to Julia, and he stared. Sarah could have sworn that all
the color left his face. "Julie!" The word was barely more
than a whisper.

Julia turned toward him slowly, as if it hurt to move. She
couldn't bear to look at him, yet she had to. "Ji—that is,
ah—" What had Sarah called him? Dr. Banks. Of course,
he had been studying to be a doctor. "Dr. Banks."

James pulled his eyes away from Julia. He tried to
recapture the thread of his conversation with Sarah. "Are
you feeling well?"

"Yes, I'm fine," Sarah replied, forebearing to mention
that he'd already covered that topic.

Julia and James both looked at Sarah, but their eyes kept
sneaking back to each other. The boy in James was gone,
Julia thought. His face was older and tired, stamped with
lines of experience. His expression was grave; the sparkle
that had once lit up his dark eyes had vanished, and his
mouth was set in firm, tight lines. Jimmy had never been
one to tease and joke and charm, as Luke had, but Julia had
the feeling that now he was not one to smile, either.

She was still beautiful, James thought. Not with that
fresh, heart-stopping loveliness he remembered, but still
delicately lovely. She was a woman now, with a woman's
fuller, more rounded body. Her pale gold hair was done up
in a tight twist, its full glory hidden. Her eyes held shadows, and there were faint lines around them. How fragile
she was—he'd forgotten over the years. He thought angrily
that Dobson was not taking good care of her. Her hands
were rough and reddened. She needed more color in her
cheeks, and she was too thin. Had she been ill?

"My sister-in-law and her children are staying with us,"
Sarah said, to fill in the awkward silence. "Julia's husband
passed away a few weeks ago."

"Oh? My condolences." That explained the wanness, the

faint air of sadness. Her husband had died, and she mourned him. The son of a bitch.

"Thank you."

James glanced at Julia again, then at Sarah. He didn't know what to say. He had never expected to see her again. Certainly, he hadn't expected to feel this rush of fierce, clashing emotions. It had been years. He had gotten over the hurt long ago. Or, at least, he thought he had. "I, uh, it was nice to see you again, Mrs. Turner. Mrs. Dobson."

It was hard to say her name. He couldn't remember what he had come into the store for. He turned and walked out the door.

Julia watched him leave. Her chest was so tight she could hardly breathe. She hadn't thought about this happening, even though it was only natural that eventually they would run into each other in a town this size. Why hadn't she realized that? Why hadn't she prepared herself to face it?

She looked at Sarah, who was studying the bolts of material again. She wondered if Sarah knew about her and Jimmy. Luke had known it; he'd practically forced her to tell him. But had he told his wife?

"I think the pale pink and the blue," Sarah said.

"What? Yes, of course, if you want."

"They'll look pretty on you. So would the red."

"Oh, no. Not the red." It was too vibrant, too blatant. She would feel like a—well, she guessed she *was* a fallen woman, even if she had saved her reputation somewhat by getting married, but she wasn't *that* sort. Not the kind to wear red.

"I guess not," Sarah agreed regretfully. It was too bold for a nice woman their age. That was too bad, because it would brighten up Julia's looks nicely.

"So Jimmy is a doctor, too?" Julia asked with great casualness.

Sarah shot her a sharp glance. "Yes. Old Dr. Banks died not long after Emily was born, and James took over his practice."

"They call him James now?"

Sarah nodded. She knew Julia wanted information about him, though she was probably embarrassed to ask. "I'm going to see him. He's the only doctor around for miles."

"No doubt he's a good one."

"That's what I hear." Sarah paused. "He lives in the house behind his office. His mother is still alive. He never married."

"Really?" Julia stared. She would have thought some woman would have snapped him up long ago.

"Not for lack of trying, you understand. Half the mothers in Willow Springs have thrown their daughters in his path."

"How odd," Julia murmured.

"People say he's married to his work."

"Oh."

Sarah wondered what had happened between Julia and James, exactly. Luke had said that James had refused to marry Julia. But Sarah had seen the look on his face when he recognized Julia, as if the building had tumbled down around his ears. And in the little time Sarah had spent with him, he hadn't impressed her as a callous man who would spurn a woman carrying his baby. He'd never married. She hadn't thought about it before, but now that she did, she realized that it was unusual for a man in his early thirties, a wealthy, handsome doctor like James Banks, to be unmarried. She wished she knew how he and Julia had parted. But she couldn't very well ask Julia.

"Well," Sarah said brightly, gathering up the cloth. "It's about time to go."

"Yes, of course."

Sarah purchased the material and the rest of her supplies, and Luke loaded them onto the wagon. Numbly Julia followed Sarah outside and climbed up into the wagon with the rest of them. Luke clucked to the mules, and the wagon began to roll. They passed through the town and out into the country, but Julia didn't see any of the scenery. Luke and Sarah talked beside her, but she was deaf to what they said.

Her mind had traveled back eleven years.

* Chapter 5 *

Harper's store was where Jimmy Banks had first spoken to
Julia. It was the week after Christmas, and she was wearing
the cherry red knitted cap that Luke had given her. Julia
cherished that cap, and she thought it made her pretty.
When she glanced across the store and saw Jimmy standing
at another counter, she was doubly glad she'd worn it. He
looked unbelievably handsome to her. She wished, achingly,
that he would see her and smile, maybe even say "hello."

As she stood there, dreaming, Jimmy turned and looked
at her. Julia realized that he'd caught her staring at him, and
she blushed and fixed her gaze on the goods behind the
counter. Old Mr. Harper handed her the flour and sugar she
had asked for, and she counted out her coins.

She gathered up her purchases and started for the door.
She heard footsteps hurrying across the wooden floor behind
her, and Jimmy suddenly went past and opened the door for
her. She looked up at him, startled, and smiled shyly.
"Thank you."

"You're welcome." He followed her outside and fell in
beside her. "You're Julia Turner, aren't you?"

"Why, yes."

Her surprise that he knew her name must have showed on
her face because he grinned a little abashedly and said, "I
asked Mr. Harper who you were. I'm sorry, but I didn't
recognize you. The last time I saw you, you must have been
only twelve."

Julia nodded. She wished she could say something clever—
or even anything at all!—to keep him walking with her, but
her mind was utterly blank.

"It's cold out today," he commented.

"Yes, it is."

"You aren't walking home, are you?"

"Yes."

"It's too cold for you to be out. Let me take you home. I'll get the buggy."

"Oh, no, that's too much trouble," she protested automatically, even as she prayed that he would insist. He did.

Julia returned to the store and waited for James to come back with the buggy. When he did, he politely helped her up into the vehicle, then took her to the little café on the square for a cup of hot chocolate. She was sure that everyone was staring at them. Imagine that she, Julia Turner, was sitting there bold as brass with Jimmy Banks! But Jimmy didn't seem to notice the other people.

Her hair was down, which wasn't really proper for a grown woman. She'd worn it that way because the weather was cold, and the fall of hair warmed her neck and shoulders. But no doubt people would say she was being brazen. Nervously her fingers went to her hair and pushed it back. She wished she could put it up or at least braid it, but she could hardly do her hair in public.

"Don't change it," Jimmy said quickly. "Your hair's beautiful."

She didn't know what to say. She didn't know how to deal with a man like Jimmy Banks. It wasn't that she hadn't been around men. Zach Sloane had tried to kiss her a couple of times, and Bobby Ray Jenks kept asking her to walk out in the trees with him. Will Dobson had been courting her for months, but Will never said anything pretty. He was rough, hulking, and tongue-tied. Zach and Bobby Ray were too slick and practiced. None of them were like this handsome, well-dressed young man across the table from her, who gazed at her with admiration and gave her a compliment without a trace of a leer on his face.

Julia sat, as tongue-tied as Will Dobson ever was, her hands nervous in her lap, and simply looked at Jimmy. He asked her polite questions about herself and her family. She was sure she answered them clumsily. He chatted about the weather. Finally, Julia thought to ask him about his schooling, and he began to talk about college, New Orleans, and medical school. Julia listened with fascination, commenting or asking questions, unaware that her discomfort had vanished.

Jimmy wound down after a while and looked embarrassed. "I'm sorry for running on like that. You must have been terribly bored."

"Not at all!" she hastened to assure him. "It sounds wonderful to me. I can't imagine reading all those books and learning so much or actually living in a city. I wish I could see those places you talked about."

He smiled. "Maybe you will one day."

She shook her head, her smile wistful. "No, I don't think so."

"Maybe I'll take you there."

She glanced at him, startled. He seemed to realize the implications of what he'd said, and he looked away quickly. "I'm sorry. I shouldn't have said that. Perhaps I'd better take you home now."

The ride home in the buggy was wonderful. Julia stored it away like a treasure in her mind. They sat only inches apart, a heavy lap robe across their legs and feet. The worst of the chill wind was cut off by the sides of the buggy. Julia had never ridden in one before. She had never sat this close to a man and felt the heat of his body. She gazed at Jimmy's hands, long and slender, sprinkled with dark, curling masculine hairs. She thought about his fingers curling around her own; she thought about him touching her. She looked at his profile, at the sharply cut lips and long, classic nose, the long, thick lashes. His skin was darker than her own. His jawline was already shadowed; he must have a heavy beard. She wondered if his chin would feel rough if she ran her hand over it; she wanted to.

When he left her at her house that afternoon, Julia was sure she would never see him again, but the next evening he showed up on the doorstep. She asked him in, her embarrassment at his seeing the humble interior of their shack outweighed by her eagerness and excitement at being with him. They sat alone—her father and Luke were both gone, and Julia's grandmother was asleep in the next room—and talked for hours.

Finally Jimmy left reluctantly. He told her that the next day he had to return to New Orleans to school. He gazed at her for a long moment, then leaned forward to kiss her cheek. Instinctively, Julia turned her face, her lips seeking his, and he kissed her. Excitement of a kind she'd never felt before shot through her. She couldn't breathe. She began to tremble. His hands gripped her arms, and she felt the rigid tension within him. He stepped back suddenly. He looked at her, his breath coming in short, rapid spurts. "I'll be back," he said hoarsely and left.

Julia lived on that kiss all winter.

It had been brazen of her, she knew, to seek his lips. He probably thought terrible things about her for doing that. Yet she couldn't regret it. She had never felt anything as wonderful, never tasted anything as sweet. She thought about Jimmy constantly, remembering the touch of his lips and the pressure of his fingers against her arms, the warmth of his breath on her cheek. She wanted to feel those things again. She wanted to see him again.

But she didn't think she would. He would be bound to forget her over the months. There were probably lots of girls that were interested in him, ones of his own class who were far prettier, brighter, and more vibrant than she. After all, she and Jimmy had shared only a few hours, only one kiss. She couldn't expect it to be as important to him as it was to her. Jimmy Banks couldn't have fallen crazily, instantly, in love with her—as she had with him.

Julia had almost convinced herself that she would never see him again when one day late in March, she heard the sound of a horse approaching the house. She glanced out the window and saw Jimmy riding into the yard. She rushed out onto the front porch as he slid off his horse. They hurried forward and stopped a few feet away from each other, grinning, surging with excitement, and suddenly shy.

They took a long walk by the creek. Julia didn't care where they went; she wanted only to see Jimmy and hear his voice, to absorb the wonderful knowledge that he was here with her.

"Is school over?" she asked hopefully.

"No. I have to go back in a week. This is just Easter vacation. But I'll be home again the end of May."

It seemed an awfully long time.

"I missed you," Jimmy said, and Julia stared at him in surprise. "I thought about you all the time."

She went all hot and cold inside. "I—I thought about you, too."

"Did you? Really? I was afraid you'd hardly remember me."

"Not remember you!" Julia gaped at him. "How could I not remember you?"

"There must be lots of other men courting you."

"Courting me?" Julia blushed. He must think she was stupid, the way she kept repeating everything he said. But his words stunned her. Could he actually be courting her?

"Yeah. Are there?"

She shook her head. "No. Only one."

"Who?"

"Will Dobson."

"I don't know him."

"He's from over Cold Springs way."

"Are you—inclined toward him?"

"No."

Jimmy grinned, and she could see the relief on his face. "Good."

After that, they both relaxed, though there was still a bubbling undercurrent of excitement between them. He stayed most of the afternoon, and they talked and laughed, the rest of the world forgotten. He left finally, reluctantly, but the next evening he returned, and for the remainder of his week's vacation he was at Julia's house every evening. Julia felt as if she were living in a fairy tale. He seemed as entranced by her as she was by him. *Her.* Julia Turner. It was unbelievable.

He didn't kiss her again. She kept waiting and hoping for a kiss, but it didn't come. The tension in her rose. She thought about his kiss, half the time not even hearing what was said, wanting only to have his arms around her and his mouth on hers. She caught him looking at her as if he felt the same way as she felt inside, and she wondered why he didn't kiss her, why he wouldn't even come close to her. The air between them was thick with unresolved longing.

The night before he left they walked again along the creek, following its meandering path. Jimmy took her hand;

his skin was like fire. They said little, too aware of his imminent departure yet not wanting to talk about it. They stopped at the foot of a large willow tree, and Jimmy laid his suit jacket on the ground for them to sit on. They looked at the moonlit water, the budding branches of the willow curving around them.

"It won't be long," Jimmy said without conviction. "Two months."

"No. You'll be back before I know it."

"I'm going to miss you."

Tears clogged Julia's throat. "Oh, Jimmy! I'll miss you, too!"

"Don't cry!" He turned to her, concerned. "Please. Not for me." He laid his hand against her cheek tenderly. His thumb wiped away a tear. He gazed at her, and she could see the hot desire in his eyes, feel the faint tremor in his hand. "You're so beautiful. Like a sylph. A wood sprite."

Julia didn't know what either of those things were, but the way he looked at her filled her with heat and elation. Unconsciously she stretched toward him. He leaned toward her. Her heart pounded inside her chest, and she couldn't catch her breath. He made a funny little groan, and suddenly his arms went around her and his mouth pressed into hers. He kissed her feverishly, hungrily, and she clung to him, dizzy with passion. His tongue came into her mouth. It surprised Julia, but she welcomed it. Bright shivers darted through her. Was this how Luke felt with women? No wonder he was so wild. She felt definitely wild herself right now. Jimmy's hand touched her breast, and she exploded into flame.

They made love there on the ground, too hungry, too eager to seek a softer, warmer place. They were too eager even to think. All Julia knew was heat and desire and the exquisite sensations his fingers awakened throughout her body. Even the pain when he entered her could not break the magical spell of her desire. Afterward, when he lay beside her, sweaty, warm, and utterly relaxed, she knew only peace and contentment.

"I love you," he whispered, though she hadn't asked for any such words from him, and tears formed in her eyes again.

"And I love you." *More than anything in the world.*

The next two months were unbearably lonely. It seemed forever until Jimmy would be home again, and Julia wasn't at all sure that she would see him again when he did return from college. She had few illusions about what a rich boy from town wanted from a Turner girl. She had known from the start that Jimmy's courtship wouldn't end in a proposal of marriage; a Banks didn't marry a Turner. There could be only lovemaking or nothing at all. Because she loved him so much, she had chosen the lovemaking, even if it meant that she was now "a fallen woman," another girl like Emma Whitehead or Tessa Jackson. But she was aware that their one night of passion might be all there would be; after he'd won her, Jimmy might not be interested in her anymore. That was the way of life; you found it out early when you grew up in a sharecropper's shack with a vicious, drunken father who was looked down upon by everyone in the county.

One night early in June, Julia was awakened by a soft tapping at the door. She glanced over to where her father lay, snoring, on a mattress on the floor. Luke wasn't home. She walked silently to the door and opened it a fraction. Jimmy stood outside on the porch, his face tight and eager.

"Jimmy!" She flung open the door and rushed into his arms. He lifted her up off the floor, burying his face in her loose, fine hair.

"Julia. Julia. God, it's good to see you again." He kissed her deeply, searchingly, a kiss born of two months of loneliness. "You're so beautiful. I've missed you like the devil." He kissed her again and again, and she could feel his hard desire through her thin cotton nightgown.

"I've missed you, too," she whispered, clinging to him.

"I just got in tonight on the eight-oh-five. I came out as soon as I could get away from the house."

Love swelled inside her chest. He had rushed to see her as soon as he got home! "I love you."

He carried her like a child into the woods behind the house, saying he didn't want her to hurt her bare feet on the twigs and rocks. They had made love in the shelter of the trees, the scent of wild honeysuckle thick around them.

* * *

Julia could smell the honeysuckle now, so strong was the memory, and she glanced around as though awakening from a dream. She was in a wagon with Luke and Sarah and the children, and there was no honeysuckle in sight. Tears filled her eyes. She thought she would give anything to feel again what she had felt back then, to be young and wildly in love, heedless of what might happen.

But then, she was exactly where she was because she had been young and in love and heedless. She and Jimmy had continued to meet all through June. He had assisted his father in his office during the day, but every evening he had been at Julia's house. They had taken long walks or simply sat together talking; but whatever they did, they hadn't been able to keep their hands from each other long, and they had made love again and again. Jimmy had murmured words of love and passion to her, and Julia had soaked them up, even as she drank in his kisses and caresses. She couldn't get enough of him because she knew that soon it would be over.

She had suspected even before Jimmy came home that she was pregnant. She had missed her monthly, and then she had started feeling sick to her stomach when she awoke in the mornings. By the end of June, she was certain. She was going to bear his child.

Julia hadn't told Jimmy. She hadn't even thought of it. She had known that he wouldn't marry her—couldn't marry her, even if by some mad chance he might want to. He was a Banks, son of a doctor and descendant of judges and bankers. And she was a Turner, daughter of a drunk and descendant of poor white trash. His parents would never have allowed him to marry her. And, sadly, she had been sure that despite his words of love, Jimmy wouldn't even want to marry her when it came right down to it. She hadn't wanted to spoil the beauty of their love by telling him. What if he thought that she was trying to force him into marrying her? He would be horrified and repulsed. She hadn't wanted to hear his refusal.

But she had been determined not to bear his child out of wedlock. She would not allow that shame to rest on her child. Jimmy's child. She would not let him carry the stigma of illegitimacy. She had gone to a doctor in another town to confirm her condition, using the money she had stored up in the old cookie jar above the sink. The doctor had told her that she was indeed pregnant, and she had known that the end had come for her idyllic love with Jimmy.

The next time Will Dobson had called on her, she had asked him if he still wanted to marry her. He had been dumbfounded, having been turned down so often that he'd given up asking. She had explained her situation, wanting him to know exactly what he was getting into. He had gazed at her for a moment, then nodded. "Sure, Julie. I want you that bad. You know I do."

They had been married on July second. She hadn't told Jimmy about her pregnancy or her impending marriage. She had planned to tell him the night before the wedding, but at the last minute she had been unable to utter the words. She had made love with him with passion, regret, and sadness that night, and she hadn't seen him again since.

Until this afternoon.

Seeing Jimmy in that store had shaken her to the core. She didn't know what she felt, exactly. Not love. That had died long ago; it had been years, after all. She supposed it was shock; she hadn't expected to ever see him again. Running into him like that had jarred loose the memories and old feelings, and she had felt them all again, like an ache in a bone broken long ago.

Oh, James! Tears welled in Julia's eyes. He was still so handsome, maybe even more so. She wondered what he had thought of her. Had he been dismayed at how old she had grown? Had it appalled him that he had once found this woman attractive? Had he noticed the lines in her face, the darkening of her hair, the roughness of her hands? But that was silly. Of course he had seen those things; he couldn't help but see them.

Julia wanted to cry, but she couldn't with Luke and Sarah sitting right beside her. The ride home seemed endless.

The children took their baths that evening in a large tin washtub in the kitchen and went straight to bed. Luke emptied the round washtub and brought in the long tub the adults used for bathing. They filled it with bucketsful of rainwater and warmed it with pots of water heated on the stove.

Julia took the first bath, and Luke and Sarah went outside to give her time alone. They walked around the barn and the animal pens, chatting about the farm, the livestock, and crop he was planting. His arm was looped over her shoulders, and hers was around his waist. They moved with the ease of familiarity, yet they were acutely aware of every place their bodies touched.

Luke loved being with Sarah like this—the quiet talk, the closeness, the intimacy. They stopped beneath the apricot tree in front. Luke reached up to pull down a branch, and they were showered with its petals. They smiled at each other and sniffed at the blossoms. Luke thought of the evening a few weeks ago when they had sat in the swing on the front porch. Sarah had smelled of the apricots she'd cooked that afternoon, tart and sweet. He remembered the scent of her skin, the smoothness, the taste, and he hardened at the memory.

He let go of the branch and reached over to brush a few white petals from Sarah's dark hair. One lay against her cheek, creamy against the pale pink of her skin and soft as velvet. He lifted it from her smooth skin. The familiar tangle of awe and love and lust for Sarah coiled in his abdomen. He rubbed the petal between his fingers, and its moisture dampened his skin. He thought of digging his fingers into Sarah's flesh, pulling her to him, sinking into her . . .

It took effort to turn away. He glanced toward the house. "Think she's through?"

"I imagine." Sarah had felt the heat of Luke's glance, and it had stirred her. She wished she weren't pregnant. She wished she could take his hands and pull him down to the ground with her right there beneath the white splendor of blossoms.

They walked slowly back to the house, each lost in his own thoughts. Sarah knew that if she touched Luke's skin, it would be blazing hot.

Inside, they found that Julia had emptied the tub for

them, and they refilled it. Julia had gone upstairs to her room. The house was quiet and dark around them. The air in the kitchen was warm and steamy. Luke began to undress, and Sarah sat down in one of the chairs, watching him. As he pulled off each garment, she felt it viscerally. Her eyes grew soft and dreamy.

Luke dropped his clothes onto the floor and stepped into the tub. He sat down and leaned back, eyes closed, luxuriating in the warm water lapping his body. He remembered how when they were first married and still sleeping apart, he used to go down to the chinaberry tree while Sarah bathed. He would stand there and torture himself with images of her naked body in the tub. Now she sat in the kitchen with him while he bathed, and he with her, so familiar, so married that they were like parts of one another. But one thing hadn't changed—the torture in his body when he couldn't make love to her.

He sighed and ducked under the water to wet his hair. He picked up the bar of soap, but Sarah took it out of his hands and knelt beside the tub. She worked the bar into suds between her hands, then began to soap his hair. "You shouldn't get down on the floor like that in your condition," he admonished her.

Sarah worked her fingers through his hair. "You're still mine. I like taking care of you."

A faint smile touched Luke's lips, and he sighed with pleasure, his eyes drifting closed. He enjoyed the touch of her fingers on his scalp, but far more pleasurable was the knowledge that she enjoyed taking care of him, that she thought of him as belonging to her. He relaxed and let her hands work their hypnotic spell. He could have fallen asleep except for the tendrils of fire her ministrations created in his loins.

Sarah took a pitcher and sluiced clean water over his head, rinsing away the soap. "Lean forward."

He obeyed her, resting his arms on his knees. Sarah washed his back, her hands slippery with soap. Tension grew in his abdomen. Her fingers slid around his ribs to the thick musculature of his chest. Luke wrapped his hands around her wrists, stopping her. He looked at her, his eyes amused, yet hot.

"You better let me finish the rest, or I'm liable to come right out of the tub after you."

Sarah sat back on her heels, smiling like a cat that got in the cream. "Maybe I want you to."

Luke caressed her cheek, leaving a trail of dampness on her skin. He knew an overwhelming desire to lick it off with his tongue. "Maybe I do, too. But Sarah . . ."

"Yes. I know. Old Dr. Banks said . . ." Sarah sighed and stood up. She started walking away, then turned and grinned impishly. "Do you think we ought to ask the new Dr. Banks?"

Luke snorted. "He'd say the same thing. Now, stop teasing me." He scowled, thinking of her talking to Jimmy Banks about such intimacies. "And if I ever hear of you talking to that man about our bedroom matters, I'll . . ."

"You'll what?" She seemed overwhelmingly unafraid.

"I'll beat you."

"Uh-huh." Sarah gazed at him with patent disbelief. "Like you always do."

"I'll keep you in bed for a week."

The curve of her lips was intentionally provocative. "Then I'll ask him tomorrow."

Luke slowly rubbed his forefinger back and forth across his lips, watching her. He enjoyed their sexual banter, the way she teased him into hardness from clear across the room. Talking to Sarah could be sexier than the naked bodies of the women he had known before. He wanted to continue the talk until he couldn't take it anymore and then come out of the tub and kiss the teasing smile off her face. But if he did that, he was sure to wind up pulling her down to the kitchen floor and taking her right there.

Luke silently picked up the rag and began to wash off. But even though there was no more teasing, the heat didn't leave his blood.

When he was through, he dried off, wrapped the towel around his waist, and sat down to wait for Sarah. He wasn't about to forgo the pleasure of watching her undress and bathe, no matter how tempting and frustrating it was.

Sarah poured another steaming kettle of water into the tub to warm it, then sat down and bent over to unfasten her shoes. It was getting more and more awkward for her to perform that task, the way her abdomen was growing. Luke smiled and went down on one knee in front of her, playfully pushing her hand away.

"Here. I'll do that."

"You don't have to."

"I want to."

Sarah straightened and leaned back in the chair with a little sigh. Luke unlaced the ties efficiently and pulled off her shoe. He set the shoe down on the floor, but he continued to hold her foot. Gently his fingers massaged her foot, and Sarah went limp all over. "Oh, Luke, that feels so good."

"Like it?"

"Yes. It's heavenly. I didn't realize how my feet hurt. They must be swelling again like they did with Emily."

His thumbs slid along the sole of her foot, rubbing away the ache. He hated to think of anything causing her pain or discomfort. "You better start resting more. I'll tell Julia to make sure you sit down with your feet up several times a day."

"But Luke..."

"No buts. You'll do as I say." He removed her other shoe and repeated the slow, gentle massage on that foot, too.

Sarah smiled down at him. She loved Luke's concern for her. Sometimes her love for him was so great that she thought she would burst from it. His head was bent, his thick silver and gold hair falling forward to hide his face. His hair was drying in the warmth of the kitchen, turning into fine, silky strands. Sarah knew just how it would feel against her fingers, slipping, curling.

She reached out and skimmed her fingers lightly across his hair. Luke looked up at her. Sarah knew the look—his mouth widening, the skin across his cheekbones stretching tautly, his eyes suddenly a blue flame. He wanted her.

His hands slid up her stockinged leg to the garter. He pulled it off and slowly rolled down her stocking, his fingers lingering over her skin. Sarah saw the sheen of moisture along his upper lip and felt the faint tremor of his fingers.

Luke watched her face for the subtle signs of passions that he knew so well. She wanted him just as much.

He pulled the stocking off her foot, crumpling it in his hand, and sat staring down at the floor, struggling within himself.

"I'm sorry," Sarah whispered, knowing full well the ache and the temptation inside him.

"Oh, Sarah." Luke moved up and forward, wrapping his arms around her waist. His body curved over the mound of her belly, and he buried his face in her breasts. "You're so beautiful. I feel like a devil sometimes, wanting you like this and knowing that it would hurt you. How could I want it so much when it would hurt you?"

Sarah hugged him to her, and her hands moved soothingly over his hair and back. "You're not a devil!" Her usually soft voice was fierce. "Don't you say that! Don't even think it. You aren't the only one who wants to make love. I want it, too."

Luke rubbed his cheek against her like a cat. "I can't get enough of you. I never have been able to. I lie awake at night thinking about making love to you, remembering how your skin feels under my hands, how you moan that soft little way."

"Luke . . ." Sarah's cheeks flushed, and her loins turned to liquid.

"I always know when we make love that you love me. That you belong to me and I belong to you."

"Of course, we belong to each other. And I always love you."

"I know, but . . ." Luke paused, unable to articulate exactly what he felt when they made love—the piercing sweetness of coming home, the joy so fierce it shattered him, the complete joining and utter closeness. Making love to Sarah was more than just pleasure; it was a need as great as the one to eat or to drink or to fight for his life. "Sometimes it tears me apart to stay away from you."

Sarah kissed his bright head. "Then make love to me."

"No." He pulled away. "I can't. It could hurt you."

"*Could.* That means only a possibility."

"Even a possibility is too much."

"But just once . . . and I'm not terribly far along. The baby's not due for over two months."

Luke's face contorted with frustration. "Sarah, please don't tempt me."

Sarah worried at her lower lip. She didn't fear any hurt to herself, and because the baby was so much a part of her, she had less fear than Luke of hurting it. She had felt no pain the last time Luke had made love to her. How could it hurt her or the baby when there was no pain, only pleasure?

Luke stood up and moved away, leaving Sarah to take off the other stocking by herself. He leaned against the kitchen counter, and watched her undress, unable to keep his eyes off her. She took off her clothes without any conscious attempt to entice him. If it had been her choice alone, she would choose to make love with him now. But she knew Luke and his intense sense of responsibility, his fear of harming her in any way. She wouldn't try to tease him into doing something he thought wrong, for she knew the burden of guilt Luke would feel if he did.

Sarah eased down into the tub with the exaggerated caution of a pregnant woman. She took up the bar of soap and began to wash. Luke gazed at her. Her breasts had grown, as they had when she was pregnant with Emily. Her wet nipples tightened in the coolness of the air. Luke's tongue stole out to moisten his lips, and his fingers curled around the edge of the countertop.

Sarah rested her heel on the edge of the tub and began to wash her extended leg. Her legs were still slim and lovely, unaffected by the weight of her pregnancy. Luke thought of them wrapped around his back, tight and strong. He crossed his arms across his chest, clamping his hands under his arms. His breath came faster in his throat. Even the mound of Sarah's belly was beautiful to him. He wanted to trail kisses across it.

Luke swallowed. He ought to turn away and not look at her. He ought to go upstairs. But he couldn't. He thought of the time when they were first married, when he had wanted her so passionately, yet had stayed out of her bed. He had managed it then; surely he could now. But then he had not made love to her. Then he had only dreamed of her body. He hadn't known her inch by inch as he did now. He hadn't felt the utter softness of her skin or the eagerness of her response. He hadn't known how glorious it was to explode within her. Now he knew all those things, and it made it twice as hard to stay away from her.

Sarah took the pins from her hair and shook it loose. It tumbled down over her white shoulders and chest, parting over her breasts so that the pinkish brown nipples peeped through. Her hair turned wet quickly in the water and clung to her skin. Luke couldn't take his eyes off her breasts, couldn't stop remembering the smell and texture of her hair. How often he had pulled it like a dark curtain across his face, burying himself in its softness. How often he had felt it trailing across his skin as Sarah moved over his body, kissing him.

He swallowed. His entire body was rigid with desire. His blood was on fire, his loins heavy and aching. He had to have her. He knew he couldn't.

Sarah washed her hair and rinsed it. Then she rose and stepped out of the tub, picking up her towel to dry off. Her hair hung, dark and wet, all the way to her hips. When it was dry, it would float around her shoulders and back like a cloud. Sometimes after they bathed, they would sit in front of the fire together and Luke would brush her hair dry, watching the play of the firelight over her face and body.

Luke broke away and went upstairs. He took his time dressing, and by the time he came back down, Sarah was dry, dressed, and sitting by the heat of the stove brushing out her hair. She smiled at him, and he managed a tight smile in return. He pulled the tub out and emptied it in the yard. Normally he would have returned to the house, but tonight he couldn't. He strolled to the corral and stood watching the horses. He walked through the barn, breathing in the familiar rich, acrid odor of animals and grain. Usually it soothed him, but not tonight.

Dark, insidious thoughts plagued his mind—images of Sarah naked and hot beneath him; memories of her breasts in his hands, infinitely soft and tantalizing; a whispering voice that told him that one time wouldn't hurt, that Dr. Banks was an old biddy without any understanding of a young man's hunger, that Sarah would welcome him. She *would* welcome him. He knew it. She never denied him anything; she gave him her love unstintingly, with no thought of herself. That was what made it so hard. He was the one who must be responsible for both of them. He had to take care of her.

It didn't matter that he imagined the feel of her lips on his body so strongly it was as if they were moving down him right now. It didn't matter that his blood pumped hot and thick through his veins, pounding in his head. He *had* to be strong.

He checked out the tack. It was all in good shape, supple and clean. There was nothing to do with it to keep his hands occupied. He went inside and took the shotgun and rifle out of the gun rack. He broke them down on the kitchen table and cleaned them. That wasn't necessary, either, but he had to do something. He couldn't go upstairs to Sarah yet. He thrust the long-handled brush into each barrel, turning it to clean them. He oiled the parts and fitted them back together. He smoothed a cloth over the polished wood stock and barrel. His hand glided slowly over the gun. He glanced down at his hands, and with a snort of exasperation, he threw down the cloth. He replaced the guns in the rack, washed his hands, and went upstairs.

Their room was dark. Sarah lay on her side in the bed. Luke slipped inside, closing the door softly behind him, and undressed in the dark. Thank Heaven she was asleep. He climbed into bed.

Sarah rolled over. "Luke."

She wasn't asleep. His heartbeat picked up. "I'm sorry. Did I wake you up?"

"No."

"Good night."

"Good night."

Luke had kissed Sarah good night before they went to sleep for three years, but he hesitated now. A good night kiss, a mere brushing of their lips. It was a gesture, that was all. It couldn't hurt. That wasn't passion, that was love, and, oh God, he loved her, too.

Luke leaned over to press his lips to hers briefly, sexlessly. His mouth touched hers. And he was lost.

* Chapter 6 *

Her mouth was soft and wet and warm. His tongue found its home in the familiar, delightful cave. Sarah's arms went around his neck, and his arms slid under her, crushing her to him. Her breasts pressed into his chest through the thin cloth of her gown. He could feel her nipples hardening against him. His mouth widened over hers, grinding into her. His manhood was like red-hot steel. He could think of nothing except burying himself in her.

Luke kissed her again and again, knowing it was wrong, but unable to stop himself. He told himself that he would do as he had done the other time, savoring her sweetness and pleasuring her without coming into her. He kissed her wildly all over her face and neck, nibbling, licking, sucking, murmuring a litany of words of love, sex, and heat.

Sarah responded without hesitation. She, too, was restless and yearning, aching for his touch. She wanted his hands all over her; she wanted his fullness inside her. She wanted to feel every inch of his male strength. She murmured his name, digging her hands into his hair, and arched up against him.

Luke sat up and unfastened Sarah's gown, impatiently jerking off two buttons that defied his clumsy fingers. He whipped it off over her head and threw it on the floor. He braced himself on his arms and looked down at her. His eyes were pale in the darkness, fierce and wild. Sarah stared back at him, her breath coming rapidly in her throat. He seemed so strange in the pale wash of the moonlight, ferocious and untamed, like a wild beast. It should have been frightening, and it was, a little, but in a way that excited her. It stirred her to think that desire for her could drive Luke to the edges of control, could unleash the primitive man hidden deep within him, but at the same time she knew, with a deep, abiding trust, that Luke would never hurt her.

His eyes moved down her face to the narrow column of her throat and lower still, over the plain of her chest to her breasts. They were full and pink tipped, the nipples pebbling. He cupped one in his brown, hard hand. Her flesh was pale against his, velvet soft to his roughness. He kneaded the lush flesh. His thumb rasped over her nipple, and it tightened in response. He took it between his thumb and forefinger and rubbed gently, his eyes darkening as he watched the nipple harden and elongate.

Luke lowered his head to her breast. His lips skimmed over the luscious mound, exploring its exquisite softness. He brushed across her nipple, then back. Once. Twice. Again. His tongue came out and circled the button of flesh, then lashed across it. Sarah strained upward, seeking the pleasure with which he teased her. He groaned and pulled her nipple fully into his mouth.

Sarah gasped. Her fingers dug into Luke's shoulders. Her nails scratched him, but he didn't feel it, too lost in his passion. His mouth left her breasts and trailed down her body, lovingly caressing her swollen abdomen. His hand glided up the inside of her smooth thigh. His breath was hot and rapid, his muscles trembling under the force of his need.

Luke's fingers tangled in the curls between her legs and found the eager dampness there. He sucked in his breath as he moved across the satiny, layered flesh, seeking the center of her heat. His head moved lower, and his hand went beneath her buttocks, lifting her up to his questing mouth. Sarah moaned as his tongue found the tender morsel of flesh it sought and he loved her gently, tenderly.

"Luke, Luke." Sarah's voice was ragged and uneven. She reached for him blindly.

Luke felt her muscles tightening, and he knew what would follow. He thought of being inside her when the waves of pleasure struck her, of feeling her clamp tightly around him. Pure, driving lust swept through him. He could not live without possessing her.

There was no conscious thought in him, only instinct and desire. He moved between her legs and slid into her. She was damp and tight around him. He groaned. Sarah circled her hips beneath him, luxuriating in the way he filled her so completely. It had been so long, so achingly long. He began to thrust within her, long, hard strokes that shook her, filled her, turned her into fire. Sarah moved with him, lost in the sensations he evoked in her. The heat built inside her, gathering into a hot, hard knot that tightened with each movement of Luke's body. It was almost unbearable, always just out of her reach, and she sobbed his name, straining up against him.

At last the sweet, piercing pleasure burst within her. Sarah cried out, arching up against him, and her movements hurled Luke into a world of new, unbelievable pleasure. He bucked against her, spilling out his hot seed.

Luke collapsed, shuddering under the intensity of his storm. His hair was damp with sweat, and Sarah combed her fingers through it lovingly. She kissed the top of his head.

"Oh, God." He rolled from her. "I'm sorry."

Sarah smiled. "I'm not." She took his hand and raised it to her lips. "I love you."

He pulled her into his arms, squeezing her tightly against him. "And I love you. Oh, Lord, I love you."

Sarah could see the guilt in Luke's eyes the next morning, but she had no regrets. His tension was gone, the taut lines around his mouth and eyes smoothed out. He was happier and more at peace than he had been in weeks. So was she. They were able to smile at each other or hold hands or kiss without being racked by desire.

Sunday was a lazy day. Sarah and Luke sat in the swing on the porch half the afternoon, gently rocking and watching the breeze play among the blossoms of the fruit trees. Julia was quiet all day, and Sarah detected a certain sadness in Julia's blue eyes. Sarah wondered if Julia was still sorrowing over her husband's death or if something else had disturbed her—such as seeing James Banks the day before. But Julia was a private person, like Luke, one who did not easily open up and talk, so Sarah didn't pry.

On Monday, Luke and Micah worked on the west forty, carrying their lunch with them. Sarah and Julia tackled the housecleaning, sweeping, dusting, and hanging out the rag rugs to be beaten. They worked all morning, and about twelve-thirty they went inside to fix lunch.

Suddenly, as they stepped inside the kitchen, Sarah felt something warm and liquid gush down her legs. Her stomach turned to ice, and she stopped dead still. "Julia?"

Julia turned inquiringly and saw Sarah's pale face. She started toward her. "Sarah! What is it?"

Sarah gazed down at her skirt as if the lower half of her body didn't belong to her. "I—don't know." She raised her skirts above her ankles. The insides of her stockings were stained bright red, and there was blood on the floor.

"Oh my God!" Julia grabbed Sarah and propelled her to a chair. "Vance! Run get Luke. Tell him to hurry."

"Julia, what is it? What's happening?" Fear was etched on Sarah's face. "Am I losing my baby?"

Luke set down the sack of seed with a sigh. "Time for lunch, don't you think?"

Micah grunted in agreement, dropping his hoe, and the two men walked to the creek, where they had left their lunch. Neither said much, which suited them both. Luke was a quiet, solitary man, and it had pleased him to discover that his new hired hand was the same. Last summer Luke had hired a man who had talked incessantly, and Luke had thought he would go crazy before they got in the crops.

Micah said little, and when he did talk, it was to some purpose. He was a good, strong worker, too, and quick to understand whatever instructions Luke gave him. In fact, it seemed to Luke as if their minds were attuned; more and more often Micah did exactly what Luke had in mind without having to be told.

They sat down in the shade of a willow beside the creek and opened the sack of sandwiches Julia had prepared for them. Luke pulled out the mason jars of lemonade that they had set in the stream earlier to keep cool. They drank thirstily and devoured their sandwiches. Their hunger somewhat assuaged, they ate the remaining sandwiches, hunks of cheese, and apple tarts more slowly, savoring the taste.

"Mrs. Dobson be a fine cook," Micah commented, sinking his teeth into his second apple tart.

Luke smiled as he brushed his hands on his pants leg to remove the crumbs. "She is that. She makes an apple dumpling that'd make you think you died and went to Heaven."

"This one'd almost get you there itself."

Luke leaned back against the trunk of the tree, tipping down the brim of his hat to shade his eyes. He felt warm, full, and happy. "Reminds me of Huntsville. We always used to talk about how good something tasted. How soft some woman was."

Micah's eyes opened wide, and he stopped chewing. He swallowed. "Huntsville? You—uh—"

"Was in prison?" Luke shot him a half-amused, half-defensive glance from beneath the brim of his hat. "What did you think? That I was brought up to this kind of life?" He made a sweep of his arm, encompassing the land around him. "Owning land, living in a house like that?"

"Yeah, I s'pose . . ."

"I wasn't." Luke paused. "I was a sharecropper's kid. Julie and I grew up in a shack that made that room in the barn look like high living."

Micah stared at Luke. He didn't know what to say. He hadn't thought about Luke's past; he had assumed he'd grown up a prosperous farmer's son. Micah didn't think of white people being poor, any more than he would have dreamed that Luke Turner had been in prison. Now that he thought about it, he could see the lines of hard experience on Luke's face. Luke's eyes weren't those of a person who had had everything handed to him. Micah realized, amazed, that the house he'd grown up in in New Mexico had probably been better than Luke's childhood home. No wonder Luke was easy to work with, comfortable to be around. He'd been on the bottom, too.

"I was lucky," Luke went on. "I found Sarah." Instinctively he glanced in the direction of the house, even though he couldn't see it from this distance. He straightened. A small figure was racing through the fields toward them. Luke rose, squinting against the light. "What's that?"

Micah glanced in the direction in which Luke looked. "I don't know." He stood up, shading his eyes. "A kid?"

Vaguely anxious, Luke stepped across the creek. He walked toward the child, and as he walked, his pace quickened, his unease increasing. Micah followed him.

"It's Vance," Luke said. He broke into a trot.

They could see that Vance was running as fast as he could, arms and legs pumping. The boy's face was contorted with effort—and fear. The alarm that had been building in Luke burst into full flower. He began to run.

"Uncle Luke! Uncle Luke!" Vance dropped to his knees, gasping for air, as Luke reached him.

Luke went down on one knee beside his nephew. "What is it? What's the matter?"

"Mama—says—to come," Vance gasped out. "It's Aunt Sarah."

"My God." Luke didn't wait to find out what had happened. He set out running for the house. Micah slung Vance up on his back and ran after Luke.

Nothing had ever taken Luke as long as it did to get to the house that day. He ran harder than he'd ever run in his life, even the time the sheriff had come for him, but still he seemed to get nowhere. His feet pounded across the dirt, and he strained forward, urging every ounce of speed from his legs. His breath whistled in and out of his lungs. His body was cold with fear despite the heat of the day, and all he could think was, "Sarah, Sarah."

When he reached the house, he took the porch steps two at a time and burst into the kitchen. He pulled up short. Sarah sat in a chair, and Julia knelt on the other side of her, holding her hand. Sarah's feet were up on the kitchen table, crossed. Her face was paper white, and the pale gold freckles across her nose and cheeks stuck out garishly.

There was blood all over her legs, all over her skirts, all over the floor.

The world jolted to a stop. "Sarah!"

Sarah opened her eyes. "Luke." Her voice was barely a whisper.

His insides went cold as ice. "What—" He dropped down beside her and looked across at Julia. He couldn't say the awful words crowding his throat. "Julie?"

Julia shook her head. "I don't know. She started bleeding a few minutes ago. She's bled a lot, but she hasn't been in any pain. We need to put her in bed. I—she was too weak to climb the stairs. And we need the doctor."

"I'll carry her. Then I'll go get Banks." His brain felt numb. He couldn't think. *Oh, God, Sarah!*

The screen door opened. Micah hesitated in the doorway. Luke turned to him with a rush of relief. "Micah. Can you ride a horse?"

"Sure. I done rode all my life."

"Go for Dr. Banks. Tell him Sarah needs him immediately. Take Jo-Jo; he's the fastest."

Micah nodded and turned, already out the door and headed down the steps. Julia came to the door after him and called, "The Banks house is the big white one on Main Street, about a block before downtown." Micah nodded without looking back as he loped into the barn.

Luke picked Sarah up tenderly, moving as if she were more fragile than glass. She leaned her head against his chest. He carried her slowly, carefully, out of the kitchen and up the stairs to their bedroom. Julia ran up before them to turn down the bed and cover one side with towels. Luke set Sarah down on the bed. She winced and breathed in sharply.

"I'm sorry. I tried not to hurt you."

Sarah shook her head. "No, it wasn't you." She looked from Luke to Julia and back. "I—it was a pain. Here." She laid her hand on her abdomen. Tears glistened in her eyes, and she spoke reluctantly, as if she could stave off what was happening by not admitting it. "I think it was a contraction."

Luke glanced at Julia. The worry was plain on her face. Sarah was losing the baby.

It was glorious to be back on a horse. Micah smiled when he touched his heels to Jo-Jo's side and the gelding leapt forward. He urged the horse into a run, relishing the thrust of powerful muscles beneath him and the rush of air past his face. When the horse reached the main road, however, Micah slowed Jo-Jo's pace. No matter how urgent the matter, he couldn't run him all the way into town.

Micah supposed it was wrong to enjoy the ride, considering the reason for it. He felt sorry for Mrs. Turner. She was a kind lady, and there was a certain sparkle about her that was appealing. Micah liked her and her husband better than he'd ever liked any white people. It was obvious that she was in trouble. Her skirts had been soaked in blood. It'd practically kill Turner if anything happened to her. Even so, Micah couldn't help but enjoy the ride.

He passed a farmer in a wagon and farther down the road went around two men walking together. All of them stared at him as he rode past, and he knew they wondered what a black man was doing on a beautiful animal like that. They would suspect that he had stolen it. When he reached the edge of town, the number of stares increased. He rode past everyone without a glance, keeping his eyes straight ahead.

"Hey, boy!" someone called from the sidewalk. Micah gritted his teeth and pretended not to have heard. But the voice came again. "Hey, I'm talking to you."

Reluctantly Micah reined in and turned to look at the man who had called to him. He was a tall, spare man in a dark business suit. Micah carefully looked to the side of the man and down. "Yessir? Sorry, but I—"

"Where'd you get that horse? It looks familiar."

"It Mr. Luke Turner's horse. I work for him." The man hesitated, his face doubtful. "I got to go now. Mrs. Turner, she need the doctor bad."

The man turned away, still frowning, but he said nothing else, and Micah seized the opportunity to leave. He kicked the horse into a trot down Main Street.

It wasn't hard to find the Banks house. It was just as Julia had described it. To one side a smaller, one-story section jutted out from the house, and beside its door hung a small wooden sign that read "James R. Banks, M.D." Micah dismounted, tying the reins through the ring of a black wrought-iron hitching post. He ran up the narrow gravel path to the office door, knocked, and walked in.

A woman with a child and another, older woman were

seated in the waiting room. They both turned, their eyes widening a little when they saw him. "Dr. Banks here? I need to see him, bad."

The older woman frowned. It was apparent she didn't find his manner satisfactory. People often didn't. Though in the recent past he had, through sheer self-preservation, adopted many of the mannerisms he saw in the blacks around him, he knew that there was something different in his stance and attitude. That was one reason he had found it comfortable around Luke Turner. Turner didn't seem to expect him to be anything but what he was.

"There's a door at the back of the house—" the woman began, but at that moment a man walked into the room from the back.

He looked at Micah inquiringly. "I'm Dr. Banks."

"It Mrs. Turner. Mrs. Luke Turner. She need you right away."

"What happened?" Already the doctor was rolling down his cuffs and reaching for his suit jacket on a hook on the wall.

"I don't know." Belatedly Micah remembered to add a "sir." "The boy called us in from the fields and when we get there, she be bleedin' a lot. Mr. Turner say to fetch you."

"I'll come immediately. I have to get my instruments." James started away, then turned back. "You rode, you say? Can you saddle a horse?"

"Yes."

"Good. Go to the stables behind the house and saddle the bay. I'll be there as quickly as I can."

Micah nodded and hurried out of the office. He cut across the front lawn to the drive on the other side and followed it down to a small carriage house and stables. Quickly he saddled and bridled the bay gelding and was leading it out when Dr. Banks joined him.

"Good. Thank you." James hooked his medical bag to the saddle horn and swung up into the saddle. He touched his heels to the horse's sides and trotted down the drive.

Micah went back to close the stall door, then started out of the stables, too. He stopped, his eyes on the driveway. The woman he had seen Saturday was strolling down the drive toward the stables. What was she doing in this part of town?

Micah crossed his arms and leaned against the doorway to look at her. She moved slowly, as though she was tired, and she rubbed the back of her neck with one hand. As he watched, she reached up to unfasten the top two buttons of her high-necked blouse, exposing the soft flesh of her throat down to the hollow. She undid her cuffs as well and rolled them up, then pulled the pins out of her hair. Her hair tumbled down in a thick black mass and she shook her head to settle it around her shoulders.

Desire sizzled through Micah. He had thought this woman was beautiful the other day, taut and restrained as she had been. With her hair wild around her face, she took his breath away. He must have made a sound, for she looked up. Her eyes fell on him, and she scowled as she hurried to refasten her blouse and sleeves.

"What are you doing here?" she snapped, pushing ineffectually at her thick, unruly hair.

"What *you* doing here?" he countered, grinning.

"*I* live here." She gestured toward the small house beside the carriage house.

Micah glanced at it. "The quarters? You work for the doctor?" A grin touched his lips. "You sure don't look like no maid."

"I'm not!" Her voice was crisp with irritation. "I teach school."

"I believe that."

"I live with my mother."

"Oh. And she's the maid."

"She is the Banks's cook and housekeeper and has been for the past twenty-five years."

He pursed his lips, amused. "La di da. Don't that make you high class? Not like the rest of us poor old niggers." He snatched off his hat and bent his head with mocking servitude.

The woman's mouth tightened. "Well, I'm certainly not like you. As I said, what are you doing here? If you want a job, I can tell you that Dr. Banks already has a gardener and handyman. If you want a meal, go to the back door of the main house, and my mother will give you a bowl of soup, I'm sure."

"I done got a job. Now, a meal with your mama sounds real nice, but not now." He gave her a little bow and set the hat back on his head. "Good afternoon, miss."

Dovie glared at him, and he gazed blandly back at her as he sauntered past. He could feel her watching him all the way down the drive and across the lawn to where Jo-Jo was hitched. He didn't mind her seeing him mount the big horse, and he couldn't resist lifting his hat to her as he rode past the driveway.

"Where the hell is that doctor!" Luke strode to the front window of the bedroom, then back to Sarah's bedside. "What's the matter with him? Why doesn't he come?"

"Luke, please." Julia leaned over Sarah and wiped away the sweat from her brow. "It hasn't been long. There hasn't been enough time for Micah to have gotten to town and for Ji—Dr. Banks to have ridden back."

Luke glanced at the clock on the dresser. Julia was right. Even if Micah and Banks both rode quickly, he couldn't have gotten here this soon. And what if Banks hadn't been in when Micah got there? What if he was out tending to another patient? Micah would have had to chase him down. It could be another hour, even more. He looked at Julia with agonized eyes. Julia looked back at him, her gaze strong and steady. He knew what she was telling him: Calm down. You'll upset Sarah.

"I'm sorry. Of course, there hasn't been enough time." Luke sat down on the bed beside Sarah and took her hand. It clenched tightly around his.

Sarah clamped her jaw together. A little whimpering sound escaped her lips. It tore Luke apart. She was having another contraction. They'd been coming steadily for an hour. Now they were almost one right after the other. Sarah's hair was lank and damp with sweat, her face ghostly pale. She had chewed her bottom lip almost raw, and there were deep red scratches in Luke's hand where her nails had dug in during the pains. Luke felt her agony all through him.

But even her anguish wasn't as bad as the blood. She just

kept on bleeding! Luke glanced down at Sarah's legs. There was blood all over the towels and sheets. How could there be so much blood in her? How could she continue to lose it and still live?

"Luke?" Sarah's voice was pitifully thin. Her eyes were closed and she breathed in quick, shallow pants. "Luke, it hurts."

"Oh, Sarah. Sarah." Tears sprang into his eyes. "Sweetheart, I—" If only he could do something! He felt so awful, so helpless, just sitting here watching her suffer.

"Please, get the doctor. I need the doctor."

"I know. Micah went to fetch him. He's on his way."

"Promise?"

"I promise."

"It hurts."

"I know it does." Her face contorted with pain, and she moaned. "It's all right, sweetheart. Let it out. Scream."

Sarah's jaw jutted out and she shook her head. "I *won't* scream. I'm not—"

"—the kind of woman who screams," Luke finished for her. "I know. But there's nobody here to think badly of you for yelling. Hell, if it was me, I'd probably shout the house down."

A faint smile touched Sarah's lips, and her hand relaxed in his as the contraction faded. But her face was still drawn, and Luke knew the pain hadn't receded entirely.

"It's so different from last time," she mumbled, wetting her lips.

"I know."

Julia bent over Sarah again and placed a damp rag between her lips. "Here, this will help that thirst."

Sarah nodded gratefully and sucked on the rag. Julia went back to her task of knotting strips of rags together. When she had finished two long, braided strips, she tied them around the foot posts of the bed. Then she wiped Sarah's face again. Her voice was low and soothing. "The doctor should be here soon."

Sarah nodded. Her eyes opened suddenly. "Emily?" She tried to lift her head.

"She's fine. Bonnie and Vance are looking after her.

Don't worry about her. I told them to stay down by the barn. She won't hear anything.''

"Thank you. Oh!" Sarah tightened as a fresh wave of pain hit her.

Julia stepped back, patting Luke's shoulder as she passed. He gripped Sarah's hand, willing strength into her. He wanted to somehow grab this enemy that was hurting her and beat it to a pulp. He wanted to run. He couldn't bear the sight of Sarah in pain. But this was the only thing he could do for her, so he made himself stand it. He thought he'd rather be eight years old and facing his father's belt again.

There was a noise out front, and Julia hurried to the window to look out. "It's him!" Relief sounded in her voice. "I'll let him in."

She flew down the stairs and yanked open the front door. James was getting off his horse. He looked strong and capable. "Jimmy! Thank God you're here." All awkwardness at seeing him again fled in the face of her relief.

James looked at her. He couldn't quell a funny little leap in his chest at the sight of her, even under the circumstances. "Julie. How is she? What happened? The hired hand said she was bleeding." He grabbed his bag and trotted up the steps to her.

"Yes, a lot. I've never seen so much blood at a birth."

"Have you been at many?"

Julia led him into the house and up the stairs. "A few. Usually I just helped the midwife, but I delivered the last one myself. The midwife didn't make it in time."

"Good. Then you'll be able to help me."

"If you'd like."

"Here. Sterilize these instruments in boiling water and get me some towels, while I go up and see the patient."

He handed her several metal tools and went up the stairs to Sarah's room. Luke stood up and turned at his entrance. James checked his steps at Luke's white, stricken face. For a moment he thought Sarah must have died, from Luke's expression, but then he saw her head move upon her pillow.

"You gotta help her," Luke said.

Suddenly James had a picture of Luke's contorted face as he had rushed at him that time on the Fourth of July, the doubled-up fist slamming into him, and he knew Luke was thinking of the same thing. He was scared to death that James would hold that against him and not save Sarah. James's mouth tightened. "I'll do everything I can for her. You must know that."

He stepped around Luke and looked down at Sarah. He picked up her hand and took her pulse, running his eyes over her clinically while he talked in a soothing voice. "Hello, Mrs. Turner. Looks like you've had an accident here."

"I didn't do anything," Sarah panted. "Julia lifted everything. I didn't. It just happened."

"Of course you didn't do anything. It's not your fault. Now, I'm going to examine you. I'm afraid it will hurt a little."

Sarah tried to smile. "It already hurts more than that."

James smiled. She had pluck. "I'll try to be as gentle as possible." He pulled off his jacket, rolled up his shirtsleeves, and washed his hands at the washstand. Then he poured carbolic acid over them to sterilize them. He came back to the bed and began to examine her.

"Luke?" Sarah's voice rose in pain and fear.

"I'm right here, honey." Luke went to the other side of the bed and reached over to take her hand. Sarah closed her eyes and clung to him, bracing herself against the pain.

"I'm afraid this baby is coming whether we like it or not," James said, stepping back and wiping the blood from his hands.

Julia walked in the door and silently handed James a hot, wet rag and towel. She carried the instruments on another towel. He glanced at her, surprised. "That was quick."

"I already had the water boiling. I figured you'd need it."

"Good. How long has she been bleeding?"

Julia described concisely and clearly what had occurred from the moment Sarah started bleeding.

"Have you touched her abdomen?"

"Yes. It's been hard like that the whole time."

"Constantly? Even when her contractions let up?"

"They don't seem to ease up all the way. She's been feeling the pain right along."

James nodded. He looked across at Luke.

"I think what has happened is what we call a placenta abruption. The placenta has torn loose from the wall of the uterus and is now between the baby and the cervix. That's why there's so much blood. Unfortunately, it usually sets premature labor in motion, and that is what is happening now. She's dilated quite a bit already."

"Am I—going to lose the baby?" Sarah asked.

James hesitated. He looked at her, his face sad. "I'll do everything I can to save both the baby and you, ma'am." He glanced at Luke.

Luke went cold inside. He knew what that involuntary glance meant. The doctor didn't think he could save the baby. Maybe not the mother, either. Luke squeezed Sarah's hand. "It'll be all right, sweetheart. It'll be all right."

The afternoon wore on. Sarah continued in pain. Luke held her hand, and Julia wiped her brow with a damp rag, murmuring soothing words. From time to time James checked her pulse and laid his hand against her cheek and arm. They waited.

"Mama?" Sarah's eyes fluttered open and she gazed up at Julia. Luke looked at James, panicked. Sarah's mother had been dead for over three years. She was out of her head.

James glanced at Sarah's face. She frowned, then whispered, "No, of course not. You're—"

"Julia. I'm Julia, honey."

"I'm sorry."

"You're just a little confused."

"Yes." Sarah's eyes closed again. She looked asleep.

James felt her pulse. "Skin's clammy. Pulse is high. She's going into shock."

Luke scrambled off the bed. "No."

"Julie, get some more blankets. We have to keep her warm. Luke, get me blocks of wood. Two of them." He gestured to indicate the size. "We have to stick them under the legs at the foot of the bed to raise it. Do you have any?"

"Yeah. Sure."

Luke raced down to the barn while Julia brought in more

blankets to cover Sarah. It was a warm April day and Julia was sweating, but Sarah's skin was as cold as ice.

"Is she going to be all right?"

"Maybe, if we can bring her out of shock. I don't think the labor will last much longer."

Luke returned with the blocks of wood, and he and James lifted the foot of the bed while Julia slid in the chunks of wood under the legs. They waited, watching her.

James took Sarah's pulse again and laid his hand against her forehead. "I think she's a little better."

Luke released the breath he'd been holding. He went around the bed to Sarah and picked up her hand again. Sarah's eyes opened, and she offered him a weak smile that tore at his heart. "You're going to be all right." Luke squeezed her hand and tried to imbue his voice with confidence. "I promise."

Sarah made a faint nod. Lines of pain were engraved in her face. She grimaced as a fresh pain struck her. Luke glanced pleadingly at James.

James shook his head. "We just have to wait. The baby will come in due course."

Luke held Sarah's hand, grateful for the pain of her fingers digging into his flesh. At least that was something he could give her, something he could do to make up for her agony—the agony he had caused.

He watched her helplessly, lacerated by fear, feeling her pain all through him, and knowing that she suffered because of him. It was his fault she was here, his fault she hovered on the edge of death, racked by pain. He had done it to her, solely to satisfy his lust. Old Dr. Banks had told him not to make love to Sarah while she was pregnant, but he had ignored the doctor's warning. Luke thought about how he had taken her without thought for anything except his own driving hunger. And now, here she was, lying in a bed of blood, losing her baby, dying. Because of him.

Luke hated himself for Sarah's suffering.

Sarah floated in and out of a hazy world, sometimes blissfully unconscious of the pain, at other times torn apart by it. She would be aware of nothing, in a black void, and then she would feel the warmth and strength around her hand, holding on to her, and she would cling to it, knowing it was her lifeline. "Luke . . ."

"I'm right here."

Tears seeped from beneath Sarah's lids. The voice gave her strength, as the hand did. She couldn't slip away, not with Luke there. "I love you."

His hand clenched convulsively around hers. "I love you, too, sweetheart. I love you, too." His voice rasped with tears. "Hold on, honey. Just hold on."

The pain was changing now. Sarah could feel it. There was a huge, unstoppable force within her, carrying her along, forcing her out of the blackness and into the awful, piercing reality. She dug her heels into the bed and pushed.

"She's pushing." That was a man's voice, one she didn't know. Sarah opened her eyes and saw a man beside her bed. He was familiar. Who was he? Oh yes, the doctor. And the woman. The woman was Julia. Luke's sister.

The pain left her blessedly. Sarah waited, panting, thankful for the sudden surcease.

Gently Julia moved Luke aside and put the braided ties in Sarah's hand. James moved Sarah's skirts out of the way and checked her again. "It's in the birth canal." His voice was tinged with excitement and an irrepressible hope. "It won't be long now."

Luke stood to one side, feeling desperate and helpless, and watched as Sarah struggled to bear their child.

Sarah felt again the huge, overpowering force within her, the compelling need to push, the rush of pain so different from what had come before. She bore down, pushing with all her strength.

"That's it. Good girl. It's coming now." The doctor's voice kept up a smooth, steady litany of encouragement, and the calm, deep tones reassured and strengthened her.

Then once again the force, the pain were gone, and she relaxed, gasping for breath. Luke crossed his arms across his chest, watching her. She was so fragile, so pale, so small. How could she possibly have the strength to do this?

He hadn't been in the room when she had given birth to Emily. The doctor had made him wait downstairs. Had it been this bad? Was childbirth always like this? No. It couldn't have been like this before. Sarah hadn't lost all this blood then. She didn't have the strength now that she had had then. She was so weak. The pains must be tearing her apart.

Luke could see her tensing up again, and it was all he could do not to cry out that it was too soon. She hadn't had a chance to rest. This would kill her. His fingers dug into his arms and he bit his lower lip, riding out the pain with her.

"That's good, Mrs. Turner," James said. "That's right. Keep on pushing." A mass of gore came out, and the sheets were flooded with blood. "I see his head!" James's hands went out to take the slippery baby as it emerged. "One more time. He's almost here. One more good push. That's it! The head and shoulders are out." His voice was laced with triumph as he pulled the tiny, bloody form from her.

Sarah slumped back against the pillows, exhausted, the braided ropes sliding from her hands, as darkness wrapped around her.

* Chapter 7 *

Julia handed James his clamps and scissors just as he opened his mouth to ask for them. He worked swiftly, clamping off the cord and cutting it. There was no movement nor sound from the baby, small and slimy with blood and mucus. James wiped the baby's face and hooked a finger into his mouth to clear it. Still, the limp form didn't move. He turned him over, holding the baby in one hand, and slapped sharply on his back. He slapped him a second and third time. James turned him back over and tried to breathe life into him. The little creature lay still in his hands. Minutes passed as he worked on the baby feverishly. Finally he straightened and looked at Julia.

There was blood all over James's face, hands, and shirt.

His mouth was grim, his eyes darkly despairing. He shook his head, and silently Julia took the child. She walked to the washstand and gently bathed the small, lifeless form. Tears gathered in her eyes and clogged her throat. It was a perfect little baby boy, too tiny to live. She wanted to cry for Luke and for Sarah, even for James and the sad frustration in his face.

James turned to Luke. "I'm sorry. The baby was born dead."

"Sarah?" Luke's face was as white as paper.

James set his jaw. "We'll save her." He had lost the baby, but he'd be damned if he lost the mother, as well. He set to work to stop the blood.

The room was utterly silent except for the sound of their breathing. Luke watched James, feeling as if his life hung suspended in the other man's hands. He wondered how often James faced this sort of life and death struggle, and he experienced a grudging respect for him for doing so. James was a good doctor, and he cared. It showed on his face and in the gentle competence of his hands. Luke would never have thought him capable of it.

"There." James straightened. "I hope we've stopped the flow of blood. It's all I can do for the moment."

Julia came over to the bed, cradling a small bundle in her arms. "I'll fetch you some clean towels and water." She hesitated, glancing at Luke, then handed Luke the bundle. He took it, gently folding back the towels from the baby's body. His fingers trembled. It was tiny, every feature formed in perfect, minute detail. It had been a boy, his and Sarah's son. And he knew he had killed it. He folded the towel back over the little head. Tears coursed, unnoticed, down his face.

Julia returned in a few minutes with a stack of clean towels and fresh water. She set them down on the washstand, and James went over to it to scrub away the blood on his face and arms. Julia went to her brother and gently pried the baby from his arms.

"I'll take him and dress him in the christening dress Sarah made."

Luke nodded. Julia reached up and wiped the tears from her brother's face. "I'm sorry. So sorry." She turned toward

James. "I put on a pot of coffee, Dr. Banks, if you'd like some."

"Thank you. Yes, I would."

Julia left the room. James dried his hands and arms and made another check of Sarah's condition. He pulled the blankets close around her. "I think the bleeding's stopped," he told Luke. "She appears to be coming out of shock."

"Then she—she's all right?"

"I believe that she is doing better. Unless she begins hemorrhaging or slips back into shock . . . yes, I think she will be all right."

"Thank God." Luke let out a breath and relaxed, unaware of how tightly he had been holding himself.

"I'm going downstairs now for that cup of coffee, if you'll stay with her."

"Yes, of course."

"Call me if there's any change in her condition."

Luke nodded, and James left the room. Luke sat down gingerly on the bed beside Sarah and picked up her hand. It seemed horribly cold to him, and her face was drained of color. He wondered how Banks could have detected any improvement. He held her hand between his, wishing he could somehow warm her.

She had almost died. She still could die.

His mother had died in childbirth. She had died bearing him. That had been why his father hated him; he had always told Luke he had killed his own mother. Luke had denied it; he had tried not to believe it. But he couldn't deny this. He had killed this baby. He had almost killed Sarah. He'd never be able to change it or forget it. Even Sarah, sweet, gentle Sarah, would blame him.

He remembered his grandmother's bitter face, her mouth twisted with hatred as she had shrieked at him, "You killed her. You and your father's selfish lust. He couldn't let her be, had to have her all the time. So she died bearing his brat. You're just the same. You'll use that sweet little thing you married for your own lust, use her until she can't bear anymore. She'll end up hating you for it, mark my words."

Stu Harper had said much the same thing when he'd warned Sarah not to marry Luke. He'd told her that Luke would make her worn and old before her time bearing his children. Men like Harper, Luke guessed, restrained themselves with their wives, held back from making love with them so that they didn't have children too often, didn't bear too many. Certainly a man like Harper wouldn't risk his wife's and child's lives by making love to his wife when she was pregnant. Luke had never understood men of that cool nature. But maybe it wasn't coldness. Maybe it was simply something in their natures that he didn't have, a goodness that made them control themselves in order to protect the women they loved.

He had thought he loved Sarah so much that he would protect her from anything, that he would die to keep her safe. But he hadn't protected her; just the opposite. It had been he who had hurt her, he from whom she needed to be protected.

Sarah was the best and kindest of women. But even she would be bound to hate him now. Luke lifted Sarah's hand and pressed his lips against her fingers. He laid her palm against his cheek. He knew she could never hate him as much as he hated himself right now.

Sarah's eyes opened groggily. "Luke?"

"Yes."

"I—" She glanced around. Her voice was barely a whisper. He had to lean down to hear her. "Where's the baby? I want to see him."

His throat closed, and for a moment he couldn't say anything.

"Luke? The baby?"

He shook his head. "I'm sorry, Sarah. I'm sorry. He was born—dead."

She stared at him for a long, silent moment, then an animal groan of pain and loss broke from her lips. "No! No!"

"I'm sorry, sweetheart." He reached out with his free hand to touch her cheek, but she jerked her head away. Pulling her hand from his grasp, Sarah rolled over on her side, away from him, and buried her face in the pillow.

Luke sat, looking down at the stiff barrier of her back. He was ice all through. He had been right. She hated him.

He slipped off the bed and left the room.

* * *

James sat down at the kitchen table with a sigh. He felt drained and weary. It was always hard for him to lose a patient, but children and babies were particularly bad. He had known as soon as he saw Sarah that she would probably lose the baby. It would have been a miracle if she hadn't. But somehow he always hoped for miracles.

Julia poured coffee into a blue enamel mug and set it down on the table before him. "Would you like some cream or sugar?"

"No." He gave her something resembling a smile. "Right now I need it black as it can be."

"Tired?"

"Yes. Aren't you?"

Julia nodded. "Would you like something to eat? I put some food in to warm up."

He started to say no, that he wasn't hungry, but he knew that part of the hollowness inside him was hunger even though the afternoon had left him with no appetite. It was late, and he supposed he ought to eat. He had to wait here awhile to make sure Sarah was all right, anyway. "Yes. Thank you."

Julia pulled out a pan of boiled potatoes and roast from the oven and loaded a good portion of each onto a plate. Belatedly she realized that for a visitor like a doctor she should have used Sarah's china, not the everyday enamel cast-iron plates. Sarah would have known to do that. Any woman brought up in James's world would have known.

She pulled a china plate from the cabinet and switched plates, sticking the metal one in the sink to be cleaned. James watched her, frowning. "What are you doing?"

"Nothing. I wasn't thinking, and I put it on the wrong plate." She set the food down in front of him and stepped back, her cheeks flushed a little with embarrassment.

James glanced at her. "What's the difference?" A more genuine smile touched his lips. "You think I can't eat off an old plate?" He shook his head. "Women."

He found it lightened his spirits to look at her. He knew he shouldn't feel that way, but he ignored the thought. Right now he needed a little lightening of his spirits. He took a sip

of the hot, strong coffee. "Mmm. That's good. Just right."
He motioned toward the rest of the table. "Aren't you
joining me?"

"I'm not hungry. I'll eat later." She hesitated. "But I
think I will have a cup of coffee."

Julia poured herself a cup and sat down across the table.
She couldn't bring herself to leave James's strength and
warmth just yet.

James ate slowly and methodically, hardly aware of what
he ate. There were deep grooves around his mouth and eyes,
and he looked unutterably weary.

"It saddens you, doesn't it?" Julia asked.

He glanced at her. "To have a baby die in my hands?
Yes, it saddens me. More than that. It makes me so angry,
so damn frustrated." He set down his fork with a clatter and
leaned back in his chair. "I'm sorry; excuse my language.
It's just that I—you'd think that we could do more, that we
could learn how to stop—" He stopped abruptly and drew a
deep breath. "I apologize. You don't want to hear this. I'm
on my soapbox again. I hate like anything to lose a baby.
It's such a waste."

"But you did everything you could. No one could ask for
a doctor to do more. You tried so hard to save him."

"Yes, I tried. Sometimes that's cold comfort."

"I know."

"You worked very hard, as well. I appreciated your
help."

"Thank you." James's compliment filled Julia with warmth.

"You're intelligent and strong." James looked at Julia's
pale face, her cheeks tinged now with color. No one would
ever guess, seeing her fair, delicate beauty, that she pos-
sessed such stamina and strength. "And compassionate.
That's even more important. You were very gentle with
Mrs. Turner."

"I couldn't be anything but gentle with her. Sarah has
been sweet and generous to me."

"I think you would be gentle with anyone."

Julia glanced down at her hands, unable to meet his eyes,
afraid that he would see how much his words pleased her.

James gazed at her bent head. There was a vulnerability
to Julia's bare, curved neck that tugged at him. Many times

over the past years, he had hated Julia for the pain she had caused him. More recently, he had thought he had nothing for her but indifference. But at the moment he could feel neither one, only a bittersweet ache in his chest. She was still so lovely it made him peaceful inside—and sad. He would have thought she wouldn't be pretty anymore. He would have thought she wouldn't still have that sweet, innocent air about her. He would have thought he wouldn't like her.

There was the sound of boots on the stairs, breaking the silence, and Luke came into the room. His face was pale and set, and there was a cold emptiness in his eyes that made James rise from his chair, fearing the worst. "What happened?"

Luke looked at him with a flat, blank gaze. "She's awake. She—asked to see the baby."

"I'm sorry." It was a hard thing to tell a woman she had lost a child—far harder, James guessed, if you loved the woman and were grieving over the loss of the child yourself. "I'll go check on her."

Luke and Julia followed James up the stairs. Inside the room, they found Sarah huddled into a ball on the bed, her back to them. James reached over to take her wrist. She didn't move or even turn her head. Julia glanced at Luke. She would have thought he would go to Sarah, but he remained standing in the doorway. He looked awful, his pale eyes lifeless.

James finished his examination and walked back to where Julia and Luke stood. "She's better. The blood has stopped. She's warmer, her pulse steadier. Barring complications, she'll be all right. Weak, of course, but she should improve. She'll need to be watched."

"I'll stay with her," Julia promised.

"Good. There are a few things I want you to do. Keep her warm and give her lots of fluids. Water, thin soup, whatever you can get down her. No food for a day or two, though I doubt she'll want any, anyway. Keep her feet elevated. And you need to rub her abdomen."

"I understand."

"Good. I'll be back out tomorrow evening to look at her, but send for me before then if she gets worse. Or even if there's just something that bothers you about her." Julia nodded. "Well, good evening then."

"Good-bye."

Luke escorted James downstairs to the front door while Julia remained in the room with Sarah. James paused at the door and turned to face Luke. Luke looked devastated, and though he'd never much liked the man, James felt pity for him now.

"I'm sorry," James said in a low voice.

"Not your fault." Luke spoke jerkily, and his movements were awkward, as though someone were moving him with strings.

"I'd suggest you sit down and have a cup of coffee. Ju—Mrs. Dobson just made some. It's hot and strong, and it will help you. Better put a shot of whiskey in it, too."

"I'm all right."

"I wish that there had been something I could do . . ."

"You did the best anyone could. You tried real hard to save the baby. And you did save Sarah. She'd have died without you here."

James paused and glanced down at the floor. "It surprised you, didn't it?"

"What?"

"I'm not sure—that I'm a decent doctor, that I tried to save her."

"There's no love lost between us."

Anger stirred in James, and he stared hard at Luke. "It wouldn't matter if I hated you. It's my duty, my oath, to do everything in my power to maintain a patient's life. You must think I'm a real son of a bitch."

Luke's eyes were as clear and hard as marbles, as lacking in life. "Yeah."

James's eyebrows rose, and he almost smiled. Whatever one could say about Luke Turner, he never had been one to pull punches. "I guess you have reason to. I never blamed you for hitting me that time." He shrugged and looked away. "In your place, I'm sure I would have done the same thing. I—what I did was reprehensible. Being young and in love was no excuse."

"In love?" A mirthless smile touched Luke's lips. "Is that what you called it?"

James met his gaze levelly. "Yes. That's what I called it." He turned away, shrugging. "At any rate, I didn't enjoy waking up with bruises all over me, but I understood it. I couldn't hate you for it. And I certainly would not let one of my patients suffer because of it." James opened the front door and walked out.

Luke watched him mount his horse and ride out of the yard, then he turned back into the house. He looked up the stairs. He couldn't go back up there. Julia would take care of Sarah. Sarah wouldn't want to see him.

He left the house and crossed the yard to the barn. He chose the best pieces of the neatly stacked lumber in the rear of the barn and laid them out on the sawhorses. He took down his saw and began to slice through the wood. It didn't take long to finish. The coffin would be very small.

He brushed his eyes with the back of his hand, clearing away the tears so that he could see his task. He fitted two small lengths of wood together and began to hammer in the nails.

They buried the baby the next day underneath the oak tree on the rise, where Sarah wanted it. She could see the tree from the window in their bedroom, and there would be shade over him in the hot summers.

From her bed, Sarah watched the small procession as they trudged up the slight incline. She was too weak to even get out of bed, let alone go with them, but it tore her heart to see them carry away the small casket and her not be there. There was Luke, carrying the small wooden box, with Julia beside him and the children straggling behind. The minister from their church was there, too. He had tried to come up and comfort Sarah, but Sarah had told Julia not to let him in.

She didn't want to see the man. She didn't want comfort. She was too consumed with rage.

Sarah hated the world. She hated Luke. She hated Julia, even the children. Everything, everyone. Most of all, she hated herself. How could they all be alive and her baby dead? How could anything dare to breathe, to live? Sarah wanted to scream and throw things, to shout like a mad-woman, to tear the room apart. Only a lifetime of training and the complete weakness in her limbs kept her from it.

Sarah had never known anger like this. Even when both her parents had died unexpectedly and tragically, she had been sad, not angry. But now . . . Now she thought she could pull out one of Luke's guns and shoot someone—anyone, it didn't matter whom—without a trace of remorse.

She surged with fury. There was nowhere to place it. And she could feel nothing else.

There weren't even tears. Her eyes were dry. Her heart was numb. There was nothing inside her, nothing but anger.

Everyone had kept away from her, and she was glad of that. Luke had slept elsewhere, and he and Julia had only come in every hour or so to check on her. Sarah had kept her eyes closed, her back turned to them, and pretended to sleep. It had been a long, bitter night. She had never been so lost and alone. Yet she had wanted no one there, wanted no hand reached out to her in sympathy. She was closed in with her rage—too filled with anger to give comfort to her husband or to receive it or even to talk about what had happened, and too ashamed of what she felt, too well brought up to let it show.

She watched from a distance as Luke lowered the tiny casket into the ground. Sarah shivered despite the quilts on the bed and the knitted shawl around her shoulders, despite the warmth of the April day. She turned her face away, unable to watch Luke and Micah fill in the grave. Sarah scooted down in the bed, further under the covers, and huddled into herself. For the first time, something pierced the numbness, broke through the anger. It was desolation.

She turned her face into the pillow and hot, hurting tears seeped from beneath her lids.

Later, Luke climbed the stairs to their bedroom and came to the doorway. He hesitated, then stepped inside. "I—uh—it's done."

"I know. I saw from my window."

Luke glanced toward the window near the bed and nod-ded. He remained in the room for a moment, looking awkward. "I'm sorry, Sarah."

Sarah pressed her lips together. Tears clogged her throat.

She looked away. It hurt to look at Luke, to see the pain in his face and to know that there was nothing in her to give him. Poor Luke. He was hurting, just as she was, and she was cold to him, yet she could not reach out to comfort him. She was too empty.

Luke saw the bleakness of Sarah's face, her averted eyes, and he knew that she wanted nothing to do with him. He had ruined her life. He looked away, focusing on the wall. "I guess I'll, uh, go out and work. Julia will be here to take care of you."

He left the room. Sarah closed her eyes and wished she could sleep. She wished she had died with the baby.

Her sister Jennifer drove out from town in her buggy that afternoon. Sarah watched her walk into the room and wished she hadn't. She couldn't talk, not even to Jen. Jennifer's lovely face looked older and not so beautiful today; her mouth was pulled down into lines of sorrow.

"I'm so sorry, honey," she said, crossing the room to Sarah.

Sarah tightened, feeling the invasion of Jennifer's presence, her crashing through the barriers of silence and isolation that Julia and Luke did not cross. She wanted to tell her to stop, to go away. But Jennifer was already there, taking one of Sarah's hands in her own and squeezing it gently. Though Sarah had not wanted it, she was suddenly glad and relieved. She clutched Jennifer's hand tightly. Jennifer sat down on the bed beside her, and they sat together in silence for a long time.

After that, Sarah couldn't quite recapture the numbness she had felt before. Gradually, as the days passed, layer after layer of her disinterest was stripped away, leaving her vulnerable to new, painful emotions.

Her anger against the world coalesced into anger against herself. She was responsible for the miscarriage. She knew that she had lost the baby because she had been careless or because she had done something she shouldn't. Maybe she had lifted something that was too heavy, not even realizing it. Or maybe it was because they had made love that night, and that was her fault, too. She had wanted Luke to make love to her for her own selfish gratification. He hadn't wanted to because of the doctor's warnings, but she had

tempted and teased him until he had. Or maybe it was that
she hadn't eaten right or—whatever the answer was, Sarah
knew that she was responsible. That precious life had been
entrusted to her, and she had failed it.

Sarah was overwhelmed with sorrow and piercing loss,
with guilt and dread, and she huddled in upon herself, like a
wounded animal retreating from the world. She couldn't talk
to anyone, could hardly bear to look at them. She was
exhausted and broken, wrapped around with misery, and
every day when she woke up, she was aware of a sharp
sense of disappointment that another day had arrived.

Dr. Banks came to check on her frequently. Sarah barely
answered his questions and ignored his attempts to offer her
comfort or to cheer her up. Julia took care of Sarah
faithfully, bringing her things to drink and later bowls of
soup to eat, checking in on her all the time to make sure she
was comfortable and well. Sarah knew that Julia would have
liked to take her hand and tell her soothing things, too, to
talk and listen to Sarah's unhappiness. But Sarah said
nothing more to her than to reply to her questions with a
simple "yes" or "no."

Sarah knew that it was wrong of her to act this way.
Everyone wanted to help her; they felt sorrow for her loss.
But Sarah could not respond, not even to Luke.

He came in every morning and two or three times during
the evening. He asked how she was, and Sarah responded
with the evident lie that she was fine. He asked if she was
comfortable, if he could get her anything, and then, after a
few more moments of awkward standing in silence, he
would leave the room, telling her to call if she needed him
or Julia. Sarah always answered him politely and listlessly.

Sarah knew that that, too, was wrong. But she felt so
bone weary, so achingly empty that she could not reach out
to Luke to offer comfort or to take it. There was no love left
inside her, no understanding or ability to rise above her
sorrow. There was only a deep, raw misery, and she could
do nothing except endure it in silence.

If Luke had come to her and taken her hand, held her
close to him, forced her to accept his love and comfort and
his own agony of loss, Sarah might have responded, as she
had with Jennifer. There was, deep inside Sarah, a faint

hope that he might, that Luke would break through the barrier of isolation and silence that surrounded her. Something within her wanted to rip through the years of upbringing that kept her still and quiet against her grief.

But Luke himself had learned to contain his feelings in an even harder school, and he kept silent now. He could not pour out his own sorrow to her, knowing that she hurt more than he and that he had caused both their sorrow. Nor did he dare to offer her his sympathy and comfort. He was certain Sarah hated him for what he had caused. He didn't blame her for not reaching out to him. And though it was like a knife to his heart to see her lying there so still and passive, no closeness or affection for him in her face, he knew he dared not hope for anything else.

A week passed. Luke drove himself mercilessly, rising before dawn and eating a cold breakfast alone, then tackling the fields and not returning until the sun set in the evening. It was as if he thought he could somehow sweat the pain out of him or atone for his sins. Sarah lay in her bed, not eating enough, frail and unhappy. Emily trailed around the house, thumb in her mouth, sticking close to Julia's side instead of playing with Bonnie and Vance.

And Julia took care of them all and worried over what was to happen to them. The only bright spots for her were the evenings when the doctor came to visit Sarah, at first every evening, then every two days. Julia found herself looking forward to his visits with an almost guilty pleasure.

She shouldn't be happy to see him, Julia thought, considering the tragic reason for his coming there. Besides, he was nothing to her, she nothing to him. Any feeling between them was over and dead long ago.

But late in the afternoon, anticipation would rise in her, and when she heard the sound of a horse's hooves coming down the drive, her heart would start to thud in her chest. She would hurry to the door to meet James, and just the sight of his face brought freshness and life into a house sunk in misery.

He would go upstairs to see Sarah, then come back down and tell Julia and Luke, if he was there, about Sarah's progress. He would compliment Julia on her work and tell her to continue what she was doing. She would pour him a cup of coffee and sometimes, if he hadn't eaten, she could persuade him to have a bite of supper. They were stiff and formal with each other in a way that would have been amusing, considering what they had once been to each other—if either of them had been able to perceive the humor in it. He called her "Mrs. Dobson" and she called him "Dr. Banks," and their conversation moved along stilted lines—questions about his work and her health and how Sarah was doing, carefully avoiding any mention of the past or any hint of former intimacy.

Sometimes Julia thought, looking at him, how very handsome James still was, and she wondered why he had never married. She couldn't suppress a funny little happiness inside that he hadn't, even though she knew that was a wicked thought. She should wish that he had married a wonderful woman and was very happy, with several children. That would be the nice thing to hope for someone she had once loved. But Julia knew she wasn't that saintly.

She wondered, too, if James ever thought about her, ever regretted what had happened. She told herself she was amazingly egotistical to think that he might. Still . . . he did always stay for a cup of coffee.

Not that she cared. Not that she had any hope of anything happening between them again. But she always checked her image in the mirror before she opened the door to him.

One afternoon, a week after the miscarriage, James came down the stairs with a worried frown on his face. Julia, who had been washing dishes, went to him, drying her hands on her apron. "What is it? Is something the matter?"

James sighed and made a negating gesture. "I'm sorry. I didn't mean to frighten you. Mrs. Turner is all right. It's just that she's not recovering as quickly as I had hoped. She is still quite weak. I'm afraid that leaves her much too vulnerable to other diseases."

He sat down at the table without waiting to be asked this time, and Julia quickly set a mug in front of him and filled it with aromatic coffee.

"She couldn't be anything but weak, the way she eats," Julia told him. "I can hardly even get any soup down her."

"She should be eating more."

"It's the grief."

"I know. She obviously closes it up inside herself, and I think that makes it even harder on her."

"She doesn't want to talk."

"But it might help her. She needs—I don't know, to somehow be raised from this desolate lethargy. Right now she just doesn't care, and that could harm her recovery." James took a sip of his coffee and looked up at Julia. "Do you think you could encourage her to talk? Maybe persuade her that she has something to live for?"

"I'll try."

He smiled, and Julia's heart warmed within her. It was amazing what power his smile still held over her. She smiled back at him.

"Would you, uh, like something to eat? Supper's on the stove."

James hesitated. He was tempted. He was tempted every time she asked him. Sometimes he refused, but it seemed as if it was easier each time to say yes. It made no sense to stay. There was little ease between them. There was awkwardness and hesitation and too many memories. Yet, crazily, he wanted to linger. It was idiocy, he told himself. Sheer idiocy. He had been unsettled ever since he saw Julia in Harper's store two weeks ago. He kept remembering too much, and too often he found her face in his mind. He hadn't needed to come out here to the Turner place practically every night, as he had. And there shouldn't be that swelling anticipation in his chest when he rode out to the Turner place.

He was a fool if he let himself get mixed up with Julia Turner again.

"I guess not." James made himself stand up. "I'd better get back into town. I have a lot of business on my desk to take care of."

"Of course. Thank you for coming by."

"It's no trouble."

Julia followed him to the door and watched him mount his horse. He lifted his hat to her and trotted down the drive. Julia closed the door. It wouldn't be right to stand at the door gazing after him. But she lifted the edge of the lace curtain on the front window and watched until he was out of sight.

Then, sighing, she went back into the kitchen and dished
up a bowl of soup for Sarah. She set the bowl on a tray and
added a thick slice of bread, warm from the oven this
afternoon and slathered with pale yellow butter. It smelled
delicious and looked just as good, but she had little hope
that Sarah would do any more than pick at it. She started to
lift the tray, then stopped and went out the side door. The
first iris of the season bloomed a bright purple at the foot of
the steps beside the house, and she bent and broke it off.
She set it in a glass and put the glass on the tray as well.

Julia carried the tray upstairs to Sarah's room. Sarah lay
propped up against her pillows, gazing out the window. Her
face was pale, her hair tumbling around it in lank disorder.
She glanced at Julia and the tray without interest.

"It's almost time for supper. I brought you some soup.
Dr. Banks said you should start eating more, so I fixed beef
and vegetables. Doesn't it smell good?" Julia set the tray
down on the table beside the bed and fluffed up Sarah's
pillows.

"I'm sorry, Julia. I don't really feel like eating."

"Of course not. Your stomach's all shrunk up. But you
take a few bites anyway. It's the only way to get back on
your feet." Julia ignored Sarah's indifference and set the
tray down on her lap. "There now. Take a sniff. Doesn't
that smell good?"

"I don't want it." Sarah's voice was mild, but utterly
toneless.

Julia picked up the spoon and placed it in the bowl, lifting
up a chunk of meat. "Just take a bite. As a personal favor for
me."

Sarah glanced at her, then took the spoon and ate the
chunk of meat. Slowly she ate another few spoonfuls.

"Good." Julia tore the piece of bread in half. "I made
this loaf of bread this afternoon. It's still a little warm. The
butter just melted on it."

Sarah took a bite of the bread and laid it aside. She
pushed the tray down her legs away from her. "I'm full
now."

With a sigh Julia picked up the tray. Sarah hadn't eaten
enough of anything, and she hadn't even noticed the flower
that Julia had hoped might cheer her up.

Julia understood how Sarah felt. No one could have understood better than she. Julia had felt exactly the same way when Pamela died. But Julia also knew that something had to change with Sarah.

She set the tray down on the table and walked over to the window, staring out of it at the big oak on the hill, with the sad dark patch of newly turned earth beneath it.

"This is no good for any of you, you know," she said quietly. "You're going to wind up sicker. And Luke and Emily are going to be even more unhappy."

She turned to look at Sarah. Sarah stared at her, surprised.

"I know. It's not my place to tell you what to do. But Luke and Emily are my family, and I love them. I can't bear to see that misery in their eyes all the time. You've got to come back to them."

"Come back? I don't understand."

"You're as far away from them as if you lived in another county. Emily keeps asking about you. I've tried to keep her out of here and to explain to her that you're sick. But she's scared and lonely. She doesn't understand why you just lie there."

Tears welled in Sarah's eyes. "I'm sorry. But I'm—I can't—"

"Yes. You can." Julia clasped her hands in front of her, struggling for the courage of say what she needed to. "I understand how you feel."

"You couldn't."

"No. I could. And I do. I had a little girl about a year and a half older than Vance."

"What?"

"She died."

"Oh, Julia, I'm sorry. I didn't know." Pity touched Sarah's face and voice.

"I wanted to lay there and die, too. It didn't seem like life was worth anything without Pammy."

"How did you—" Sarah's voice broke, and she started again. "How did you ever manage?"

Julia shrugged. "I had to, that's all. I had a baby to take care of. I had to live for him. I had to feed and bathe and clothe him. I had to rock him to sleep. So I couldn't give way. I had to live for somebody else. And, finally, it got easier. Then I began to want to keep on living. You've got people to live for, too.''

"I guess I have.'' Sarah's eyes were huge green pools of sorrow. "But I don't know how I will.''

"The strength will come to you. You'll see.'' She picked up the tray and set it back on Sarah's lap. "And you can start by eating a little more. You have to work to get well.''

Sarah looked down at the soup with distaste, but she picked up the spoon and grimly ate several more bites.

That evening when Julia called the children in to supper, Emily came in the door with tears in her eyes. She carried her rag doll under one arm, and in the other hand she carried the doll's arm, stuffing trailing from it.

"Aunt Zulie,'' she wailed, holding out the doll and its dismembered arm. "Vance bwoke.''

"Vance!'' Julia cast a fulminating glance at her son, who was loitering uncertainly in the doorway. "How could you!''

"I didn't mean to. It was an accident.''

"Fix. Pwease?''

Julia looked down at the little tearstained face, her heart pulled by Emily's innocent sadness. She reached out for the doll, then stopped. "Honey. I have a better idea. Why don't you run upstairs and see if your mommy can put it back together. All right? Here, I'll give you the sewing basket.''

Emily's face brightened instantly. "Mommy fix,'' she agreed.

Julia gave her the sewing case, and Emily ran up the stairs with doll and basket as fast as she could. "Mommy, Mommy, dolly's bwoke!''

She burst into Sarah's room and stopped. Her mother looked so pale and different that it scared her. She swallowed and backed up a step. She thought of her aunt and the warm kitchen below, and she started to run back to that safety.

But Sarah's voice stopped her. "Emily.'' Sarah gazed at the small figure with its tearstained face and grubby hands, her dress torn around the hem. Sarah's eyes flooded with tears, but she smiled. "Sweetheart. Come here, and I'll fix it."

Emily came over to the bed, and Sarah took the doll. She leaned out of bed and pulled her daughter into her arms and held her close. Tears coursed down her cheeks. "I love you. Oh, sweetie, I love you."

* Chapter 8 *

Sarah's health began to improve steadily. She forced down the food Julia brought her no matter how uninterested she was in eating, knowing that she couldn't regain her strength unless she did. She had to regain her strength. She had to go on. She realized that now. Emily needed her. Luke needed her. She had duties and responsibilities. And she had never been the kind to just lie down and die.

Before long she began to get out of bed with Julia's help and sit for a few minutes in the chair. The times she sat up grew longer and more often. Then she started walking around the room and out into the upstairs hall, at first with Julia's supporting hand under her arm, and later on her own. Gradually her strength returned.

In less than two weeks she was able to come down the stairs to supper with Julia's help. When Luke walked in that evening and saw her sitting at the table, a smile of pure, surprised joy spread across his face. "Sarah!"

He started toward her, his hands going out automatically, his eyes alight. "Sarah!"

For a moment Julia thought that everything was suddenly working out, that Sarah and Luke would now be as they had once been to each other. But before Luke reached Sarah, he stopped abruptly, as if remembering the situation between them, and the blazing smile on his face subsided into something far fainter and more polite. "I—you must be feeling better."

Sarah had looked up at his entrance, and as he walked toward her, her eyes had softened, the corners of her mouth curling up, but when he stopped, the small signs of life drained from her face. "Yes. Thank you."

She laced her fingers together in her lap. She didn't know what to say to Luke. She never did anymore. He came to her room every morning and evening, but the rest of the time she rarely saw him. When they were together, they said little, talking stiffly and awkwardly, as if they were strangers. Their sorrow lay like a wall between them.

For just a moment, Sarah had known a spurt of feeling when he smiled, a funny tightening in her stomach and a lightness around her heart. Once, she knew, she had felt that every time she saw Luke, only more so. But the last few weeks there had been nothing in her except an absence of feeling. Apparently Luke was the same. He avoided her except for those brief, almost formal visits. He slept in another room.

Sarah had been relieved when Luke stayed away. She hadn't wanted to talk to or be close to anyone. It hadn't occurred to her to wonder why Luke avoided her so assiduously or why he was so stiff when he was around her. But now, suddenly, she did. Was it that his grief, like hers, cut him off from the world? Or was it that he blamed her for their baby's death?

Luke stood awkwardly in front of Sarah. When he saw her, it had been such a surprise that he had almost run to her and taken her in his arms. He had almost babbled out his relief and happiness at seeing her downstairs and dressed, obviously feeling better. It was only just in time that he remembered that Sarah didn't want hugs and kisses or congratulations from him. She wouldn't want anything from the man who had put her in this condition.

But oh, she looked pretty and sweet in that pink and white striped shirtwaist. It was one of his favorites. Her hair hung over one shoulder in a braid as if she were a girl, and there was a faint brush of pink back in her cheeks for the first time since she lost the baby. Luke wanted to squeeze her to him tightly and tell her how much he'd missed the sight of her in their kitchen, waiting for him to return from the fields. He wanted—how he wanted!—for things to be as they had been.

But they weren't. They could never be.

Supper was quiet. Luke said little and Sarah said even less, so that only Julia and the children carried the burden of the conversation. Their efforts soon lagged. When the meal was over, Sarah stood up to go back to her room.

"I better carry you," Luke offered. "That's too hard for you."

"No. I should do it myself. It's the only way I'll get stronger."

"All right." Luke linked his hands behind his back, restraining himself from reaching out to help her. She was so frail it hurt his heart to look at her. She wasn't strong enough to climb the stairs. But he knew why she had refused his help. She didn't want him to touch her.

Many times over the past two weeks, Luke had hoped that Sarah would reach out a hand to him or tell him of her sorrow and hurt. If only she would look at him with even a hint of love in her face! He had wanted desperately to believe that she might love him despite it all, that she needed him, no matter what. But every day it was harder to keep such dreams alive. It was clear that Sarah didn't want him around.

He didn't blame her. She couldn't dislike him any more than he disliked himself.

James trotted down the stairs from Sarah's room, a smile on his face. Julia, watching him, smiled back. She knew that only part of her smile was for Sarah's improved health. The rest was simply for the man coming down the stairs. It was wrong that James could still call forth such a response from her. But he did.

"She's doing much better than when I was here a week ago."

"I'm glad to hear you say it. I thought she was. Would you—"

"Yes." His smile broadened, and there were light and

laughter in his eyes that Julia hadn't seen there since she'd come back to Willow Springs. "Yes, I'd like a cup of coffee, and yes, I'd love something to eat. I've been running since sunup, and I haven't had dinner."

"All right. Good." Julia was unaware of the way her smile lit her face, tinting her cheeks with pink and adding sparkle to her eyes. "I mean—" She stopped, flustered. "Well, not good that you didn't have anything to eat. It's good that you have time to eat now, I mean."

She turned away to hide her embarrassment and began dishing up food onto a plate for James. "Is roast pork all right?"

"Perfect."

Julia added a steaming hot sweet potato and a large spoonful of black-eyed peas to the plate and set it down on the table. She added a dish of butter, a bottle of hot pepper sauce, and a plate of cornbread, hot from the oven.

"Mmm. It smells delicious." James sat down quickly. He really was hungry, though he knew he would have stayed even if he hadn't been. "Aren't you going to join me?"

"Yes, if you'd like." Normally Julia would have waited for Luke and the children, but she couldn't resist the opportunity to sit down at the table and eat with James. She was glad that the others wouldn't come in to eat for another hour.

She dished up a much smaller plate of food for herself and sat down across from James. The flutter of excitement and anticipation in her stomach that she always felt around him made it difficult to eat. She pushed the food around on her plate, taking a few bites, and watched him eat.

His hands on the fork were long and slender, capable, agile. Masculine. She remembered them curled around Sarah's wrist, taking her pulse, and working over the poor, dead infant. His fingers had been quick and efficient, yet tender as well. Julia remembered their tenderness on her own flesh years ago.

Julia shook the image from her mind. It was foolish to think of such things. "Will Sarah be all right now?"

"She's doing very well. You've taken good care of her, and she's young and healthy. Barring something unexpected, she should recover."

"That's good."

"I'll check on her again in a couple of weeks, just to make sure she's all right." There probably wasn't any reason to, really, but he wanted to.

"Thank you." It lifted Julia's spirits to think that he would be back in two weeks. She had assumed that she wouldn't see him again.

"I guess you and the children will be living here now," James commented. *Until she met a man, of course; until she married again. A woman as pretty as Julia was bound to marry again.*

"Oh, no, only until Sarah's feeling better. As soon as she's strong again, the children and I will move." When Sarah was well, she wouldn't need Julia's help anymore, and Julia knew that then her family would become a burden. Besides, perhaps Luke and Sarah would work out this trouble between them if they were alone. Julia suspected that she and the children acted as a buffer between Luke and Sarah. Without Julia there, they would come up against each other more. They would have to talk. They would have to deal with each other.

James looked surprised. "Really? Why?"

"I can't continue to live on Luke's and Sarah's charity."

"But they're your family."

"I have to make a life for myself and my children. I don't want to be a burden to Luke, and, well . . . I want my own home. I want Bonnie and Vance to have their own place, to not be dependent on their uncle. I'm able to stand on my own two feet."

James didn't understand. It was in the nature of things for a woman to depend on male relatives in her time of need, just as it was the man's duty to care for his sister or mother. Never having known the sting of poverty, he couldn't comprehend Julia's pride and dislike of charity. "But what will you do?"

"I'll move into town and rent a room. I can get work cooking and cleaning, or maybe I'll take in laundry."

James stopped in mid-motion and set down his fork. "You can't do that."

"Why not?" Julia smiled. "It's what I've done ever since I can remember."

The idea of Julia cooking and cleaning for someone appalled him. James thought of her on her hands and knees, scrubbing floors for someone like Mrs. Whitfield, who had a tongue like vinegar and no hesitation about using it. Even -if she worked for a kind woman, it was backbreaking work. A woman like Julia should have her own home and a maid to help her, not be slaving away in another woman's house. It was too hard, too humiliating. He couldn't let her do it.

"But you've done those things in your own home. That's different," he reminded her.

Julia lowered her eyes. James looked horrified. She must have committed a social error. No doubt the women of his acquaintance didn't hire themselves out to clean, no matter how poor they were. "I'm sorry. I don't know what else to do."

"Stay here. It wouldn't be for long. You'll—marry again, I'm sure." The words stuck in his throat. He picked up the fork, his fingers clenching around it unconsciously.

Julia's head came up. Her cheeks were pink, and her eyes flashed blue fire. "No. I'm not marrying a man just to have a roof over my head. That's no better than selling yourself, and I won't do that again." She stopped abruptly and jumped up from her chair. She walked quickly toward the stove. "I'm sorry. I shouldn't have said that." What would he think of her now, as good as saying that she had sold herself to Will Dobson?

James froze. What had she meant? That she had sold herself to her husband? But why? Or had she meant that she had sold herself earlier, not to Will Dobson, but to himself? It didn't make sense, but then, very little about their brief time together made sense to him. There was a faint ache in his chest, like the pain of an old wound.

"Julia . . ." In the emotion of the moment, he forgot that he addressed her formally now as Mrs. Dobson. "I didn't mean it like that. I wasn't implying that you would marry a man just to have a house and a—a means of support. I was simply saying that you are bound to—fall in love and marry again. I'm sorry if I offended you."

Julia turned back to face him. "I'm sorry, too, for flying off the handle. But I . . . well, I'm not likely to marry."

He wondered, with a wicked little stab of satisfaction, if

that was because she hadn't enjoyed her first marriage. On the other hand, perhaps she was still too in love with Dobson to fall in love with another man. It shouldn't matter to him, anyway, any more than it should matter whether she scrubbed someone's house in order to live.

But it did matter.

Julia returned to the table, and they began to eat again. James didn't notice that Julia only poked at her pork and peas. He was too busy watching his own fingers crumble a piece of cornbread into tiny bits.

The children came bounding in the back door, and Julia was grateful for the distraction of their presence. James looked at them and smiled a little stiffly, in the way of an adult who isn't used to young ones. "Hello, Bonnie. Vance." He hesitated for a second. He had heard Julia say their names that day in the store; they were implanted on his brain. But what was the other one's name? "Emily."

Julia was surprised that he knew her children's names. She couldn't think when he would have even heard them. Yet apparently he knew theirs better than Emily's.

"Good afternoon, Dr. Banks," Julia's two replied. Their mother had drilled politeness into their heads. Emily simply gave him one of her irresistible smiles. The children's eyes went to the stove, and James smiled.

"It must be time for their supper."

Julia nodded. "Soon." She turned to the children. "Wash up, now, and you can eat soon as Uncle Luke gets in."

James watched them cross to the washstand and clean their faces and hands. Bonnie's and Vance's hair was dark, but he could see Julia in the fine bone structure of their faces and in their large, grave eyes. Dobson had been dark, as James himself was. Would his and Julia's children have looked like this, their coloring his, their features Julia's?

He stood. "I'll get out of your way now."

He picked up his medical kit. He was always awkward leaving Julia's house. He remembered how when they were young he had lingered over saying good-bye, kissing her again and again, until the last thing he wanted to do was walk away. "Well. Good-bye."

"Good-bye, Dr. Banks."

* * *

During the next two weeks, Sarah grew stronger. She came downstairs for much of the day, going back to her bed for only a nap or two. At first she simply sat, but soon she began helping Julia with the chores that could be done sitting down: sewing, mending, chopping vegetables, polishing the silver. By the end of the week, she was setting the table, sweeping the floors, and doing some of the other light chores. Julia was sure that when James saw her again, he would declare her well.

That meant that soon Julia would have to leave the house. She knew that she would be only a burden to them now. Luke, Sarah, and Emily needed to be a family by themselves again. They wouldn't dream of asking her to leave. They were too kind, too loving. She would have to take the initiative.

As soon as James said Sarah was well, she would go into town to look for work, Julia decided. She quailed at the thought of going from door to door, asking if there was work available, but she didn't know what else to do.

She didn't mention her plan to Sarah or Luke. There would be time enough for that when she was ready to go. She didn't look forward to telling them. She didn't look forward to going. She had never lived as comfortably and pleasantly as she had since she came here. It would be so easy to stay. But it would be better for all of them, Bonnie and Vance included, if she and the children moved into a home of their own.

James came to the house two weeks later, as he had said he would. Sarah herself opened the door at his knock.

He smiled. "No need to ask if you're feeling better."

Sarah's smile was slower and less brilliant than it had been in the past. "Yes, I'm fine, thank you, Doctor."

"Then you won't have to see me again for a while."

They went upstairs for the examination. James came down alone a short time later. He paused in the doorway of the kitchen. Julia stood at the stove, stirring the contents of a pot. She hadn't heard his entrance, and he watched her unobserved for a moment. Her back was slim and straight. Soft stray hairs had come loose from her twist and clung damply to her neck, darker than the almost white fairness of the rest of her hair. She was graceful, her movements smooth and economical. It was pleasant to watch her.

Julia turned, sensing his presence, and a flush rose in her cheeks. "I'm sorry. I didn't realize you were there. Would you like something to drink?"

He shook his head, a faint smile touching his lips. "No, not today. I'd like to talk to you . . ." He hesitated, wanting to call her Julia, but knowing he should be more formal. It was difficult to call her Mrs. Dobson, as if they had never been anything to each other. As he usually did, he wound up not saying any name at all.

"Of course. Is there something wrong with Sarah?"

"No. Not at all. I'm sorry. I didn't mean to alarm you. Sarah is doing quite well. I wanted to talk to you about what we discussed the other day—your seeking employment."

"Oh." Julia nervously straightened the edges of her apron. She disliked arguing, particularly with James. "Please, there really isn't any point. My mind's made up."

"I won't try to change your mind, at least not about your decision to work. I wanted to talk to you about a specific job."

Julia's eyes widened. It surprised her that he was taking the time and trouble to help her.

Sarah's heels sounded on the stairs above them.

"Would you rather discuss this alone?" James asked.

"Yes. Thank you. Why don't we go outside?" Julia walked out the side door and down the steps. She turned to face James, her body tense. She wanted to know, yet she didn't. "Do you know someone who wants a cook or housekeeper?"

"No, not exactly. It's—I'm the one who would like to hire you."

Julia stared. "You want me to clean your house?" She couldn't do that. Anything but that. She simply could not be a maid in James Banks's house, once his lover and now his servant.

"No, of course not." He looked offended. "I wouldn't think of asking you to—no, I want you to assist me in my office."

"What? I don't understand."

"It would be a great help to me if someone could take information from my patients when they come in, keep my files up-to-date, and do the book work. I haven't the time for it. I could show you how to keep the records. You could do that, couldn't you?"

"I guess I could," Julia replied slowly, even more stunned by this request. Working in his office! She had never dreamed of doing anything like that. "But surely you could get someone better than me. I mean, someone who knows what she's doing."

"But you do. You know the important things. Keeping the records is only part of it. I need someone to help me with the patients. To hold a broken limb in place while I'm setting it. To calm a frightened child. To hand me the instruments I need. I need a nurse, like the ones in the hospital where I worked in New Orleans. But there aren't any here. I've needed one for quite some time, but I have struggled along by myself. Then, when you told me you wanted to work, I realized how perfect you would be for the job."

The truth was, he had racked his brain for days trying to think of some way to talk Julia out of her decision to hire herself out as a cleaning woman. Then, suddenly, this idea had popped into his mind. It was perfect. He did need an assistant, and he thought Julia could do the job. He could pay her decent money, and she wouldn't have to do menial work.

"But I don't—I'm not a nurse."

"No, but you do have a lot of practical experience. I'm not likely to find a nurse in this area. The best I can do is find someone with natural talent and train her for the job. You've tended sick people. I saw how good and efficient you were during Mrs. Turner's delivery. You knew what I needed and got it even before I asked."

"I have attended several births, but that doesn't mean I could do anything else."

"You're calm; you're good with people; and you're not squeamish. Those are the basic prerequisites. I can teach you what you need to know. I'm not asking you to practice medicine, just to help me. I know you'd catch on quickly."

Julia gazed at him silently. She didn't know what to say.

What he had suggested to her seemed like Heaven. She wouldn't have to go from door to door, humbly asking for work. She wouldn't have the hard physical labor involved in cooking and cleaning. She knew James would not be a difficult taskmaster. The work would be interesting, not dull. She had always enjoyed helping people. It was exhilarating and joyful to help a baby into the world. It was satisfying to see a sick person take a turn for the better. Julia knew she would love the work. That wasn't the problem.

The problem was that she would be working with James. Julia wasn't sure she could stand that. It would be wonderful, of course. Whenever he was around, everything was suddenly a little brighter, a little more colorful, a little more exciting. She didn't love him—not yet, anyway—but she knew that the seeds of her old love for him were still there, deep inside her. Working with him all the time, watching him save people's lives, seeing him at his best, his most glorious—it would be horribly easy to fall in love with him again.

It would hurt even worse this time if she did. There was no hope of her love being returned; James wouldn't even desire her now. She was too old, too careworn. She was the mother of two children, after all! James Banks could have his pick of the most beautiful and charming young women in town. He wouldn't have the slightest interest in her; any love or desire she had for him would be completely unrequited. And Julia no longer had the resiliency of youth. She wasn't sure she could recover from a broken heart now.

Yet, how could she refuse his offer? How could she turn down something so perfect, so appealing?

"I'd pay you better than you would make as a house servant," James went on, misinterpreting her hesitation. "You wouldn't have to pay for a place to live, either. I have a rent house that's unoccupied, and you could have it. It's not large, but I think it would be ample for you and your children."

A house of her own! Julia had been sure that she would be able to afford no more than a room in a boardinghouse for herself and the children. A salary, a place to live, interesting work—how could she turn it down? James was being more than generous.

"You're very kind, too kind, really," she began.

To her surprise, a dark flush rose along his cheekbones, and his face hardened. "I'm not trying to obligate you! I swear. I wouldn't use this job or the house as a way to force you to—"

"Oh, no!" Julia gasped, horrified that he should have misinterpreted her reluctance in that way. "I know that. I didn't think that. You're far too good a man."

James's face softened, and he smiled ruefully. "I'm not so sure about that." He paused. "Then what is it? Do you dislike the work? Would it be distasteful to you to work with me?"

"No. I know I would enjoy the work very much."

"Then why are you hesitating?"

She couldn't tell him her real reasons for holding back. Julia glanced down at her hands; she couldn't look him in the eyes. "I'm not sure. It's so sudden. I never thought about something like this. It's—I'm not sure I could do it."

"Why don't you let me be the judge of that?"

"I'm afraid you're offering this to me just to be kind."

"Why should I do that?" James's mouth thinned. There was no reason for him to do it. He shouldn't feel responsible for her, shouldn't care what happened to her. She had hurt him as badly as a woman could hurt a man. He ought to hate her. Yet he couldn't. Nor could he keep from trying to take care of her. He could remember too clearly the smooth feel of her skin beneath his fingers, the way her face loosened with desire, the passion-bruised look of her mouth when he kissed her. In some way, she would always be his.

"I don't know," Julia responded honestly. It didn't make sense. There was no reason for James to be kind to her, except that it was in his nature. She had known the kindness in him years ago when they were lovers, and she knew that had not changed. She had seen it in him when he delivered Sarah's stillborn baby. "I—it's hard for me to take a favor."

"*You* are the one who would be doing me a favor. I've needed an assistant for months."

Could she work with him and not fall in love with him again? A grown woman ought to be able to control her feelings, Julia thought. How could she refuse? How could she throw away a home for her children and work that she would love? It was a dream come true, something so good she would never even have thought to wish for it.

"Yes," she said softly, afraid to look at James. "I'd like to do it, very much—as long as you're sure that's what you want."

"I'm sure." He was too sure, James thought; it scared him how much he wanted it.

"All right." Julia looked up at him then and smiled. Her smile tore right through him, as it always had.

James smiled back, aware of an urge to pull her into his arms and kiss her. He would have to be careful around her in the future, he thought, or this could turn out to be the worst mistake of his life.

* Chapter 9 *

Luke and Sarah reacted much as Julia expected when she told them she was going to work for James Banks.

Luke scowled and jumped up from his chair. "Absolutely not! What in the hell are you thinking of? You can't work for that man!"

Sarah looked surprised and hurt. "Are you unhappy with us?"

Julia sighed. "No, I'm not unhappy. Please don't think that. No one could ask for a kinder sister-in-law than you, Sarah. I've been very happy here. But I want the children to have a home of their own."

"Your home's with us," Luke put in.

"You were kind to take me in, and don't think I'm not grateful. But it's time for me to be on my own."

"There's no need for it."

"I think there is."

"Well, you don't have to work for Jimmy Banks!"

"Would you rather I cleaned someone's house or took in

laundry?'' Julia asked her brother exasperatedly. ''That's
what I was planning to do until Dr. Banks offered me this.''

''No, of course I don't want you cleaning some rich
woman's house! I don't want you to work, period.''

''Dr. Banks is paying me a generous salary, more than I
could earn doing anything else, as well as giving me the use
of a house.''

Luke's brows drew together thunderously. ''Good God,
Julie, are you blind? Can't you see what he's doing?''

''I see that he's being very kind.''

''He's 'being kind' to himself. He means to obligate you.
He might as well have declared that you're his mistress—
setting you up in a house, paying you.''

''Luke! That's a terrible thing to say to Julia!''

''I'm saying what everyone else will think. What Banks
will do his best to make a reality.''

''You're wrong!'' Julia cried. ''He won't. He wouldn't
think of it.''

''Like hell. Any man would think of it.''

''He swore to me—''

''Oh, that's wonderful. You believe the promises of the
man who seduced you before?''

''Luke!'' Sarah protested.

Luke pressed his lips together and stared down at the
floor, pushing his anger back under control. ''I'm sorry.''
He looked up at Julia. ''I just don't want you to make a
mistake.''

''Sarah, do you mind if I talk to Luke alone for a
moment?''

''No, of course not.'' Sarah had always thought Luke and
Julia were alike in coloring, but never before had she seen
Julia's face set in the same angry, stubborn lines that Luke's
could assume. She wouldn't have thought it possible—until
now. Julia's arms were crossed, her jaw set, and her eyes
were alight with a cold blue fire. She looked a match for
Luke. Sarah smiled to herself and left the room.

''I want to set something straight with you,'' Julia began
in a low tone, her voice trembling with anger. ''Jimmy did
not seduce me. I went into it with my eyes wide open; I
knew exactly what I was doing.''

"He took advantage of you, and he'll do it again if you give him half a chance."

"You're wrong. Even if you weren't, you have no right to interfere. I'm a grown woman, Luke. I make my own decisions."

"Julie, this is insane. There's no reason for you to leave here. You don't have to hire yourself out to anyone. Sarah and I both want you here."

"Maybe you do. But you don't need me here. Just the opposite. There's something wrong between you and your wife. I'm not asking what; I don't want to pry into your personal affairs. But I know you'll work it out easier if you don't have an extra woman and two kids around."

"That's not true."

"It is. You know it is. You and Sarah have to be alone together."

Luke sighed and moved away. "I think that's the last thing we need."

"Luke. I sit at the dinner table every night. I talk to you. I talk to Sarah. But you and Sarah hardly exchange two words. You don't sleep with her."

"She just gave birth," he replied stiffly. "Do you think I'm going to—"

"I think a woman's husband ought to be lying beside her at night. He ought to be there when she wakes up in the dead of the night, feeling so empty. Then's when she needs you to hold her and let her cry her heart out."

"You think I don't want to be there? That I don't ache to comfort her? She doesn't want me there, Julia. She doesn't want me."

"I don't believe that. Sarah loves you as much as you love her."

He shook his head. "She realized, finally, what she married. She understands why everybody warned her against me."

"You're talking crazy."

"Am I?"

"Of course you are. Why would Sarah have changed her mind about you?"

Luke shook his head. "Just believe me. She has." He paused, and when he spoke again, it was in a voice so low

Julia had to strain to hear it. "She turned away from me, Julie. She hates me."

"No."

"It's the truth."

"How do you know? Has she told you?"

"I can tell. She won't talk to me anymore. It's like I'm a stranger."

"You have to talk to her about it. You've got to straighten it out. That's why you need to be alone."

"Your leaving won't change what's between Sarah and me."

"Maybe not. But I have to go, anyway. The children and I need to have our own life. We should be a family together. I want to be on my own; I don't want to be dependent on someone else, not even you. You can understand that, can't you? Didn't you always want a home, something you could call your own?"

"Sure. It's just . . . you're my sister. I want to take care of you. You shouldn't have to work."

"I've worked all my life, Luke. The difference is now I'll get paid for it. Now I'll enjoy it."

"I don't want you to get hurt again."

"I won't be, I promise. I'm an adult now. I won't let myself . . . be so foolish again."

"Hell, Julie. You don't know what you're getting into. I should have protected you last time, and I didn't. I was too selfish, too careless. But this time I will."

"I don't need protection. James won't hurt me. He wouldn't be interested in me anymore, and even if he were, he wouldn't force himself on me. Do you think that I'm so stupid that he'll be able to trick me into his bed?"

"Of course I don't think you're stupid."

"Then admit that I can take care of myself."

"You shouldn't have to."

"I want to."

Luke sighed. "Obviously I can't stop you." He paused. His eyes were hard and glinting. "But if he hurts you this time, I'll kill him."

* * *

Two Saturdays after that, Julia moved into town. Micah drove the wagon, loaded high with the furniture Luke had retrieved from Julia's neighbor's house. The children sat excitedly on the high seat beside him, and Luke, Sarah, and Julia followed in the buggy.

Julia was surprised to see James standing on the front porch of the rent house, waiting for them. He smiled and hurried across the yard to help Julia out of the buggy.

"Mrs. Dobson. Mrs. Turner. I'm glad to see you're feeling better."

"Thank you." Sarah hid a smile. The doctor had barely glanced at her as he greeted her. His eyes were on Julia, and the expression on his face was too eager for that of a landlord or an employer. It confirmed Sarah's suspicion that James Banks felt more for Julia than either the simple kindness or lust that Julia and Luke attributed to him. Sarah was equally certain that Julia was not entirely immune to the doctor, either.

Though she knew Luke would have been furious to hear her say it, she was hopeful that Julia's move might encourage a romance between these two. With that idea in mind, Sarah had sewn up two more attractive shirtwaists and skirts for her sister-in-law and had spruced up Julia's other dresses and blouses with bows and touches of eyelet embroidery or lace. She had worked on the clothes happily, not even noticing that for the first time since she had gone into labor she was interested in something.

"Our housekeeper is here getting the place ready for you," James told Julia. "I dropped by to see that everything was in order." He didn't add that he had dropped by an hour ago and had been loitering around ever since, trying to look as if he were doing something. He wouldn't admit, even to himself, that he wanted to be there when Julia arrived, that he wanted to see her face as she went through the house.

"That was nice of you." Julia looked past him to the house. The children were already racing across the lawn toward the front door.

It wasn't a big house, only one story tall and two rooms wide, but it was cunning in its smallness, like a dollhouse. A small porch, adorned with gingerbread, ran across the front. The house was white, with blue shutters and trim. A white picket fence edged the small front lawn.

Julia swallowed. Her throat was almost too tight to speak. It was beautiful, a perfect little dream of a house. "It's lovely."

James smiled and relaxed. "I'm glad you like it. Come in and see the rest." Belatedly, he remembered to turn to Luke and Sarah and include them in the invitation.

Inside, the house was split by a wide hall running the length of the house, with rooms opening off on either side. There were a parlor and a dining room at the front of the house, and behind them were a spacious kitchen and two bedrooms. A screened-in porch stretched across the width of the house at the back.

The hardwood floors were waxed to a golden gleam, and the walls were freshly painted. The kitchen was a cheery pale yellow. The larger bedroom was papered in a pattern of twining pink roses. In the backyard were two cherry trees, already laden with hard green fruit, and the grass was thick and green.

Julia could already see herself picking the cherries with the children, already imagine the kitchen sweet with the aroma of baking cherry pies. She would put her braided rug in her bedroom, and she would make a new, brighter one for the parlor. The sofa would go here, the chairs there. In the summer, Vance would love to sleep on the screened porch, where the breeze could touch him. There was even a mantel over the fireplace in the parlor.

She turned to James, tears springing into her eyes. "It's perfect. I love it." She could say nothing else, or she knew she would cry. She pressed her lips together and turned away. James looked at her. Just for a moment, before his good sense returned, he wanted very much to take her into his arms and hold her.

But he didn't. He stepped back. "I'm glad you like it." He glanced around. He couldn't think of anything to say, any reason to stay longer. "Well. I guess you're eager to move in. I'll just get out of your way." He walked to the front door and turned. "If you need anything, let me know."

"I will. Thank you."

"Take your time getting settled. You needn't come in to work until you're all squared away here."

"Thank you. But I'm sure I'll be there Monday."

"I'll see you then." He paused, then nodded once, briefly, and left the room.

Julia revolved slowly, gazing at the parlor. It was beautiful. Everything was beautiful. She couldn't have wished for a lovelier home.

And Jimmy had given it to her.

She wanted to cry and laugh and throw her arms around him. She wondered if he had any idea how much this house meant to her. With the luxury he'd grown up in, no doubt it seemed like nothing to him. But it was the world to her.

Luke and Micah carried the furniture into the house in silence. It was obvious to Micah that Luke wasn't in too good a humor about his sister's moving into town, so he figured the best course was to keep his own mouth shut, too.

They carried in the sofa for the parlor together. Then Micah returned with one of the parlor chairs. He glanced down the hall as he was leaving the parlor and came to a dead stop. At the other end of the hallway a tall, slender black woman emerged from a room. She wore a faded calico blouse and skirt, and an old kerchief was tied around her head to protect her hair from the dust. From her clothes one might have mistaken her for a maid, but Micah recognized her instantly. It was his schoolteacher.

He dipped the front brim of his hat with a finger. "Mornin'."

Her cool gaze looked through him, and she turned around and walked right back into the kitchen without a word. Micah shook his head, looking after her, then grinned. He made sure that he and Luke brought in the kitchen table next. The woman was cleaning the kitchen windows with a soapy rag. Another, heavier black woman washed the windows from the outside. The other woman looked in curiously at them, but his schoolteacher kept her rigid back to them, silently scrubbing away.

"Mornin'," Micah said again to her, knowing that she would be forced to be polite with Luke there.

She turned, forcing a smile. "Good morning."

"Hello, Dovie," Luke replied.

Dovie. So that was her name. It was a pretty, soft name. Micah repeated it in his mind. It sounded good, but not at all like her. She was too regal and prickly and classically beautiful.

The two men went back to the wagon for more furniture, and as soon as they were out of earshot, Micah said casually, "You know her?"

Luke glanced at him. "Dovie? Sure. Everybody knows her. She teaches school over at the Negro schoolhouse." For the first time that morning, Luke smiled. "Why? I take it, you don't know her?"

"Not much as I'd like." As soon as he said it, Micah realized it was the sort of thing he wasn't supposed to say. It was too free and easy a way to talk to a white man. But that was the nice thing about Luke Turner. He didn't notice such slips.

Luke's grin grew broader. "I see. Well, she's Lurleen Mitchell's daughter. Lurleen's worked for Dr. Banks ever since I can remember. The old doctor sent her off to college, so I reckon she must be smart." He cast Micah a sideways glance. "She's not married, far as I ever heard, if that's what you're wondering."

Micah smiled. "I didn't think so."

Luke made no effort to help Micah carry in the chairs to the kitchen table. Instead, he picked up an end table for the parlor. Micah smiled and picked up a kitchen chair under each arm.

When he entered the kitchen and set the chairs down, Dovie ignored him, studiously scrubbing away at the windows.

"Those gonna be the cleanes' windows in Texas."

She didn't turn around. "I believe in doing a job well."

"You workin' for the doc this mornin'?"

"I am helping my mother."

"Do that a lot?"

"When I can. When she needs me."

"You helpin' her tonight?"

"No."

"They be dancin' at Opal's place tonight."

Dovie said nothing.

"I thought maybe I see you there."

"I don't go to 'Opal's place.' " Dovie injected the two words with a world of scorn.

"How'd I know that?" Micah grinned and perched on the edge of the table. "You don' dance?"

"I don't drink." She turned around finally and faced him, her hands on her hips. "And I don't keep that kind of company."

"Oh." Micah couldn't help but smile. He liked looking at her. He liked the sparkle in her eyes and the tilt of her chin. "Company like me?"

"Precisely."

"You sure a pretty woman to be so mad all the time."

"I am not mad 'all the time,' only when someone is annoying me. Which is what you are doing right now."

"You even pretty in that dress 'stead of your teacher clothes. But I wish you showed your hair. You got pretty hair. I be steady thinkin' about it—seein' your hair all spread out on your shoulders."

"Mr. Harrison!" Dovie was taut as a bowstring. He saw the faint tremor in her fingers and a certain softening of her mouth that told him she wasn't as indifferent to him as she'd like him to think. "This is not something I wish to discuss."

"Why? You too fine to think 'bout takin' your hair down? 'Bout me takin' it down for you?"

Dovie curled her hands up into balls. The image he evoked sent heat all through her. She thought about his hands, big and rough, calloused, but working smooth as silk through her hair. She imagined her knees trembling, giving way so that she had to lean against the hard breadth of his chest. "Please."

"Please what?" Micah slid off the table and walked toward her.

Dovie backed up until the windows stopped her. "Don't."

He watched the quick rise and fall of her chest, the softening of her mouth, but he also saw something like fear in her eyes. That brought him up short. "You scared of me?"

"Of course not." The pointed chin came up a fraction more. "I'm not scared of you or anyone."

"No need to. I won't hurt you."

Dovie wasn't about to explain that she wasn't afraid of him, but of the involuntary response he brought out in her. She shouldn't feel anything like that for a man like him. It was dangerous. "Mr. Harrison . . ."

"Micah."

She was tempted to say his name, but she refrained. "I am not interested in . . . any of this."

"Any of what?" His voice was low and warm, and it, too, had a dangerous effect on her.

"I don't want to talk to you. I don't want to see you."

"Why you runnin' so scared, girl?"

"I'm not scared. I'm just not the kind of woman you're obviously used to."

His smile was slow and suggestive. "I could get used to you."

"No. Now please leave me alone."

Micah hesitated. He wanted to move closer to her, to reach out and touch her, to pull her up against him and kiss her. He thought she would kiss him back. But there was that fear in her, too, and that stopped him.

The back door opened. "Honey? What you doin' in here?"

The large black woman from outside puffed into the room. Micah stepped back. He'd forgotten all about the fact that there were people around.

Lurleen stared at Micah. It wouldn't have surprised him if she'd lit into him for making advances toward her prim daughter. But she smiled. "Well. Dovie. You holdin' back on me."

Dovie grimaced. "Mama, this is the Turner's hired hand."

"You got a name?" Lurleen asked him, still grinning.

"Micah Harrison."

"That's a nice name. Where you from, Micah?"

"Mama." Dovie looked pained.

"New Mexico." Micah grinned back at Lurleen. Obviously Lurleen didn't have her daughter's concern about strangers.

"So, you workin' for Luke Turner. Nice folks?"

"Yes. Seem like."

"Dr. Jim tol' me about that poor Mrs. Turner. Sad thing, losin' her baby."

"Yes'm."

"You know many people in town yet?"

"Mama." Dovie shot her a significant look. "I'm sure he needs to get back to work."

Micah looked at Dovie and smiled to let her know he knew why she had stopped her mother from continuing. "Yeah. I better get to work." He nodded to Lurleen. "Nice meetin' you."

He left the kitchen. Behind him he could hear Lurleen's voice. ". . . good-lookin' man."

"Mama, hush!"

"Don't tell me you ain't interested in him—a man with shoulders like that."

Micah paused, listening.

"Well, even if I were, it wouldn't do any good, now, would it?" Dovie retorted heatedly. "A man like him is nothing but trouble."

Micah smiled to himself and walked out the front door.

Sunday dinner at the Turner house the following day was quiet. There were no guests, no Julia and her children to make conversation, and the silence was oppressive. Emily said a few things, but her conversation was limited, and after a while even her childish prattle ceased, weighed down by the stilted atmosphere.

It had been this way since Julia left. Yesterday after they returned from Willow Springs, Luke had gone out to the barn to do his chores while Sarah prepared the food. They had said nothing at supper except to ask that a dish be passed. Then Luke had returned to the barn and not come in until Sarah had gone to bed. She had listened to his footsteps on the stairs. He had walked past her door to Vance's room, where he'd been sleeping the past few weeks. Sarah had lain awake in their big bed, loneliness filling her with cold. She couldn't remember when she'd been so lonely. The baby was lost to her, and now it seemed as though Luke was, too. She wished he would hold her; she was so empty and cold. When she had first lost the baby, she hadn't wanted him to hold her or talk to her. She had been beyond sympathy. But now that the numbness and shock had faded, she needed comfort. She wanted to talk to Luke and hear his soothing voice. She ached to lie in the strength and safety of his arms.

But there was no comfort from Luke.

He sat at the opposite end of the table, six feet away, as removed from her as he had been last night, sleeping in another room. Without Julia there, they had nothing to talk about, no one to talk to. Sarah remembered how once she and Luke and Emily had sat at their table, happily chatting or simply enjoying being together when there was silence. Only weeks ago, she had been so close to Luke it seemed as if they could read each other's thoughts. Now they were strangers. She had no idea what he thought or how he felt. Did he blame her for losing the baby? Did he hate her? Why were they now so separated, so far apart?

Sarah laid down her fork. She had no appetite. "Would you—care for anything else?" she asked, searching for something, anything, to break the silence. "Maybe some preserves for the biscuits? I have peach and strawberry."

Luke shook his head. "No, thank you."

He knew how stilted and formal his words came out. He wished they could talk naturally to each other again. But then, nothing was natural between them anymore. Sarah didn't want to have anything to do with him. He couldn't blame her. He had wrecked their lives. She would never forgive him for killing their child. He would never forgive himself.

He watched her as she bent her head over her plate. She wasn't eating, just pushing the food around. She didn't eat enough. She had lost the weight she'd gained during her pregnancy, and more. Her face was too thin, too pale. She looked fragile.

He wanted to take her in his arms and hold her. He wanted to feel her arms around his waist, her head resting trustingly against his chest. He was so empty without her. The nights were long and lonely, and he didn't sleep well. He lay awake thinking about Sarah, missing her warm body curled up against his. He missed talking to her. There was so much inside him that in the past he would have released by telling Sarah. Now it stayed within, festering.

He missed making love to her. That fact racked him with guilt; he felt like an animal. Despite how fragile Sarah was, despite what his desire had cost them, despite how recently she had lost the baby, he still wanted her.

At first he had been too angry and disgusted with himself to even feel desire. But lately it had been creeping back into him. When he had seen Sarah standing on the back porch a few days ago, calling to Emily, the breeze tugging her hair from its knot and molding her skirts to her body, hunger had stirred in him. Today when she leaned across the table to set down a dish, he had noticed how the material of her blouse strained across her breasts, still a little large from her pregnancy, and he had wanted to bury his face in that lushness. He lay awake at night, thinking about her lying in their bed across the hall and remembering what they had once done together there. She was still the most beautiful woman in the world to him, and his body responded to her, even when his mind told him it wasn't decent.

Having to hide his desire made Luke even more tongue-tied and awkward around Sarah. She would be thoroughly disgusted if she realized that he wanted to make love to her again. He was afraid that his eyes would give him away or that he would let something slip. So he avoided looking at and talking to her.

Luke ate quickly, and got up from the table as soon as he was through. He planned to spend the rest of the day as he had yesterday, finding chores to do outside that would keep him out of Sarah's presence.

There was the sound of a buggy pulling up beside the house. Luke groaned inwardly. The last thing he wanted was to have to sit in the house all afternoon with company, trying to act as if everything were normal.

"I wonder who that is." Sarah rose and went to the window. A buggy stood in the driveway, and a woman was alighting from it. Sarah stared. She had never before seen a woman who looked like this one.

Their visitor wore a vivid blue satin dress. It had enormous puffed sleeves and was cut far too low in the front, so

that much of her milk-white chest showed. A wide blue hat
with an extravagant feather curling around its brim sat on
top of high-piled blond hair, arranged intricately in curls.
Her skin was pale, her mouth and cheeks unnaturally red.
She walked with a sway, and she held her skirts too high off
the ground, showing an indecent amount of ankle and calf.

Even though Sarah had never seen one, she knew exactly
what this woman was. "My goodness." She turned to
Luke, her eyes round with amazement. "Luke, come look."

He crossed the room quickly and looked out. He stared,
his eyebrows rising. "What in the—" He broke off and
glanced over at Emily.

"Who is she?" Sarah asked.

"I haven't any idea." They continued to watch as the
woman made her way to the side steps. "Good God!"

Sarah glanced up at Luke. He appeared stunned. "What?
Do you know her?"

"I think—I think it's Tessa Jackson."

"Tessa Jackson!" They stared at each other. How could
she have the nerve to come here? It was she who had sent
Luke to prison on a false rape charge so many years ago.

Luke's face went hard and blank, and suddenly he looked
as Sarah remembered him from the past. "I'll take care of
her. You stay here."

He strode through the kitchen and opened the door just as
the woman raised her hand to knock. She stepped back,
startled, and drew a quick gulp of air. "Luke!"

"Who else did you expect?"

"No one. I—you surprised me, that's all."

Luke looked down at her. She was a year younger than
Sarah, but she appeared years older. Lines radiated from the
corners of her heavily painted eyes, and her skin sagged
beneath the makeup. She was garish and cheap. Luke
wondered how he could have slept with her. Sarah's natural
feminine sexuality was far more stirring than Tessa's obvious, well-used lures. But he hadn't known Sarah then. He
hadn't known love at all.

Luke stepped out onto the porch, closing the door behind
him. Tessa glanced at the closed door, and her mouth drew
into a bitter smile. "My, come up in the world, ain't ya'?

Afraid the sight of me will contaminate your little high-class wife?''

"My wife is not a topic for you to discuss." Luke walked down the steps, so that Tessa had to follow him. She grimaced with irritation, but went after him, holding her skirt high enough that he would get a good glimpse of her shapely legs.

Tessa stopped inches away from Luke and smiled up invitingly, her hand straying to her throat so that his eyes would be drawn to the exposed tops of her full breasts in the low-cut dress. "You're still a powerful good-looking man, Luke. Maybe even better looking." She trailed her forefinger down the front of his shirt. "I wonder, are you still as good in—"

Luke grabbed her wrist, his fingers biting into her skin, and almost flung her hand away. "Believe me, there's no chance of you finding out." He backed up, his mouth tight with disgust. "Do you really think I'd have any interest in you?"

Tessa shrugged, her chin going up defiantly. "A lot of men do." She braced her hands on her hips, pulling her elbows back to emphasize her breasts. "I reckoned you weren't getting much, with that dried-up little church-going wife."

"I told you not to talk about Sarah." Luke's eyes blazed. "Now, unless you'd like me to throw you up in that buggy and send you on your way, you better tell me what you came for. And tell it quick."

Tessa's eyes flamed, but she pulled her anger under control. "I come to ask a favor of you."

"A favor! My God, Tess, why in the hell do you think I'd do you a favor? You're lucky I didn't come out of that door with a shotgun in my hand. You sent me to five years of hell. You think I would welcome you with open arms? Help you out of whatever trouble you're in?"

"I didn't want to hurt you! I didn't have any choice! Daddy kept on hitting me, 'til I couldn't take it no more. I couldn't let him hurt the baby."

"You could have done a lot of things. You could have come to me."

She snorted. "I didn't know what a family man you was.

Besides, you wouldn't've taken me in. You wouldn't've
married me. You'd a said it wasn't your kid. There wasn't
no way to know.''

"I wouldn't have let your father hurt you.''

Her shoulders sagged, and she glanced away. "I didn't
know that. I couldn't count on you—or none of the other
boys I'd been with. I couldn't think of nothin' else to do.''

"So you cried rape.''

She nodded, still not looking at him. "I'm sorry, Luke. I
always felt real bad about it. I know—I know I ain't your
favorite person.''

"That's putting it mildly.''

"And you got no reason to help me." She paused, then
lifted her head. Luke was surprised to see that her eyes were
wet with tears, making the thick makeup run. "But I ain't
askin' for me.''

"Then for who?''

She swallowed. "For your son.''

"What?" He stared at her blankly.

"Your son. That baby I had—it was yours, Luke.''

✳ *Chapter 10* ✳

Luke stiffened. His lips curled with distaste. "You think I'm
an idiot? You didn't have a clue who the father of that baby
was.''

"I didn't back then. But when he got older, I knew. Cal
looks just like you.''

Luke's heart picked up its beat. His son? No, it was
impossible. With all the men Tessa had lain with, anyone
could have been the father. "I don't believe you. What is it,
Tess? You need a little cash?''

Tessa's eyes hardened. "No. That ain't why I come here.
I make good money in Fort Worth. I don't need to beg from

you. But I—it ain't a good life for the boy. I kept him with me some at first, but it's hard.''

"I can imagine a child would cramp your style.''

She shot him an angry look. "You didn't use to be so mean.''

"It's something you learn in Huntsville.''

"I'm sorry.'' Tessa's lower lip quivered, and she pressed her lips together to stop it.

Luke felt a flash of pity. "All right. What's this favor?''

"I want you to take Cal.''

"Your son?''

"He's your son, too. I swear it. My life ain't a decent one for a kid. He sees things he shouldn't; he gets into trouble. So most of the time I've left him at home.''

"At your father's?''

She nodded. "Yeah. I didn't want to, but I didn't have nowhere else. He's been living there all the time for a couple of years. I just see him now and then, when I can get home—and when Daddy'll let me in. The thing is, well, you know how Daddy is.''

"Yeah, I know.'' Every time Luke had visited Tessa when they were young, her father had launched into a long diatribe about how worthless and godless Luke was. George Jackson was a brutal, sanctimonious man with puritanical beliefs. He believed that he was the absolute ruler of his house, and he beat any family member who didn't conform to his rigid ideas of right and wrong. Most of his children had left his house as soon as they were old enough, and generally they had turned out to be the opposite of what he had tried to make of them. Tessa had turned whore; one of her brothers had died in a knife fight in Dallas; and another brother was in Huntsville for armed robbery.

"He's mean to Cal. He's worse than he was with me and Rachel and the boys. Ma's not there anymore to calm him down. He says that Cal's full of sin 'cause he was born out of sin.''

Luke sighed. "Poor little bastard.''

Tears spilled out of Tessa's eyes, streaking her cheeks with black. "Cal ain't bad, Luke. Not deep down. But he's like Bobby always was; he defies Daddy, and then Daddy's even harder on him. Cal hates me; he'll hardly talk to me.

Who can blame him? But I can't take him out of there; he can't live with me. It's just no life for him. I saw him this weekend, and it broke my heart. And I thought—maybe you would take him. He could grow up here; you could teach him how to act. And he'd have a—a good woman for a ma. I promise, Luke, if you'd take Cal in, I wouldn't ever bother you. I swear it. I wouldn't try to come see him or anything. I'd stay clean out of your lives.''

"Tessa, I'm sorry for the boy, but . . .''

"You don't think he's your kid.''

"I don't know how you could tell.''

"Go look at him.'' Tessa grabbed his arm with both hands. "Then you'll know. He's yours, Luke. I ain't lying. Just go over to Daddy's place tomorrow and look at him. You'll see.''

Luke sighed. "All right. I'll ride over to see him tomorrow morning.''

A smile burst across Tessa's face. "Oh, thank you! Thank you.'' She squeezed his arm and let out a giggle. "I know you'll do the right thing. Then I won't have to worry about him being there anymore.''

"Tessa, I didn't say I'd take him in.''

"I know, but once you see him, you'll believe that he's yours. And you won't leave your own son with Daddy.''

She wiped the tears from her face with her hands and climbed into the buggy. She picked up the reins, then paused and looked down at him. "You know, Luke,'' she began, her voice low and almost shy, "you was always the best. You was the only one who didn't treat me like dirt.''

She slapped the reins and the horse started forward. Luke watched her turn the buggy and drive out onto the road. He walked over to the steps and sat down heavily.

It couldn't be true. It just couldn't. Tessa had to be lying—or else she wanted to believe it so much that she had convinced herself that it was true. She knew that he, of all the boys she'd given her favors to, now had the means to take care of a child well. She knew that he would do the right thing. So she told herself that the child looked like Luke, that he was Luke's child.

And yet . . . what if it was true? What if the boy was his son? It was possible, of course. God knows, he'd visited

Tessa often enough when he was young. It could have been his seed, and not some other man's, that had taken hold inside her.

A son. What if he had a son? Had had a son all these years and never even known it? How old must the boy be now? Nine? Was his son growing up in poverty and hate, just as Luke himself had done?

Luke closed his eyes. He couldn't bear the thought. He had sworn that his children would never be touched by the hunger and anger that had haunted his life. The thought of a child of his flesh being in George Jackson's hands made him ill.

And what was he to do if he couldn't tell for sure whether Cal was his? How could he leave the boy if there was even a possibility it was his son? How could he leave any child with that man?

He heard the kitchen door open behind him, and he turned, flooded with relief. Sarah would know what was right. She would show him the way; she always had.

"Luke?" Sarah stood in the doorway, her face puzzled. "What is it? Why did she come here?"

He rose. "She wanted to ask me a favor."

"A favor! You're joking." Sarah came down the steps to him.

"I wouldn't do it as a favor for her, of course. But if what she said is true . . ." He paused. "She wants me to go to the Jackson place tomorrow to see her boy. The child she was carrying when she testified against me."

"Why?"

"Because she says he's mine. My son."

"What? No!" Sarah backed up. "He couldn't be. How could she know?"

"She says he looks like me."

"There are other blond men around."

"I know. At first I figured she was lying, too. But she was so sure. I think she believes it."

"If it were true, why didn't she come to you before? Surely she needed money then, too."

"I was in prison until four years ago."

"And since then?"

"I don't know. Maybe it took her awhile to get the courage to do it."

"It took nerve, all right. She's trying to use you. What does she want? Money?"

"No. She wants me to take him in. She's a, well, you could see what she must do for a living. She can't have the boy with her, and she doesn't want to leave him at her father's any longer. George Jackson is a brute; I'm sure he makes the boy's life hell."

Sarah's stomach turned to ice. "She wants you to bring him here to live?"

"Yeah. I'll go see him tomorrow. If I can tell that he's mine, there won't be a problem. I'll bring him home. But if he doesn't look like me, I don't know what to do. He—"

"No!" Sarah interrupted fiercely. Panic rose in her throat. Her son had just died; Luke couldn't mean to bring in another boy in his place. He couldn't be that callous and unfeeling. "He's not yours!"

"But I don't know that. He could be mine. Even if he doesn't look like me much, he could still be mine."

Sarah's hands knotted together. "You aren't going to bring him home. Luke, tell me you're not."

He frowned. What was wrong with Sarah? "Well, of course I'd bring him home if he's my son."

His son. The words cut like a knife through her. Luke thought he had a son—the son she had failed to give him.

"No. Please, I couldn't bear it."

"What do you mean?"

"My son is dead! I won't have you trying to put another child in his place."

Luke went still. "I would have thought you would like it. That you'd want a child here, someone you could love and care for."

Sarah's face was deathly white, the faint sprinkling of freckles across her nose and cheeks standing out starkly. "You think that I can replace my baby with some other woman's child? Do you think his death means that little to me?"

"Of course not." Luke reached out to her, but Sarah jerked away from him.

"Does it mean that little to you? Does it? My son, Tessa's son, what's the difference? Is that how you feel?"

"Sarah, you're being hysterical." Her reaction amazed him. He would never have dreamed that Sarah, of all people, would show so little concern for the child. The Sarah he knew would have cried at the thought of a poor little boy in Jackson's house. His Sarah would have been urging him to bring the child home, no matter whose it was.

"I am not!" Sarah's hands clenched in her skirts. She couldn't believe that Luke could be so cold and callous to her. Did he really believe that she would want to take in a strange boy when her own son had died only weeks ago? How could he think that Tessa Jackson's son by God-knows-whom could take the place of her own child? "How can you ask that of me? How can you do it yourself?"

"If he's my son, I don't know what else I can do."

"He's not your son! I won't have you bringing that boy in my house!"

Luke stared at her for a long moment, his eyes cold and blank. "I never would have believed that you could turn so hard."

He wheeled and walked off. Sarah sat down on the steps. She felt stiff and cold. She wanted to cry—she ached to cry. But she couldn't.

Julia settled in at her new house quickly. She and the children didn't have enough possessions to make unpacking a time-consuming chore, and James's housekeeper had left the place so spotless that there was no cleaning to do. It seemed as if she spent most of the time walking around the house, admiring it.

Saturday afternoon Julia walked to the grocery store— what luxury to live only five blocks from the stores!—and purchased their supplies with the salary James had insisted on giving her in advance. Sunday at noon, her family sat down to their first real meal in their new home. Looking at Bonnie and Vance on either side of the table, Julia felt more at peace than she could ever remember. At last she was able to give her children a lovely, peaceful home and ample food on the table. She couldn't forget that it was James who had made it possible.

Bright and early Monday morning Julia walked to James's office. The front door was unlocked, and she stepped inside tentatively. The waiting room was unlit, the shades closed. "Dr. Banks?"

She walked down the hall leading off the waiting room. Dark rooms lay on either side. She almost tiptoed, feeling like an intruder and unsure what she should do. A stream of light fell across the hall from the room at the end. Julia went up to the door and peeked inside.

It was James's office, and he sat behind his desk, a stack of files and a tray of food before him. He ate as he read through a file. He glanced up at the sound of Julia's footsteps, and broke into a smile. "Ju—I mean, Mrs. Dobson."

"Dr. Banks. I hope I'm not disturbing you. Am I too early?"

"No, of course not. Come in. Here, have a seat." He rose and pulled a chair up to the side of his desk. "I'm sorry that you find me so—" He cast a glance down at himself. His jacket and tie were off, and his vest hung open. His sleeves were rolled up to his elbows. His shirt front was open one button down. His hair was mussed, and a black stubble covered his jaw. He looked like a man barely out of bed. "—so informal. I was called out in the middle of the night, and I've just now gotten in. I decided to eat a quick breakfast while I caught up on my files."

Julia sat down in the chair he offered. It made her a little uneasy to be here with him. There was an intimacy about the scene, as if they were a husband and wife at the breakfast table together. She glanced at his arms, bared by the rolled-up sleeves. His arms were very masculine—brown, with prominent tendons and silky black hairs. His hands were long, competent, and strong. She had lain with this man. His hands had stroked her breasts. She had nestled against his chest.

Julia swallowed nervously and looked down at her hands. This was no way to start off her employment. She and James were merely acquaintances now. He was her employer; she worked for him. There was no intimacy between them. There couldn't be.

"I didn't realize what time it was," James went on. "I've been at Joe Miller's place since four this morning. His wife Margaret had a baby."

"Really?" Julia smiled. "Boy or girl?"

"A boy. Their third. I think poor Mrs. Miller was sorry not to have a girl, but Joe was pleased. He says he needs the farmhands." He grinned and picked up a piece of buttered toast. "Would you like something to eat?"

Julia shook her head.

"A cup of coffee, at least. Lurleen gave me a whole pot."

"Well, all right."

He poured a cup of coffee and handed it to her. He, too, was very aware of the casual state of his clothes, the suggestion of intimacy. If Julia had been his wife, he thought, they would have sat together just this way. She would have waited up for him until he returned this morning and made him a pot of rich black coffee. She would have fixed him a big breakfast and perhaps rubbed his tired shoulders and neck while he ate it. And he would have been happy and content, loving the way she took care of him.

"Was the baby all right?" Julia asked, sipping her coffee.

"Perfect. There weren't any problems. I'm probably just lucky she let me have a part in it."

Julia smiled.

If she were his wife, she would have asked him questions like this while she rubbed his shoulders, James thought. She would have known he needed to release the built-up excitement and energy within him. Maybe later they would have gone upstairs and celebrated the joy of new life in their bed.

James set down the cup so hard it rattled against the saucer. This wasn't a good way to start. Julia was his assistant, not his wife.

"Are you settled in?" he asked, trying to instill some formality into his voice.

"Oh yes."

"You needn't work today, if you'd like more time to unpack."

"No. I've done it, really. I'd like to begin today, if you don't mind."

"Good." He gave her a perfunctory smile and rose, picking up the tray. "I'll take this back into the house and, uh, get ready for the day."

Julia watched him leave, then walked back down the hall to the waiting room. She opened the shades to let in the early morning light. The glare of daylight revealed the sorry condition of James's waiting room. Dust gathered on the furniture, and the chairs were scattered around the floor in haphazard fashion, their cushions flattened and worn. However good a doctor James was, he obviously wasn't adept at keeping his office in order. Julia quickly straightened the chairs and arranged them so that there was more space in the room. She turned over the cushions and plumped them up. Then she searched until she found some rags in one of the examination rooms, and she started dusting.

She had finished the waiting room and was working on his office by the time James returned from the house. When he saw her busily wiping off the glass-fronted bookshelves, he said, "There's no need for you to do that. I didn't hire you as a maid."

Julia turned, smiling. "I don't mind. And it needs it desperately. The examination rooms are all spick-and-span, but obviously you don't lavish the same sort of care on the rest of your office."

He shrugged. "I never think about the rest of it."

He went to the reception room and looked around. Julia followed him, waiting anxiously for his opinion. He turned, surprised. "Why, it looks ten times better. What did you do?"

"Just a little simple housekeeping."

He smiled. "Thank you. Obviously, I needed help in areas I didn't even know. You ready for some more?"

Julia nodded.

"All right. First, the files . . ." He pulled open the top drawer of an oak filing cabinet. "Whenever a patient I've seen before comes in, I want to review his file. They're alphabetized, as you can see." He gave her a rueful smile and opened the bottom drawer. "But these are the patients I've seen the past couple of months. I haven't had time to put the files back where they belonged."

Julia looked down at the drawerful of jumbled files. She pursed her lips to hide a smile. "I'll get them in order."

"Would you?" He seemed vastly relieved.

"Yes, of course."

"It would also be helpful if you could keep the patients in some sort of order as they come in."

"I'll enter them on a roster."

"You're a jewel. Now let me show you around the office."

He gave her a tour of the place, starting in the examination room. He pointed out the location of his instruments, explaining their use. Seeing the panic beginning in Julia's eyes, he reassured her, "Don't expect to remember it all at once. As we go along, I'll try to explain everything to you, so you'll learn gradually what I use and when."

Their tour was interrupted by the first patient of the day, and after that, there was little rest for either of them. Julia greeted the patients as they arrived and took down their names, then dug each one's file out of the cabinet. While James examined the patients, she busied herself with straightening the files. Twice James called her into one of the examination rooms to help him, once to calm a small boy as he checked out his ear and another time to help him set a broken leg.

Julia soon had the patients moving in an orderly procession, placing one into an examination room to wait while James saw another patient in the second room. By mid-afternoon James wondered how he had gotten along without her for so long. His office had never run so smoothly, and she had added precious minutes to his busy schedule. For the first time in ages, he actually had time to lunch, and by four-thirty, the last of the patients was gone.

James gazed around the waiting area, unable to believe that it was empty. He looked over at Julia. She was on her knees, straightening files in the bottom drawer. The day had been warm, even for the beginning of June. Several stray hairs had come loose from Julia's neat bun and clung damply to her neck. A faint sheen of perspiration lay across her forehead. It made him think of the way she had looked when they had made love in the hot summer evenings, the sweat darkening her hairline and clinging to her translucent skin. He thought of her eyes closed in passion, her mouth opening beneath his.

He tore his eyes away. "Well," he said with all the heartiness he could muster. "You've certainly worked wonders in just one day."

Julia looked up at him, smiling. "Thank you. I haven't really done that much."

"It seems like a great deal to me. You've made it all easier."

"I was terribly clumsy, helping you."

"You did fine. With a little practice, you'll probably run the place without me."

"I doubt that." She rose to her feet in a smooth motion. James enjoyed seeing it.

"Do you have a few minutes?"

"Yes."

"Good. I wanted to take you inside the house and introduce you to my mother."

"What?" Julia's hands flew to her hair. "I can't. I must look a mess."

"You look fine. She'll enjoy meeting you."

Julia knew she wouldn't. Mrs. Banks would think her messy and common. She would wonder why her son had chosen someone like Julia Turner to work in his office. What if she had a suspicion about what had happened between them eleven years ago?

James took Julia's arm and gently pulled her forward. "Come on. She doesn't bite."

She had no choice but to go with him, though her stomach was twisted into knots. James led her through the office into the house. Nothing she saw there calmed her fears. She had never been in a home that was so large and elegantly furnished. It seemed as if everywhere she looked there were silks and damasks and heavy, carved furniture. In the foyer a wide mahogany-railed staircase curved up to the second floor. A crystal chandelier dangled from the high ceiling, and the floor was a black and white checkerboard of marble. The rugs on the smooth wooden floors were thick and richly designed.

They walked down the hall to the back parlor. Past the stairs a rectangular wooden box with a mouthpiece jutting out from it hung on the wall. Julia recognized it from pictures she'd seen in one of Sarah's magazines. "James!" she gasped. "Look! Is that a—"

He smiled down at her, enjoying her obvious delight. "Yes. It's a telephone. A doctor needs one, or at least that's the excuse I used. Several people in town have one now." He took the earpiece from its hook. "Would you like to talk to anyone? The operator, perhaps. It's Red Pierson."

"Oh, no." Julia backed up quickly, shaking her head.

James chuckled and waggled the earpiece at her. "Come on now, it doesn't bite either."

Julia giggled, but she continued to shake her head. "Oh, no, you don't. I'm not making a fool of myself."

"Don't be silly." James reached out and pulled her over to the telephone.

"James!" she protested, but took the earpiece he held up to her. He turned the handle on the side of the box. It made a tinny ringing sound. Suddenly a voice spoke in her ear, and she jumped.

James leaned against the wall, arms crossed, watching her and grinning. "Say something."

"Hello?" she said cautiously, stretching up to put her lips close to the mouthpiece. She felt like an idiot, talking into a box, but there was James, grinning at her, making her giggly and excited.

"James?" An older woman's voice came from the doorway behind them.

Julia jumped and whirled, the earpiece falling from her hand and thumping against the wall.

A white-haired woman stood in the doorway. She was dressed all in black silk. Jet earrings dangled from her earlobes, and a matching jet brooch closed the collar of her dress. Her hands were gnarled, but soft and well kept. A large diamond flashed on her left hand. She looked as elegant and wealthy as the house. Julia was very aware of her simple white cotton shirtwaist and dark skirt and the stray hairs that had come loose and straggled down the back of her neck.

"Oh, hello, Mother." James turned and smiled. He picked up the earpiece Julia had let drop and set it back on its hook. "We were coming in to see you."

"How pleasant." Anthea smiled at Julia, only her bright brown eyes giving away any of her curiosity.

"I wanted you to meet my new assistant. Mother, this is Julia Turner. I mean, Dobson. Mrs. Dobson, this is my mother, Anthea Banks."

"I'm pleased to make your acquaintance, Mrs. Dobson," Anthea said politely.

"Thank you. It's an honor to meet you, Mrs. Banks."

Anthea smiled and cast James a loving, playful glance. "I hope my son hasn't been too hard a taskmaster."

"Oh, no, ma'am. He's very nice." Julia colored a little. "He's easy to work for."

"That's only because Julia is such an efficient employee." James smiled at her.

Julia glanced from him to his mother. She wondered what Mrs. Banks thought. Julia imagined the woman had been horrified to hear James laughing and teasing with the hired help in the hall. She probably thought Julia was brash and forward. Julia wished she knew how to act in a situation like this.

"Won't you join me in the parlor? I'll have Lurleen bring us coffee—and perhaps something sweet?"

"Didn't Lu make her Mississippi mud cake? I'd love a slice of that." James turned toward Julia. "You haven't lived until you've eaten Lurleen's Mississippi mud cake."

Anthea studied her son thoughtfully. There was a light-hearted, youthful quality in his face that she hadn't seen there in years. Her eyes went to Julia. She suspected the change in James's attitude had something to do with this girl. There was something about the way they stood, the way they looked at each other—not quite as if they were in love, but as if they were extremely aware of each other. They weren't simply acquaintances nor just employer-employee. She wondered what was going on.

"Oh, no," Julia protested quickly. "I couldn't. I'm sorry, but I can't stay. I, uh, the children are waiting for me at home. I have to get back and fix their supper."

"Oh. Of course." The light in James's face dimmed, and he turned formal. "Then I'll see you tomorrow."

"Yes." Julia looked at Anthea. She felt as if she ought to curtsy, Anthea was so regal looking. She struggled to remember the lessons in manners her schoolteachers had given so many years ago. "It's nice to have met you, ma'am."

Anthea smiled. "The pleasure was mine. I hope you'll visit again someday when you can stay longer."

Julia nodded. She didn't know what to say. She took a step back.

"I'll walk you to the door," James offered.

"Thank you." Julia walked awkwardly beside him down the hall to the front door, feeling Anthea's eyes on them every step.

She was glad when James opened the massive door for her, and she was able to escape. She hurried across the lawn to the office to get her hat and gloves, then left the office by its front door. Involuntarily she glanced back at the main house. James still stood on the front porch. She was surprised to see him, and an unthinking smile broke across her face. He smiled back and raised a hand in a wave. Shyly she waved back, then ducked her head and walked away.

James watched her back until she reached the corner and turned out of his sight. She was as slim as she had been as a girl. The sun glinted gold on her hair where the hat didn't cover it.

He sighed and went back into the house. The day seemed to have ended too soon.

✳ *Chapter 11* ✳

After breakfast Luke went out to the barn and saddled a horse. Sarah stood at the sink, washing the breakfast dishes, and watched him lead the saddled horse out of the barn and mount it. He rode out of the yard without a wave or even a look toward her. He hadn't told her where he was going, but Sarah knew. He was going to see that boy.

She wouldn't think of him as Luke's son. He wasn't. He couldn't be.

She finished the dishes. There were plenty of other chores to do, but at the moment she couldn't summon up the energy or interest to do them. She felt leaden inside. Sarah sat down at the kitchen table and braced her head against her hands, elbows on the table. She stared down at the wood grain of the table, her eyes filling with tears.

Luke had hardly spoken to her since yesterday afternoon. She had seen the disillusion in his eyes when she told him that she didn't want him to bring Tessa Jackson's son home. Luke had always thought she was so good, so perfect. Now he was seeing her as she really was, and he didn't like her.

She closed her eyes, and the tears rolled out, plopping onto her cheeks. She couldn't bear to have another child in her dead baby's place. She remembered the dreams she had had for their son. She had imagined him tagging behind Luke out to the fields, the sun gleaming on his white blond hair. She had dreamed of him growing up straight, handsome, and strong, just like Luke but without the sorrow and pain that Luke had experienced. She would have given their son all the love that Luke had never had, all the happiness and joy. They would have been tight knit, the four of them, strong in their love for one another.

But he was dead, and so were those dreams. She wouldn't have the tow-headed boy—and she could not take another child in its place. Luke was trying to replace her baby with this other child. She couldn't do that, and it hurt to think that Luke could, that it was that easy for him. Yet he had called her hard!

What would she do if he brought the boy home? Luke would be furious if she refused to accept him. It would likely be the death blow to her marriage, already crumbling around her. But she couldn't take him in. She simply couldn't!

Luke's thoughts were grim as he rode to George Jackson's farm. He hardly noticed the warm June day around him. He kept thinking about what Tessa had told him, as he had constantly since yesterday afternoon. Had Tessa spoken the truth? Would he be able to tell if the child was his? And if Cal was his son, what would he do?

Sarah didn't want Cal. Luke still found it hard to believe that Sarah, his sweet Sarah, had so coldly rejected a child who needed their help. He knew she was grieving for the baby she had lost. He, too, felt the pain and the empty ache inside. But he couldn't imagine Sarah, even grief stricken, not reaching out to help a child. She was a stranger to him now.

They had never had a real argument, a serious disagreement, in the whole time they'd been married. Luke had never ridden roughshod over her or ignored her wishes. There were husbands, he knew, who ruled like despots over their families, but Luke was not that kind. To him, his wife was a gift to be cherished and cared for, not commanded. He hated the idea of arguing with her. He hated even more to go directly against her wishes. But if Tess's boy were really his, he could not turn his back on him.

Luke turned his horse onto the dirt path leading to the Jackson house. It gave him a funny feeling, going up the path that had once been so familiar, but on which he hadn't set food in nine years. He stopped in front of the Jackson house and sat, looking at it. It was the same: a small, square frame house with a narrow lean-to attached to it, the faded white paint peeling from its walls. He remembered Tessa standing on the porch, looking for him. He would round the corner and stand until she saw him, then cut off to the left into the trees. She would leave the porch and meet him there. She had always been so hot and eager, and it had only added to the excitement to know that if her Bible-thumping father discovered them, he'd probably take a shotgun to Luke. That was the way it had been with Tessa, all excitement and danger—the way it had been with all of them. He hadn't known love in lying with a woman until he'd had Sarah, and then he'd discovered that it provided an excitement far more intense than any he'd ever experienced.

Luke slid off his horse and looped the reins around the narrow porch pillar. He knocked on the door, and after a few moments a tired-looking woman answered it. Her brown hair was screwed up into a tight knot atop her head,

and she wore a faded calico skirt and blouse. Her face was
as faded as her clothes. Luke couldn't figure out who she
was. She looked older than Tessa, but he was sure that
Tessa had said that her mother had died.

The woman's eyes widened, and she stared. "Luke?"

"Yes."

His puzzlement must have shown, for she chuckled
mirthlessly and said, "You don't know me, do you? I'm
Rachel, Tessa's sister."

"Rachel." He tried not to let his surprise show. Rachel
was a year younger than Tessa, but she looked far older. He
wasn't sure which of them was worse off, Tessa selling her
body in the city or this girl, staying at home and slaving for
her tyrannical father, growing older and more careworn
every day.

"It's been awhile." Rachel paused. "Pa'll kill you if he
sees you."

"I didn't come to see him. I want to talk to Tessa's boy.
Where is he?"

Rachel frowned. "You oughta go."

"I'm not leaving 'til I see him."

She gnawed on her lower lip. Finally she said, "He's
down slopping the hogs." She hesitated, then added, "Pa's
out in the fields, but he'll be back by noon."

Luke nodded and walked away. As he approached the
outbuildings, nerves began to jangle in his stomach. A boy
came from behind the barn, carrying a large pail. He was
barefoot and dressed in patched calico shirt and trousers, so
faded that they were no particular color. A rope tied around
his thin waist acted as a belt.

The boy climbed up on the low fence and poured the
contents of the pail into the pigs' trough. He stood with his
back turned to Luke, so that all Luke could see was his wiry
frame and a cap of dark blond hair. He turned at the sound
of Luke's footsteps. His face was thin and suspicious,
dominated by large, pale blue eyes. Luke sucked in his
breath sharply and stopped.

The child was his.

He knew it instantly, all through him. There was no
mistaking it. The boy's hair was a darker blond than Luke's
had been as a child (though up close Luke thought that was

as much due to dirt as to natural color). But the sharp blue eyes, the skin color, the facial structure were all his. He might have been looking at a mirror image of himself as a child. Even the narrowing of his eyes, the closed expression, the defiant, sullen stance, were exactly as he had stood and looked. It was eerie, like seeing a ghost of himself.

There was a purpling bruise just below Cal's left eye and another, yellowish one on his neck. Luke's hands tightened into fists. He was certain Jackson had beaten the boy. His son. A fierce, cold anger swelled in him.

Cal backed up a step, but continued to face him, his chin thrust out. Luke knew that the anger on his face had scared the child, so he forced himself to relax his taut muscles and smile. "Hello."

The boy nodded, saying nothing.

"My name is Luke Turner." Cal's eyes widened, and he backed up again, until he was stopped by the railing of the sty. "What's yours?"

"Cal. Cal Jackson."

"You're Tessa's boy."

"What of it?"

"Nothing. I'm just trying to strike up a conversation with you."

"I don't have nothing to say."

"How old are you?"

"Just turned nine. What's it to you?"

Luke sighed and gazed off at the trees for a moment. How in the hell was he supposed to say this? It was suddenly very important to him that the boy not hate him. "Your ma came to see me yesterday. She told me something that I'd never known. She told me that I had a son."

Cal's mouth curled in disgust. "She's always lying. I wouldn't believe what she said. Don't you know what she is?"

"Yeah. I know. She's lied about me before. But she wasn't lying this time. She told me that you were my son. I can see it with my own eyes."

"Grandpa says you hurt her. He says you forced her to have his baby. He says you got sent to prison for it."

"What does your ma say?"

He shook his head. "She's a liar."

"I didn't hurt your mother. I never forced her to do anything. But I did go to prison—because she lied about me."

"Grandpa says you're wicked. Even wickeder than Ma, 'cause you put the devil in her."

"Well, I may be wicked. There's those that think so. But I'll tell you one thing: I never hit a kid."

He reached out to touch the bruise on Cal's face, but the boy twisted away. He stood with his shoulders hunched, jaw set stubbornly, and stared down at the ground. Luke knew, as surely as he knew himself, that the boy would be hell to raise.

"Do you like it, living here with your grandfather?" Luke asked.

Cal shot him a single, flaming glance. His mouth twisted. "I hope the old son of a bitch dies."

A laugh escaped Luke. "Tell you the truth, that's the way I feel about him. Look. You're my son. I want you to come live with me. That's what your mother wants, too."

"Maybe I don't want to."

"I thought you hated living with your grandpa."

"I do."

"How much worse could it be with me?"

He shrugged. "None, I reckon."

"It'll be a lot better. I guarantee you. At least you'll be fed well and you won't get beaten." Luke wanted to reach out and touch the boy's head, but he knew better. He also knew better than to tell Cal that he would be loved and his life would be happy. Cal would assume he was lying.

Cal shrugged.

"Go on in the house and pack, and we'll go back to my place."

The boy pressed his lips together. "Grandpa says you live in sinful splendor."

Luke's face lifted in amusement. "Does he, now? I wouldn't call it splendor. But you'll like it, I think."

"I reckon," Cal said slowly, "if you're wicked, you won't care so much about my being wicked."

"I doubt you're wicked. You're young for that."

"Grandpa says I was born in sin."

Luke contemplated hanging around long enough to beat

George Jackson to a pulp. He drew a breath. "I'm no preacher, but I can tell you, you weren't born sinful. And you'll never be as full of wickedness as that old man."

"Grandpa?" Cal's eyes rounded in amazement, and, unexpectedly, he grinned.

"Yeah, Grandpa. Come on, let's pack your things." He laid a hand on the boy's shoulder.

Cal flinched away. "I ain't got nothin' much to pack."

Luke followed the boy to the house. When they reached the front porch, where Luke's horse was tied, Cal stopped. He gazed for a moment at the horse, then up at Luke. There was awe in his eyes. "Is he yours?"

"Yeah. His name's Jo-Jo."

Cal reached out a tentative hand toward the horse, then drew it back, glancing at Luke.

"Go ahead. You can touch him. He's not ornery."

Cal touched his nose, and the horse bent his head to nuzzle at him. Cal slid his hand along the horse's neck, and there was a mingling of tenderness and longing in his face. "Sometime, do you think you'd let me take care of him?"

"Sure. You can help brush and feed him. You can learn to ride him if you'd like."

"Really?" Cal stared. For an instant his face was eager before it returned to its habitual closed expression. Reluctantly he moved away from the horse. "I'll be back in a minute."

He went inside the house, and Luke waited for him on the porch. Inside he could hear a woman's voice raised in exclamation. Then the door opened, and Cal came out, carrying a small bundle. Rachel followed him, her face drawn with worry. She went to Luke.

"You can't do this. Don't take him. Pa will be fit to be tied when he finds out where he's gone."

Luke's lips drew back over his teeth in a smile that contained no humor. "Tell him to come over to my place, and I'll be real happy to discuss it with him."

"Luke, you can't!"

"I'm sorry if your father takes his anger out on you, but there's nothing I can do about that. I won't leave my son here for George Jackson to beat and vilify and ruin his life the way he did to all his children. Your father likes to talk about everyone else's sin and wickedness, but I'll tell you plain: He's got a blacker soul than anybody I know." Luke turned. "Come on, Cal."

He swung the boy up onto the horse and mounted behind him. They rode out of the yard, leaving Rachel standing on the porch, gazing after them.

Sarah wrapped the pad around the handle of the flatiron and lifted it from the hot stove, replacing it with the cool iron in her other hand. She turned and started toward the ironing board, but stopped at the sound of a horse's hooves in the yard. Slowly she walked over to the window and looked out.

Luke was riding Jo-Jo to the corral. A small figure sat on the horse behind him, his arms around Luke's waist. Luke had brought the boy home.

How could he! Knowing how much she disliked the idea, he had brought the child home anyway. He might as well have said that what she wanted, what she felt, didn't matter. All that mattered was what *he* wanted. He had never before gone against her like this.

Sarah's stomach quivered. She wanted to cry. Luke no longer loved her; that was the only explanation. He was angry with her because she had lost their son, and he was determined to replace him, with no concern for Sarah's feelings.

Sarah set her jaw. Well, he would find out that it wouldn't be that easy. She didn't know what she could do, but she would do something. She refused to have that boy here. He would be a constant reminder of everything that she had lost. It was impossible. If it meant she had to take Emily and go into town to live with Jennifer, then she would.

Luke unsaddled the horse and turned it loose in the corral. He started toward the house, the boy trailing behind him. Sarah drew a breath and went out the side door to meet them. She stood at the top of the steps, waiting, her face set and cold. Luke was being cruel to her, and that knowledge slashed her like a knife. But she was a fighter, however much she loved him, however much she was hurt. She wasn't about to give in.

Luke's steps slowed. He didn't want to reach the porch. He stopped at the bottom of the steps. "Hello, Sarah."

She answered him coolly. "Luke."

Luke reached behind him and pulled Cal forward. "I've brought Cal home."

Sarah looked down at the boy. He stood with his hands in his pockets, shoulders hunched. He glanced up at her, then quickly away. Sarah grasped the porch rail. She couldn't speak. He *was* Luke's son. It was written in every line of his body, every bone of his face. The way he stood, the way he looked up at her and away were exactly as Luke had stood and looked at her that first day he came to their farm. His mouth was set in an identically sullen expression, and there was the same hard, lonely defiance in his eyes.

He wasn't simply Luke's son. He was a replication of him. It wasn't just face and form. It was what was inside him, too. He had been hurt, as Luke had been as a child. This boy had known the same rejection, the same pain.

Sarah's heart twisted within her. She knew she couldn't send the child back. She couldn't deny him, as Luke had been denied. She couldn't condemn him to the same fate Luke had suffered. It would be a betrayal of Luke himself.

"Hello, Cal," Sarah said evenly, though tears glinted in her eyes. "Welcome home. Have you eaten lunch?"

Luke relaxed. Sarah hadn't changed. Love swelled in his chest. He smiled. "No."

Cal said nothing, pushing the dirt around with his toe.

"Go on in and clean up. I'll get lunch on the table."

Luke guided Cal up the steps in front of him. As he passed Sarah, he reached out and took her hand. He smiled down at her, his eyes warm and loving. "I knew I could count on you," he whispered. "You're too kind to turn him away."

Sarah leaned against his arm. For a moment she felt close to Luke, a part of him as she had been for three years and no longer was. He bent and kissed the top of her head.

Luke and Cal entered the house. The moment was over. Sorrow swept over Sarah, and she gripped the railing, staring out over the yard. It was as if that brief moment of intimacy had reminded her afresh of all she had lost, opening a crack in the well of her grief. She was suddenly filled with longing, sadness, and pain. She sat down on the top step and leaned against the post of the railing and cried.

Cal stepped inside the kitchen and stopped, gazing around him in awe. He'd never been inside a house like this. The truth be known, he'd never been much of any place. Grandpa never took Cal with him when he went to town because he said he didn't want Cal getting any new ideas of wickedness—he was wicked enough on his own. Nor did they visit other people much. The only other house he'd seen was the Henderson place, but it was nothing like this grand house.

The kitchen was enormous, and its walls were a pale blue. Cal had never seen inside walls painted a color, but the next room, which he could see through the open door, was even stranger. A fancy slat of wood ran around the middle of the walls, and above the wood, the wall was covered with flowered paper. Not only that, there was an eating table and set of chairs in that room, as well as the table and chairs in the kitchen. The table in the next room was massive and dark, and it was covered with a cloth as fragile as spiders' webs, so that the gleaming dark wood showed through.

Cal couldn't understand what you would do with two tables to eat on; he wondered if they had that many people living here. But then, that other table surely wasn't for eating, not with the fancy cloth on it. There was other furniture besides the elegant table—a long chest and a tall, glass-fronted cabinet filled with delicate, painted dishes. He didn't know what you'd do with that many dishes, either.

Luke led Cal to a washstand in the corner of the kitchen. At home, the wash pitcher and bowl were on a low table on the back porch. In winter he often had to break the skimming of ice to get to the water. He didn't use it much.

Luke poured water into the bowl and washed his hands with a big yellow bar of soap. He handed the bar to Cal, and Cal reluctantly soaped his hands. It didn't sting like the lumps of soap Rachel made, so washing wasn't so bad, even when Luke went back over his hands again with the soap.

Cal couldn't figure Luke out. Why did Luke want him to live here? He knew Luke was his father; his ma and grandpa had told him that often enough. But he hadn't wanted Cal since he was born. Why would he start now? There must be a reason for it. Maybe he was big enough now that Luke figured he would get some work out of him. Whatever the reason, Cal was glad to leave his grandpa. The old man had hated him, and Cal had hated his grandfather right back. He would have been glad if Grandpa had dropped down dead one day. He knew that made him wicked, but he didn't care. That's how he was.

He wasn't so sure how to feel about Luke. Grandpa said he'd hurt and shamed his ma, but Ma said he was a good man. Luke said he didn't hit children. Cal couldn't imagine that. Men punished their womenfolk and young 'uns when they were bad; everyone knew that. And Cal knew that he was bad often enough that Luke would hit him fairly often.

But there was something special about Luke, something that had made Cal want to go with him. He didn't know what it was, just a thing inside, a need that had made him hang on to Luke with both arms as they rode. It was a feeling that rose in his throat, part fear, part hunger, whenever Luke took him by the arm or laid his hand on Cal's head. It was crazy, but he thought—he thought that Luke might like him.

The woman didn't, though. He'd seen that plain enough when she met them at the top of the steps. He had figured she was going to tell him to get, and his stomach had turned sickly. She hadn't said that, though, which surprised him. But he'd seen the tears in her eyes, and when he'd looked back, she was sitting on the step, crying. He didn't know what he had done to make her cry, but he was sure it was his fault. He had made his mother cry a lot, too.

Sarah came into the kitchen. Her eyes were red, but she was no longer crying, and she bustled about the kitchen putting things in bowls and setting them on the table. She plunked down utensils and dishes and more food than Cal had ever seen in his life. There was a little bowl of butter and a loaf of bread. There was a plate of meat that smelled so good it made Cal's stomach knot and the saliva flood his mouth. There were bowls of peas, greens, and little new

potatoes, with butter melting goldenly on them. The crown-
ing glory was a cherry pie with a fancy latticed crust on top
and thick cherry filling oozing out.

Cal swallowed hard and glanced at Luke. Surely they
couldn't mean for him to have whatever he wanted of all
this. Luke pressed his lips together and looked like he was
going to start cussing, but he didn't. Instead, he took Cal's
plate and put something on it from every bowl.

Cal crammed the food down as quickly and in as big
amounts as he could, suspecting that all this bounty would
be taken away from him. Sarah stared at him, at first in
amazement, then with growing pity. Poor thing; he acted
like he'd never eat again. Finally, Luke had to stop him for
fear he would make himself sick.

Sarah began to clear the table, and Luke got up to help
her. Cal stared. He'd never seen his grandfather lift a hand
to help Rachel with the food.

"Where's Emily?" Luke asked. Cal wondered who Emily
was, but if there was one thing he'd learned, it was not to
ask questions.

"Upstairs taking her nap." Sarah glanced at the clock.
"She should be getting up in thirty or forty minutes. In the
meantime, I think it would be a good idea if Cal took a
bath."

"Sure." Luke grinned. He had figured Sarah wouldn't let
the boy's present state of dirtiness pass.

Cal came to his feet. "I don't wanna take a bath."

"Well, you must," Sarah replied calmly. "Everyone
bathes in this house."

Cal crossed his arms across his chest and looked sullen.
"I don't have to."

"Oh yes, you do." Luke paused on his way out the back
door to get the washtub. "You'll do whatever Sarah says."

"And if I don't?"

Luke met the boy's defiant gaze with a flat, cool stare.
"Then you'll answer to me."

Cal felt a familiar prickle of fear. For all that Luke didn't
thunder like Grandpa or look at him like he wished him
dead and in hell, there was something about him that was
even more powerful. Cal looked down at his feet, tacitly

giving in and disliking himself for his cowardice. Next time, he thought, next time he'd let Luke see he wasn't boneless.

Luke brought in the large round metal tub in which Emily bathed while Sarah pumped out big pots of water at the sink and put them on the stove to heat. Luke filled the tub halfway up with water, and Sarah added the heated water to it. Cal unbuttoned his shirt reluctantly and took it off. He kept his eyes averted. It embarrassed him having Sarah in the room with him while he undressed. He'd never taken off his clothes around Aunt Rachel.

Sarah, seeing his embarrassment and understanding the reason, left the room, saying, "I'll run up and get some of Vance's old clothes for him."

She glanced at Cal as she left the room, and one look at his bare chest and back brought her to a halt. "Cal!"

Several purpling bruises decorated Cal's back and chest. Scars, some old and white, others new and red, stood out across his back.

Cal looked up at her. Her eyes were flashing. Cal didn't know what he'd done to make her angry, but obviously he had. He raised his chin and set his face, waiting for the storm to break.

Sarah turned to Luke, and he nodded, his mouth grim.

"Oh!" She burst out, her voice furious. "I'd like to get hold of that George Jackson for just ten minutes!"

Luke chuckled. "I'd bet on you."

Again, for a moment, there was the old closeness between them, the familiar warmth. Sarah smiled at Luke. She wanted to go to him and have him put his arms around her. But she wasn't sure that he would, anymore. She turned abruptly and left the room.

Sarah busied herself upstairs, giving Cal time to bathe in private. She had put Vance's old clothes in the attic, intending to tear them up for rags because they were so worn and patched. But they were a long sight better than what Cal had on now. She'd get started on sewing a new set of clothes for him tonight; she had enough material in the attic for that. Saturday when they went into town, she'd buy some more material.

Sarah smiled, thinking about driving into Willow Springs Saturday with Cal. That would start the tongues clacking. It had been a long time since she and Luke had provided the town with any good gossip. She imagined Julia's face when she saw Luke's son, and her smile grew broader. She knew Julia would love him immediately, simply because he looked so much like Luke.

Sarah took the clothes down to Luke, then returned to the attic for the material and pattern she and Julia had made for Vance. When she came back down the narrow stairs from the attic, she found Emily sitting in the hall outside her room, playing, and she took her downstairs. Cal and Luke were already gone from the kitchen, leaving Cal's old clothes in a heap on the floor. She picked them up and threw them in the pile of trash outside to be burned; there was no salvaging those things.

They found Luke and Cal in the barn. Cal looked even more like Luke now that his hair was clean. With the dirt and grease gone, his hair was several shades lighter than it had appeared, though still not the white blond that Luke's had been as a child.

Emily stopped dead at the sight of the other child, and a sunny smile lit up her face. "Who zat?" she asked, pointing at Cal.

Cal stared back at her. He'd never seen anyone as beautiful as the little girl in front of him. Pale blond hair curled riotously around her head. Her eyes were huge and blue. Her face was all roses and cream in color, like a porcelain doll. She looked like the cherubic angels he'd seen in the pictures in Grandpa's big Bible, only prettier.

"This is Cal, honey," Luke said, putting his hand on the boy's shoulder. "He's your brother."

Emily giggled delightedly. "Bwuzzer?" Sarah doubted that she had any idea what that meant, but still she liked the idea. She liked Cal—and with an immediacy and intensity that was far greater than what she had shown for Vance and Bonnie. Sarah wondered if somehow the little girl sensed that he was closer to her.

Emily ran to Cal and held up her arms to him. He froze with astonishment, but after a moment he bent awkwardly toward her. Emily threw her arms around him and hugged him tightly. She was soft and sweet. He'd never smelled anything so good. A funny feeling twisted through him, part sweet, part sad, and painfully intense. His arms tightened around her.

Emily bussed him soundly on the cheek, then stepped back. "See horsies." She tugged at his hand. "See horsies."

Luke chuckled. "Okay. We'll show Cal the horses. I think he's as interested in them as you are."

Sarah returned to the house to finish her work while Emily and Luke showed Cal around the farm. Late in the afternoon a huge black man came into the barn. Luke greeted him easily, and Emily ran over to him, talking a mile a minute in her baby chatter, but Cal retreated a step, fear written all over his face.

"What is it? What's the matter, Cal?"

Cal looked at Luke, then back at Micah. "I—he—"

"The boy's scared of me."

"No, I ain't," Cal retorted quickly, but Luke could see the truth in his eyes.

"Why?" he asked. "Micah won't hurt you. He works for me."

"He around all the time?"

"Yes. What's wrong, Cal?"

"He's a Devil's child."

"A what?"

"That's what Grandpa says. There's a family of 'em that lives on the way to church. Grandpa says they're black all over 'cause the Devil spawned 'em."

"Your Grandpa is a godda—well, he's a fool. Look, Cal, Micah's a man. That's all. He's not going to hurt you. I promise."

Cal glanced at Micah, unconvinced.

"Your grandpa thinks he's holy, but what he is is cruel and sanctimonious."

"Sanc—what?"

Luke grinned. "Sanctimonious. What I'm saying is, he thinks he's better than anyone else, but he's not. And he doesn't know everything; hell, he doesn't know much of anything at all. He said I hurt your mother, didn't he, and that wasn't true. He's told you things about yourself that weren't true, either. He's a pious man, but he's not a good one. And he's wrong in what he told you."

He paused. "After you've been here awhile, you'll see

that I'm telling you the truth. Things aren't like he told you."

Cal looked at Luke. He was afraid to believe him. It was too good, too easy. Things were never like that. He shrugged and turned away from Luke. "I ain't scared."

Luke glanced at Micah. The other man's face was impassive. "I—uh, I'm sorry. His grandfather's a crazy, mean man. Cal'll come around."

Like Cal, Micah shrugged. "It don't matter."

They did the evening chores and went back to the house for supper. As they walked, Emily put her hand trustingly in Cal's. Cal said nothing, but his hand closed tightly around hers.

Inside the house they sat down at the big table in the room adjoining the kitchen. The room intimidated Cal, but Emily hopped up into her chair and patted the seat of the one next to her, beaming at Cal. He eased his narrow body into the seat she had indicated. He glanced at Sarah and Luke beneath his lashes, half expecting to be told to get off the chair, but they said nothing. He looked at the table in front of him. It was heaped with even more food than had been on the kitchen table at lunch. The aromas made his mouth water.

Everyone bowed their heads, and Cal followed suit, resigning himself to a long, fearsome prayer of the sort his grandpa gave at mealtimes. It had always been torture to sit through them with his stomach empty and the food right there within reach. But Luke's prayer was blissfully short. Afterward they passed the food around, and nobody seemed to care how much he took.

Cal wasn't very hungry because he had eaten so much at lunch, but still he piled heaps of food on his plate, afraid to let anything pass without taking a helping. He ate until he was stuffed, and when he couldn't take another bite, he stuffed a couple of rolls into his pockets. He didn't know when he'd eat like this again. He couldn't conceive of it happening everyday.

As they ate dessert, there was a loud knocking on the front door. Sarah rose and went to answer it. Everyone watched her, curious to see who it was. She pulled open the door. A short, stocky man in sweat-stained work clothes stood on the other side. His blocky face was set pugnaciously, and his gray eyes were as cold as the winter sky.

Cal drew in his breath, rising involuntarily from his seat. He was suddenly cold all over. "Grandpa!"

* *Chapter 12* *

George Jackson stared right through Sarah. She had never seen such malevolence directed at her before, and she stepped back instinctively.

"I'm here for Cal. Where is he?" Jackson barked.

Luke jumped out of his chair and hurried into the entry hall to position himself between Jackson and Sarah. The two men faced each other silently for a long moment. Cal watched them, his hands gripping the edge of the table so hard his knuckles turned white. He would have to go back now, he knew, and he wanted desperately not to.

"Cal is staying in this house." Luke's voice was as calm and cold as Jackson's was heated, but it was even harder.

"My grandson's not spending even one night in this godless household. You have no right to take the boy away from me."

"I have every right. I'm his father."

"You're not a father; you're just the man who raped his mother."

Luke looked at Jackson levelly. "We both know that isn't true. And we know why Tessa claimed it—to keep you from beating her to death."

"She spoke the truth."

"She would have said it was John Wesley if she thought that was what you wanted to hear. But the name you wanted was mine, and the word you wanted was rape."

"You're the devil's own. And your boy's got the devil in

him, too, but I aim to see that the devil's rooted outta that child. He's gonna grow up in God's way.''

"What the hell do you know about God's way?" Luke's eyes flashed blue fire. "You think it's God's way to beat religion into a boy?"

"The Lord's path is a hard one. Calvin's prone to all the pitfalls. But I'll see to it that he don't fall in with sin.''

"You'll see to nothing. He won't be with you. He's staying right here.''

"You're not fit to raise a child. I'll go to the law and get him back.''

"Fine. We'll go to court. I'm the boy's natural father. His mother wants me to have him. I have the means to take care of him. Who do you think they'll give the child to?"

Jackson's face turned red, and veins stood out at his temples. "You have 'em all fooled, don't ya? You dress so fine and act so high-and-mighty, they forget what you are, what you did to my daughter. Well, I don't forget. You can seduce a weak woman like her.'' He gestured toward Sarah. "Sweet talk her into marrying you and giving you her daddy's land. But you can't sweet talk me. I know you for the vile sinner you are.''

Luke's hand shot out grabbed the other man's shirt, and he jerked him forward. "Don't you ever, *ever*, talk that way about my wife again. I don't even want to hear her name in your mouth. Do you understand?" He twisted his hand around Jackson's shirt, closing it tightly around his throat. He wound it one more turn. "Do you understand?"

Jackson nodded shortly, hatred in every line of his face.

"All right.'' Luke uncurled his hand slowly and dropped it back down by his side. "Now. Cal is staying here. I want you off my land. If you ever show up here again, I'll meet you with my shotgun.''

Jackson glared and his hands doubled up into fists. But Luke stood poised, ready for him, and Jackson stepped back. "You'll regret this, Turner.''

Luke said nothing, simply keeping the same cold stare on him. Jackson made a low growl of frustration and left.

Luke closed the door and turned around. Sarah was smiling at him, her face pink with pleasure and all the old love in her eyes. It made his heart start to hammer.

He looked into the dining room. Cal stood stock-still, and his tanned skin was pale, his eyes huge.

"Cal? You all right?"

Cal wet his lips and nodded. He'd never seen anybody stand up to his grandfather before. He would never have believed it possible. But Luke had done it. Luke had faced the terrifying old man down—and he'd done it for him.

"Don't worry about it, son," Luke told him gently, and the blue eyes, a moment ago so cold and hard, warmed. "He won't get you back. I won't let him."

Cal's legs began to tremble, and he sat down abruptly. Luke walked past him and ruffled his hair. Cal had never before felt a gesture of affection from a man, and tears started in his eyes. He blinked them away, hating his weakness.

"Well," Sarah said, restoring the moment to mundane reality. "It's almost time for bed. Why don't you children go play while I do the dishes? Then I'll put you to bed."

Playing wasn't something Cal was used to either, for Grandpa firmly believed in the axiom that "idle hands are the Devil's playground." Emily was happy to introduce him to the concept. Sarah smiled, listening to her daughter's squeals of laughter from the other room. The boy had a good heart, she thought, like Luke.

When Sarah finished the dishes, she made up the bed in the room Julia had occupied when her family stayed at their house. She couldn't put him in the room Vance had used because Luke was still sleeping there. Sarah felt a fresh stab of hurt at the thought. It was so lonely in her bed at night.

She sent Cal to his room to undress, giving him a nightshirt Vance had worn, while she dressed Emily for bed and read her a story. When she was through listening to Emily's baby's prayer, she went into Cal's room.

He stood in the middle of his room, dressed in the faded nightshirt. He looked pitifully thin and alone to Sarah.

"Well." Sarah smiled at him. "Looks like you're all ready." She went to the bed and turned down the covers. She patted the sheets. "Hop in."

Stiffly Cal climbed into the bed and sat there. Sarah pulled up the covers over his feet. "Are you too big a boy for a bedtime story?"

He looked at her in confusion. "You mean, readin' from the Bible?"

"Well, if you want, I could. But I meant a bedtime story, like the ones I read Emily."

"I don't know." His face became shuttered. Sarah had seen the look often enough on Luke's face when she first met him to know what it meant. Cal wasn't sure what she was talking about and was embarrassed by that fact.

Sarah got the book from Emily's room and sat down on the side of Cal's bed. She chose one of the fairy tales with action and adventure as more suited to his age and sex. He listened intently, his eyes fastened on the colorful pictures in the book, his mouth slightly open. When she finished the story and shut the book, he gazed up at her in wonder.

"Did you like that?"

He nodded.

"Good. We'll read another one tomorrow night. Now it's time to say your prayers and go to sleep."

Cal knelt beside the bed with Sarah, thinking that this time the prayer was bound to be long and full of sin and repentance. But Sarah folded her hands and merely thanked God for the day and its blessings, ending by saying, "And thank You most of all for bringing Luke's son to us. Please help us to become a strong and loving family in Christ. Amen."

She rose, and Cal opened his eyes in amazement. He scrambled to his feet before she could change her mind. He got into bed, and Sarah pulled the covers up around him. They looked at each other for a moment, then she leaned down and softly kissed the top of his head. Cal froze. Her scent was all around him, sweet and warm. He wanted to throw his arms around her and hold on. But he didn't.

Sarah straightened and walked out the door. Cal looked around the room. It was twice as big as the one he'd shared with his grandpa back home and far lovelier. The bed was soft and deep, and the sheets were cool and clean, scented with the outdoors. The window was halfway open, and the curtains moved in the slight breeze. It was all so soft, so nice, so good.

He slipped out of bed and padded softly around the room. He touched the posts of the bed, the colorful quilt folded across the foot, the dresser top with its long lace runner, the mirror, the china figurine, the washstand. It was his room. All his. He wanted to believe it. But he didn't dare let himself. He didn't even dare let himself hope. It couldn't last; it couldn't be what it seemed to be.

They would grow tired of him. He would do one of the bad things he always did, and they would realize what a mistake they had made. They'd send him back to Grandpa, and he'd lose the wonderful room, the soft bed, the little sister, that kind woman. His father. His home. Those were things he couldn't count on. He'd found out long ago that it was worse than useless to want something; it was painful.

The door opened, and Luke entered the room quietly. "Cal? What are you doing up?"

Cal shrugged and jumped back into bed, afraid that Luke would be able to read his face and see the hope there. Luke sat down on the bed. He brushed an errant strand of hair back from Cal's forehead. "I never thought I'd find me a half-grown son." He paused. "I meant what I said down there. There's no way I'll let George Jackson take you back."

Cal wanted to throw himself against Luke's hard body, to find safety in his strength. But he was sure Luke would recoil from him. Besides, it would reveal to Luke how weak he was, how scared. Cal was determined that no one should ever find that out.

"I know it must seem awfully strange to you right now," Luke went on. "But you'll get used to it. You'll come to like it here. You'll see." He paused. He didn't know what to say to reach this boy, yet he found himself wanting to find the key to unlock him. But that wouldn't happen tonight, he reminded himself. There were years of pain to be gotten through before he reached Cal inside.

"Good night, son." He leaned down, like Sarah, and brushed his lips against Cal's forehead. He rose and walked out of the room.

Cal watched him until the door closed. He slid down in bed until he was lying down. He pulled the sheets up high around his shoulders, burrowing into the softness of the down mattress. Then, suddenly, tears came out of nowhere like they sometimes did at night. He buried his face in the pillow to muffle the sounds, and he cried.

Luke went downstairs to the kitchen. Sarah was sitting at the table with a glass of lemonade before her. She looked up at him and smiled. "Would you like a glass?"

"That'd be nice." He sat down at the table while she poured him the last of the lemonade from the pitcher.

They sat for a moment in silence, sipping at their drinks. There was a comfortableness, a rightness, between them that hadn't been there in a long time. "I was proud of you this evening," Sarah said quietly, "the way you stood up to George Jackson."

Luke's lips curled into a sneer. "He ought to be horsewhipped."

"Yes." Sarah paused. She stared down intently at her glass as she methodically ran her thumb and middle finger down the sides of the glass over and over. "Luke . . . I . . . I wanted you to know how sorry I am."

"For what? What are you talking about?"

"For the way I acted yesterday. What I said about not wanting Cal. It was wrong. Will you forgive me?"

"Forgive you? Oh, Sarah, there's nothing to forgive. I'm nobody to be forgiving you."

"But I was mean and cold, like you said."

"I was angry. I don't think that. I couldn't think that of you. You're the kindest woman in the world."

Sarah smiled faintly at his hyperbole. "Hardly that."

"Close enough." He reached out and touched her fingers with the tips of his.

Her skin was smooth beneath his fingers. Just the feel of it sent desire snaking through him. He wanted her, as he had always wanted her. He wanted to be with her, to lie with her, to have her head on his shoulder, to hear her voice beside him in the darkness. He wanted her soft body beneath him, her legs locked around him, taking him into her.

He felt like a scoundrel for wanting her. He had killed their baby and almost killed her with his lust. He hated himself for that, yet he couldn't control the lust. Merely touching her hand brought it surging up within him. He thought about kissing her, about sliding his hand up her arm and onto her body. He thought about her breast cupped in his hand, the nipple tightening at his touch. Already he was hard and pulsing.

He lay in bed at night thinking about Sarah, remembering their lovemaking. Every night was a torment: desiring her and despising himself for it. He was an animal. She was barely healed. She must dread his touch after what had happened. He could *not* take her.

This evening it had been worse than usual. She had looked at him glowingly when he got rid of George Jackson, just as she had looked at him in the past, full of love and pride. Several times today there had been a moment when they were close, when there was warmth between them and no barriers. Those tastes of remembered love had been like a match to straw, igniting the passion in him that was never far below the surface.

He wished desperately that it could be like it was once more. He knew it could not.

Luke pulled his hand back from Sarah's. He cleared his throat and took a gulp of his drink. "Well. I guess it's time for us—time to go to bed." He took the glass to the sink and rinsed it out. He set the glass on the counter and stood for a moment, his hands gripping the edge of the sink. He wanted to turn around and take her in his arms. It took everything he had not to.

Sarah stood up, too. Perhaps now Luke would return to her bed. Maybe the closeness they had shared today had ended the separation between them. She wanted to fall asleep in his arms again, to feel his warmth and strength encircling her.

She climbed the stairs to their bedroom. She heard Luke rattling around downstairs, latching the screen doors and turning off the lamps. Sarah stood in her room, taking down her hair and brushing it, listening for the sound of Luke's footsteps. She heard him coming up the stairs. He paused at the top, and she stiffened, scarcely breathing, waiting.

Luke looked through the open door at Sarah. Her hair hung loose around her shoulders, thick, dark, and inviting.

He knew exactly how it would feel beneath his fingers. He knew its softness and scent. His breath came faster in his throat, and his heart raced.

He turned the other way and went into the bedroom he used now.

Sarah slumped. She wanted to cry. Luke didn't want to be with her. She was alone. For the first time in weeks, her loneliness was more missing Luke than sorrow over the baby that had died.

It was an adventure working in James's office, and Julia loved it. She felt uneasy about leaving Vance and Bonnie at home while she went to work, but as the days passed and the children did well on their own, she gradually relaxed. After all, Vance was nearly ten years old and a responsible boy; he was capable of looking after Bonnie. Besides, the neighbor lady on one side was a friendly middle-aged woman, and she had assured Julia that she looked in on the children two or three times a day.

As her fears about the children eased, Julia was able to enjoy her work even more. It took her only a few days to get the files and bookkeeping organized. She was appalled at the amount of money James allowed people to owe him. It warmed her heart to think of his generosity, but her practical nature rebelled at the idea of letting the practice go on unchecked. She made sure that each patient paid at the time of his visit, and if they were unable to, she arranged a schedule by which they would pay the doctor gradually. Some of the payments were in chickens or eggs or vegetables, to be sure, but at least she made sure James received some recompense for his work. James might have plenty of money to live on from his inherited wealth, but Julia wasn't about to let anyone give him less than what he deserved.

James laughed at her vehemence on the matter and was relieved to be rid of the burden of keeping books. Seeing how quickly Julia caught on to everything in the office, he taught her more and more about medicine. He called her into the examination rooms to assist him, and as he worked, he explained to her what he was doing. He showed her the supplies and tools and taught her the name and function of each. Sometimes Julia thought her head would burst from trying to remember all the new information, but she kept on determinedly.

She delighted in working with James. He was kind, patient, and bright. He didn't snap at her mistakes, and he answered her questions without condescension. He was never too tired or too busy to explain something to her. She enjoyed talking to him. She enjoyed his smile. She enjoyed his laugh when she said something that amused him.

Yet it was painful to work with him—and for the same reasons. He was too easy to like, too easy to fall in love with all over again. Julia couldn't allow that. She could never have any place in James's life other than that of his assistant. Loving him, wanting to be the love in his life, would bring her nothing but heartache. She had to resist the lure of his smile, the tug in her chest when he looked at her, the treacherous curiosity that wondered what it would be like to feel his lips on hers again. She struggled to hide her feelings, even from herself. She ignored the warmth inside her, hoping that somehow it would not grow.

On a warm afternoon in the middle of June, Julia was sitting in the reception room, working on the books. It had been a slow day, and she had had to assist James very little, so she had taken the opportunity to catch up on some of her clerical work. As she sat, toting up figures, the door burst open and a young boy tumbled in. He was breathless, and his words were almost incoherent.

Julia quickly came around the desk and grasped his shoulders. "Shh. Now wait, calm down."

Her quiet, even voice and steady hands reassured him, and he drew a breath. "Daddy's sick. Real sick. Ma sent me for the doc. He's gotta come. Ma says he can't waste no time."

"All right. Let's talk to the doctor." Julia led him down the hall. "What's your name?"

"Walter, ma'am. Walter Purdon."

Julia stuck her head inside the examination room where James was working. He left his patient and joined them in the hall. "What is it?"

"This boy's mother sent him for you. He says—"

"Daddy's sick!" the boy interrupted agitatedly. "You gotta come. Right now."

James squatted down beside Walter. "What's the matter with your father, son?"

"He's got a pain in his side. Right here." He laid his hand below and to the right of his stomach. "He had it all night long. Ma's scared."

"Is he vomiting?" The child looked puzzled, and James said, "Can he hold down his food?"

He shook his head. "It comes right up."

"Does it hurt if you touch him there?"

"Oh yessir." Walter nodded emphatically, his eyes getting rounder. "Ma laid her hand on him, and he hollered."

"We'll ride out to your place." He looked up at Julia. "Tell my patients I'll be gone the rest of the afternoon. Then lock up and come with me. I may need your help. I'll finish up with Mrs. Jarvis and hitch up the buggy."

Julia hurried to do as he instructed. Minutes later the three of them were in James's buggy, heading out of town. Walter gave them directions to get to the house. James kept the horse at a quick pace.

Julia sat on the buggy seat between James and the boy. James's arm touched hers as his hands moved on the reins. A fold of her skirt lay against his leg. She tried not to look at his leg. She tried not to look at his hands on the reins. This was serious, she reminded herself; there was no place for wayward thoughts. Julia folded her hands and gazed determinedly ahead.

James glanced at Julia. She was staring directly in front of her, so that he saw her delicate profile. He looked at the curve of her lips and the creamy skin. There was more color in her face today, the cheeks pink, her lips rosier. He supposed that the excitement of rushing out to an ill patient had put the color there. In her hurry, she had forgotten to put on her hat, so that her pale gold hair glinted in the sun. He ached to touch it.

The last two weeks had been a blend of heaven and hell for him. He had found himself arising in the mornings filled with goodwill, eager to get to work, and he had had to admit to himself that it was because he would see Julia there. He enjoyed seeing her and talking to her. It gave him pleasure to watch her walk across the floor, to hear her voice outside with a patient, to have her calm presence beside him, helping him. She made life comfortable and easy. More than that, she made it fun. James liked the idea of Julia's being there in a place that belonged to him, in the midst of the work he loved. It made her in some way his.

But she wasn't his at all. That was the hellish part of it—to watch the curve of her breasts beneath her gown and know that he could not touch her, ever; to look into her eyes and know that they would not glow for him; to have her take care of him and know that she did it only as a job. He wanted her; he could not stop himself from wanting her. When she stood beside him in the examination room, he breathed in her lavender scent and felt tingles of heat all through him. When she looked at him with those clear blue eyes, her face solemn, he wanted to pull her into his arms and kiss her. When he saw her with patients, her bright head bent down to theirs, he wanted to unfasten the tight knot of her hair and watch it cascade down her shoulders, feel it slide like silk through his fingers. But he had no right. She had given him no encouragement. Falling in love with her would be asking for trouble.

It was difficult to remember that she had broken his heart. But it was folly to forget it.

James turned the buggy in at the small lane that Walter pointed out, and they reached the Purdon house. It was small and unpainted, its simple lines not softened by trees. Walter jumped out of the vehicle and ran up the steps, followed more slowly by James and Julia.

"I'm afraid it sounds like appendicitis," James told her in a low voice. "We'll have to operate here if that's so. It won't be good conditions. I'll need your help. I just hope it hasn't been going on too long."

Julia nodded, fear beginning to flutter in her stomach. She didn't know enough. She would fail him.

They stepped inside the Purdon house. It was small and airless, stiflingly hot. There was only one window in the front room, and the light was dim. However, it wasn't too dark to see that the place was filthy. Dust from the fields lay everywhere. Walter was waiting for them, three smaller children clustering shyly behind him. He led Julia and

James into the next room, a bedroom far smaller than the living room, but equally dirty. The room was small, and there was only one window high up on the wall. It was so hot that Julia felt perspiration beading on her forehead as soon as she stepped inside.

A man lay on the bed, curled up on his side, a quilt atop him. His face was contorted with pain and unnaturally pale. He sweated profusely. A woman sat beside him on the bed. Her clothes reflected the same lack of care as the rest of the house; the skirt was ripped near the hem, and her blouse was splotched with stains. Her hair was curled loosely into a bun low on her neck, but most of it had pulled loose from the knot and hung lankly around her face. Her face was round and Julia suspected that usually it wore a cheerful expression, but today it was lined with worry.

She jumped up when James and Julia entered the bedroom. "Dr. Banks! Thank God you're here! He's so sick."

James went to the bed and pulled the quilt away. "Mr. Purdon, I have to examine you." His hands moved over the man's abdomen and stomach, and suddenly Purdon jerked and cried out. James drew his hands back. "How long has he been like this, ma'am?"

Mrs. Purdon began to cry. "Too long. We was workin' in the fields yesterday, him and me and Wally, weedin'. An' he started sayin' his stomach hurt, an' it got so bad that he come back to the house early yesterday afternoon. I shoulda sent Wally for you last night. But I figured Joe just had a stomachache. He ate too many of them wild raspberries the young 'uns picked the other day. An' I thought, we can't afford no doctor." She brought her hands up to her face, sobbing. "Oh, God, I killed him, didn't I?"

"No, of course not, Mrs. Purdon," James replied quickly. It would have helped, of course, if the woman had sent for him earlier, but there was no point in adding to her guilt. "You say the pain was in his stomach?"

She nodded, gulping back her tears. "Yessir, not where it is now, though. More right in his stomach, but then it sorta moved down some."

He nodded. "Your son said he had been nauseated—throwing up."

"Some."

"I'm afraid your husband has appendicitis."

"Oh, Lord."

"Which means we will have to operate."

"You're goin' to cut on him?" Her face turned ashen at the thought.

"Yes, and we'll have to do it here. He's in too much pain and time is too short to take him back to town."

Mrs. Purdon knotted her hands together. "Oh, Lord. Oh, Lord."

James looked at Julia. "Why don't you take Mrs. Purdon to the other room?"

Julia nodded and led the woman out. She settled her on the sofa in the front room and left her there with her children, then hurried back to James. He took her arm and drew her over to the corner.

"We can't operate in this house. It's too dirty. The chances of him getting infection are enormous." Though he knew some older doctors who weren't too particular about the standards of cleanliness when they operated, James was a firm believer in the theory of antiseptic surgery. "Besides, it's as dark as the Black Hole of Calcutta in this place. I can't see well enough to operate."

"But what can you do? I thought you said we can't take him back to town."

"I can't." He sighed and closed his eyes for a moment. "We'll have to rig up an operating table outside."

"Outside!"

"I know. But the outside air is cleaner than in here. There's no wind today to blow the dust in from the fields. And I'll have enough light to see."

"What do you want me to do?"

He smiled. Thank heavens for Julia's calm readiness to work. He couldn't have chosen a better assistant. "Let's talk to Walter. He seemed like a smart kid and cooler in a crisis than his mother."

With Walter's help, they located two sawhorses in the barn and set them up outside. James unfastened one of the inner doors from its hinges and laid it across the sawhorses for a table. Julia scrubbed the door thoroughly, first with soap and water, then with carbolic acid while James pulled off the clothes Purdon wore and wrapped him in the cleanest sheet from the linen chest. With Mrs. Purdon's help, he walked the man to the makeshift table outside.

When they had gotten Purdon up on the door, James ordered his wife and children back into the house. Purdon glanced apprehensively at Julia. Gritting his teeth against the pain inside him, he asked, "What's she doing here?"

"Mrs. Dobson is my assistant. She will help me operate."

"A woman? But I ain't got no clothes on!"

James suppressed a sigh. "She's a widow. Besides, she'll be far too busy to be shocked. Now, I'm going to hold this pad up to your nose. It will smell bad, but it will make you sleep and keep you from feeling the pain."

While James administered the chloroform to Purdon, Julia sterilized James's instruments. Her heart hammered inside her chest, and her stomach was a knot, but she'd been scared too many times in her life to let fear paralyze her.

"All right. He's ready." James looked at her and smiled. "I meant to teach you to help me in surgery, but I hadn't planned introducing you to it in quite this way. Will you be all right?"

"I think so. I have a strong stomach."

"Good. If it gets to be too much, go back into the house. I can manage on my own."

Julia nodded. She was determined not to do that. James needed her, and she refused to let him down.

James lowered the sheet to expose Purdon's abdomen and washed the area with carbolic acid. He took the scalpel from Julia's hand and made a diagonal incision on the right side of Purdon's abdomen. Julia glanced away, unable to watch the metal slice into the man's skin, but she forced her eyes back immediately. The cut was the worst part. Even though her stomach flopped at the sight of the exposed fat and muscle, she was able to swallow her gorge and stand firm. She had spent all her life on a farm and had helped at several births, and she was familiar with wounds and blood.

James worked quickly and competently, slicing through the fat and muscle and tying off the arteries. "Damn. It's already gangrenous. That makes it more difficult." He carefully snipped off the tube of the appendix and removed it. He tied off the nub, and Julia saw his shoulders relax. He began to suture. Julia watched him, her queasiness forgotten in her awe at James's skill. He was so careful, so good, even operating under these primitive conditions.

With smooth stitches, he completed the operation and pulled the sheet up over Purdon's chest. He turned to Julia. His forehead was dotted with sweat from the heat of the sun and the tension of the makeshift operation. A grin broke across his face, making him look almost boyish. "We did it!" He laughed.

Julia began to laugh, too, giddy with the aftermath of tension and adrenaline. James picked her up and swung her around, and they giggled like children.

"This'll be one to tell our children," he said. He froze, suddenly aware of what he had said. He released Julia, and she slid slowly to the ground. James looked down at her.

Julia's dress was damp with sweat between her breasts. Her eyes shone a blue as bright as the sky. Her face was soft and dewy, her lips rosy, her cheeks pink with excitement. Her chest rose and fell rapidly, her breasts clearly outlined beneath the soft fabric.

James didn't stop to think. He simply bent his head and kissed her.

✳ *Chapter 13* ✳

James's kiss was soft, slow, searching. His lips moved over Julia's, rediscovering the taste and feel. Julia stretched upward, pressing her mouth against his, unable to stop herself. Her fingers curled into his shirt. It felt so good, so much the same, yet far better than her memories. Memories were too pale.

At Julia's response, desire slammed down through James like a fist. His mouth burrowed into hers, opening her lips, and his tongue slid inside. His tongue roamed her mouth, exploring the serrations of her teeth and the ridges along

the roof of her mouth, twining around her slick, warm
tongue. He wrapped his arms around her, squeezing her to
him. Her soft breasts flattened against his chest, and he felt
the points of her hardening nipples even through their
clothes, God, she felt good!

Julia threw her arms around his neck, not considering
how brazen he would think her. She thought only of the heat
of his body against hers, hotter than the sun pouring down
on her back, and the heady taste of his mouth. She'd almost
forgotten how sweet, how wonderful it was to kiss him. She
tightened her arms around James. Her tongue curled around
his and slid away, returning in an erotic dance. He moaned,
pressing her even more tightly into him. She could feel the
full length of his body against hers.

His mouth left hers, and he kissed her all over her face.
"Julia," he breathed. "Julie, oh, Julie."

Julia's hands dug into his hair. It was soft and thick
between her fingers. His mouth moved over the ridge of her
jaw and down onto the soft flesh of her neck. Julia arched
her head back, exposing her throat to the pleasure of his
lips. Her skin was alive with nerves, aware of every sensation—
the hot kiss of the sun, the breathy touch of the breeze, the
weight of her clothes, but most of all the velvet nibbling of
James's lips.

His mouth traveled down her throat hungrily until it was
stopped by the high starched collar of her shirtwaist. He
froze. The prim, businesslike piece of clothing brought him
back sharply from the timeless limbo in which there had
been nothing but the taste of her mouth and the softness of
her body in his arms. He recalled where they were and what
they had just done. He remembered who they were and all
that had happened between them.

His arms dropped away from her and he stepped back
suddenly. Julia gazed up at him, shocked, her eyes wide and
lambent with desire, her lips reddened and slightly open.
Then she, too, remembered, and her face flamed with
embarrassment. They had been standing outside in full view,
kissing passionately. And with a patient lying right beside
them! Julia turned away, her hand flying up to her cheeks as
if she could cool them.

"Oh, my Lord!" she whispered. She wanted to run away,

as fast and far as she could. What would James think of her now? That she wanted to start up again where they had left off years ago? That she was loose and sluttish? But of course he must think that; she had proven it to him years ago—and proven it again just now! All he had to do was kiss her, and her passion flamed into life. She had never felt this way with her husband, never responded to his kisses and caresses as she had a minute ago to James. She thought of how she had molded her body to his and flung her arms around his neck. She had been bold and brazen. He must think her cheap. Any man would take advantage of the favors a woman gave so freely.

"I'm sorry." James turned back to the operating table and began to clean his instruments. He was an idiot. A fool. What did he think he was doing? He couldn't fall in love with Julia; it would be asking for misery. You'd think he would have learned the first time around. She didn't love him. She hadn't loved him before; she had just played him along until she got what she wanted out of Dobson. It would be insanity to believe in her again.

Julia shook her head, unable to say anything, and walked quickly back to the house. She paused for a moment to collect her frazzled nerves before she opened the door. She smoothed back her hair and straightened her skirts. Then she took a deep breath, knocked on the door, and walked in. She found Mrs. Purdon and the children sitting huddled together on the sofa. Mrs. Purdon's hands were folded in prayer, and her eyes were shut tight, her lips moving silently.

Julia was swept with relief. They hadn't been watching from the window. "Mrs. Purdon?"

The woman's head snapped up. Her eyes were wide and fearful.

"Dr. Banks is through with the operation."

"Is he—"

Julia smiled. "He's alive. But I'll let the doctor tell you how he's doing."

Mrs. Purdon jumped up from the sofa and rushed past Julia out the door, the children following her. Julia watched as she ran to James and talked to him. Mrs. Purdon clasped James's hand in hers and began to cry. She wiped her eyes with her apron and bent over her husband and cried again. Julia remembered her own reaction when her husband had died, and she felt anew the sting of remorse and guilt. She hadn't been able to work up that much emotion over Will's death. She wondered what it must be like to live with a man you loved, to be his wife and share a bed and house and children out of love, not necessity.

She turned away, swallowing back her unruly tears. She would never know what it was like. She was certain of that, for now she knew that she still loved James. That kiss out by the crude operating table had torn away all the years, all the pretenses she had built up, and exposed the truth. She loved James. She would always love him, she guessed; there didn't seem to be much hope of it dying now. But she could no more have him now than she could have years ago.

Sarah rose from the breakfast table and began to pick up the dishes. She was looking forward to this morning. It was Saturday, and they were going into town. They hadn't gone in two weeks; there had been too much work to do, what with the regular farm work and the peaches coming ripe. Besides the picking, Sarah had been inundated with canning and preserving. They hadn't even gone to church last Sunday, trying to get the peaches in before a hailstorm hit. So it had been a long time since Sarah had had any female companionship, and she had missed it sorely. She had gotten used to Julia's being around, and it was hard not having a friend to talk to, especially considering that she and Luke hardly spoke anymore.

"Cal, Emily, help me clear the table so we can leave sooner."

Cal looked at her scornfully. "I ain't doin' that. That's woman's work."

Sarah sighed inwardly. She frankly didn't know what to do with Cal. He'd been with them for over a week now, and most of the time he had been surly and uncooperative. He had refused to do chores often, but it wasn't laziness, for he worked with a will at other times. It seemed to be sheer orneriness. He never smiled except at Emily, and his responses to anything Sarah or Luke said were short and often defiant. It was almost as if he wanted to antagonize them.

"Cal!" Luke's voice cracked out, and the boy straightened, casting him a sideways look of fear and something that was almost anticipation. Luke clenched his jaw, saying nothing. When he spoke again, his voice was quieter and calm, though firm. "You carry those dishes into the kitchen, then run out to the barn and help Micah get the team ready."

Cal's thin face brightened. If there was one thing he loved, it was the horses. He had taken over most of the chores of feeding and grooming them. This was the first time he had gotten to help hitch up the team, and he was eager to do it, even if it meant working with Micah, who still scared him. Cal grabbed several dishes and carried them into the kitchen. He came back for two more loads, then dashed out of the house and across the yard to the barn. Luke, carrying in the last platter and bowl, watched him from the window. He shook his head.

"Sometimes I don't know what to do with that boy."

"Nor me." Sarah began to scrape the plates and stack them in the sink. "He's so hard. I don't know how to handle him. He acts as if he doesn't like anybody or anything."

"He tries your patience," Luke agreed. "He keeps on wearing on my nerves until there are times when I think I'll explode."

"But why? I thought he was happy to be here. I thought he would like us. But he seems to get angrier and more distant every day."

"He's scared."

"Of what? Surely he knows that we won't hurt him, that we won't send him back to his grandfather."

"No, he doesn't know any of those things. All he knows is what he's had. What he's scared of is liking us—liking it here and wanting to stay."

"That doesn't make sense."

"Not to you." Luke smiled faintly. "But it does to me. I was just like him. I never let anybody do me any kindness. I remember I wouldn't let old Mr. Harper give me a stick of penny candy whenever I went in his store. I didn't want his pity."

"But he gave those sticks of candy to all the children."

"I know. But I couldn't take them. I was a lot easier with people hating me than with them being kind."

"Oh, Luke." Sarah turned to him, her eyes wide and warm with love and pity. The sight of her feelings for him turned Luke inside out, as it always did. He wanted to take her in his arms and kiss her until they couldn't breathe anymore. Instead, he took a step back.

The look in her eyes died, and she turned back to the sink. "Then you think Cal won't ever like us?"

"Someday he'll let go, but I'm afraid it'll take a long time and a lot of effort. He won't be easy, Sarah."

Neither had Luke been, Sarah thought, but she had managed to crack his shell. She'd manage it with Cal, too. After all, Luke and Emily would be working with her to do it, three against Cal's obstinate one. "At least he likes Emily."

"How could he help it?" Luke paused. He wanted to apologize for moving away from her like that; he hated how the love in her eyes had vanished. But he couldn't apologize, any more than he had been able to talk to her about anything the past few weeks. His guilt and desire were a wall to anything normal between them, freezing his actions and inhibiting all conversation. "I better get out there and make sure all the chores are done before we go."

"All right. I'll be ready to go before long. All I have to do is wash these dishes." Luke walked out the door. Sarah concentrated on her task. "Emily! Come help Mama do the dishes."

Emily came bounding in from the stairway, where she had been playing, and hopped up on a chair to dry the dishes. This was her favorite job, for she and her mama always sang while they did the dishes. Emily loved to sing. She had sung her favorite songs to her new brother and was amazed that he didn't know them. All he knew were slow, heavy songs like some that they sang in church. But he didn't know "O, Come, Angel Band" or "Shall We Gather at the River," the church songs she particularly liked. Nor did he know "Oh, Susanna" or "Swanee" or "Green Grow the Lilacs" or her favorite, "After the Ball Is Over." Unfortunately, she could sing just a few of the words; only Mama knew

them all. Cal shook his head when Emily tried to bring
Mama in to sing them. But he hung around more often while
they did the dishes.

By the time they finished the chore, the wagon was ready.
The wagon bed was half full of bushel baskets of peaches
that they would sell to the grocery store. Micah sat in front
of them, his legs stretched across the width of the wagon.
Emily clambered into the rear of the wagon with Micah, her
favorite place to sit. But of course she did not sit, but stood
up, holding on to the side of the wagon and bouncing with
excitement. Cal, standing in the yard, looked at her in
surprise.

"Cal! Cal!" Emily called. "Come here. Come sit wis
me."

"You're going to town, too?" he asked, startled.

"Yes. Yes. To town." She bobbed her head in emphasis.
"To Aunt Zenny. And stowuh. And park."

Cal looked over at Luke. He was helping Sarah into the
wagon. The whole family was going into town, not just
Luke. Grandpa never took him or Rachel. Luke turned
around and saw the surprise, the questioning and hunger
that Cal tried to hide. He realized that Cal hadn't understood that he would get to go, too, that even now he wasn't
sure that he wouldn't be left behind alone.

"Come on, boy, get in the wagon," Luke told him.
"Unless you aren't planning on coming."

Cal grinned, and his face suddenly glowed with a happiness and excitement he was unable to conceal. Luke's heart
twisted within him. Poor little kid. At least Luke's father
hadn't been a religious fanatic determined to squeeze out
the sin in him—he'd only hated Luke for killing his wife.

Cal jumped into the wagon, and they started off. It wasn't
a long trip into Willow Springs. Cal spent the entire time
kneeling by the sideboard and staring out at the land they
passed, gripped by excitement. He'd never been anywhere
or seen anything new, and he was filled with anticipation.

It turned out to be more than he could have dreamed of.
The road got wider and wider, and finally there was a house
and then another house not a hundred yards past it. Before
he knew it, there was house after house, sitting right next to
each other, with only little strips of land in between. Some

of them had green grass growing in front and rows of
flowers. The houses gave way to big, long buildings with
huge boards covered with writing hanging on them. In front
of the buildings were wooden walkways, raised off the
ground. There were wooden hitching posts and wrought-iron
hitching posts. The buildings had big windows with things
sitting in them that you could see. One had bars over its
windows, and Micah told him that was the bank; but when
Cal saw another one and said there was another bank,
Micah told him no, that was the jail.

Strangest of all, there were people everywhere. They were
walking up and down the wooden sidewalks and across the
streets. They were riding horses and driving buggies and
wagons and surries. He had never seen anything like it.
There were more people even than he saw in church on
Sundays, and he couldn't imagine what so many people
were doing here all at one time.

They stopped before one building, and Cal helped Luke
and Micah carry the bushels of peaches into the store while
Sarah and Emily went inside and bought things. The store
was full of food—sacks of flour, sugar, rice, and potatoes,
big barrels with all kinds of things in them, even a barrel of
brine filled with dill pickles. They carried out Sarah's
purchases, and Micah left them. They rode on to what
Sarah called the "post office." It was a brick building.
Inside, the walls were lined with little boxes, each with a
number and a dial on it. Sarah twisted the dial on one
several times and opened the little door. She pulled out
letters from it and two magazines with slick, colorful fronts.

Sarah often read aloud to them after supper out of
magazines like that. They were fascinating stories that
always left you wondering what was going to happen at the
end. Cal had been amazed by the stories and loved hearing
them, but he hadn't realized where they came from. "Do
you buy those here?" he asked.

Sarah looked amused. "Oh, no, we buy these from a
company in New York City, and they mail them to us. This is
where all the mail comes and where you send your letters
that are going to other towns."

"Other towns?"

"Yes."

He found it hard to imagine that these magazines sitting in Sarah's hands had come from another city. "Is it far? New York City?"

"A long way. Hundreds and hundreds of miles."

He couldn't conceive of that. He had never imagined what the world was like.

They left the post office and walked along the wooden sidewalk. Cal liked the hollow sound it made beneath his feet, and he tried to peer down between the cracks to see what lay beneath the walkway. People nodded to them and said hello. It seemed like Luke and Sarah knew everyone.

They went inside another store, far larger than the first one. It had big tables piled with goods in the middle of the store and long counters around the walls. Below the counters were cases with all kinds of articles in them, and there were things in the shelves behind the counters and hanging on the walls. There were shoes, denim overalls, ladies' bonnets, bolts of material, nails, tools, buckets, even posthole diggers and hoes. Out in back, there were still more objects that were too big for the inside, like rolls of barbed wire and plows. Cal had never seen so many things jammed together in one place. It was exciting and awesome.

A man with black hair stood behind the counter at the front and punched keys on a big gold box that rang and had a drawer that zipped out, full of money. He greeted them, eyeing Cal curiously, and handed Cal and Emily each a stick of peppermint candy. "Who's this, Emily?" he asked, jovially. "You got another new cousin?"

"This is Luke's son, Cal," Sarah told the man, and he looked like he'd swallowed his tongue. Cal could see Sarah smiling as she turned away nonchalantly and went to shop.

Cal followed her. Here in town he didn't like the idea of getting far away from Luke or Sarah. Sarah looked at several materials, asking Cal his opinion of the colors and patterns. He didn't understand why, and when he asked, Sarah chuckled and said, "Why, they're for you, that's why."

He stared. "All of them?"

"Yes. You need several new everyday shirts and a couple for Sunday, as well as a suit for church. In a minute we'll go over there"—she pointed to a different part of the store—

"and buy you some denim overalls, shoes, and the other things you need."

Cal glanced away. He didn't know what to say or do. Sarah was always making him feel that way. He wanted the clothes, wanted them so much it made him a little sick inside. It wasn't just the clothes; it was her giving them to him. It was the idea of her liking him enough to do it. He didn't want to want that. It made him feel too desperate, too scared. She would find out about him; she'd realize how awful he was. Then Sarah would regret the things she had done for him; she would take them away. She'd take away her smile and the sweet feel of her hand on his shoulder and the touch of her lips against his forehead each night when she tucked him in. Ma had done that from time to time, sweeping into his life with smiles and hugs and kisses, then sweeping out again, leaving him to wonder what he'd said or done that had made her leave. It was better, easier, not to want Sarah's love.

Sarah didn't expect Cal to thank her for the new clothes. She would have been surprised if he had. She got the pieces of cloth she wanted, then took Cal to another section to purchase the rest of his necessities. When they had finally made all their purchases, Luke piled them in the back of the wagon, and they left the store. Luke didn't turn the wagon toward home, however. Instead they drove into another part of town that was all enormous houses. Some of the homes were plain brick or wood, but some had little towers and fancy carved wood trim. One even had a funny little square room jutting up from the center of the roof. Luke pulled the wagon into the driveway of one of the houses and stopped.

It wasn't as big as some of the houses Cal had seen today, but it was larger than Luke's house, which until now Cal had thought the biggest place in the world. This house was painted a pale blue, with white shutters and white carved trim on the porch. The door was white, too, and high up on it was a big brass door knocker shaped like a lion's head. At the street side were two black wrought-iron horse-head hitching posts and in between them lay a long stone block for stepping down out of vehicles.

"Aunt Zenny!" Emily told Cal gleefully and pointed toward the house. "Aunt Zenny's house."

Cal followed the others up the long flagstone walk to the house. A black woman answered the door and let them in. Cal gazed around him, his eyes wide, as the woman led them through the entry hall and into a parlor. The rooms were large and high ceilinged, with fancy plaster moldings on the ceilings and dark wood paneling on the walls. The furniture was dark and massive, the seats covered in rich materials. Cal felt utterly out of place.

A woman rushed into the parlor, her arms stretched out to Sarah.

"Sarah! I'm so glad to see you. And Emily." She bent and gave Emily a big squeeze, lifting the child up into her arms. "How's my sweetheart? Do you have a kiss for your Aunt Jenny?"

Emily gave Jenny a big smack on the cheek. Cal stared at her. She was beautiful. He had thought Sarah beautiful, but she was not as lovely as this woman. Jennifer was dressed in a pink cotton dress with thin, puffed sleeves, fancier than what Sarah wore around the house. Her hair was done up in an intricate style, and tiny jeweled ear bobs danced in her ears. Her hair was dark; her big, expressive eyes were green; and her skin was like white porcelain tinted pink at the cheeks. Her features were lovely, but there was an animation in her face that made her even more striking.

Behind her came two girls and a chubby little boy, all laughing and crying greetings. The boy was a little older than Emily and wore a blue sailor suit with a wide piped collar, white stockings, and shiny black shoes. The girls were in white dresses sprigged with pink flowers, adorned with ruffles at the neck and sleeves and three around the hem of the skirt. Their skirts ended at their knees, and below them were pristine white stockings down to the high-topped, buttoned black shoes. Their hair was arranged in long, fat sausage curls and ornamented with large pink bows. The older girl, about seven, was pretty, but the younger one, like her mother, was beautiful. Her hair was coal black, and her eyes were a sparkling emerald green. She looked like a doll Cal had seen in the dry goods store. Or she looked like one of those princesses in the stories Sarah read to him and Emily at night. Cal knew, with a sick feeling, that she would not like him, that she would think him awful, crude, and poor. And he wanted her quite badly to like him.

Jennifer set down Emily, who was immediately seized and hugged by her cousins. She looked at Cal. "Well, now, who are you? You aren't Vance."

He shook his head.

"This is Cal," Sarah put in, sliding her arm around Cal's shoulder. "Cal, this is my sister Jennifer. Why don't you call her Aunt Jenny like Emily does?"

Cal saw the surprised look Jennifer shot at Sarah, but she said only, "Hello, Cal. I just fixed some lemonade and cookies out in the kitchen. Why don't you children have some and then run outside to play?"

The children disappeared toward the kitchen, Cal following behind the others reluctantly, while the adults sat down in the parlor to talk. Sarah could see that Jennifer was bursting with curiosity about Cal, but she didn't say anything until Luke left the room a few minutes later. Jennifer was immediately all questions, and Sarah told her Cal's story. As kindhearted as Sarah, Jennifer was full of sympathy for the boy. Sarah didn't tell her the problems she had had with him. She didn't want to give her a bad opinion of Cal. Besides, Jennifer would be the last person to have useful advice about a poorly disciplined child. Her own three were sweet-mannered children whom Sarah had rarely seen even mess up their clothes.

Luke returned to the room, and their talk turned to the Fourth of July dance, coming up in two weeks. It was the biggest social event of the year in Willow Springs. There would be speeches and a parade in the afternoon, followed by a picnic supper and dancing in the park. As usual, the Turners would share one of the long tables with Jennifer and her family. Sarah and Jennifer discussed what foods and supplies each of them would bring, then went on to the more interesting topics of the clothes they would wear and who would be there and with whom.

Their conversation was interrupted by a long, loud wail and the clatter of footsteps down the hall. Little Jonathon burst into the room. His face and silky dark hair were splattered with mud, and his suit was stiff with it. He was crying loudly, his tears cutting rivulets through the mud on his face.

"Jonathon! What happened!" Jennifer went down on her knees beside her son and took him in her arms, mud and all. He continued to weep, unable to get out any words.

Sarah felt Luke stiffen beside her, and she glanced at him. His mouth was drawn into a tight line, and she knew that he was thinking that whatever had happened was Cal's fault. Sarah hoped not. Cal kept pushing Luke, until Sarah was afraid that finally Luke's temper would snap.

Before Jennifer could get Jonathon calmed down enough to answer her, there were shrieks outside, followed by a slamming back door, and the girls ran in. Melissa, the younger one, was crying, too.

"He put a worm down her back!" Penny announced in a voice high with outrage. "That boy! Cal! He pushed Jonny down in the mud, then he put a worm down Missy's dress, and I had the most trouble getting it out, 'cause she kept on hopping around and—"

"Damn." Luke stalked out to the backyard. That boy seemed determined to get into trouble. Not a day went by that Cal didn't test Luke's temper. More than once this past week he had been tempted to turn Cal over his knee and paddle him, but he had restrained himself, remembering the treatment Cal had received at the hands of his grandfather. But each time it got harder to hold back.

He stepped out onto the back steps, letting the screen door bang shut behind him. Cal stood by himself in the middle of the yard, arms crossed over his chest, chin thrust out, waiting for Luke. The defiant stance irritated Luke. He could remember standing that way himself, and now he wondered why somebody hadn't taken him down more often than they had. It was a look guaranteed to raise one's hackles. But Cal was a pathetic figure, too, alone in the big yard, awaiting his doom and trying to look as if he weren't scared. Pity twisted through Luke, enabling him to remain calm.

"What did you do that for?"

Cal shrugged without answering.

"It doesn't seem very smart, does it? Antagonizing people you're going to have to be around the rest of your life? Making enemies of them instead of friends?''

"I don't need friends," Cal returned scornfully. "'Specially not sissies like them. Jon's a crybaby, and so's the girl.''

"He's only three. He and his sisters didn't grow up tough. There's nothing wonderful about having to. You had no reason to hurt or scare those children.''

"Reckon I'm just mean, like my pa.''

"I was. That's nothing to be proud of, either. Look, those children belong to Sarah's sister, and Sarah's real fond of both them and her sister. It'd break her heart not to visit her sister because you can't control your actions. I'm not going to let that happen. Now, I want you to go inside and apologize to the kids and to Jennifer. Then we're leaving.''

"I won't.''

"What?" Luke's voice was rigidly controlled, the anger seething beneath it.

"I won't say I'm sorry.''

"When you do things like you just did, you have to. Remember that the next time you want to push somebody into the mud. Look at me.''

Cal tilted his face up and met Luke's eyes. Sometimes they were warm, but right now they were as cold as the sky on a clear winter day. Cal swallowed and looked away; he couldn't hold his gaze. "All right.''

They went inside, and Cal made his apologies with ill grace, mumbling the words and looking steadfastly at the floor. Jennifer accepted his apology smoothly and whisked Jon upstairs to change. Luke and Sarah left the house, Cal trailing along behind them. Emily walked beside Cal, but this time she didn't slip her hand into his. Cal felt the loss keenly. He looked down at her. Her face was troubled, and it made his insides twist. He was awful and wrong, and he hated everyone for it.

"I think we should go home," Luke said.

Sarah touched his arm. "Oh, no, we have to see Julia. You know how much she would want to see Cal.''

Luke set his jaw. Maybe Cal would act better at Julia's. No doubt the boy had been intimidated by Jennifer's grand house and beautiful children. At Julia's little place, in

Julia's easy, down-to-earth presence, he might do better. "All right. We'll try it."

They drove to Julia's. She came out onto the front porch, smiling, when they pulled up in front. Her mouth dropped open when she saw Cal, and she turned to Luke.

"Is this—"

Luke nodded. "Yeah. This is my son, Cal."

A smile spread across her face, and she went to Cal and squatted down in front of him. "Hello, Cal, I'm your Aunt Julia, your father's sister." She put her arms around him and hugged him, despite the fact that Cal remained stiff and unyielding in her arms. She kissed him on the cheek, then stood up, blinking back tears. He was so much like Luke that it hurt. "Let's go inside. I know your cousins will love to meet you. You look about my boy Vance's age."

Julia took Cal's hand too tightly for him to pull away and led him into the house. There she introduced him to a boy and a girl. Cal decided he didn't like them any better than the other ones, but when Vance asked if he wanted to see his fort out in back, Cal went along.

After the children left, Julia turned to her brother. "Luke, where did he come from? Who is he? You could have knocked me over with a feather when I saw him, he looks so much like you did."

"He's Tessa Jackson's boy."

"Tessa!" Her eyes widened. "Oh, my goodness."

"She came to the house a couple of weeks ago and told me about him. He's been living with her father."

"That awful man? Poor child!"

"Yeah. So I brought him home."

Julia glanced at Sarah. She couldn't help but be happy that Luke had a son, particularly one who looked so much like him, but she wondered how Sarah felt about it. It wouldn't be unlikely for a wife to resent taking in her husband's illegitimate offspring, particularly when the mother was Tessa Jackson.

"I hope you'll all be happy." Julia paused, not knowing what to say. She glanced around. "Well. This must be the first time you've visited my new home since I got squared away. What do you think of it?"

"It's lovely," Sarah answered promptly. "It's a darling house, and you've made it look so homey."

Julia smiled. "Thank you."

"Give us the grand tour," Luke prompted.

"All right. If you really want it."

"Of course we do."

Julia showed them around, pleased that they liked her home. She loved the little house and kept it neat as a pin. She was always doing something for it—braiding a rag rug for the hallway or crocheting antimacassars for the parlor chairs or digging a little flower garden out front. She had never had such a lovely home before, nor one that was all hers, and she was determined that it be perfect.

They sat down in the parlor and chatted. They talked about Cal, and Julia told Luke and Sarah about her work, carefully expurgating any mention of what had happened between her and James the day before. Sarah asked Julia if she had decided what dress she would wear to the Fourth of July picnic and dance, and Julia shook her head.

"I don't think I'll go."

"What? Why not? You have to come." Sarah looked shocked.

Julia smiled. "Do I?"

"Certainly. Doesn't she, Luke?"

He nodded. "Yes, come, Julia. We'll stop by and pick you and the children up. They'll have a grand time."

"But I don't know anyone, and I—"

"Nonsense," Sarah declared. "You know us. And you know my sister Jennifer; we'll eat with them. The food will be delicious; Jen's a much better cook than I am."

Luke chuckled. "You're fishing for compliments."

"It's the truth."

He snorted. "Her apricot tarts don't compare."

Sarah gave a slightly smug smile that made Luke want to lean over and kiss her hard. "Well, I will admit that my apricot tarts are better." She turned to Julia. "Say you'll come. Please. It won't be as much fun without you."

Julia hesitated. It was hard for her to face the people in town, and the idea of seeing so many of them at once terrified her. She was certain they would whisper about her and point her out as that slutty Turner girl who had had to get married. James would probably be there. He might even be squiring some girl to it. He would dance with women, certainly, and Julia didn't want to have to watch that.

She glanced at Luke. He understood how she hated to be in public.

"We'll be there with you," he reminded Julia softly.

"Well, I—yes, I guess so."

"That's wonderful! It'll be so much fun." Sarah's eyes sparkled with anticipation. It was the first time in a long time that he had seen that, Luke thought, and he wished he could keep the light in her eyes.

"Mama! Mama!" Bonnie tumbled into the room, her pigtails flying. "Come quick. Vance is fightin'."

Luke was the first one out of the room, with Julia and Sarah on his heels. He raced down the hall and out the back door. The two boys were rolling in the dirt down by the oak tree. Luke took the steps in two bounds, ran across the lawn, and, planting a hand in the shirt collar of each boy, he yanked them to their feet.

"What in the hell do you think you're doing!"

Their arms and legs stopped flailing. Vance looked ashamed and turned his head away. His mouth was bloody, and his eye was already purpling. Cal stared mulishly at Luke.

"Damn it, this is the last straw!" Luke surged with fury. He let go of Vance, and the boy backed away uncertainly. Luke grabbed Cal by both shoulders and faced him.

Julia took her son by the arm. "Just what do you think you were up to, young man?" she asked crisply. Vance couldn't meet her eyes. "Come along and get washed up."

Julia looked at Sarah. Sarah hesitated, making a vague gesture toward Luke and his son. "You go on. I better stay out here."

"There's nothing you can do. They have to work it out by themselves."

Sarah cast another look toward the man and boy, so alike, so hard, and sighed. "All right."

They went back inside, leaving Luke and Cal in the yard by themselves. Julia sent her son upstairs to clean up, and the two women stayed by the back door, looking out.

"You've done it once too many times," Luke told Cal fiercely, punctuating his word with quick shakes of the boy's shoulders. "What did you think I would do? Keep on taking it and taking it and never bring you up short? What in the hell is the matter with you? Sarah and I have given you the best home we know how, but all you can do is sass and back talk and get into trouble. And now this. You terrorize every child in our family!"

Cal set his jaw, trying to wipe out all traces of fear from his eyes. "You want me to cut the switch now?"

"What?"

"I said, you want me to cut down the switch? Grandpa always made me cut down the switch 'fore he strapped me with it."

Luke went still. He stared at the boy for a long moment. "You're trying to make me whip you like your grandpa did, aren't you? That's why you've been doing all these things— to make me break down and beat you."

Cal's mouth tightened, but he said nothing.

Luke sighed. The rage drained out of him. He went down on one knee in front of Cal, his hands still on the boy's shoulders. "I don't know why you want that. I don't know what you're trying to prove. But I can promise you, I'm not going to whip you. Do you understand? You can do what you want, but that won't happen."

Luke let go of Cal, and his hands went to the front of his own shirt. He unbuttoned it and pulled it down off his shoulders, exposing his tanned back. He turned his back to Cal. Cal stared. Luke's hard, muscled flesh was browned by the sun, but thin white scars slashed the darker skin.

"See those?" Luke asked quietly, the tinges of an ancient pain in his voice. "I've got the same scars you have, only a few more, 'cause I had to live with my daddy longer than you've lived with your grandpa. I got them the same way you did." He turned back to face Cal, shrugging his shirt back on. "That's why you don't have to be scared of me whipping you. I won't. Ever. So you don't have to try to make me do it."

·They looked at each other. Cal backed up a step. "Well, if you ain't gonna whip me, then I don't have to do nothin' you say, do I?"

"Oh yes. You'll obey me." Luke's eyes bored into him steadily. "You'll do what's right. Not because you're scared of me, but because inside you know what's right. No matter what trash your grandfather told you about yourself, you're good inside.''

"You don't know nothin'."

"I know you. I'm your father. And I was just like you. I know you through and through."

Luke put his arms around Cal and pulled him close. Cal stood stiffly within the circle of his arms, but Luke continued to hold him. At last Luke felt the hesitant touch of Cal's hand on his cheek. He buried his head into the crook of the boy's neck. Cal's arms went around Luke's neck. Luke's eyes filled with tears, and he hugged Cal to him tightly.

* *Chapter 14* *

Sarah watched Luke and Cal as they knelt in the yard, their arms around each other, and tears pricked at her eyes. "I used to daydream about Luke with his little boy, about how close they would be, how much alike. Now he has that."

"Except that the son isn't yours," Julia put in softly.

Sarah glanced at her sister-in-law sharply, but saw only concern in Julia's face. "Yes. Except that he isn't mine."

"How do you feel about Cal's living with you all? When Luke told, I wondered whether you wanted Cal, too, or just Luke."

Sarah sighed. "At first I didn't. When Luke told me what Tessa had said, I refused to believe it. I thought I wouldn't be able to stand it, that every time I saw him I would be reminded of the baby I had lost. I was afraid it would be too painful."

"And has it been?"

"No. I've been surprised. It isn't often that Cal makes me think of my son. Maybe it's because he's older. But I find I simply think of him as himself. Just now, when I was thinking how I'd wanted a son for Luke, for the first time I didn't feel horrible despair because I hadn't given him one. I just—I envied their closeness!'' Sarah turned away, hugging herself tightly, trying to push anguish back down inside her.

Julia frowned. "I don't understand."

"It's so awful! I don't think Luke loves me anymore."

"Nonsense! I've never seen anyone love a woman as much as he loves you."

"He's changed. Used to be, after supper we'd sit together and talk. It didn't matter about what. It was enough just to be there, with his arm around me and listening to his voice. We were so happy! We were so in love! But nowadays, I hardly see him. He gulps down his food so he won't have to sit long at the same table with me. He rushes off to the fields early in the mornings and doesn't come back until dark.''

"There's a lot of work in the summer on a farm."

"But it's not like the other summers. He makes excuses to get out of the house. He goes down to the barn to check on something, or he just walks around the yard. Anything to avoid being with me. He—'' Sarah blushed "—he sleeps in another room.''

"Oh, Sarah. I'm sorry. I had hoped that you and he had made up.''

"We didn't fight. There's nothing to make up. He just doesn't want to be around me! I think he hates me.''

"No, that's impossible."

"Yes. He hates me for losing the baby. For losing his son.''

"That's ridiculous. As if you could have done anything to stop it! I know Luke wouldn't blame you for that.''

"Why else would he be so cold to me? We're like strangers. Every once in a while, for a moment, we'll be close, like we used to be. Then Luke draws back, as if he's remembered why he dislikes me.''

Julia took Sarah's hand and squeezed it. "I'm sure you're wrong. Luke wouldn't change that much." She paused. "I hope you won't take this the wrong way. I'm not trying to put any blame on you. I understand how you felt. But right after you lost the baby, you shut yourself off from the rest of us. Do you remember?''

Sarah nodded. "Yes. I felt awful and angry. I didn't want to see anyone. I hated everything, and it seemed like too much effort even to live.''

"I know. I was the same way after Pamela died. I understand why you didn't want anyone around, why you didn't want comfort. But I'm not sure Luke did. You shut him out then, Sarah. You turned away from him. Maybe he thought that you didn't want him.''

"But I did! At least, after a little while I did. I wanted him to take me in his arms, but I couldn't reach out to him. I just couldn't! I couldn't ask him for comfort. He was too cold, too remote.''

"Maybe he felt the same way. He was grieving, too. He needed comfort. At the time perhaps neither of you had comfort to give, but that could have created the distance between you.''

Tears brimmed in Sarah's eyes. "I don't know. Maybe so. I've been so confused. Nothing seems right anymore. I want it back the way it was. I want to be happy again. But I don't see how it can ever be like that again.''

"It can't be exactly the same," Julia agreed. "But you and Luke can be happy together again. I'm sure of it. There was too much love between you for it to die.''

Sarah looked back out in the yard at her husband. Tears ran unheeded down her cheeks. "I hope so, Julia. More than anything in the world, I hope so.''

All the way home, Sarah thought about what Julia had said. She remembered how she had turned her back on Luke when he came toward her right after the baby came. He had been offering her comfort, and she had refused it. Refused him. For days she hadn't wanted to see anyone. She recalled Luke coming and standing beside her bed, awkward and unsure. Often she had pretended to sleep, and when she hadn't used that pretense, she had answered only in mono-syllables. How selfish she had been! How she must have hurt Luke.

It was no excuse, she thought, that she had been deeply hurt. Luke had suffered, too, but she hadn't thought about that. All she had thought of was her own grief. Even later, when she had gotten better, when she had wanted Luke's comfort, she hadn't made any real effort to heal the breach. She had seen the wall between them and had been hurt by it, but she hadn't done anything about it. Again, she had been too wrapped up in her own misery.

Poor Luke. He had been turned away and denied so many times in his life that he had come to expect it. It wouldn't have surprised him; it probably didn't even anger him. But Sarah knew it must have cut him like a knife, another rejection of him laid on the lacerations of countless others. A less sensitive man would have paid little attention to her turning away from him that time or to her subsequent silence. A more secure man might have realized that she was numb with grief and didn't mean any rejection of him. But not Luke.

He wouldn't have said anything. That wasn't his way, just as it wasn't her way to pour out her grief and ask for comfort. He would have silently withdrawn into himself. He would have left her alone, as she seemed to want. He would have lived with his own grief and not let it show.

Sarah wondered why she hadn't realized it before, why Julia had had to point it out to her. But then, that was obvious, wasn't it? She had been concerned only with herself, too selfish to think of what Luke was suffering. Her own pain had blocked out everything else, even her love for Luke.

She was afraid she had ruined her marriage by the way she had acted. What if Luke couldn't forgive her for rejecting him? She couldn't bear to live the rest of their lives with this coolness between them, especially knowing that it was her fault. She had to do something to mend things between them. She had to explain it to Luke and ask him to forgive her. Her stomach quailed at the thought that he might not accept her explanations, that he might cut her off coldly. Still, she had to try.

That evening, after they had put the children to bed, she stopped Luke before he could make one of his excuses to leave the house. "I'd like to talk to you for a minute, if you don't mind."

Luke turned and looked at her. There was something odd in the tone of her voice. She looked so serious his stomach dropped. "Of course."

"Shall we sit on the porch where it's cool?"

He nodded and followed her out to the front porch. There was the barest slice of a moon in the sky. It was a velvet dark night, warm and close, holding the scent of the roses in front of the porch. An unexpected whisper of breeze touched Luke's skin, damp from the heat of the day, and a shiver ran down his spine.

Sarah sat down on the swing, but Luke sat upon the railing of the porch across from her, one foot on the floor, his hand curled around the narrow, carved post. Sarah looked down at her lap, where her fingers carefully pleated the material of her skirt. She didn't know how to begin. "Uh, Cal seemed better this evening."

"Knock on wood." He rapped the railing lightly.

"Your talk with him this afternoon must have helped. You're very good with him."

Luke shook his head ruefully. "I wish I was. Most of the time I'm groping in the dark. Hoping I'll do the right thing."

"I think you must have. He didn't get out of hand the rest of the afternoon and evening."

Luke grinned. "Maybe he'd just worn himself out. No, I think we got somewhere. I convinced him that we aren't going to beat him every time he does something wrong. He's been testing us, trying to goad us into whipping him."

"But why?"

"I don't know. It sounds crazy. But this afternoon when I was so furious with him, he asked me if I wanted him to cut down a switch. He said Jackson made him cut down the switch before he whipped him with it."

"Oh, Luke, how cruel!"

"I know. I'd like to have that man's throat in my hands right now." He made an encircling gesture with his hands. "But when Cal said that, I saw something in his eyes—like he was expecting a beating. More than that, almost antici- pating it. I realized he was trying to push me into it. Maybe he wanted to prove to himself that we would eventually turn out to be like Jackson, after all. Or perhaps he feels lost without the old hypocrite's rules and punishments.''

''I don't understand.''

''How could you? I hardly do myself. But you give him what he needs. Love and care and compassion.''

Sarah swallowed. ''I haven't been very generous in those areas lately.''

''You always are.''

''No. Not—not after I lost the baby.'' Sarah studied her nervous hands. She couldn't look at him. ''I was talking to Julia today, and I realized a few things that I'd been too wrapped up in myself to notice before.''

''What are you talking about?'' Luke frowned. He didn't like to hear her criticize herself in any way.

''The way I acted when I lost the baby. I remember that I—'' She paused, and when she spoke again, her voice was low and pebbled with tears. ''I turned away from you when you wanted to comfort me. I was so cold and distant; I hardly spoke to you. I didn't mean to hurt you. I was just—I felt so horrible! I didn't want to be comforted. I was so angry; I hated the world.''

''You had every right to be angry. To hate me.''

''No. I had no right at all. It wasn't that I hated you; I hated everything and everyone, but mostly me.''

''Sarah, no.''

''Yes. I hated myself for losing the baby. At the same time, I was full of self-pity; you'd have thought I was the only woman who'd ever had a baby born dead. It was wrong. I know I must have hurt you.'' Tears filled her eyes, and she looked up at him. ''I'm sorry. You can't imagine how sorry. Please forgive me.''

Luke's insides wrenched at the sight of Sarah's damp, luminous eyes. He would have killed for those eyes.

''Forgive you! You must be joking.'' Luke sat down on the swing beside her, taking her shoulders between his hands and turning her to look at him. ''You shouldn't be asking my forgiveness. My God, Sarah. I'm the one who should go on my knees to you.''

''No. Not ever.'' Her voice shook, and the tears poured down her cheeks. ''Luke, do you still love me?''

"Still love you!" He pulled her against his chest. "How could I not love you? You're all in all to me."

Sarah wrapped her arms around him. She rubbed her cheek slowly, tenderly against his chest. "I've been so lonely the last few weeks. I've missed you. I was afraid you hated me for losing your son. And when I didn't want Cal, you thought I was heartless."

"No. No." Luke squeezed her even more tightly to him. His lips brushed her hair. She smelled sweeter to him than the rose-laden air. She was soft and warm in his arms. Desire rose in him, thick and hot.

"I was so wrong. I never wanted to hurt you. I love you, Luke."

His arms trembled around her. He buried his face in her hair. He wanted to take it down and wrap it around him, tie them together with its sable softness. "Sarah." He kissed her hair. "Sarah." He kissed her forehead. His breath was hot against her skin.

Something stirred deep inside Sarah. Her skin felt suddenly tingling and alive all over. She hadn't felt this way in a long, long time. She had thought all passion was dead inside her; but now it stirred, and she flushed with anticipation. "It was lonely every night," she murmured. "I wanted your arms around me."

Luke made a peculiar, throaty noise. He kissed her eyes and cheeks, her ears, her hair. His breath rasped in his throat. He wanted to bear her back on the seat of the swing and sink into her. He wanted to feel her taking him in and hear her satisfied sigh as he filled her.

"Sarah." Her name was a moan. He couldn't stop kissing her face. He knew if he touched her lips, he'd be lost.

"Can we be together now? Will you come back to our room?"

His fingers dug into her. He wanted to scream with frustration. He couldn't take her. He couldn't. She had told him she loved him. They could have their old love and closeness again. Why couldn't that be enough for him? Why did he have to want her body so badly?

He had killed their child and almost killed her. He

couldn't risk that again. His lust would not put her into the grave, as his father's lust had done to his mother.

But how could he sleep with her and not make love to her?

How could he refuse to sleep with her and watch the hurt return to Sarah's eyes?

"Luke?" There was a hint of worry in her voice.

"Yes. Yes. Of course I'll come back to our room. If you want me to. I didn't want to disturb you."

Her laughter was like silver. "I'm not sick now."

They sat holding each other in the dark for a long time. Now and then Luke kissed the top of her head. He allowed himself nothing more. Later, they rose and went up to their bedroom. They changed clothes, self-conscious in a way they hadn't been since they were first married. Luke tried to look anyplace but at the glimpses of her white flesh that were revealed as she took off her clothes and put on her nightgown.

Sarah kept her back turned to Luke, a little embarrassed and feeling foolish about it. She could see him in the mirror of her dresser. He peeled off his shirt and trousers. She looked down, but her eyes crept back up to gaze at him. Luke's chest was already browned by the early summer sun; it was padded with muscles. A thin line of hair ran down from his chest to the shallow well of his navel. His arms were corded, the hair on them the same sun-touched color as on his head. There was something rawly sexual about Luke. There always had been. No number of years of respectability could alter the sensual shape of his mouth or the blue promise of his eyes or the challenge of the way he moved.

Sarah's abdomen went warm and liquid. A prickle of anticipation started between her legs. She finished undressing quickly and put on her light cotton nightgown.

They got into bed together, each pulling up his own side of the sheet. Their eyes avoided each other. They lay down, inches apart. It was strange to be this close to each other after all these weeks. It seemed even stranger that it felt so odd. Sarah waited for Luke to touch her, to lean over her and kiss her. He did not. She glanced at him shyly. The room was so dark she could see only the shape of his face. His eyes were deep shadow. He lay looking up at the ceiling, his arms crossed behind his head.

She wondered what he was thinking. She knew, looking at him, that he would not make love to her tonight. She didn't know why, and it hurt. For a while downstairs she had thought they had broken through the barriers between them. But apparently there were still others she hadn't even known about. She rolled over onto her side away from him.

Luke's muscles were as taut as stretched wire. He kept his arms linked beneath his head for fear that if they were free they would reach for Sarah, no matter what. It seemed as if he couldn't stop wanting her, couldn't stop remembering the taste of her mouth, the feel of her skin beneath his fingers, the tight fit of her body to him. His pulse throbbed. He wanted her. The harder he tried not to think about her, the more he did.

She turned onto her side, moving farther away from him. He thought it might make it a little easier, but it didn't. He lay awake, unable to sleep, unwilling to satisfy his desire, caught and aching. It was hours before he finally fell asleep.

✻ *Chapter 15* ✻

Sarah tied Emily's straw boater hat firmly on her head. "There. You look perfect." She stood up and began to put on her own Sunday bonnet, walking out of Emily's room into the hall as she did so. "Luke?"

"Down here." Luke stood at the bottom of the stairs.

"All right. Be there in a second. Cal?" Sarah knocked on the door to his room. "Cal? Time for church."

There was no answer. Sarah knocked again, then eased the door open. The room was empty.

Sarah turned, puzzled, and went downstairs. Luke and Emily were in the kitchen. "He must be down already."

"Here?" Luke looked surprised. "I haven't seen him."

"He's not in his room."

"Maybe he's waiting outside." Luke stepped out onto the porch and called Cal's name. Sarah walked through the bottom floor of the house, looking for him.

"He's not in the house." Sarah joined Luke on the porch. He frowned. "I'll check the barn."

Sarah waited, Emily fidgeting beside her. Sarah checked the watch that hung on a chain around her neck. They would be late to church if Cal didn't appear soon. Where could the boy have gone?

Luke emerged from the barn. He shrugged as he hurried across the yard to them. His face was tight with worry. "He's not in there."

"But where is he?"

"I'm afraid he's run away."

Sarah stared. "Why? I thought he was better last night."

"I did too. Maybe he was pretending, trying to lull us into thinking everything was fine."

"Why?"

"God knows. But I'm going to start looking for him."

"I will, too."

"All right. I'll take the road. You start toward the fields."

Luke loped off in the direction of the road. Sarah took Emily by the hand and headed for the fields, calling Cal's name. They trudged along the corn rows, sighting down each row as they went. Sarah's shoes and the hem of her skirt got dusty, and after Emily had stopped to investigate a few worms, puddles, and rocks, she was splotched with mud. Sarah soon had to peel off her gloves and the short jacket that matched her skirt. The high lace collar of her shirtwaist was damp and itchy in the heat.

They reached the stream, and Sarah hesitated. Should she go across the stream or start up it to the north pasture? There was so much area to search! Just as she was about to start toward the pasture, Emily let out a shriek. "Cal! Cal!" She jumped up and down, pointing to a clump of bushes by the water. "Me find."

She darted over to the bushes, and Sarah hurried after

her. She peered into the clump of greenery, and, sure enough, Cal was squatting in the middle of it. She would never have spotted him, but Emily, close as she was to the ground, had seen his feet beneath the bushes.

"Me hide." Emily suggested cheerfully, thinking it was a game.

"You will not. We are all going home. Cal, come out from there."

Cal crawled out on his stomach. He was barefoot and thoroughly dirty. Sarah stared at him in exasperation. "What do you think you're doing?"

Cal shrugged. "Hiding."

"That's obvious. Why? Are you running away from home?"

"No."

"Then what?"

"I don't wanna go to church."

"What?"

"I don't wanna go to church."

"You mean you hid out here and worried us all to death just so you wouldn't have to attend church?"

He bit his lip and turned his eyes downward. "I didn't think you'd look for me this hard."

"You think that if you disappeared, we wouldn't be anxious and concerned? That we wouldn't try to find you?"

"I figured you'd go on to church."

"How could we go anywhere not knowing what had happened to you?"

He squirmed. "Grandpa would. He'd just paddle me afterwards."

Sarah sighed. "Cal . . . why do you want to miss church so badly?"

He stuck his hands in his pockets and raised his face to her. His eyes were remote, and his mouth was set stubbornly. "I won't get up and say them things."

"What things?"

"You know. 'Bout what I did yesterday."

"I don't understand. To whom are you going to say them and why?"

"You know. Confess to everybody about the sins I done yesterday. Hittin' Vance and all. Ruinin' you all's day."

"Confess? You mean to the congregation?" Sarah stared,

nonplussed. "Why would you get up in front of everybody
and tell them that you got into a fight yesterday?"

Cal looked at her oddly. " 'Cause it's church. 'Cause I
sinned. Grandpa always made me stand up during the
'invitation' an' confess all the things I'd done wrong during
the week. He'd lead a prayer for me, you know, for special
help, on account of my bad blood. I figured with what I
done yesterday, you'd make me, too."

The blood drained from Sarah's face, and the exasperation she had felt fled. "He what?" Her eyes flashed so
fierily that Cal took a step backward. Sarah squatted down
on his level, heedless of her skirts trailing the dirt. "Now,
you listen to me. Luke and I won't make you do that, ever.
That's not the way we are, and not the way our church is.
We go to church out of love, not fear and hate. You
understand me?"

"Yes'm."

"Good. Then let's go back to the house." She took Emily
by the hand and laid her other arm around Cal's shoulders.
He was stiff beneath her touch, but he didn't shrug off her
arm, and as they walked, he inched closer to her side.
Sarah suspected that beneath the spiky exterior, Cal was
desperately hungry for a loving touch. The problem was,
she had to practically fight him to let her give it to him.

They walked back to the house, where they met Luke
returning from his search. Sarah took Luke aside and
explained to him what had happened. The anger and worry
drained from his face, and he said nothing to Cal about the
worry he'd caused them, only asked him if he'd like to help
unhitch the buggy.

Because it was now too late to go to church, Sarah put on
her apron and set to work on dinner. The Crowleys were
coming over to eat with them.

When the Crowleys arrived, Sarah, Luke, and Emily
rushed out to meet them, exchanging happy greetings and
hugs. Cal hung back, eyeing the Crowley children suspiciously.
Sarah sighed inwardly, hoping that Cal's reactions to these
children wouldn't be a repeat of what he had done the day
before. She introduced Cal to the Crowleys and sent the
children out to play while she and Mary Etta finished
dinner. She watched the children anxiously out of the kitchen

window while she worked, her mind only partially on Mary Etta's chatter.

Cal stood a little to one side of the others, watching. They were setting up the rules for a game of tag, and it was obvious that Cal wasn't sure what to do. Mary Etta's youngest daughter leaned close to him, whispering, and he nodded. He smiled at her, a rare, sweet smile, and joined the rest of them as they ran away from home base.

Sarah wanted to laugh and cry, all at once.

"Who's that boy?" Mary Etta asked, joining her at the window. "Luke's nephew? A cousin?"

Sarah shook her head. "No. That's our son."

Dovie swayed a little to the music as she sang. She loved to sing, though her voice wasn't as good as her mother's, who stood on the other side of her. When the hymn was over, the choir sat down, and the preacher took his place at the lectern. He spoke in a melodious, compelling voice, and Dovie drifted along on the rhythm of his words. Reverend Bascomb was always filled with the spirit, so that it was a pleasure just to listen to him, though Dovie would have liked now and then to have taken hold of his grammar.

She glanced over the congregation of the Mt. Zion Baptist Church. All of them were decked out in their Sunday best, flowery straw hats on the women and most of the men in suits. Her eyes touched a man sitting near the rear of the church and moved on. She looked back. Her Bible slipped out of her hands and she had to grab it to keep it from falling to the floor. Micah Harrison was in her church!

Dovie couldn't concentrate for the rest of the service. She kept sneaking glances at him, and every time she did, she found him looking at her. His gaze was steady; he didn't pretend to be paying attention to the sermon. He didn't even have enough shame to look embarrassed when she caught him staring. He just kept on looking. It rattled Dovie. She lost the thread of the sermon, and one time when the choir stood up to sing, she stayed in her chair, and Lurleen had to poke her arm to get her attention. She jumped to her feet, trying to remember what they were supposed to be singing.

The others started, and she stumbled along with them. She glanced surreptitiously at Micah in the audience. He had the gall to grin at her! Dovie felt like sinking through the floor.

She was relieved when the service was over and she was able to escape into the back of the church, where the choir took off their robes. She told her mother that she would meet her at Aunt Martha's, and she slipped out the side door. She knew that Micah intended to talk to her—he'd never come to Mt. Zion before—and she was determined to avoid him.

When she stepped out the door, she found Micah standing in the side yard, his arms crossed, waiting. Dovie stopped. "What are you doing here?"

"I knowed you'd come this way. I seen you goin' to the back."

Dovie's lips twitched in irritation. She turned and strode through the yard to the street. He fell into step beside her.

"Thought I'd walk you home from church this mornin'."

"I don't want you to." He continued to walk beside her. "And I'm not going home."

"I take you where you goin'."

They walked. Dovie tried hard not to look at Micah, but found it hard to resist. She glanced over at him. He was watching her, his black eyes warm and amused. He was laughing at her. She stiffened her spine even more.

"You get much straighter, girl, you gonna break in two."

"Why do you keep bothering me?"

He smiled. "Maybe 'cause you bother me."

"What do you mean?" she began, then caught the sexual undermeaning of his words. Her lips tightened.

He chuckled a little. It was a warm, rich sound, and her body softened unconsciously in response to it.

"You sure pretty when you singin'."

"Thank you."

"You lose that prickly pear look. I like watchin' you."

"Well, I didn't like you watching me." That was a lie, she knew, at least partly. Disturbing as it had been, there had been some sort of perverse enjoyment in it, too.

He knew that as well. She could see it in the dark amusement in his eyes. Dovie glanced away, unable to meet his gaze, even though she knew how much that gesture gave her away.

"What I don't understand," she said, "is why you persist in pursuing me. I've made my feelings plain, I think."

"You done that."

"I'm sure there must be lots of other women who would be happy to spend time with you. Why do you keep following me?"

He looked at her for a moment. His eyes were dark and intense, and Dovie found that she couldn't look away. Her heart began to beat faster.

"I like you," Micah replied simply. "I don't want 'other women.' You the one I want."

Dovie didn't notice that they had stopped walking and were standing still on the side of the street, facing each other. "But why?" she persisted.

A slow smile lit up his face. "Why? You want the truth?"

"Yes."

" 'Cause I like that long body you got, 'cause watchin' you move makes me itch. I wanna take your hair down; I wanna feel it 'gainst my skin. I like hearin' you talk, an' I like watchin' your face while you doin' it. I think you one hell of a woman, an' I wanna be the man you want."

His words melted Dovie. Her face went hot, and her knees suddenly had the consistency of putty. "Micah." For once she couldn't think of anything to say.

He laid his hand against her face. His hand was big; it covered her cheek. His fingertips and palm were rough with calluses. Dovie knew he must feel the heat of her skin, and he would know how his words affected her. She ought to step away from him. But she didn't move. She only waited and watched him as he bent toward her, his features growing larger until she closed her eyes. His lips touched hers, and a little tremor ran through her.

"Dovie." He slanted his head in the other direction, and his lips met hers again. His kisses were light and brief, teasing, and she knew an urge to make him stop and stay, to feel the fullness of his kiss. Her hands came up between them and curled into his shirt.

His kiss deepened, and his tongue teased at her lips. She opened her mouth to him, and his tongue filled her. She had never let another man kiss her like this, and it went like a shock wave though her. She wanted to moan. She wanted to press herself into him and feel the line of his body all up and down hers.

Slowly, reluctantly, Micah ended the kiss. He drew back from her. For a moment their eyes held. Then, abruptly, as if released from a spell, Dovie realized where they were and how brazenly she had behaved. She jerked her hands back from his shirt as if they had been burned and whirled away. What in the world had she been doing! Standing on the street corner kissing a drifter like she was trash! If anyone had seen her, she would never hear the end of it. Lots of people thought she gave herself airs and would enjoy seeing her humiliated.

She glanced around anxiously. There was no one on the street, but there was no telling who might have been watching from their windows. She hurried away from him, almost running. She should have slapped him. She should have pushed him away. She shouldn't have let him kiss her! But at the time she hadn't been able to move; it was as if he had mesmerized her.

Micah caught up with her. She shot him a seething glance. "Why are you following me? Haven't you done enough already?"

He smiled, unrepentant. "No. Not near enough."

"Don't grin at me like that, like a . . . like a crocodile!"

"Can't help it. Lookin' at you makes me happy."

Dovie made an exasperated noise. "Why can't you get it through your thick skull? I don't want you around!"

"I couldn't tell it back there. Kissin' a man like that ain't no way to tell him to move on. It jus' makes him want to stay."

"All right, I kissed you." Her voice was agitated and rapid, slipping more and more into the accent she had carefully stripped from her voice. "That don't—doesn't mean I want you around. It was a—a slip, that's all."

"It come from in here." He tapped his chest lightly. "'Stead of your head. That makes it truer."

"No."

He frowned. "Why you so set against me? You 'gainst

me—or any black man? You thinkin' that some white fellow gonna come along for you? Your doctor maybe?''

Dovie gasped and came to a stop. Anger flooded her. ''What! You think I—'' She pressed her lips together and paused, pulling herself back under control. ''You think I'm in love with Dr. Banks!''

He shrugged. ''You real partial to the man.''

''I grew up with him! We played together when we were little. Of course I'm fond of him! And his family has done lots for me. Old Dr. Will paid for me to go to school. If it wasn't for him, I'd be scrubbin' some white woman's floors instead of teachin' school.'' Dovie drew a deep breath, struggling for calm. She was not going to let this man make her create a scene on the street.

''You so fond of him you clean that house of Mrs. Dobson's.''

''I was helping my mother! There was no school that day, so I helped her. That's not a crime, is it?''

''No.''

''Nor does it mean I'm in love with James Banks. I'm not! Nor am I hankering after any other white man!''

''Why not? You sure try to be white yourself.''

''What are you talking about?''

''Look at you. Your hair, your clothes, the way you talk, the way you act. You done everything 'cept take bleach to your skin.''

''That's not true! Just because I try to better myself doesn't mean I'm trying to—to—deny my heritage! I don't want to be poor or ignorant or looked down upon by everybody else. That doesn't mean I'm trying to change the color of my skin. You think we're ever going to get anywhere by not being educated? You think it would raise me higher in life to talk like I've never been off a farm? Knowledge is there to be used, and a person'd be a fool not to! The only way to get respect or money or any of the better things in life is to work at it. You have to make people respect you, and that means acting uprightly, talking correctly, and working hard.''

''Oh? I thought it mean playin' up to the rich white folks.''

"Is that what you think I do with the Bankses? I told you, I like them! They're good people, kind people."

"You can't trust a white man," Micah stated flatly.

"Don't be silly."

"You the one that's silly. You think any of your precious Bankses would help you out if you got in trouble?"

"Of course they would."

He snorted. "You has lots of college, girl, but you don't know much 'bout real life. They kind to you, like they kind to one of their dogs, but they drop you like a hot potato if you get outta line."

"That's not true."

He shrugged. They started walking again, both of them moving with the quick strides of anger.

"If you disapprove so much of me and what I think," Dovie snapped, "then why in the world do you keep pursuing me?"

He grinned at her in that irritating way. "Maybe I like a good fight."

Dovie grimaced. "I might have known you'd have an answer like that."

"Like what?"

"Annoying."

"Ever wonder why I annoy you so much?"

Dovie gave him a speaking glance. "Because you're fresh and rude and—"

"And you don't scare me. That's why I get under your skin. 'Cause you know this man can handle you."

Her eyes flashed. "You're crazy."

He smiled. "An' maybe I like you for the same reason."

Dovie glanced at him, surprised. They continued to her aunt's home in silence. Dovie stopped at the path leading up to the house. Micah glanced at her questioningly.

"This is where I'm going."

He nodded toward the porch. "I walk you to the door."

"No. There's no need." She moved away from him.

At that moment Lurleen stepped out onto the front porch, her eyes bright with curiosity. "Dovie? What you doin' hangin' 'round out here, girl?"

"Sorry, Mama." Dovie started toward the house.

"Aren't you gonna invite your friend in?"

"He's not my friend."

Lurleen turned to Micah. "You the one I met at Dr. Jim's rent house?"

"Yes, ma'am. Micah Harrison."

"Well, come in, come in. You welcome to stay for Sunday dinner."

"I 'preciate that, ma'am. I'd like to stay and eat with your family."

Dovie shot Micah a fulminating glance, but he smiled blandly back at her and moved past her to the porch. Her mother bustled him inside the house, talking a mile a minute. Dovie felt like screaming. She stomped after them into the house.

Julia hurried into the First Baptist Church, holding her children's hands. They were almost late. The service was about to start, and the only seats left were near the front. She walked down the center aisle to the vacant place in the second pew, feeling as if every eye in the place were on her. She thought people were wondering what a woman like her was doing here in church. She was sure that they resented her presence. She and her family had come to this church almost every Sunday since they moved into town, but usually she had made sure to sit near the back where they weren't noticeable.

As she went down the aisle, she saw James and his mother sitting a few rows back from the front. They turned to glance at her as she passed, but she didn't pause or look at them. She wouldn't put Anthea Banks in the position of being forced to speak to her in public.

But when the service was over and Julia followed the crowd out the wide front doors, she found herself right behind James and Mrs. Banks as they stood in line to shake hands with the minister. Julia quickly started to skirt the knot of people waiting, but Anthea turned and saw her. Anthea smiled.

"Why, it's Mrs. Dobson. Hello, my dear."

"Good morning. I mean, good afternoon." James turned at his mother's words and looked at her, too. "Dr. Banks."

It was strange to address him so formally, remembering how he had kissed her the other afternoon. Her cheeks went hot as she thought about it, and she saw in his eyes that he was thinking of the same thing.

"Mrs. Dobson." James watched the color rise in Julia's face, tinting her cheeks pink. He thought she looked like a spun sugar confection, all white and gold and pink. She was so beautiful that he wanted to take her in his arms and kiss her right there. He wondered how he was going to get through the days working with her now, with the knowledge of that kiss between them. Desire had been burning in his gut ever since that day.

"These must be your children," Mrs. Banks went on in a friendly way, smiling down at Vance and Bonnie.

"Yes. This is my son, Vance, and my daughter, Bonnie. Children, say hello to Mrs. Banks." They chorused a polite greeting, and Julia was relieved they had responded properly.

Anthea glanced at her son. There was something in his face when he looked at Julia; it had been there the other time she'd seen them together, as well. She was intrigued. "I haven't seen much of you since we met. I'm afraid my son makes you work too hard."

"Oh, no." Julia rose quickly to James's defense. "It's more that it takes me a long time to understand things."

"Nonsense," James protested. "Julia has a sharp mind. She catches on quickly."

Anthea smiled. Their quick defense of each other raised her curiosity even further. "Well, whatever the reason, I do hope that we will have time in the future to chat."

"Of course, if you'd like." It amazed Julia that this woman would want to talk to her—unless she had heard rumors and wanted to make sure Julia knew her place in James's life. Her stomach froze at the thought.

"Why don't you come have dinner with us now?" Anthea suggested brightly.

Julia's insides grew even colder. "Oh, no, really. That would be an imposition."

"Not at all. Lurleen always has an enormous dinner sitting on the stove for us on Sunday. You must come."

Julia glanced at James. It would be awful to sit there with him under Mrs. Banks's eye, unable to get that kiss out of her mind yet having to act like any worker with her employer. "Well, I . . ."

James said nothing to help her.

Julia looked down at her children. "I can't leave Bonnie and Vance."

"Of course, I include Bonnie and Vance in the invitation, too. It will be nice to have children in the house. It's been so long. My son has been exceptionally stubborn about marrying and giving me the pleasure of grandchildren."

Anthea watched with interest as Julia blushed a fiery red and kept her face turned determinedly away from James. Anthea was certain that she was on to something important here. She glanced at her son. He was looking only at Julia, and there was a strange, drawn expression in his face that was akin to pain.

"Thank you. We'd be glad to come to dinner." Julia didn't know what else to say. She couldn't be rude to Mrs. Banks, no matter how awful it would be to eat with them.

"Good, then, that's settled." Anthea turned back to the line of people greeting the minister, and when her turn came, she pulled Julia forward and introduced her to the minister. Afterward, they walked together to the buggy, and James drove them back to his house.

Julia could see her children's eyes widen when they pulled up to the large house, with its round tower on one end and ornate wooden gingerbread carving. But their awe was nothing compared to what they felt when they walked inside. Bonnie and Vance stood in the marble-tiled entryway with its grand mahogany staircase winding up to the second floor, and simply stared around them, their mouths little O's.

"It's beautiful," Bonnie breathed.

Anthea smiled. "Why, thank you, dear. My father built it just before he died. Before that Dr. Banks—the late Dr. Banks, that is—and I lived in the house where you live now."

"Really?" Julia turned to her, surprised. "I didn't know that."

"Oh yes. I have a special fondness for that little house. It's where James was born, you see."

Julia wondered if Anthea resented James's turning a

house which had such special meaning over to a stranger like herself.

"We lived there several years. How old were you when we moved here, James?"

"Six or seven, I think."

"Then you must remember the other house well." Did it have special meaning to James, also? But if so, why had he given it to her—and rent free? Julia had assumed it was just a small house from which James received such negligible rent that it was little loss to let her have it without charge. But now that she thought about it, Julia realized that it couldn't have been just any old rent house. It was too neat and well cared for.

"Oh yes, I remember it," James replied. "Fondly. When we moved into this place, I was scared to breathe, it was so big and formal."

"As I recall, you weren't in awe of it too long," Mrs. Banks put in tartly. "You made a hole in the back wall with your slingshot."

James's smile was rueful. "Yes, I seem to recall that."

"And do you recall the marks on the parlor furniture legs from your wagon?"

"All right, all right. Are you going to reveal all my misdeeds to Mrs. Dobson?"

Anthea smiled. "I'm sure I don't know all of them."

She led them into the formal dining room. The table was set for only two people, but at each place there was a multitude of china dishes, silver eating utensils, and crystal goblets. The table was laid with an ecru lace tablecloth, and linen napkins edged in lace lay beside each plate. In the center of the table stood an ornate silver bowl filled with fruit. More china and crystal sparkled in the large glass-fronted cabinet. A heavy silver coffee service sat upon the sideboard, along with a large crystal vase full of fragrant summer flowers.

It was lovely and far richer than anything Julia had ever seen. She wondered what you ate with all those forks and spoons and what you put in the various dishes, and she knew she would look like a bumpkin trying to figure it out. What if the children broke a glass or spilled something on the delicate lace tablecloth? She wanted to run for home.

Neither James nor his mother seemed aware of the awful splendor of the room. Anthea went to the china cabinet and began to pull out more plates. Julia hurried to help her set the extra places. It was hard to imagine Mrs. Banks, with her regal carriage and elegant silk dress, doing any domestic task. But when the table was set, Anthea went into the kitchen, donned a full apron, and began to dish up food from the pots on the stove.

"Except on very special occasions, Lurleen has Sundays off," Anthea explained to Julia. "Fortunately, though, she leaves us a wonderful meal."

"Won't you let me do that for you, ma'am?"

"Heavens, no." Anthea's eyes sparkled with humor. "I have even on occasion been known to cook a meal."

"Of course."

Anthea handed Julia a large bowl of green beans, and Julia went to put it on the dining table. Anthea watched Julia as she left the room, and she frowned a little. There was an anxious look in Julia's eyes that Anthea didn't understand. It was almost as if she were scared. Anthea could understand a little nervousness; the house—even she herself—could be a trifle imposing. But surely that didn't explain the tumult of emotions that she sensed in Julia Dobson.

Julia and Anthea carried the rest of the serving dishes into the dining room, and they sat down to dinner. Bonnie and Vance stared in dismay at the lineup of eating utensils before them. Julia wished she could help them, but she knew no more than they what everything was for. She had thought Sarah's Sunday dinner table was elegant, but it paled next to this one. What could you do with so many spoons? She'd never seen potatoes sliced up and mixed with white sauce and cheese.

Dinner was a miserable experience. Julia watched Mrs. Banks closely to see which utensil to use, then tried to silently relay the message to her children. She watched Bonnie and Vance like a hawk to make sure they didn't make a mess. She avoided looking at James altogether. Julia was sure that if she met his eyes, Mrs. Banks would see everything in her face—the past, what she had felt for James, the kiss they had shared the other afternoon, her confusion about her present feelings.

Conversation limped along, with Anthea supplying most of what little there was. Julia replied to the questions Anthea put to her, sure that she sounded like a dolt. She could think of nothing to say on her own. James watched Julia, but, like her, hardly spoke unless spoken to. Julia was aware of his gaze, and it made her even more nervous.

James could see how nervous Julia was. He would have liked to lay his hand over hers and assure her that everything was all right. But of course he couldn't. He tried not to look at Julia too much, knowing it would arouse his mother's interest, but it was difficult not to look at her. She was so pretty in that blue cotton dress that turned her eyes the color of the sky. He looked at her mouth and thought about kissing it. He remembered how soft and warm and eager it felt beneath his lips. He recalled their kisses years ago—and the one just days past. All of them were unbearably sweet.

He wanted to grab Julia and start kissing her and never stop. His palm itched to curve around her breast. Her breasts were heavier now. Her nipples, too, would look different after having borne and suckled children. He thought of how she must have looked nursing her children, and desire thrummed in him. There would be other changes in her body; he yearned to know each and every one of them. He wanted to have her in his bed, to explore and touch and taste at his leisure. Just the thought of it made him ache.

Julia was relieved when the meal was over. She offered to help with the dishes, but Anthea refused politely, saying that Lurleen would take care of them later. Julia was afraid she had showed her ignorance of social etiquette by even asking. She tried to say her good-byes and leave, but Anthea insisted on showing her the flower garden in back.

James didn't come with them, and Julia felt more at ease. At least she knew something about flowers and growing things, even if she had never had the money to buy all the fancy flowers Mrs. Banks grew. The two women strolled through the garden, and Julia exclaimed with delight over the varieties of roses. When they had finished their tour of the garden, Julia left as quickly and gracefully as she could. She murmured a polite good-bye and thank you to Mrs.

Banks and to James, forcing herself to look into his face as she did so. But as soon as she looked at him, she glanced away and, taking the children by the hand, she hurried out the front door.

Anthea and James stood at the door, watching them walk away. "She seems to be a nice girl," Anthea commented, her eyes on her son rather than Julia.

"Yes."

"I like her."

"Yes. I like her, too." Anthea waited for him to continue, but James said nothing else, only turned away and closed the door. "I think I'll go in back and smoke a cigar."

Anthea watched him leave. The dinner had made her more curious than ever about Julia and her son. Julia had been hardly able to look at James, and James had been hardly able to do anything but look at Julia. Anthea was sure that her son was interested in Julia. But then why had there been that touch of bleakness in his voice when he said he liked her? Why had the young woman avoided him so? Puzzled, Anthea sat down in the back parlor and took up her needlepoint, contemplating when and how she would find out what was going on.

James strolled through the garden, smoking his cigar, hardly noticing the beauty around him. He was restless and bored. He had been this way ever since he kissed Julia two days before. He had been unable to think of anything but that kiss. He kept remembering the past and imagining what it would be like to make love to Julia now. It would be nothing short of foolhardy to become involved with her again, he told himself. Only an idiot would set himself up for a second heartbreak with the same woman. She didn't love him; she had played him for a fool before. Yet he couldn't stop the rush of desire whenever he thought about her or looked at her. It was crazy. Crazy. But he still wanted her.

* Chapter 16 *

It seemed to Dovie as though everywhere she turned during the next few weeks, Micah was there. He was at the June Teenth picnic, the celebration held on June nineteenth each year to commemorate the day blacks in Texas learned of the Emancipation Proclamation. He almost forced Dovie to dance with him and then sat down beside her just as if he had the right to. Her mother, of course, was no help; she just smiled and talked to him. Later, when the party grew rowdy, he walked Dovie and Lurleen home. Lurleen went straight to bed. Micah lingered at the door with Dovie and kissed her. Once again, she had been somehow unable to free herself from his arms.

She just stood there and let him kiss her and kiss her until she was melting in his hands. Only the sound of the back door closing at the big house brought her to her senses and sent her fleeing back into their little house.

He was at her church the next two Sundays, and one Saturday afternoon she found him sitting on her aunt's porch, telling stories to her cousins' children. He charmed everyone in her family. Her mother and aunts were impressed with his looks, his quiet strength, and his slow, devastating smile. Her cousins, nieces, and nephews were entranced by his stories of the West and life on a ranch.

When Dovie commented rather tartly that he had certainly entertained the children with his wild stories, he smiled and asked, "You like them, too?"

Dovie tried to look her most severe. "I have no liking for the Wild West, thank you."

He grinned in that irritating way of his. "Oh, I bet you got more wildness in you than you ever guessed."

She didn't know what to do with a man like that.

It wasn't as if she hadn't been around other men. She had. And some of them had been charming, far smoother than Micah Harrison. But there was something about him— the way he stood, the way he walked, the way he looked at her—that pulled at her. He was tough; he was experienced. But there was no cruelty in him and no braggadocio. He had seen things she never would, known things she could only imagine. He intrigued her, much as she tried to pretend that he didn't. He spoke to something inside her that she hadn't even known was there before. Dovie was afraid that he might be right—that there really was a wildness in her that she had always suppressed. Even worse, she was afraid that he might be able to release it.

Dovie wanted to avoid him. She didn't want to see him again. But every weekend found her taking particular care with her clothes and hair, and she walked to church on Sundays with a jumping excitement in her stomach that wasn't engendered by the thought of Reverend Bascomb's sermon. She had to admit that however much she might not want to see Micah, she wanted to see him ten times more.

Cal settled in at the farm. He did his chores, usually well and without protest, and he was no longer as sullen or defiant. Though only Emily could make him smile and sometimes even laugh, he listened to Luke and Sarah without the defensive hunching of his shoulders and the blank look to his face.

He was finally beginning to believe that his life had changed. Luke and Sarah hadn't given up on him and sent him back to his grandfather. Luke hadn't beat him, no matter how surly or bad he had been, and Sarah was consistently patient and kind. Luke taught him things in such a way that Cal didn't feel stupid or wrong not knowing them in the first place. He gave Cal chores, but he didn't wear him out with work. For the first time Cal could remember, he had plenty of time to play and explore the farm.

Luke talked to him in a different way from the way his

grandfather ever had. No sermons or parables came out of his mouth. He just plain talked, as if Cal were a regular person. He told Cal about his life. At first Cal couldn't believe that it was true; Luke couldn't have been a ''bad boy'' too. But then he realized that it was true—and that all the things Luke said about how he'd changed must be true, as well.

Cal found himself thinking about what Luke said at night before he went to sleep. Hope crept through him like the tendrils of a climbing plant, and it scared him. He didn't want to believe. He didn't want to hope. He didn't want to love it here. Yet he couldn't stop.

He was still wary of Micah. The man was too big and too dark. He couldn't forget the things his grandfather had told him about men like Micah. But Micah had a way with the horses, and that drew Cal to him. Despite his unease, he slipped into the barn when Micah was grooming the horses to watch his skillful hands and hear his low, soothing voice.

One day Micah turned and caught sight of Cal watching him. Micah looked at him. Cal's chest tightened, and he thought about running. Then Micah said, "You like horses?"

Cal nodded.

"They fine animals. Nothin' like them." He paused. "You ever ride one?"

Cal shook his head.

"Now, that's a shame. I done rode horses all my life. Best feelin' in the world, sittin' up on a good horse." Almost as an afterthought, he added, "You like to learn?"

"To ride?" Cal came forward a step.

"Sure. I teach you."

The boy hesitated. Desire won out over his fear. "Yeah. I'd like that. Will you? Please?"

Micah's smile was so swift and faint that later Cal wondered if he'd even seen it. "Yeah. I jus' do that."

After that, Cal spent part of almost every evening with Micah, learning how to ride. His fear of Micah soon turned to liking and awe at his riding skills, until he couldn't remember why he had been scared of the man before.

The Fourth of July holiday came, and the family went into town for the celebration. Sarah had spent all the day before cooking in preparation for the picnic, so that the morning of the Fourth all she had to do was pack the food baskets and dress.

She put on a new pink and white striped cotton dress that she had made especially for today. She wanted to look her best. Maybe if she looked pretty enough, Luke would want her again.

Even though Luke had returned to her bed two weeks ago, he still had not touched her. Sometimes Sarah awoke to find their arms and legs tangled around each other, and she hoped that Luke would awaken wanting her, as he had so many times in the past. She would keep her eyes shut, pretending to be asleep, but when Luke awoke, he slipped out from her embrace and got out of bed.

However much Luke might say he still loved her, he obviously didn't desire her anymore.

She ached to know why, but she couldn't ask him. She was shy around him now. It would be too humiliating to say, "Why don't you want me anymore? What's the matter with me?"

How could desire die that quickly, that suddenly? Did the thought of the stillbirth repel Luke? Or was it that she was now unattractive? Pregnancy had thickened her waist and dulled her hair, but she had thought the signs of pregnancy were gone. Her figure was slim again, and her skin had lost the slightly muddy look; her hair had regained its luster.

Sarah leaned closer to her mirror, peering at her face up close. She always wore a bonnet outside to protect her skin, but even so the weather had worked on it. There were freckles across her nose, and her skin was dry. Tiny lines had formed around her eyes, and there were even the beginnings of creases on her forehead. She was too tanned. This land was not kind to a woman.

She thought of Tessa Jackson. She looked cheap, but she was also white and soft, her breasts and hips lush, her waist cinched in. Sarah considered her own uncorseted body. Her waist was wider than fashion indicated, and her hips were narrow. Her breasts weren't as full as Tessa's. Was she too thin? Sarah wondered what Luke had thought when he had seen Tessa that day. He hated Tessa for what she had done to him, but had he felt desire for her despite that? Had he

found her more feminine than the spare, unornamented farm
woman who was his wife?

Sarah shivered. She didn't think she could bear it if Luke
never wanted her again. Some women would be happy to
have their husbands leave them alone in bed, Sarah knew.
But she was not one of those. She had enjoyed her husband's carnal knowledge of her body. No, more than enjoyed—
she needed it, as she needed air, water, and food. Last night
she had awakened with a dark throbbing between her legs.
She had been dreaming of Luke's lovemaking, and her face
had been drenched in sweat, her loins warm and heavy with
passion. She had buried her face in her pillow, her teeth
clenching on the pillowcase, remembering Luke's hands on
her, his mouth, his thick shaft buried within her. Little pulses
had broken in her, pale reminders of the waves that had
drenched her whenever he took her. It had given her no
surcease, but left only a sweet ache and a desire for more.

Sarah pulled her hair up on top of her head in the soft
pompadour style that she knew Luke liked best. Around her
neck, she fastened the cameo that he had given her last
Christmas. She dabbed perfume at her temples and neck.
She hesitated, then unbuttoned the top button of her dress
and slipped a touch of perfume into the hollow between her
breasts. She started to refasten the button, then stopped. It
wasn't lewd this way, really, but if Luke looked down at her,
he could see the shadowy tops of her breasts. She bit her
lips and pinched her cheeks to bring color to them.

She looked in the mirror one last time, then went downstairs to join her family.

They were waiting for her in the kitchen. The table was
loaded down with food baskets and jugs of water and
lemonade. Luke wore a light summer suit and a white shirt
with a tiny blue stripe through it and a stiff white collar and
cuffs. He looked so good it made her throat close up. She
never saw the celluloid collar and cuffs without thinking of
Luke taking them off: unbuttoning the collar and laying it
down atop his tall chest of drawers, unsnapping the cuff
links and sliding them through the slits in the cloth, and
placing both cuffs and links beside the collar. Just the
thought of that routine sent a piercing shaft of desire
through her viscera. She was starved for him, she thought,

and knew it was something a truly good woman wouldn't have felt, much less admitted. But goodness had little hold on her when it came to Luke.

Luke stood up when Sarah entered the room, and his eyes ran down her involuntarily. When he looked back up at her face, Sarah thought she saw the familiar blue gleam of hunger there.

"Oh, Mama, you pretty!" Emily clapped her hands with pleasure. Emily wore a white dress ruffled with eyelet embroidery and decorated with pink ribbons, and she reminded Sarah of some sugary concoction atop a cake. By the end of the day, though, the ruffles would doubtless be dragging and the dress liberally sprinkled with dust, mud, and food.

Beside Emily, Cal smiled. His pale eyes sparkled with excitement. He wore a pair of trousers and a shirt that Sarah had made him. It warmed her to see him clean and happy.

Sarah's beauty struck Luke like a blow to the gut. She was fresh and vibrant, her face alive with color and her hazel eyes bright. Her lips were red; it made him think of the way they looked when he kissed her.

He had gone through hell the last two weeks, sleeping with Sarah without making love to her. He didn't know how much more of this torture he could take. He lay awake every night, looking at the soft curves of her body beneath the sheet, thinking of her without sheet, without gown, without anything between her flesh and his hands. He imagined waking her with his kisses. He imagined touching her. He imagined sinking into her and feeling her molten heat close around the throbbing core of his desire. The blood had pooled between his legs, heavy, pulsing, demanding its animal release. Luke wasn't sure how he had managed not to roll on top of Sarah and take her in pure, instinctive lust.

But each time his love for Sarah had conquered his hunger. He awoke in the mornings feeling as if he hadn't slept. His face had become drawn, the lines biting in deeply beside his mouth and eyes, and there were blue smudges like bruises beneath his eyes. He feared each night when he went to bed that this time he wouldn't be able to protect her from himself.

They walked out to the wagon. Luke watched the gentle

sway of Sarah's hips beneath her dress. He helped her up
into the wagon, very aware of the bare flesh of her arm
beneath his hand and of the flash of stockinged leg that was
exposed as she climbed up into the high seat. Luke sat down
beside her on the seat. He glanced down at Sarah. The top
button of her dress was undone. He could see little but
shadows, but just the thought of the soft swell of her breasts
beneath the dress was enough to set his pulse skittering. His
hands clenched around the reins, and he snapped them
across the mules' backs with more force than usual. This
was going to be a hellish day. Luke wondered how he was
going to get through it.

They drove into town to Julia's house. Julia and her
children were waiting for them on the porch, a basket of
food beside them.

Julia had thought a hundred times about not going to the
celebration. She didn't want to see James in a social
situation. It was bad enough being with him at the office,
remembering their kiss and pretending not to, trying to
avoid the touch of his hand when she handed him a piece of
paper or a medical instrument. But to have to see him in
public—to watch him dance with other women and to have
others see her looking at him with her heart in her eyes—
would be almost unbearable.

She didn't want to go. But she couldn't disappoint the
children; they had their hearts set on seeing the parade and
the fireworks. Besides, Sarah and Luke would plague her
about why she didn't want to go, and she couldn't tell them
the real reason.

So she forced herself to smile when Luke and Sarah
arrived and climbed into the wagon with them. They drove
to the town park, where they unloaded their baskets and
found a long, shaded table. Soon Jennifer and Stu and their
family joined them, and after that, the large Crowley clan
claimed the table next to them. There was a great deal of
friendly chatter and laughter as the families settled in. The
women set up the food while the children ran off to play, and
the men grouped together to talk. Julia's nerves relaxed a
little. She hadn't even seen James or his mother. Perhaps
the whole day would pass without her seeing him, and she
would find that she had had nothing to fear.

By the time the women had finished unloading the baskets, the tables were jammed with food. There were platters of fried chicken and ham and bowls of potato salad and coleslaw, as well as thick baked beans, still warm from Jennifer's oven, and a variety of cobblers and pies for dessert. In addition, there were jugs of cold iced tea, lemonade, and water, and side dishes of sliced tomatoes, onions, hot peppers, pickles, and relishes. At either end of the table were plates piled high with thickly sliced bread, squares of cornbread, and round dinner rolls. It looked like enough to feed an army, Julia thought, but when the menfolk and children returned to the tables, they made a sizable dent in the wealth of food.

After they ate, the women cleaned off the tables, stuffing the remainder of the food back into the baskets for supper later that evening. The children went to play again, but the adults were content to sit beneath the shade in the fierce heat and talk quietly or doze. Julia sat on one of the benches at the table, her elbow on the table and her chin propped on her hand. Mary Etta Crowley was explaining a quilting pattern to Jennifer and Sarah, and her voice was soothing. The insects droned in the somnolent heat. Julia's eyelids drifted lower.

"Hello, ladies."

Julia's eyes popped open. James Banks. She looked up and saw him standing a few feet away from their table. He had just tipped his hat to them and was returning it to his head. He wore a cream-colored linen summer suit, and he had taken off his jacket in the heat and carried it slung over one shoulder. His shirt was pastel striped, and he wore no tie. The top button of his shirt was unfastened, and sweat glistened in the hollow of his throat.

"Good afternoon."

"Dr. Jim."

"Doctor." The other women answered him. Julia said nothing. All she could think was how good he looked. She had a wicked desire to touch her tongue to that shallow indentation below his throat.

James looked directly at her. Julia felt heat rising up her throat and hoped it didn't show in her face. "Good afternoon, Dr. Banks."

"How is your mother?" Jennifer asked.

He turned his head toward Jennifer and smiled. "Fine, thank you. She's here today, holding court over on the west side of the park." He motioned in the direction of the picnic table where Anthea sat.

"I'll have to run over to see her later."

Vance and Cal came racing up to the table. Their shirttails were out, and Cal had a long streak of mud across one trouser leg, but their faces were so alive with excitement that neither Julia nor Sarah could bring herself to admonish them. "The parade's started! It's coming!"

They darted off, with Bonnie and Emily running after them. Both Julia and Sarah hurried after the girls, afraid they would get lost in the crowd. They reached the street just as the parade came into sight. Luke joined them and lifted Emily onto his shoulders. Julia picked Bonnie up, but she still could not see well.

"I wanna go higher," the three-year-old complained.

"But sweetheart, this is as high as I can lift you."

"Here, let me." Julia turned. James was standing behind her. He held out his hands, and Bonnie went unhesitatingly into them. He placed her on his shoulders. She squealed with delight at being so high, able to see everything.

"Thank you." Julia's breath came and went unevenly. James was so close to her that she could smell the scent of his shaving soap. She tried to keep her eyes on the parade, but she couldn't stop herself from glancing back to James again and again. She enjoyed looking at his clean profile, at the white line of the collar as it cut across his neck and the way his hair curled over the edge of the collar in back. Some devil inside her urged her to reach out and slide her fingernails into those curls. She remembered the thick springiness of his hair.

James turned his head and Julia glanced away, afraid he would read her thoughts in her eyes. The last thing she wanted was for James to know how easily she would fall into his bed again. All he had to do was crook his finger, and she would go to him. It was sinful—and foolish. His lovemaking could bring her only shame and pain. She was no more the kind of woman James Banks could marry than she had been eleven years ago. He would want nothing from her but a brief, easy affair. A mistress. She didn't want to be that, not even for James. But she was terrified that she wouldn't be able to resist if he should ask her.

Julia was glad that James didn't linger with them after the parade was over, but wandered off to talk to other people. After the parade, there were speeches from the mayor and the Democratic candidate (the only candidate, since no one ever ran on the Republican ticket opposite him) for the state seat from their area, followed by the winner of the high school oratory contest last school year. The program ended with a half hour of patriotic songs sung by the combined choirs of the First Baptist and Main St. Methodist Churches.

Julia and Sarah remained at their table, watching the program from a distance. Neither of them had any interest in the speeches. It was more important to get Bonnie and Emily down for their naps on folded quilts beneath the tree. While the girls slept, Julia and Sarah chatted in low voices. They talked about the crops and Julia's job and their children, but neither of them spoke of what was uppermost in their minds.

They ate supper late, a casual meal of leftovers from the extensive lunch. Dusk fell, and the stifling heat dropped. The night insects began to whir, and the frogs started up over by the pond. The new gas lights around the park came on. Then the fireworks display lit up the sky with colors, and everyone who watched let out gasps of admiration.

All too soon it was over, except for boys setting off an occasional firecracker. Many of the families started toward home. Julia saw James leave with Anthea and thought with relief that he would not be there for the dance. She wouldn't have to see him with some other woman in his arms, circling around the floor.

The dance floor was a raised wooden platform built out from the bandstand, and all around it wires were strung from the corner posts, with brightly colored paper lanterns hanging on the wires. The candles inside the paper lanterns were lit, and the musicians took their place on the stage. They tuned their instruments as people began to gather on stage from all around the park. Luke turned toward Sarah, his eyes questioning. Julia could see the energy and excitement coursing in him, ready to burst its bounds in dancing. Julia looked at Sarah. There was an answering electricity in her, too. Sarah held out her hand, and Luke took it, and they walked to the platform. Julia thought they would have liked to run.

The first tune the band played was fast. Luke and Sarah joined a set of couples in the Texas Star. It was followed by a Virginia reel. But the next song was a waltz, and Luke pulled Sarah into his arms. They were only inches apart, and though their bodies didn't touch, Sarah could feel the heat emanating from Luke and see the drops of perspiration dotting his upper lip and forehead. His hand burned against the small of her back. His other hand curled around hers; she could feel every callus, every dip and curve. Sarah's breath was uneven, and she knew it wasn't entirely due to the fast-paced dances they had just finished.

Luke looked down at Sarah. He couldn't keep his eyes off her. Some of the tension inside him had been released as they whipped through the fast steps of the dances, but it hadn't burned off nearly enough steam. He felt as soaring and fiery, as explosive as the fireworks that had shot up earlier. He'd had a drink down by the pond with Jake Crowley and Stu Harper, but it hadn't really relaxed him, only unsnapped a few of the leashes he kept in control.

Sarah was beautiful. He wanted her. He looked at her lips. He knew those lips: each line and curve, the fullness, the softness, the taste. He wanted to taste her again, to kiss her right here on the dance floor. He wanted to eat her up. He thought of the first time they had danced together. It had been at a housewarming party at the Crowleys. He had drunk too much that time, and when they reached home, he had danced Sarah around the yard in the fierce white moonlight. That night they had made love for the first time. The memory didn't help the state of his nerves.

He looked at Sarah's smooth white brow, the twin curves of her dark eyebrows, the firm line of cheek and jaw. He knew her face more intimately than he knew his own. He'd spent almost four years memorizing it. Yet it was always fresh and beautiful to him. His eyes moved lower, to the shadowy triangle of flesh revealed by the open neck of Sarah's dress. A sheen of moisture glistened on her chest.

He thought of how her skin grew slick and damp when they made love. She was beautiful naked and gleaming, his sweat mingling with hers on her skin.

The scent of perfume rose from her, warmed by her body. It was dizzying, intoxicating. When they danced close to the lights, he could glimpse the soft, trembling tops of her breasts. He thought of them in his hands, pure white against his browned skin, the essence of softness. He wanted to feel their heaviness, to trace the pink brown circles of her nipples and watch them tighten for him. God, he was growing hard just thinking about it.

Once he had thought it would be enough to be married to Sarah. Then he had thought it would be enough to make love to her, but finally he had realized that he had to have her love as well. All of her—body, mind, soul, heart—that was the only thing that could really satisfy him. He had learned that once, and he was rediscovering it more and more painfully every day. No part of Sarah was enough. He had to have her all. And he couldn't.

Sarah glanced up at her husband. Luke's eyes glittered even in the dim light. He wanted her. She could feel it in the heat of his hand and see it in the fierce glow of his eyes. She knew the stamp of desire on Luke's face, and it was there now. Sarah smiled, unaware of the seductive triumph in the curve of her lips. But she heard the quick intake of Luke's breath, and it sent a fire licking through her abdomen.

Her hand slid up from his shoulder and curled around the back of his neck. His skin was tender there, soft against the hard bone and swelling musculature. He tightened; she could feel the muscles bunching beneath her hand and arm. Her fingertips brushed the soft edges of his hair. Sarah stared up into his eyes, a kind of challenge in her face. Once Luke would have answered the challenge by pressing her tightly against him and letting her feel the hard ridge of his desire. Once he might have pulled her from the dance floor into the darkness of the trees and kissed her until neither of them could think anymore.

But now he just continued to follow the steps, holding her the correct distance from him, and inside he grew tighter and tighter, like a clock wound up too far. Sarah saw the hunger in his face and felt the taut refusal of his body. She didn't understand it. Why was he torturing them both?

When the waltz was over, Luke stepped back from her, his breathing more labored than the dance warranted. "Sarah..."

"What?" She waited, her stomach beginning to knot in anticipation.

Luke drew a deep breath. "Nothing. Thank you for the dance."

"Luke." Sarah put her hands on his arms. Her touch was like fire to him. "Why won't you—"

"Sarah, please. Don't."

"I don't understand."

"I—would you mind if we left early tonight?"

"You don't want to dance?"

"Not anymore."

Sarah smiled dreamily. She thought she understood what he wanted. He didn't want to dance anymore because he wanted to be in bed with her.

Her smile went through him like a flood of molten iron, almost buckling his knees. He realized how foolish it was to run from the dance back to their home because he couldn't stand the beckoning sexuality of dancing with her. It was like jumping from the frying pan into the fire. At home they would be alone together in bed.

"Of course," Sarah said in a low voice. "Shall I ask Jennifer or Julia to take the children home with them?"

For a moment Luke couldn't speak because of the desire surging in him. He thought of being alone in the house with Sarah, something that hadn't happened since Emily was born. He thought of being able to make love to her in any room, doors open. Erotic images twisted in his head.

"Luke?"

"What? Oh. No. Better not. We'd, uh, just have to drive back in tomorrow and get them. Take too much time from the fields."

"Oh. I guess you're right." Her voice dropped with disappointment.

Luke swallowed, trying to ease his dry throat. He wanted to lead Sarah to the far side of the park, in the black shadows, and take her, hard and fast, half their clothes still on. He wanted to see her face melt with pleasure, feel her tremble uncontrollably beneath his hands. He wanted to hear the breathy little moans she uttered as he drove her higher. He wanted his tongue in her mouth. God, how he wanted that.

"Let's go." He took her by the hand and hurried off the dance platform, walking as if he were being pursued. But the devils that chased him were deep inside.

✳ Chapter 17 ✳

Julia watched Sarah and Luke dance, a smile playing on her lips. They were a handsome couple, and so much in love. Neither of them had looked anywhere but at each other while they danced. Julia hoped that meant that they had worked out whatever had been troubling them.

"Would you care to dance?"

Julia jumped, startled, and whirled. "James!"

"Julia."

She wished that just the sight of him didn't make her insides start to shake. Somehow, here in the warm darkness, they seemed much closer to the people they had been eleven years ago. "I thought you had gone home."

"I took Mother back to the house. She was getting tired. But I returned for the dance."

"I see." Then she *would* have the painful task of watching him dance with other women.

"Well?"

"Well, what?" She glanced up at him, confused.

"Would you care to dance with me?"

"Oh." Her heart skittered all over her chest. She didn't think she'd ever wanted anything as much. "Uh, yes. Yes, I'd like to."

James smiled and took her arm. The dress she wore had short puffed sleeves, and his fingers touched her bare skin.

She hoped he didn't feel the flood of heat that poured through her at his touch. They started toward the bandstand.

Halfway there they ran into Luke and Sarah. "Julia." Luke glanced awkwardly at Julia, then James, and back. "Uh, we'd decided to go home early. Would that be all right with you? I hate to make you leave the dance, but . . ."

"Oh." Julia struggled to keep the disappointment out of her voice. "No. That's fine."

James retained his hold on her arm. "Mrs. Dobson and I were just about to dance. I'll be happy to escort her home later, so that she can stay and enjoy the dancing."

Luke hesitated. He didn't want to leave Julia with Banks. But at the moment he felt torn in so many different directions, he couldn't think straight.

Sarah settled the issue for him. "Why, how nice! Then we won't have to spoil Julia's evening. Thank you."

"Yeah." Luke stared at the other man, his hard eyes reminding James that this time he wasn't dealing with an unprotected girl. "I'm sure you'll be very careful."

"Of course." Banks's voice was about as warm and friendly as Luke's. The two men nodded to each other, and James and Julia walked past them to the dance floor.

The fiddlers and guitarist were playing a slow, sad tune. A harmonica wailed. James drew Julia into his arms, and they began to move around the floor. Julia knew how to dance; Luke had taught her and he was probably the best dancer in the county. But in all the years since she had married Will Dobson, she had danced only once or twice, and she was afraid that she had forgotten how. But she hadn't. She moved easily in James's arms. He was a smooth dancer, and he held her exactly the proper distance from him. Julia knew with a certain amount of shame that she would have liked for him to hold her closer.

Julia looked up into James's face. She thought she could have gazed at him forever. The faint light highlighted the planes of his face and turned his eyes and hair dark as midnight. His mouth was firm and sharply etched. She remembered the feel of it against her lips two weeks ago, the hot lash of his tongue, the taste of him. Julia lowered her eyes, afraid he would read the desire there.

James was shaken by how good Julia felt in his arms. He

hadn't known there could be such pleasure in simply dancing with a woman. "We never danced together."

Julia's head came up. There was a wealth of memories
behind that statement, a reminder of all that they *had* done
together. They stared at each other, suddenly awkward.

A hundred questions pushed up inside James. Why had
she married Will Dobson? Had Julia ever loved him? Why
had she thrown him over without even a word of explanation? Had every word, every sound of passion she'd uttered
been a fake? He wanted to ask her. He wanted to take her
by the shoulders and shake her until she answered him. He
wanted to spew out how much he had loved her, how he had
hated her after she left, how his heart had been ripped out of
him. He wanted to kiss her roughly, consumingly.

He looked away and so did she. "Perhaps—perhaps I
ought to go now, after all," Julia murmured.

"No. Don't." He felt as if he would beg. "Stay for
another dance."

She stayed for three more and danced them all with him.
She would have liked to dance with him all night, but she
knew she had pushed the limits for gossip with four dances
with the same man. James knew that, too, and he didn't
protest when she said she must sit down.

He walked her back to the table where her family had sat
and took a seat on the bench beside her. Julia glanced down
at the foot of the tree. Bonnie was sound asleep on a quilt
beside Jennifer Harper's little boy. Julia smiled.

"Poor thing. I guess I better get her home." She stood up
and looked around for Vance.

"All right." James stood with her.

She turned to him. "You don't have to take us home.
We'll be fine."

"Walking alone at this time of night? Don't be silly."

"Nothing will happen to me here."

"I'm seeing you home."

Julia couldn't suppress a warmth in her chest at his
adamant words. "All right. Thank you."

Julia saw Vance and signaled to him. She started to reach
down and shake Bonnie awake, but James stopped her.
"Don't do that. I'll carry her." He bent and lifted the little
girl off the ground. Bonnie snuggled against his chest,

sound asleep, and the sight of James carrying her child filled Julia with tenderness.

He carried Bonnie to the buggy. Julia climbed into the front seat, and he laid the little girl in her arms. Vance hopped in beside her. James unclamped the chain and weight that hung from the horse's harness to keep him in place, stowed them in the buggy, and climbed in. He picked up the reins and clicked to the horse, and they started off.

It was a warm, damp night, softly seductive. The sky was black and very far away, the stars bright even here in town. The steady plop of the horse's hooves was lulling, and beside Julia, Vance drooped, his head sinking against her arm. Julia herself would have liked to lean her head against James's firm arm and rest. Forever.

When they reached the house, James carried Bonnie inside. Julia directed him to the girl's bedroom while Vance stumbled sleepily onto the screened-in porch, where he slept. They tucked Bonnie into bed. She slept soundly through the process. Julia looked up at James, sharing the intimacy of putting a child into bed. James laid his hand on Julia's back and slid it slowly down to her waist. Julia wanted to arch her body like a cat against his hand, but she suppressed the desire. She walked out of the room without looking at him.

James followed her. Julia went straight down the hall to the front door. She had to get him out of here. It was as if she must circumvent herself. She reached out to turn the doorknob. James laid his hand over hers, stopping her. Her fingers began to tremble beneath his, and she looked up at him. James's eyes were dark and intense. Julia couldn't move; she could only gaze at him.

His hand tightened on hers, and his other hand came up to her face. His fingers spread wide across her cheek. He leaned forward and kissed her. A long tremor ran through Julia, and she couldn't stop herself from kissing him back. Their tongues met and tangled. They kissed forever. He wrapped his arms around her, pressing her body into his.

He pulled his mouth away from hers and kissed her cheek and ears and neck. "So sweet," he mumbled, his voice thick with passion. "It's just like it was."

James lifted his head and stared down into her eyes. His

hands cupped her face, holding it immobile. His eyes were fierce and compelling. "Do you remember that, Julia? Do you remember how it was between us? How good it felt, or was that only me?"

"Of course I remember!" She was amazed that he could think she wouldn't. "How could I possibly forget? I've treasured it ever since. It was the most beautiful time of my life!"

"Then why?" His voice was laced with anguish and confusion. "Why did you leave? Why in the hell did you marry Will Dobson?"

Julia went cold and still. She had never thought to hear that kind of pain in his voice. "I—I had to. I was—" Her voice dropped. "I was carrying your baby. I had to marry."

His hands dropped away from her, and he stepped back, stunned. "You what?"

"I was pregnant."

"With my child?" James's face was suddenly pale, his eyes too dark. "My child!"

Julia nodded, her stomach twisting inside her.

"But why? Why did you marry *him*? Why didn't you tell me?"

Julia swallowed and looked away. In the face of his stunned pain, she felt suddenly guilty and small. "I was afraid that you'd think I was trying to force you to marry me. I thought you might be furious, even hate me for it. I didn't want it to end like that. It had been so beautiful."

"My God! So you married someone else? So you didn't even tell me I had a child?"

"I knew you wouldn't marry me. You couldn't. You were a Banks."

"Does that make me not human? Jesus Christ, Julie! I loved you! I'd told you that a million times. How could you think I would not marry you? I wanted to marry you. I planned to marry you. I loved you!"

Julia stared at him silently. She felt as though she'd opened a vein and her life blood was pouring out. Could she have been married to James all these years? Had she thrown away her future? "No. It was impossible. You couldn't have—your parents—"

"Damn my parents!" His eyes were blazing now. He

wanted to crash his fist into something, wanted to storm and rage. "I would have married you. But you didn't even love me enough to tell me. You didn't believe me, didn't trust me. Did you think everything I said was lies? That I'd said I loved you just to seduce you? Was that your opinion of me?"

Julia shook her head miserably, tears starting in her eyes. "No. I knew that you believed you loved me. But that didn't mean you would marry me. You couldn't have. I couldn't have been a doctor's wife."

"Why the hell not? Goddamn it, Julia!" He swung away, stiff with fury. "You broke my heart."

The tears spilled out and coursed down her cheeks. "Oh, Jimmy, no! You got over it. You were bound to get over it quick enough."

"Oh yeah, I got over you. After years of thinking about you, missing you, wondering why in the hell you'd married Will Dobson when you'd said you loved me! I couldn't see any reason for it except that you had lied to me, that you didn't really love me but had just used me to bring the man you wanted into line."

"No. My Lord, no! I didn't want Will!"

"You didn't want me, either. Not enough to tell me." His voice was low, and somehow his quiet fury was worse than when he had shouted. "How could you have kept my child from me! What happened to it?" He took a step toward her. "It couldn't be Vance; he's not old enough. Where's the baby that was mine?"

Julia drew a ragged breath. She looked away. "She's dead. She died of scarlet fever when she was a little less than two years old."

James simply stood and looked at her, dazed by her revelations.

"I never meant to hurt you." Julia was equally astounded by James's reaction. She would never have dreamed that he had loved her that much, that he had been heartbroken when she married another man. She had assumed that he would be hurt for a while, but that he would recover quickly. After all, there had been so many girls who had wanted him, girls of his own class whom it would have been proper for him to love. He had desired Julia, been infatuated with her, but she had never imagined that he wanted to marry her. "I wouldn't have hurt you for the world. I loved you."

"So you say." James gazed at her levelly. "Yet you robbed me of my wife and daughter. Is that love, Julie?"

"James." Tears poured from her eyes. She didn't know what to say.

He reached around her and opened the front door. He walked out of it and down the walk to his buggy without looking back.

"James." Julia watched him go, leaning against the door and crying. She had lost him all over again.

Sarah rode on the high wagon seat beside Luke, not saying a word. The two children were asleep in the back, stretched out on a quilt. She glanced at them and smiled. They were worn out. She was glad; she didn't want their childish chatter spoiling the mood.

She cast a sideways glance at Luke. He sat stiffly, staring straight ahead of him. He'd hardly looked at Sarah the whole ride out from town. Sarah didn't mind. His silence and avoidance of her were as clear a signal of his desire as if he had his hands all over her. He was taut with tension and very aware of her.

Sarah laid her hand casually on Luke's thigh. The hard muscle jumped beneath her palm, and she gave a tiny smile of satisfaction. Oh yes, he was aware of her.

Luke caught the little cat-in-the-cream smile on Sarah's face. It stirred him even more. She was teasing him, enticing him; she wanted him to lust after her so much he broke the bounds of his control. Such evidence of blatant desire in his proper Sarah always aroused him.

His hands tightened on the reins. He tried to blank out of his mind what would happen when they reached home, to ignore the clamoring in his nerves and the heavy need in his loins.

When they reached their house, Luke jumped down from the wagon, then reached up to help Sarah. She leaned out, putting her hands on his shoulders, and he placed his hands on her waist. He lifted her down, her body sliding slowly through his hands. His thumbs brushed the soft sides of her breasts. Even that brief touch speared him with desire. She was too close to him. He could smell the faint scent of her perfume and see the undisguised invitation in her clear hazel eyes.

Why did she want him when he had caused her such pain? Why didn't she protect herself against him, instead of leaving herself so open and vulnerable?

They carried the children upstairs to bed, then Luke returned to unhitch the team and let them loose in the corral. He added hay to their trough and checked their water, then stood for a moment, leaning against the corral fence, delaying his return to the house.

He ought to sleep in the other bedroom tonight. It was pushing his limits too far to lie in that bed with Sarah again. Maybe another man could do it, a gentleman like Stu Harper or James Banks. They could probably leave their wives alone in order to protect them from having children. Banks would no doubt find a loose woman to slake his sexual desires. But Luke was too loyal to Sarah to do that; hell, he didn't want any other woman but Sarah. And his blood didn't run cool enough to make it easy for him to stay away from her. Now here she was, acting seductive. It was too much. The best thing would be to remove himself from the danger.

Luke went upstairs with that purpose in mind. He would tell Sarah he was sleeping elsewhere. He stopped at the doorway to their bedroom.

Sarah was seated in front of her vanity table, dressed only in a chemise and petticoat, taking down her hair. Luke watched her. He couldn't speak. He couldn't move.

She pulled out the pins from her hair one by one and dropped them into a flat porcelain box. Her hair hung heavily as the pins released it, then slowly tumbled down altogether. Her hair was long, reaching to her hips, thick and buoyant from having been pinned up. Luke thought about sinking his fingers into her hair and combing through it, and fire danced in his abdomen. Sarah picked up her silver-backed brush and ran it through her hair. Slowly she ran it down the length of her hair, pulling the heavy mass out a little from her body, so that it settled back at the end of each stroke, crackling.

Once, when they were first married, Luke had stood and watched her brush her hair this way, every fiber of him charged with passion. But that was a time when he had made love to her only once, briefly. He hadn't known what it was like to bury his face in her hair and smell the faint scent of lavender that clung to it, to feel its silken texture against his skin. He hadn't known what it was like to have it spread across his chest like a soft, dark cloud, hadn't had it trail along his skin as she kissed him all over. Luke drew in his breath with a hiss.

Sarah looked up and saw her husband in the mirror. She smiled. She watched Luke's eyes drop down her body, taking in the soft tops of her breasts and the tightening of her dark nipples beneath the sheer cotton chemise. Her eyes grew dark and dreamy. She made no effort to put on her robe.

Luke walked over to her, pulled by dark, unreasoning desire. There was no thought to him, only need and hunger. Sarah rose, pushing back the stool upon which she sat, still watching his reflection as he drew closer. Their eyes met in the mirror.

He put his hands on her upper arms and bent his head to hers, burrowing his face in her hair. He breathed deeply of the scent, his heart pounding faster with each breath. He kissed her hair. He lifted it and kissed the tender skin of her neck underneath. Sarah's eyelids fluttered closed. Luke's lips skimmed up her neck to her ear. His breath was hot and rasping, sending shivers through her. His tongue touched the shell of her ear and slowly, lovingly traced its convolutions. His teeth teased delicately at her earlobe. Sarah's mouth opened slightly, her breath coming faster.

Luke laid his head beside hers and looked at their reflection in the mirror. His hands moved from her arms onto the plane of her upper chest. Sarah's eyes came open, and together they watched as he moved his hands over her chest onto the globes of her breasts. He cupped the full orbs, and his thumbs eased over the nipples until the nubs stood out thick and pointing against her chemise. He squeezed her nipples gently between his forefingers and thumbs, rolling them. A flush rose to Sarah's face, and her chest rose and fell with her quickening breaths. Luke smiled, loving to see the desire he could bring to her. He ignored the insistent little voice in his brain that told him he was wrong, wicked and wrong.

Luke's fingers moved lower on her body, gliding down her flat stomach and abdomen to her thighs, flattening the cotton of her chemise and petticoat to her skin. He moved back up to her waist and untied the string that held up her petticoat. He released it and let the garment slide to the floor. His hands went to her chemise and unfastened the buttons that held it together. He slid the wide straps off her shoulders, and they hung in dangling loops around her arms. He spread his fingers wide across her chest, his skin startlingly brown against her white flesh. Both of them watched in the mirror as his fingers moved down over her breasts, shoving the chemise off. Luke stared into the mirror, his mouth dry as dust. With his forefinger he circled one nipple, barely touching it, and watched it prickle.

He groaned and nuzzled her neck. "Oh, sweetheart. God, I'm about to burst, wanting you."

In response Sarah smiled and rubbed her hips provocatively against his groin. He grunted and sank his teeth lightly into her neck. His hand went to the cotton-covered V between her legs and pressed her even harder against him. His shaft was thick and hard under her bottom, and she felt its pulse as he rubbed her over him.

Luke gazed at Sarah's face in the mirror. It was soft and slack, her eyes lambent and hazy with longing. Her lips were parted slightly; her tongue came out to moisten them, leaving them shiny. She looked as though she were melting, lost in desire, and he loved the look. It made him hard and hungry, the animal of desire barely kept in check. His hand pushed into the cleft between her legs, and they parted slightly, giving him access. He rubbed rhythmically. Sarah stirred against him, her head lolling back on his shoulder, and gave a small groan of pleasure. The noise sent another spurt of heat to his groin. The cloth turned damp with the moisture of her desire, and Luke sucked in his breath sharply.

Sarah turned in his arms. "Don't tease me now. I want

you too much." Her arms went around his neck, and she stretched upward to kiss him.

Her kiss was full and deep, her tongue coming boldly into his mouth, caressing, coaxing his own tongue out. He thrust into her mouth then, hard and demanding, grinding his lips into hers as if he would consume her. Sarah pressed up into him, her breasts flattening against his chest, the nipples pricking at him. Luke's hands swept up over her body and grasped her hair, holding her head immobile, as though she might escape his predatory mouth. He rubbed his pelvis against hers, seeking release, seeking his home.

Sarah's hands slid down his back and dug into his buttocks. Luke made a noise deep in his throat, and backed her up against the vanity table, knocking over bottles and jars with a clatter. His knee went between her legs, parting them, and she rubbed her body up and down against his leg. He was wild with hunger for her, his hands moving everywhere on her body. He was desperate to have her, yet unwilling to stop their kisses or the exploration of his hands long enough to get rid of their clothing and move to the bed.

He lifted her, one arm beneath her hips, and walked her over to the bed. They fell onto the bed together, their hands tearing at their clothes as they kissed and caressed, unable to stay away from each other long enough to undress completely. They rolled across the bed, scattering their clothes across it and tossing them haphazardly onto the floor. Sarah unbuttoned his shirt but did not remove it; she was distracted by the sight of his firm, brown chest and kissed his nipples. Luke was struggling to remove her underwear but stopped— his fingers digging into her flesh—at the exquisite torment of her tongue circling his nipples. She bent to remove his boots, but at the sight of her bare back and hips, Luke had to pull her back up and kiss each knob of her backbone. Sarah unbuttoned his trousers but found more urgent things for her hands to do than push the garment down his legs.

Somehow they managed to get undressed, so that they lay full length against each other, luxuriating in their nakedness. Sarah explored Luke's body with her hands, rediscovering the different textures of the male body—the smooth flesh of his back, the furred skin of his thighs, the silken hair centering his abdomen, the satiny hardness of his manhood.

She dug her fingers into the fleshy mounds of his buttocks, delighting in his low, animal groan in response. She loved him with her fingers, lips, and tongue, and he writhed beneath her ministrations, so pounding with desire that he thought he would explode, yet unwilling to cut short her delightful caresses.

He laved her skin with his tongue, kissing and teasing at her flesh. He nipped her buttocks with his teeth and tenderly kissed the inside of her thighs. His fingers sought out the hot, slick folds of her femininity and the hard little button of flesh that made her groan and twist, seeking release. She panted his name, opening her legs to him. "Please, Luke, please."

Luke slid inside her then. She winced slightly as he entered her, and he paused, fighting to hold back the surging tide of his passion. Then her face relaxed and her legs encircled him, urging him on. He moved in, finding his hot, tight home. It felt so good that he quivered and went rigidly still to keep from exploding in her too soon. Sarah clamped her legs around him and circled her hips, and he began to thrust within her. He could not move gently, with careful consideration for her tender body. He could only pound into her mindlessly with his hard, hungry flesh. But Sarah didn't notice his lack of care. She was as hungry and desperate as he, her pelvis churning in rhythm with his, welcoming each deep thrust.

It had been so long that it came quickly for them both, sweeping them along on an uncontrollable tide. Luke groaned hoarsely, shuddering as he spilled his seed into her, and all around him Sarah melted into her own hot spasms, crying out at the long-missed pleasure. They clung together, lost for a moment in eternity, utterly one.

They lay together, spent and at peace, unwilling to separate themselves. Finally Luke rolled off her, but his arms were tight around her still. Sarah snuggled into the hollow of his shoulder, her hair fanning out over them, and they slept.

Luke awoke slowly, aware at first only of a deep sense of peace. Sarah slept curled up beside him, her back fitted against his chest and his arm flung across her. It was the way they usually slept. At least, it had been the way they usually slept; they hadn't done so in weeks now. Luke remembered that fact, and he was suddenly full awake. He remembered what he had done last night and why he shouldn't have. He bit back a soft groan.

Damn! Why had he given in to the temptation to enter Sarah's room last night? He should have gone to the other bed. She could be pregnant even now. His hand moved down to her abdomen and curled over it protectively. He was relaxed and content for once, more at ease than he had been at any time since Sarah lost the baby. But he had purchased his own satisfaction at the price of Sarah's safety. He was washed with guilt.

Luke kissed the top of Sarah's head softly and started to ease away from her body, but Sarah stirred and awakened, turning to him with a smile on her lips. Her hair was tangled, and it tumbled down over her bare shoulders, veiling the smooth white flesh. She looked warm and sleepy and well loved. Heat started anew in his loins.

"Good morning." Her voice brimmed with good humor.

Luke swallowed. "Good morning."

Sarah sat up, stretching, and the sheet fell down to her waist, exposing her breasts, covered now only by the curtain of her hair. It was worse than no cover at all, revealing as much as it hid and letting her nipples peek through coyly.

"Isn't it a beautiful morning?" Sarah flipped her hair back over her shoulders, without shyness with him.

"Yes." Luke looked quickly away and concentrated on the far wall. "It's time we should be up."

"Why? It's Sunday."

"Emily."

Sarah smiled. "Cal will take care of her."

There was nothing Luke wanted more than to lie down and spend a few extra minutes holding Sarah. But that would lead to other things, and it would be disastrous. "Church."

"It's still early yet." Sarah ran her hand lightly down his arm. His muscles turned to iron at her touch. "You know, one would almost think that you didn't want to stay here with me."

"Oh, Sarah," he groaned and sat up, moving away from her hand. "I want to stay with you. But I can't."

"Luke . . ."

"No." He swung out of bed and stood up. He found the trousers he'd discarded so hastily the night before and pulled them on, as though they would afford him protection from his own desires.

"What is it?" Sarah frowned, watching him. "What's the matter?"

Luke turned back to face her. "What I did last night was wrong. I'm sorry. I shouldn't have allowed it to happen. I was . . . weak. But it won't happen again. I promise you. I'll start sleeping in the other room."

Sarah started. "Wrong! What are you talking about?" Suddenly she felt naked and embarrassed, and she pulled the sheet up over her torso, jackknifing her knees and huddling into herself. Tears started in her eyes, and she dropped her gaze down to the sheet. "You think it was wrong for us to make love?"

"It was criminal of me."

When Sarah had awakened, she had felt happy and free of the sorrows that had haunted her for the past few weeks. At last she felt there was hope for the future. But now, at Luke's words, her world crumbled down around her ears once more. Sarah couldn't stop the tears that overflowed her eyes and rolled down her cheeks. "Why? Because I lost the baby? Do you hate me for losing your son?"

Luke stared at her, astonished. "What? No, of course not! How could I hate you for that? It wasn't your fault. It was mine! I was responsible for our son's death. I was to blame for the anguish you suffered. That's why I hate myself for taking you last night and why I won't do it again. I won't let you suffer like that again."

Sarah's head snapped up. She wiped at her tears with the palm of her hand. "I should have known you would blame yourself. Why? How are you responsible for my losing the baby?"

"You know why." Luke's voice was low and tormented. "Because I slept with you that night. The doctor had told us not to; he said it would hurt you and the baby. But I was so hot for you, so selfishly, damnably lustful that I ignored his warnings. I took you anyway.''

''It wasn't lust! And you didn't 'take' me. We made love.''

''What difference does it make how you term it? I made love to you, and two days later the baby came two months early. I caused it. It was because of me you almost died, because of me that you bled and bled and were wracked with pain. Don't you understand? How can you possibly not hate me? How can you even stand for me to touch you?''

Sarah's throat closed with unshed tears. ''Oh, Luke. You're so hard on yourself. You always are. It's not a question of my 'standing' for you to touch me. I want you to; I long for it. I've been going crazy the past few weeks wondering why you wouldn't.''

''Sarah, you're too good, too generous—''

''Nothing of the kind. I just love you. Look. I don't hate you because there is no reason to hate you. It wasn't your fault. Maybe you're right, and it was because of that night we made love. But you weren't the only one involved, you know; I was equally to blame.''

''I gave in to temptation, like I did last night. I invaded your body. I was wickedly selfish, thinking of nothing but my own desire.''

''Who do you think did the tempting? If you were wicked and selfish, so was I. If you were lustful, so was I. Luke, you didn't invade my body. I invited you. I welcomed you.''

Luke let out a low moan and turned away from her. God, even her warm, openly desirous words made him stiff and aching again. He crossed his arms over his chest like a man in pain and went to the window. He stared out blindly. ''You deserve a better man,'' he told her in a stifled voice. ''A moral man, one who'll protect you first instead of indulging himself.''

Sarah jumped out of bed and followed him. ''There isn't a better man!'' she snapped. ''And if there were, I wouldn't want him. I want you. Do you think I wish you were any different from what you are? I don't.'' She laid her hands on his arms and slid them downward. His flesh quivered beneath her touch. "Yes, you're a healthy, lustful man. I like that." She kissed his back.

"Sarah, don't." He moved away. "I was irresponsible. I shouldn't have slept with you that night."

"You're right. We shouldn't have. But we did, and it's over and done with. There's nothing we can do about it now, except do better next time. When I'm pregnant again—"

"No!"

"When I'm pregnant again," she went on, ignoring his hoarse cry, "we'll follow the rules to the letter. But you can't change what happened by denying us both the pleasure of our bed now."

"I can change the future. I can make damn sure it doesn't happen again."

"But I'm not pregnant now. Why—"

He whirled. "I hope to God you're not! And I don't intend for you to be again. Even if you don't lose another baby, I won't let you go through the anguish of birth again to have my child. I'm not like my father. I care for you more than I desire you, more than I want to please myself. I won't murder you by making you bear my children. I refuse!"

"Luke!" Sarah started toward him, hands outstretched, but he stopped her with a look.

"No! I won't sleep with you again. I swear it." He turned and left the room.

Sarah slapped her hand against the wall. "Damn!" Why did Luke always take all the guilt, all the blame for everything upon himself? Why did he think he had to be perfect? He was going to ruin both their lives by trying to protect her from himself, when he was the last thing she needed to be protected from! She threw herself down on the bed and sobbed her heart out.

* Chapter 18 *

Julia didn't go to church the next day. She couldn't bear even the thought of seeing James, let alone perhaps having to talk to him and Anthea. The children were glad of a chance to stay home and play, so she let them run out in the backyard while she sat in the kitchen, keeping an eye on them and thinking.

She couldn't stop thinking. James said he had truly loved her. He said he would have married her. She wondered if he really would have, or if it was just the rosiness of memories speaking, untempered by the force of reality. Would he have stood up to his mother and father, risking their wrath and perhaps endangering his medical career? Would he have accepted her pregnancy without anger or resentment or suspicion? She wasn't sure he would have, that the boy would have done then what the man would now. And yet . . .

What if he would have married her? What if she had thrown away a life with James? Her life would have been so different. She would have worked with James, been the loving wife waiting up for him when he came in worn out from saving or losing a life, as she had dreamed about. She would have known his kisses and his searing, loving touch instead of the brutal pawings of Will Dobson. There wouldn't have been hunger and want for her children. There wouldn't have been loneliness and emptiness for her. Pamela might even have lived . . .

But no. She pulled herself back from the direction her mind was taking. Things had happened the way they had, and there was no use wondering what might have been. She had to remember that she wouldn't have had Bonnie and Vance if she had married James, and she couldn't wish for

that. She had done what she did, and her life had taken the
course it had. She couldn't go back, and it was too late to
cry over it.

Still, Julia couldn't get rid of a feeling of guilt about what
she'd done to James. She had never thought about what had
happened from James's point of view. She hadn't considered
that he might want to know about the baby, that he had a
right to know. She had deprived him of a family for all these
years. She hadn't realized it at the time, of course; she had
assumed that he would forget her quickly, that he would
marry and have children. But now she realized that she had
wronged him. He hadn't gotten to see Pammy; he'd never
known the joy and pride of watching her crawl or walk or
talk for the first time. She had given him pain and sorrow;
she had robbed him of his daughter. That had been cruel
and unthinking of her, and she regretted it bitterly.

Poor James. Her eyes filled with tears, thinking of him
and his loss. She couldn't undo what she had done; she
could never make it up to him. He must despise her for it.
He probably would never want to see her again. Tomorrow,
when she went to work, she would make it easy for him and
tell him that she was quitting.

James, too, couldn't stop thinking about Julia's revela-
tion last night. He was in a black mood all day, not
accompanying Anthea to church and barely speaking to her
at dinner after she returned. They sat in the front parlor, as
they usually did on Sunday afternoon, but they had little
conversation. James was either restlessly moving about the
room and staring out the window or sitting in his chair,
brooding. When Maida McPherson and her daughter came
to call, he jumped up and left the room.

After the callers left, Anthea sat for a moment, thoughtfully working on her embroidery. Finally she stuck the
needle into the cloth and went up the stairs to James's
room. He was sitting in his room with the door open, a book
lying unread in his lap, and staring blackly at the floor.

Anthea tapped lightly on the door frame. "James?"

He glanced up. "Hello, Mother."

"May I talk with you for a moment?" She had been a formally raised woman. She wouldn't have dreamed of going uninvited into his room and, indeed, she felt a little awkward being in a grown man's bedroom at all, even if he was her son.

"Of course." He stood up politely.

"Why don't we go into my sitting room?"

He followed her down the hall into the small room adjacent to Anthea's bedroom, where she liked to sit most of the day. She took a seat beside the window where her frame of needlepoint stood, and James sat in the straight-backed chair opposite her. He looked restless and resigned and as if he'd rather be any place but there.

"I like to think that I am not the sort of mother to pry," Anthea began. "I suppose that's always what one hears right before a person pries."

James smiled faintly. "No, you never pry."

"I've held my tongue for quite awhile, but I—I'm worried about you. You seem unhappy."

"I'm in a black mood today. It happens. Nothing for you to worry about."

"You forget; I've known you for thirty years; I know your black moods. This is more. It's been building up for weeks. It's something to do with Mrs. Dobson, isn't it?"

He glanced at her, startled. "What makes you think that?"

"Come now, James," she returned tartly. "Do you think I'm blind? Or simply stupid? How could I not see that there is more between you and your assistant than a working relationship?"

"There is nothing going on between us. Julia is a good woman."

"How quick you are to jump to her defense. I wasn't implying anything bad about Mrs. Dobson. Quite the contrary, I rather like her. But I've seen the way you look at her, and she at you. I've watched you mooning about ever since she came to work here. Last night you hustled me home obnoxiously early, then returned to the park to dance with Mrs. Dobson."

"I'm sure that inveterate gossip Mrs. McPherson was happy to report to you on each dance, too."

Anthea's lips quirked up. "She did happen to mention

that you danced four times with Mrs. Dobson and with no other young woman. She also pointed out that you left early to take Mrs. Dobson home.''

''I hope you put a scotch to her rumors.''

''My dear boy, of course I showed not the least interest or concern, but it would take a force far stronger than I to shut Maida McPherson's mouth. But I'm not interested in Maida's gossip. I'm merely pointing out that it's obvious (and not just to me) that you have a particular interest in Julia Dobson. What I want to know is why is it making you so unhappy? I hate to see you like this. I want to help you.''

''No one and nothing can help me.''

''Not even a listening ear?''

James sighed. ''No. It's not the sort of thing—''

''I'm sure that I have heard things that would make your hair curl, and I haven't fainted. Gentility is not the same thing as ignorance.''

''I don't want you to—think badly of Julia.''

''Why would I think badly of her? Did she break your heart?''

He glanced up, startled.

''I have had some experience with the world, James, and I'm not stupid. I saw your sadness years ago, and I've seen the way you act around Julia. It didn't take much to guess that they were connected. Have you loved her all these years?''

He made an impatient gesture with his head. ''I don't know. I swear, I don't know. I thought I had recovered from the heartbreak long ago, but when I saw her again—'' He sighed. ''I don't know whether I never got over her or if I just fell in love all over again. I don't even know if it's love. I feel such anger toward her, such sadness and such—'' He stopped, his gaze flickering away from her. ''Er, other things.''

''Yes,'' Anthea put in dryly. ''I can well imagine what 'other things.' Yet, despite this anger and sorrow, you want to protect her. You're concerned that I might think ill of her.''

''She had a hard life. She wasn't raised as you were. Her family—''

"I know what the Turners were like. Yet even the youngest oy didn't turn out so badly."

"They're good people inside. Luke had his reasons, that me he hit me."

"His sister?"

James nodded, not looking at her.

"Was she—"

"Yes. Yes! And I was the father."

"Oh, James."

He looked at her entreatingly. "It wasn't like you think. he wasn't bad or easy. I was to blame. She—well, she oved me. Or so I thought."

"Why didn't you tell us? Why didn't you marry her?"

"I didn't know!" His eyes widened with shock. "Can you onestly think I'd desert a woman who was carrying my aby? A woman I loved?"

"No. I don't think that. But I don't understand what appened."

"I didn't, either, until yesterday. At the time I had no idea ulia was . . . with child. One day I went to her farm, and he wasn't there. Her father told me she'd married Will Dobson."

"I see."

"She didn't tell me! I had no idea. Even when Luke beat ne up I just thought he had found out about Julia and me nd was furious with me for leading her astray. I was naive. : never occurred to me that that was why she married Dobson. Or maybe I was simply too full of my own hurt to ink about her."

"Why didn't she tell you?"

"I don't know!" His voice was agonized. "Last night I sked her why she left like that, why she had married Dobson, and she told me about the baby. I couldn't believe ; I couldn't understand it. She said she knew I wouldn't arry her. She said you and Dad wouldn't have let me, even ' I'd wanted to. She was afraid I would think she was trying o force me to marry her. She didn't trust me! She didn't elieve in me enough to know that I would stand up to my arents for her. I loved her; I wanted to marry her, and she idn't trust me. She didn't love me enough."

Unshed tears glinted in his eyes, and he stared down at

his hands, locked together. "How could she have done that
Mama? I loved her. She yanked my heart right out of me
All these years, and I never knew I had a little girl."

"A little girl. But who—where—"

"She died." His voice rasped. "She died when she was
little more than a baby. If only Julie had married me . . ."

"Stop it! You aren't God; you don't know that the child
would have lived if Julia had married you. Perhaps it would
have, and perhaps not. That's too hard a burden to lay on
Julia. Too easy for you to say."

James closed his eyes. "You're right. I shouldn't say it.'
He sighed. "But I feel betrayed by her all over again
Betrayed in a different way."

"I'm sorry." Anthea reached across and laid her hand on
her son's clenched hands. "The mistakes we make always
seem to come back to haunt us."

"Why couldn't she have trusted me?"

"James, I'm going to say something to you, and I hope
you won't get angry. But . . . did you ever think that maybe
Julia had reason?"

His head came up and he stared at her in shock. "Reason
not to trust me?"

"Reason to think you wouldn't marry her. To think you
would be angry with her for getting pregnant. Now, before
you blow up, listen to me: Julia came from a family that no
one in their right mind would want to marry into, and she
knew it. She knew what her place in society was, and what
yours was, and there was very little hope that the two of
them could ever meet."

"But I loved her! She knew how much I loved her."

"A lot of young men love easily. You know the reputation
her brothers and father had. I suspect that Julia knew a lot
more of the cold, hard realities of life than you did at that
time. She didn't know any romantic, worthy young men like
you. I'm sure she never dreamed that there was any way
that she could have you, except in her bed. And what did
you do to change her mind?"

"What do you mean?"

"I mean, you slept with her without benefit of marriage
That didn't show respect for her. You kept her a secret from
your father and me, and that didn't show respect for her

either. Maybe she knew that you desired her, that you even thought you loved her. But you gave her no reason to think that you respected her enough to marry her. You didn't show her that you thought she was good enough to be your wife. All you showed was that you thought she was the kind of woman you could sneak around and take to bed.''

James stared at Anthea, horrified. ''It wasn't because I didn't respect her! I wanted her so much I didn't think about anything else. I was crazy in love with her; I was—you can't understand.''

''What? That you were a young man whose blood was so hot you didn't think about what was right or what was best for Julia? Oh, I understand that, all right. Maybe it's even excusable. But can't you see why it would make Julia think you wouldn't marry her? A young man introduces the girl he wants to marry to his parents; he doesn't hide her from them.''

''I wanted to keep her to myself! I didn't want to have to share her. I didn't want to spoil it. Hell, I just didn't think!''

''Tell me truthfully, James, weren't you at least a little bit ashamed of her?''

''No! How can you say that?''

''It seems to me that there must have been more reason than you said for carrying on a secret affair. You must have been embarrassed or scared to tell us, or something.''

''I loved her!''

''I know you did.''

James rubbed his hands slowly over his face and up into his hair. ''Oh, God. I did love her. I wasn't ashamed of her. I thought she was the most beautiful girl in the world.'' He sighed. ''But I didn't want you to know. I was afraid you would disapprove of her. If I had told you and Dad about Julia, I figured you would argue with me and try to keep me from seeing her. I didn't want you all interfering with Julia and me. It was so beautiful, so easy.''

James rose and walked to the window. ''That was awful, wasn't it? I never realized it until now. I didn't think about it then. I just acted. I was a coward. I guess Julia saw that more clearly than I.''

''You weren't a coward,'' Anthea retorted staunchly. ''You were simply young. It was a natural reaction for any boy your age. You were afraid we wouldn't approve, and you were probably right. At that time, no, I can't imagine my thinking that the Turner girl would be a proper mate for you. I would have raised a huge fuss and probably forbidden you to see her. Infatuation, I would have called it, or perhaps worse. It's not unusual for a nineteen- or twenty-year-old boy to hide something like that from his parents. But remember that Julia was even younger than you. Yes, she was wrong to withhold that information from you, but you weren't entirely blameless, either. She probably did the best she could, just as you did. It doesn't mean that she didn't love you or that she wanted to hurt you. But she was no doubt frightened and confused; she didn't know what to do.''

''And I hadn't given her any reason to think that I would help her, had I? I'd acted like any rich boy from town, out looking for a good time.''

''Don't be too harsh on yourself.''

''How can I not be?'' James leaned his head against the window frame. ''She must have felt so alone and scared. I was furious with her, and all the time she was in trouble. I didn't even think about what she might be going through, what sort of pain she might be in. Last night, when she told me, I blew up at her. Once again, all I could think about was myself.''

He turned away from the window. ''Excuse me, Mother. I have to go see her. I have to apologize.'' He strode across the room and paused at the door. ''Thank you.''

Anthea smiled. ''Once I would have wanted only a girl from a proper family for you. Seeing your loneliness the last few years, now all I want is for you to be happy.''

James shook his head. ''I don't know if that's possible.''

''It is, if you want it enough.''

When Julia answered the knock at the front door and found James standing on her porch, her heart sank. She knew he must have come to tell her that he no longer wanted her in his office. She stood with her hand on the door, looking at him, not quite sure what to do.

"Dr. Banks."

"Don't you think this formality is a little absurd at this point?" he asked.

"I don't know what else to call you."

"James. Jim. Jimmy. I answer to any number of things."

"All right. James."

"Could I—do you think I could come in for a minute?"

"Yes, of course. I'm sorry."

Julia led him into the front parlor. She sat down on the edge of one of the chairs, and he sat on the couch across from her, equally stiff and uncomfortable.

"Where are the children?" he asked after a moment of silence.

"Playing in back. They love it out there." Julia bit her lip. She shouldn't have said that, not if James was here to tell her she would have to leave the office and this house.

"I'm glad. I enjoyed playing here when I was a child." He paused. He had taken off his hat when he entered the house, and now he held it in his hands, turning it around and around, watching the movement.

"You don't need to tell me," Julia said softly. "I understand."

James glanced up, surprised. "What?"

"That it wouldn't suit . . . us working together anymore. It would make you uncomfortable, and me, as well. I was planning to tell you tomorrow that I will look for other employment."

"You're quitting?" He looked amazed, and not pleasantly so.

"Isn't that what you came to tell me? That you didn't want me to—"

"No! Not at all. Of course, if you prefer not to work for me, I can't stop you. I can understand why you wouldn't want to, after the way I acted last night. That's why I came here today—to apologize for what I said last night. I had no right to say those things. It was cruel and selfish of me. Not the first time I've been that way with you."

"No, don't say that," Julia put in quickly, her heart squeezing at the sorrow and guilt in his eyes. "You've always been most kind to me."

He smiled faintly. "It's like you to say that. But it isn't

true. My words were harsh last night. I was hurt and angry, but that didn't give me the right to take it out on you.''

"No, you were right. I never thought about it—that I was depriving you of the chance to know your child. I didn't mean to hurt you. I see now that it would have been better to tell you and let you decide what you wanted, instead of assuming.'' Tears sparkled in her eyes. ''It was just that I was scared of what you'd say. I hated for it to end bitterly, when it had been so beautiful.''

James swallowed hard, but it didn't get rid of the lump in his throat. He wanted to reach out and cup Julia's delicate face in his hands, to smooth away the tears and the lines of worry in her face. ''I'm glad you still think it was. I'm surprised. I behaved badly. I was young and foolish. I loved you, but I didn't act as I should have. I seduced you, and that was the act of a scoundrel.''

"No.'' Color tinged Julia's cheeks. ''You didn't have to seduce me. I wanted it to happen.''

"I should have waited until we were married. Then none of this would ever have occurred. You were so beautiful, and I wanted you so much. I couldn't wait. I remember sitting in my room at school, trying to study, and thinking about you, thinking about you, until I was practically crazy.'' He looked away. There was silence. He cleared his throat. ''Anyway, I apologize for the way I acted then, and I apologize for what I said last night. I was in the wrong. I can understand if you don't want to work for me any longer, but I'd like you to stay, if you can bring yourself to.''

Julia wanted to cry. She wanted to grab his abused hat from his hands and toss it aside and cover his face with kisses. Dear God, how much she still loved him! Her voice trembled a little as she answered him, ''I'd like to stay.''

"Good.'' He looked up at her and smiled. He would have liked to go down on his knees in front of her and kiss her hands and face, but he was afraid to spoil the delicate balance between them. There was no reason to think she still felt anything for him. No reason to think she ever would. Their love was in the past, and he wasn't sure how he felt, let alone how she did.

"I'll see you tomorrow.'' James didn't know what else to say. He had no excuse to linger. He stood up, and so did

Julia. She walked him to the door. James lingered for a moment in the open doorway. "Julia . . ."

"Yes?"

"What was her name?"

She knew immediately whom he meant; she didn't have to ask. "Pamela."

"Was she pretty?"

"Very. She looked like you. I'm sorry that you never got to see her. She was a wonderful child."

"Where is she buried?"

"Near Gideon, where we lived."

"I'd live to see her grave. Would you take me there?"

"Of course."

"Thank you." He looked at her for a moment, then nodded once and walked away.

Julia watched him go. She felt relieved and glad and sad and uncertain, all at once. She didn't know what was going to happen with them. She wasn't even sure what she wanted to happen.

James and Julia spent the next week working together in restrained formality, a little distant and uncertain. What they had discovered about each other and themselves had shaken them.

They drove out to Gideon the following Saturday. James picked Julia up in his buggy early in the morning. Most of the way to the gravesite they rode in silence. The closer they got, the more Julia's nerves clanged inside her. When she had left here a few months ago, she had wondered if she would ever see her daughter's grave again. Now she was returning to it with James. She was afraid that the anger James had felt against her would come again when he saw Pammy's grave. Yet at the same time she couldn't deny the pleasure she felt at being alone with him like this. Both the feelings were equally disturbing.

Julia directed him to the Antioch cemetery. When they reached it, he came around and helped her down from the buggy, then took her arm. Julia walked with him to Pamela's grave. James looked down at the small grave with its simple wooden marker. He wasn't sure what he felt. The child buried here was his flesh and blood, the fruit of his seed. Yet he had never known her. He didn't even know what she had looked like or how her voice had sounded. He'd never heard her laugh or seen her tears. The ache he felt seemed more for that loss than for anything else.

"What was she like?"

Julia smiled, remembering. "She was a special child. Beautiful, like an angel, like a gift from God. She had dark brown hair, just as thick and straight as yours, and big, soulful brown eyes. When her eyes filled up with tears, I wanted to cry, too, and when she smiled, it turned the whole world bright. I loved her so much. If only I'd told you, if only I hadn't married Will, maybe she would still—"

"No!" James interrupted fiercely, grabbing her by the shoulders and pulling her to him. His arms sheltered her. "Don't say that. You can't second-guess fate. What happened, happened. It wasn't your fault that she died. She might have died anyway, if not in that way, then in another way, at another time."

Tears spilled out of Julia's eyes, and she clung gratefully to James. "I was so wrong not to tell you. I'm sorry."

"Hush." His hand smoothed down her back. "I don't blame you. I just wish I had been there with you, to share your sorrow, to comfort you." He kissed the top of her head. "I'm sorry you had to bear it all alone."

Julia leaned against him, her eyes closed, soaking in the comfort of his hard masculine strength. If only he had been there . . . "She was so sweet." She began to tell him stories about Pamela—the precious things she'd done, the funny, lisping way she talked. The pain receded, and gradually Julia moved away from him, until they were standing separately, the sorrow once more in the past.

"I'm glad you brought me here," James told her. "Thank you. I thought—if you don't mind—that I might have another marker put up, a small one in white marble, with her name on it."

"And a lamb." Tears sparkled in Julia's eyes, but they were tears of happiness and gratitude now. "That's what I wanted for her, but we didn't have the money. Thank you. It would be very kind of you."

"It's not kindness. She was my daughter." He looked back at the small grave. "You know, I never thought much about children. What they'd be like, whether I even wanted any. But now I . . ." He drew in a breath. "I think about how much I've missed. I want children."

He glanced at her. He knew that what he wanted was children of her body.

"You should have them." Julia didn't look at him. It pierced her heart to think of another woman bearing his children.

James wished she would look at him. He wished he knew what she was thinking. He wondered if she had any feeling left for him after all that had happened. He wondered if she could love him again, if she would even think of marrying him. It was what he wanted. Suddenly everything that had seemed so confused and murky the past week became crystal-clear. Except for what Julia thought, what Julia wanted.

He moved to the side, thinking, his hands clasped behind his back. He glanced down at the ground in front of him and saw Will Dobson's grave. It was fresh, the earth still raw, the marker legible. He didn't like to think of Will Dobson. Most of the time it was easy to block him out of his mind. He'd never seen the man; Julia didn't speak of him; there were no reminders of his presence. But now, with his grave right there, James couldn't keep him out.

"Did you love him?" His voice was low.

"What?" She glanced at him and saw where he was looking. "Oh. No."

"Not at all?"

"No. Not in any way."

Her statement only partially eased the tension in his chest. "Did he know?"

"That Pamela wasn't his? Yes. I told him before we married; I couldn't go into marriage with a lie like that."

"Yet he married you anyway."

"Yes."

"He must have loved you very much." The idea burned in him; he didn't like to think of another man's loving Julia. Even worse was the thought of another man taking care of her, helping her when she needed it, instead of him.

Julia shrugged. "I don't know. He wanted to marry me. He was obsessed with it. But I don't know if it was love or just . . ."

Her voice trailed off. James knew what she didn't say: just desire, just lust. He knew what Dobson had felt; he'd felt it often enough himself. Just last night he'd dreamed about Julia and awakened stiff and throbbing. But Julia hadn't been there in the bed with him when he woke; with Dobson, she had. Revulsion crawled in him at the thought of the other man's touching her, taking her, having the right to claim her body. But even worse he hated knowing that she had had to submit to him, even without love.

"Was he good to you? Kind?" Did he hurt you? Force you? Hit you? The words screamed inside him, but he couldn't say them.

"He wasn't a bad man." Julia saw the strange look in James's eyes, the unaccustomed wildness, and she didn't want to tell him the truth. He would feel too guilty, too angry, but with no one at whom to lash out.

"What does that mean?"

Julia shrugged. "That he was like most husbands, I guess."

"Like your brother is with his wife?"

"Like Luke? Oh, no. No. Luke is so . . . sweet, so loving."

"And Dobson wasn't."

"No. James, must we talk about this?"

He reached out and grasped her arm. "Yes. I have to know. Did he take it out on you that the child wasn't his? Did he yell at you or—or raise his hand to you?"

Julia pressed her lips together tightly and turned partly away. "Sometimes he yelled, of course. He got angry. Every once in a while he would . . ."

"Would what?"

"Hit me."

The color washed out of James's face. "Oh, Julia." His hands went out to her, but he didn't quite know what to do. They settled lightly on her arms. "I'm sorry. God, I'm sorry."

"It happens. He wasn't so bad. Daddy was worse."

"Sweetheart." He wrapped his arms around her from behind, pulling her back against his chest. His cheek rested upon her hair. "I wish I could take all that out of your life. I wish I could go back and change what happened."

"You can't. Nobody can." She slid her arms over his. It felt so good and warm in the circle of his arms. "Like you said awhile ago, what happened, happened. We can't go around thinking how it could have been different, or what we should have done."

He kissed her hair. "I can't bear to think of him hurting you." His fingers lightly stroked down her cheek. "Of that lovely skin being bruised. I can't even stand to think of him touching you, sleeping with you."

"I slept with him because it was my duty. But he never touched me inside like you did. I never made love with him."

"Julia." The word was a whisper, a sigh. He rubbed his cheek against her hair. Her words stirred him. He wanted to kiss the delicate pink shell of her ear, so temptingly close. He wanted to bury his face in the flesh of her neck. He wanted to touch her all over, and with his touch obliterate the memory of Will Dobson's hands on her.

But they were standing in a cemetery, beside the graves of their daughter and Julia's husband, and he could not. She was not his. He didn't know if she ever would be. He didn't even know if she would welcome his touch or resent it.

Again he kissed the top of her head, then let his arms fall away from her. He stepped back. Julia felt empty at the loss of his arms, but she said nothing. She smiled at him a little awkwardly. "Well. Shall we go now?"

He nodded, and they walked back to the buggy. This time he did not take her arm as they walked.

They left the cemetery and drove into Gideon, and there they stopped at the little café on the square to eat lunch. Julia hadn't eaten in a restaurant since that time years ago when she and James had first met. She was delighted at the treat of having a meal served to her. James watched her enjoyment, smiling, and wished he could have given her things like this for years. He watched her hands, delicate and white, as she held the utensils. He watched the fork carry a bite of food to her mouth and saw her lips close over it. He gazed at her smile and the sparkle of her eyes. And he wanted very much to pull her over into his lap and kiss her. He wondered what she would say if she knew what he was thinking.

After they ate, they drove back to Willow Springs. James's hands were lax on the reins. He enjoyed sitting next to Julia like this, alone and free from the rest of the world, and he had no desire for it to end.

When at last they did reach Julia's house, she invited him in for a glass of lemonade. James accepted with alacrity. He followed her into the kitchen and watched her while she made the drinks, even though she protested that he sit in the more comfortable parlor. He preferred the cozy intimacy of her kitchen and seeing her perform the simple domestic chore. He thought of her being his wife, preparing his food and drinks for him. He thought of her small hands on his clothes, on his furniture, making his bed—their bed. Heat started deep in his abdomen.

He glanced around, searching for a safe topic to think about. "Where are the children?"

"Luke and Sarah took them out to the farm. They'd been wanting to stay out there again, and it seemed like a good opportunity, with me being gone all day."

They were alone in the house. The thought increased the heat inside him. It wasn't proper to be alone in the house with an unmarried woman. He could understand why; it led to all sorts of licentious thoughts. He wondered what would happen if he kissed her. Probably better not to think about that.

He wished he knew how she felt about him. He wanted to pour out his feelings to her, but he was reluctant, too, afraid she would find his love ridiculous after all these years.

Julia brought the pitcher of lemonade to the table and poured each of them a glass. "Would you like to sit in the parlor?"

"I like it fine here."

"All right." They sat and sipped at their lemonade, neither of them saying anything. Julia was as aware as James of the intimacy of their situation. They were alone. There were no parents, no children, no servants. Only the two of them, and the memory of the love they had shared long ago.

Julia looked at James. Her forefinger slowly, rhythmically

circled the top of her glass. Little beads of sweat formed on the glass like balls of crystal and rolled down its smooth sides. James watched Julia's hand, mesmerized by the movement of her finger on the glass. He could feel it on his own skin, cool and wet, arousing him with delicious circles. He gripped his glass tightly and tried to think of something else. Something besides the kiss they shared weeks ago; something besides the hot blood gathering in his loins; something besides Julia's mouth and breasts and legs.

Julia saw his face change, saw the faint slackening, the heaviness of his mouth, and the darkening of his eyes. Her hand trembled on the glass. "James."

He touched her, his fingers sliding down hers and along the back of her hand to her wrist, feather light. Sensations raced from Julia's hand through her body, sparkling and light, delightfully shivery. His thumb inched back up hers. Desire pulsed through him. Her skin was so soft and inviting. His fingers curled around her hand and brought it to his mouth. He kissed the back of her hand, his eyes closing at the aching sweetness of tasting her flesh again.

His voice shook. "I love you."

"Oh, James." She had not expected to hear him say that. That he desired her, yes—she had seen that in his face—but not love.

He pulled her out of her chair and into his lap; she went easily. One hand went around her shoulders, the other came up to cup her face. "You're so beautiful."

He kissed her. His mouth was gentle, his arm loose around her, as though to let her escape if she needed to. But Julia's arms went around his neck; her lips answered his. His kiss deepened, his tongue filling her mouth, his lips moving eagerly on hers. His arms crushed her to him. They kissed again and again, long, hungry kisses that sought to wipe out the memory of eleven lonely years. Passion swelled in James, fierce and demanding, sending his blood racing through his veins and his lungs laboring for air.

James buried his hands in her hair, popping loose the pins and sending her heavy hair tumbling down over his arms. He ached to feel it against his bare skin. His hand slid down her neck and over her chest, finding the sweet weight of her breast. He stifled a groan. She felt so good, so right, as if he'd come home after years of searching. He broke away from their kiss and buried his face in her neck.

"God, I want you. I love you so much."

"I love you, too."

His arms tightened convulsively around her. "Thank God."

Julia slipped out of his arms and stood up. He looked up at her, startled and confused. Her hands went to the top button of her dress and unfastened it. They slid down to the next button. James understood what she was doing. He jumped to his feet and took her hands, stopping her.

"No. Wait." He drew a long, calming breath. "That's not what I want." He smiled wryly and shook his head. "At least, not all I want. I love you. I want to make love to you. But first, I want to marry you."

"What?"

"I want to marry you. I'm not a kid anymore, so hungry to have you, so selfish, that I can't think of anything else, including your good name. I don't want to take you secretively or hastily. I want to sleep with you in my bed. I want to make love to you all night long and not worry about anyone seeing me leave your house. I don't want just tonight or a few nights. I want you every night. I want my ring on your finger. I want you to bear my name." His hand went to her stomach and spread out over it possessively. He smiled with a purely male pride. "I want you to carry my children."

"Oh, James." Her eyes filled with tears.

"Well? Will you marry me?"

She looked down at the floor. "No."

"What?" James stared at her as if he'd been poleaxed. "But you said you loved me."

"I do!"

"But not enough to marry me."

"That's not it. I love you enough for anything, even refusing to marry you."

"I don't understand."

"I love you. I want you. I'd go upstairs with you right now. But it wouldn't be right for us to get married."

"Why not? Don't you think we've waited long enough?"

"It's not that. I'm not the right person for you now any more than I was eleven years ago. I'm not good enough for you. I'm a Turner. You're a Banks. You're a doctor! You need someone else, someone better. Someone your own kind, a woman like your mother. Refined and elegant.''

"Damn it! I have a *mother* like my mother. I don't need a wife like her. I want you, not someone else.''

Julia shook her head. "No, please. I don't know how to act around people like your mother. I'd embarrass you. Heavens, that day at your house when we ate dinner, I didn't have any idea what all those spoons were for. I couldn't give parties right. I couldn't talk to your friends. The kind of people you know would think I was ignorant and low class. You'd regret it.''

James sighed. "I don't know why this should surprise me. You've never been able to see yourself as you really are. You are a jewel, a treasure. Any man would be happy to have you for a wife, and I, most of all. If people thought you were ignorant or low class, I wouldn't want them for friends. And I can't find it in me to love a woman because she knows what the spoons in the table setting are for. I'm far more impressed by the fact that you know what my medical instruments are for. If that kind of thing worries you so much, Mother can teach it to you.''

"Your mother won't want me in your family.''

"I think you'll be surprised by my mother. Why don't you give her a chance? She likes you. She's the one who pointed out how wrongly I acted eleven years ago.''

"You told her!'' Red surged up in Julia's face. "She knows that we—that I—ohhh . . .'' She turned away on a moan of humiliation. "She must think I'm terrible. Cheap. She would die if you married me!''

"She would not. She doesn't think badly of you, I swear.''

"That's not true. She must think I'm a slut.''

"Don't say things like that! She does not. I told you, she likes you, and she wants me to be happy. Even if she did dislike you, it wouldn't make any difference. I have no intention of marrying to please my mother. I will marry to please myself, and it will please me to marry you!''

"We can't.''

James slammed his hand down flat on the table. "Damn, but you're exasperating! You're bound and determined to make us both miserable, aren't you?''

Julia began to cry. "No. It's because I don't want you to be miserable."

"I have been miserable for the past eleven years because I *didn't* marry you, and I don't intend to spend the next eleven years of my life the same way. I won't accept your answer. I am going to court you."

"James . . ."

"No. I'm leaving now, but I'll be back tomorrow morning to take you to church with Mother and me."

"James, no."

"Yes." His voice was flat. It took all the willpower he had not to put his hands on her or kiss her again, not to take the willing offer of her body. He stuck his hands in his pockets and left the kitchen. Julia trailed after him to the front door. He turned. "You be ready at ten forty-five. And you're having dinner with us, too."

"Please. You can't."

"I can." He pointed his forefinger at her. "You, young lady, are going to marry me. I am going to court you the way I should have courted you the first time, until you say yes. Do you understand?"

He opened the front door and walked out. Julia slumped against the wall, stunned.

✳ *Chapter 19* ✳

The long, searing days of summer slid by. Luke, Micah, and Cal picked the food crops from the garden—green beans, black-eyed peas, squash, tomatoes, onions, watermelons, cantaloupes, beets, cabbage, spinach, mustard greens. It was the time of year when they were overflowing with fresh vegetables and fruits, and Sarah was constantly busy canning and preserving. The canning kettle remained on the stove, and the kitchen table was lined with clear Mason

ars, waiting for the food that would be stored in them.
Whenever Sarah got a chance to sit down, there was always
a big stoneware bowl in her lap and she was shelling peas.

Late in July the first hay crop was ready for bailing. In
August the corn ripened, and not long afterward, the
cotton. Harvesting the cotton made their earlier work seem
as nothing. They spent all day bent over the plants or
creeping along the ground beside them, long tow sacks
hooked over their shoulders and dragging the ground behind
them. The sun broiled down on their backs, and the sacks
grew heavier as they filled up. By the end of the day it was
hard to straighten up. Pulling the cotton with gloves on was
awkward, but without them the cotton and hard bolls abraded
their fingertips until they were raw and sore.

Cotton was their best cash crop, and it was important to
pick it as quickly as possible. They didn't want to lose the
crop to some summer storm that might come up, but more
important, the first loads in to the gins brought better money
than did the later ones, when the market was glutted. So
Luke hired one of the migrant families of workers that were
always around at this time of year, and Sarah donned a
shovel-brimmed poke bonnet and joined them in the fields.

Luke, of course, worked the hardest of all. He left early
every morning after a quick breakfast and came home late
in the evening, usually after Sarah and the children had
eaten. After he ate, he would return to the barn to finish his
chores and finally come back to the house late to tumble
into bed—alone. Sarah knew he worked dawn to dark for
the same reason he slept in the empty bedroom. He was
doing his best to avoid her. To avoid temptation.

She had proved to herself that he wanted her. He didn't
stay away because he didn't desire her, but for precisely the
opposite reason. He desired her too much, and he thought it
was wrong. He was determined not to seek his pleasure with
her if it might cause her future pain. But Sarah was equally
determined that they have that pleasure again.

She desperately missed Luke's touch. Sometimes she would
awaken from a dream about Luke, her heart pounding in her
chest, her skin on fire, desire dampening her thighs, and it
would be hours before she could go back to sleep. At those
times she thought about going to his room and crawling into

bed with him and kissing him until he wanted her as much
as she did him. Once she even got as far as his door, but her
nerve always failed her. Sarah was afraid that he might
reject her again, and she couldn't bear that.

She tried in more subtle ways to entice him—touching the
precious perfume behind her ears even on ordinary days,
wearing the dresses Luke particularly liked, often unbuttoning
them farther down than was proper, brushing against his
arm as she set something down at the dinner table. One
evening as she was about to get into bed, she spotted a
long, fuzzy centipede crawling across the floor, and though
Sarah was more than capable of dispatching the creature
herself, she fled to Luke's room for help. She was dressed
only in her nightgown and she purposely didn't grab her
wrapper. It was dark inside Luke's room, and she knew how
the light in the hall behind her would outline her form
through the thin cotton gown.

When she burst into his room, Luke rose up on his elbow
in his bed. The sudden tension in the room was palpable.
The moonlight slanted through the open window and fell
across Luke, glinting on the pale gold of his hair and
touching his naked torso with light. The muscles of his arms
bunched. It was so still Sarah could hear his breath rasping
in and out of his throat. She thought of the thick, oppressive
stillness just before a tornado-carrying storm, of how the air
seemed heavy, weighing them to the ground. This was like
that moment, waiting, sultry, robbing one of air. Her throat
closed up; she couldn't speak. She couldn't even remember
why she had come in here.

Luke moved, breaking the moment. "Sarah? What's the
matter?"

"What? Oh." She glanced toward her room, suddenly
shy. "Uh, there's an awful, ugly bug in my room."

Luke smiled and went to get rid of the creature. He tossed
the centipede out the window and turned back to her. The
lamp was still lit in her room, and they could see each other
clearly. They were both intensely aware of how they were
dressed. Sarah stared at his naked chest. It had been weeks
since that night they had spent together. Luke had lost
weight, even more than he usually did in the summer, so that
he was all bone and muscle, hard and honed. She knew just

how strong he was, just how tough. Excitement sizzled through her.

For a long moment they gazed at each other, and Sarah saw in his eyes how much he wanted her. It started an ache low in her abdomen. She wanted him just as much. Finally, he turned and walked out of her room, his hands clenched at his sides, and leaving Sarah roiling inside with unsatisfied desire.

That was the problem. Every time she tantalized Luke, it tantalized her, too. Each time his eyes lit up with passion, she felt an answering fire inside herself. And whenever he turned away, it left her aching and empty. It had been easier when they had first been married, for then she hadn't known the delights of love. But now she did. She remembered all the ways Luke had touched her and kissed her, the times he had brought her to a heart-stopping peak of pleasure. Erotic images crowded her mind, even in the day, in the midst of the backbreaking work of pulling cotton.

Once, when they were sitting down to lunch in the fields with the others, Luke glanced up at Sarah. She had been dreamily thinking about lying between the cool sheets of their bed with Luke, his mouth and hands roaming her body. Her expression must have revealed where her thoughts were, for a dull red flush swept up Luke's neck and his hand clenched around the peach he was eating. Juice oozed out of the peach onto his palm, and Sarah knew a desire to lick the sweet juice from his palm.

She looked into his eyes. He was thinking the same thing. Sarah reached over without a word and took the peach from his hand. Luke's eyes never left her. She bit into the ripe fruit. The warm juice spurted in her mouth. Luke swallowed, and his hand closed around the sticky moisture in his own palm. He could taste the peach on his tongue, mingled with the sweetness that was uniquely Sarah's. For a moment it was as if their breaths were together, their skin one, their hearts thudding with the same rhythm. He had never wanted her more than he did in that moment.

Abruptly Luke rose and walked away from the rest of them into the trees. Sarah followed him. She caught up with him at the stream, where he was squatting down to wash his hands. He lifted his head at her approach. His eyes were as fierce and bright as a summer sky. "Sarah, no. Go back."

She shook her head. "I want to be with you."

His eyelids closed in a gesture of pain. "You think I don't want to be with you?"

"It seems like it these days. I never see you anymore."

Luke looked back down at the water. "I want to be with you. I miss you. I think all the time of what I want to tell you, of how you'll smile at this or how your eyes'll light up at that."

"Then come back to me." Her words came out fast and low, almost a whisper. She wanted him so much all pride was forgotten. Even the fear that he would reject her seemed as nothing compared to the burgeoning need inside her. If Micah and the children hadn't been sitting so nearby, she thought she would have stripped right there and begged Luke to take her.

"I can't." His voice was tortured. "It kills me to be around you."

His words were like a slap in her face. Luke turned and saw the pain in her eyes, and he leapt to his feet.

"No. Sarah, I didn't mean it like that. I love you. I love being with you. I'm so lonely without you. But when we're together, I want you ten times worse. Just looking at you sets me on fire. I'm afraid I won't be strong enough, that I'll break down like I did before."

"Then—"

"No! I won't. I refuse to make you suffer for my pleasure."

"I won't suffer!"

"You would. I can't risk it. I want you; I've wanted you from the first moment I ever saw you, standing there at your pa's kitchen door. But I love you more than I want you, so I'm not taking you to bed."

"You love me? Truly? How long do you think that will last when you aren't ever with me? When you won't talk to me? How can our love be nourished if we're strangers to each other? Luke! I want my husband back!"

Luke felt as if a dark chasm suddenly yawned at his feet. "I am your husband." His voice sounded desperate, as though he battled with his back to the wall. "I will always be your husband."

"You call this being my husband?" Tears filled Sarah's eyes. "Never seeing me? Never touching me? Never even talking to me? How long will this go on? For the rest of our lives?"

Luke turned aside. Her questions pierced him. He had tried not to think about the future, only hanging on day by day. But she, of course, being Sarah, wanted to meet everything head-on. "Sarah, I love you. I can't harm you!"

"You're harming me now! You're killing my heart! Can't you see that?"

"No. Don't say that." He pulled her into his arms and crackled her tenderly against his chest. "I love you. I love you."

Sarah's hands curled into his shirtfront, and she buried her face in his chest. It was wonderful to feel his arms around her, to be held in his strength and love. She luxuriated in the scent of him, in the heavy, secure thump of his heart beneath her face. Like a cat she rubbed her cheek against his shirt.

It was all Luke could do not to groan and shove her hips tightly against him, to rub her crudely against his already stiffening, aching manhood. She was so soft and warm, so willing. Her scent filled his nostrils. He could think of nothing but coming into her and feeling her tight and hot and welcoming around him.

She needed his love and comfort, not his passion. The problem was he wasn't able to separate the two.

Sarah lifted her face. Her eyes glistened with tears, and her lashes were stuck together in starry points. Her lips were lush and red and a little wobbly from her bout of tears. She looked heartbreakingly vulnerable and yet so desirable it made Luke shake inside. She went up to tiptoe, offering her mouth to him. His heart crashed inside his chest; his breath came fast and hard. She was so close; she was everything he'd ever wanted. Her eyes drifted closed. A long shudder ran through Luke, and he kissed her.

Kissing her was like drowning in rose petals and honeysuckle, so sweet and soft that disappearing, even dying, was desirable. He murmured her name against her lips, the sound swallowed by their hungry, seeking mouths. His tongue plunged into her, tasting what it had not had in so long. His fingers dug into her back, pressing her into him. His hands slid slowly down her back to her hips, flattening her against him all the way down. He squeezed her buttocks and lifted her up and into his body, moving her slowly, delicately over his pulsing shaft. Sarah felt the hard thrust of him and smiled, melting like warm butter in his hands.

She loved him. She was his. He had every right, every reason. God, he wanted her. He couldn't live without having her.

Sarah whimpered softly in her throat, and the sound went through him like a red-hot spear. His mouth widened over hers, as if to consume her, and he began to pull her down to the ground.

"Mommy? Mommy?"

It took a moment for the sound of their daughter's high voice to register with them.

"Mommy?"

Luke froze. He released Sarah and spun away, going over to the stream and crouching down beside it as if in pain, his back to the trees through which Emily was picking her way.

"Over here, sweetie," Sarah called to Emily, surprised that she could even speak. She smoothed at her dress and hair. Thank God it was only Emily, who wouldn't understand the passion that must be written on her flushed face.

Emily hopped out of the trees. "Look at me, Mommy! I'm a bunny! See?" She bounced across to Sarah. Sarah swung the girl up into her arms and kissed her.

"I see. Well, little bunny, we better get back to work, huh?"

Emily grinned sunnily, thinking of the piles of twigs, leaves, and cotton bolls she had been stacking. "Yes. Me help."

"Come along, little Miss Me Help." Sarah set her daughter down on the ground and turned toward Luke.

"Luke?" she began tentatively, unable to stop the catch in her throat at even speaking his name.

He nodded. "I'll be along in a second." He reached down into the stream and splashed cool water on his face. He could hear Sarah walking away with Emily. "Sarah?"

Sarah turned. "Yes?"

He twisted his torso to look at her. His face was drawn and tight. "If you love me, please don't torture me."

Sarah was swept with fierce regret and frustration. Why had Emily had to come along at that moment? She was furious with everything and everyone, including Luke. "All right," she replied, tight-lipped. "If that's what you want."

He wanted to say that it wasn't what he wanted at all, but Sarah gave him no chance to answer, turning and stalking off so fast that Emily's chubby little legs had to run to keep up with her.

Luke looked back down at the water. Now Sarah was angry with him. He cursed slowly and viciously. He stood and paced alongside the stream, kicking a rock into the water. He felt as if he might explode. Why in the hell couldn't he control himself? Why in the hell wouldn't Sarah understand? And why in the hell did everything always have to be so difficult? So goddamned impossible!

Sarah worked through the afternoon on a wave of fury, pointedly avoiding even looking at her husband. If that's the way he wanted it, then fine! That's the way it would be. Let Luke keep his precious nobility, his wonderful sacrifice. Let him be a martyr and a saint. He'd find out when it was too late that he had ruined both their lives. But she wouldn't throw herself at his feet again.

Anger carried her through the afternoon, but by the time she returned to the house and fed the children, her anger had dissipated. When Luke came in and sat down to his solitary supper, she had difficulty leaving him alone in chilly silence as she had intended to do. He kept casting little sideways glances at her, guilty, uncomfortable looks that reminded her of a boy who knows he's in Dutch and can't figure out how to squirm out of it. It was infuriating to find that it worked on her, as it always did. She had never been able to maintain a decent anger with Luke for any length of time. Especially not now, with those dark smudges beneath his eyes and the lines of weariness on his too thin face.

As always, Luke expected too much of himself. He would work himself into the ground trying to escape the desire inside him. He would condemn and restrain himself beyond reason because there lived inside him the conviction that he was bad, that somehow he was always at fault. He put her on a pedestal, but he was ready to flay himself over every transgression.

Sarah sighed and sat down across from him at the table. She laid her hand across his. She could feel the tension vibrating in him. He was a man on the edge. It occurred to her that she could go to him tonight, dressed in her gown with her hair down, and he would pull her into his arms, unable to resist the temptation.

But she also knew how he would feel afterward, how he would blame himself for giving in. Luke never punished others, only himself, and he would put himself through hell for sleeping with her. She couldn't do that to him, no matter how hard it was to stay away. She refused to damage Luke's self-respect. All she could do was wait and hope that eventually he would realize that he wasn't responsible for her pain and would come willingly to her bed.

Dovie looked across the table at Micah. She was getting used to seeing him there. She had lost count of how many Sundays he had had dinner with them.

She knew she ought to put a stop to it. She was drifting into dangerous territory. She was reaching the point where she approached Sundays with anticipation, even excitement. She looked forward to seeing Micah again, eager to engage once more in their lazy, sexy verbal sparring.

And that was risky. Micah Harrison was a traveling man. He wouldn't stay here long; he wouldn't put down roots. He wasn't the kind of man a woman like her should be interested in—or fall in love with.

Dovie shook that thought from her mind. She stood up. "Would you like any more coffee?" She looked at Micah, and he nodded, his eyes sliding down her like a caress. Dovie's voice was a little breathless as she turned toward Lurleen. "Mama?"

"No, sugar. I'm goin' over to Bessie's. She be steady havin' that ache in her back, and I better see how she doin'. I done told her, she got no business liftin' them heavy things like she do. But when did that woman ever listen to sense?"

"She must be like her sister," Dovie remarked, a smile touching her lips.

Lurleen laughed and shot her daughter a mockingly stern look. "Don't you go talkin' 'bout your mama like that."

"Yes, ma'am." Dovie's smile grew.

Micah watched her. He liked to see Dovie's smile. It was something rare and wonderful. It softened her face and touched her dark brown eyes with a faint gold. He thought about her smiling a lot, imagined her looking at him like that, only softer—and hotter.

Lurleen called a cheerful good-bye to them and left. Dovie brought a pot of coffee back from the kitchen. She leaned around Micah to refill his cup, so close he could smell her scent. Micah thought about turning and pressing his face against her, drinking in the sweet musky odor, reveling in the softness.

Dovie stepped back, setting the pot down on the table where Micah could reach it should he want it again. She sat down across from him. He got the message. She had seen the look in his face, and she wanted to make sure that there was a table between them.

"A man ever hurt you? Or you jus' naturally shy?"

Dovie's eyebrows rose. "I beg your pardon?"

Micah smiled. That prissy way she talked never failed to start a heat inside him. "You know what I mean. You sure always backtrack from me fast."

"Maybe I think you're dangerous."

"Then you oughta not be sittin' here alone with me."

"The thought had occurred to me."

Micah looked at her with a steady, unwavering gaze. Dovie stared back at him with all the calm she could muster. She knew it wasn't wise to be alone with this man—and as soon as Lurleen got back, she'd let her mother know exactly how she felt about that little bit of treachery. She ought to ask him to leave. Yet she couldn't open her mouth to say so. Her gaze shifted and fell to the table. She began to trace the whorl of the wood with her forefinger.

Micah watched her. She was as nervous as he'd ever seen Dovie, and it gave her an appealing air of vulnerability. For that reason he backed off. He took a sip of his coffee and began to talk about the Turners. He could see the relief in every line of Dovie's body. He wondered if there was any disappointment in her, as well.

"That Luke now, he goin' through hell," Micah commented.

"What makes you say that?" Dovie looked back up at him, glad to have a safe topic of conversation.

Micah shrugged. "He be sleepin' alone ever night."

Dovie felt the heat rising in her face. It wasn't so safe a topic after all. "He told you that?"

"Don't have to. It plain on his face. He look like a man that ain't had enough res' in weeks. He drive himself like a devil. She don't look too happy, either."

"I don't really think that this is a fit topic of conv—"

"He gonna put himself in the grave 'fore too long, if he don't watch it. They got something powerful 'tween them, them two, and it be killin' them to keep it in."

"You sound awfully concerned about these white folks of yours. I thought you didn't care anything about any white man." Dovie arched her brows challengingly.

"Maybe the way you think rubbin' off on me." Micah paused, and the faintest trace of a smile touched his lips. It was a smile that didn't make Dovie comfortable. "Or maybe I jus' got fellow feelin' for a man that been achin' for a woman too long."

Dovie jumped up and moved away from the table. One hand flew up to her hair as though to make sure it was still screwed tightly into its bun. It wouldn't have surprised her if it had come loose, just as everything inside her had at Micah's words. "Ah . . ." She glanced around, searching for something to say, and quickly. Her thoughts were flying around in her brain like buzzing bees, wild, furious, and loud, with nothing logical or decent that could be picked out to be said. She glanced into the kitchen. "Oh! Oh yes." Her mind found something ordinary and clung to it. "There's a cabinet in the kitchen that the, uh, door won't stay on. I— Mama thought you might fix it when you came today. That is, if you don't mind."

Micah watched her. She never once looked at him while she talked. He enjoyed her confusion; it was rare to see Dovie not in full control, and he liked it. He liked causing her to lose it. "Sure. I don't mind." He stood up and sauntered toward the kitchen. "Which one?"

"Which one what?"

Micah smiled. "Which door? Which cabinet?"

"Oh." Dovie caught his knowing smile, and it made her feel even more like a fool. He knew his effect on her and fully enjoyed it. She ought to throw him out. She already would have had he been any other man. She ought to at least lecture him on the way he had spoken to her. But she was afraid that would only make her appear even more foolish.

Dovie followed Micah into the kitchen and pointed out the offending door, standing a good three feet away from him as she did so. He glanced pointedly at where she stood, and though the smile wasn't there, she could see the amusement— and the satisfaction—in his eyes. Damn him! It pleased him to put her at such a disadvantage. She swung away, starting back to the living and dining area.

"Wait."

Dovie turned, trying her best to recapture the haughty expression she was normally so good at.

"Where're the tools?" She looked at him blankly. "To fix the door?"

"Oh!" She'd been so busy trying to pretend that he didn't affect her that she'd practically forgotten what she had asked him to do. "Uh, here." She went to a drawer and opened it. He came up close behind her and reached around her to take out the screwdriver. She could feel the heat of his body and his hard strength as his arm curved around her.

Dovie sidestepped out of his reach and left the kitchen. Her hands were trembling. She clasped them together and stood rigid, willing herself to be calm. She was, after all, a grown woman, one used to being in control. There was no reason for her to feel like this, as fragile and helpless as a boat tossed about upon the sea.

She busied herself cleaning up the table and carrying the dishes into the sink in the kitchen. She carefully avoided looking at Micah as he worked. Finally, when the table was cleared and her nerves had relaxed somewhat, Dovie poured herself a cup of coffee and sat down at the table. She glanced into the kitchen and immediately wished that she had not.

Micah had removed his Sunday jacket and tie and rolled

up his sleeves to work. The top button of his shirt was undone, exposing a narrow V of dark skin, glistening with the faint sheen of sweat. The muscles in his arms moved as he twisted the screwdriver, the long tendons pushing against his skin. How large his hands were, wide-palmed, with long, agile fingers. The paler skin on the inside of his hands was heavily callused; they would be rough to the touch.

She watched him work. He was so big that he dwarfed the kitchen, yet his large hands were light and quick, not clumsy. There was skill in him as well as strength, and intelligence, too. He was the kind of man you could be proud of, the kind you'd smile about when you introduced him around.

Dovie swallowed and looked away from him. *That* kind of thinking was dangerous. He wasn't the kind of man who could be her man. She wanted marriage; she wanted stability. Micah Harrison was a drifter. He might seem almost domesticated, walking her home from church on Sundays and staying for dinner, repairing the little things that broke around the house. But he wasn't. He had too much wildness in him.

She remembered the sight of him on Turner's horse. There had been power in him, and freedom. He didn't fit here; he belonged in that wild country where he had been born. And he would return to it before long, while she would stay here.

That was why it did no good to look at him and feel the things she did inside; why she ought to stop herself before it was too late.

Micah turned, as though he had felt her gaze upon him. Dovie couldn't look away. He rose slowly, lithely to his feet and came toward her. The air was suddenly twice as hot. She could hardly breathe. A gust of breeze lifted the curtain and curled around her in a cool caress. He had seen her thoughts on her face. She ought to deny them. She ought to tell him to stop, to go away. But she couldn't say anything. She hadn't the strength; the fire in his eyes drained it from her. Anyway, she'd never been good at lying.

"Dovie." His voice was low, a mere breath of sound. He stopped in front of her, so tall she had to crane her head back to see him. She dropped her gaze. "Baby."

Micah's hands touched her hair. She felt his fingers working on the knot of her hair, unfastening it with quick, sure movements. She should protest. But the sensations running through her at his touch were too sweet to stop. She wanted only to lean into him. Her hair came loose and tumbled down around her head, free. His fingers sank into her hair, gathering it up into thick handfuls.

"You sure a beautiful woman. Sometime I think lookin' at you's all a man could ask for. But right now, it ain't enough."

He smoothed her hair from her face, gently pressing her head back until she was looking up at him. He loomed over her, but somehow his size wasn't frightening; it was exciting. He slid his hands down her hair and onto her shoulders. He pulled her up from her chair. Dovie was a tall woman, but she was small against him. Her hands came up between them and rested on his chest. She was breathless, her heart pounding, and she didn't know whether to run or to throw herself into his arms.

His hands moved down her back, crossing to pull her in tight against him, and he kissed her. Dovie went up on tiptoe to meet his mouth. The kiss went on and on, unending, thrilling, and all the time he pressed her into him tighter and higher, until her feet were dangling off the floor and the breath was almost squeezed from her chest. She didn't protest. She hardly noticed. There was nothing in the world for her at that moment but his mouth and his arms around her.

Dovie clung to him, returning his kiss passionately and straining to be closer to him. For once, all thought and logic fled her, and she was aware of nothing but pure, raw emotion. His arm went under her bottom, pulling her up and into him, so that she felt the force of his hard maleness. She squirmed against him, wanting to feel it fully. There was an ache between her legs that made her yearn and hunger and . . . She moved her legs restlessly, and he groaned.

"Oh, sugar." He made a sound that was part laugh and part pain. "I want you." He released her slowly, letting her slide down until her feet touched the floor.

Dovie gazed up at him, her eyes soft and luminous.

"Mama won't be home all afternoon. She always stays the whole day when she goes to Bessie's."

She could feel the tremor in his arms, lightly looped around her. "You tellin' me you want me to stay?"

"Yes." Her voice was as unsteady as the heart rocketing about inside her chest, but it was passion, not uncertainty, that made it so. There was no doubt in her, only desire and rushing, pounding need. His kiss, his touch had turned her into fire. "I want you to stay."

"I will. Oh, baby, I will."

He lifted her into his arms and carried her into the small bedroom that was hers. There he set her on her feet and began to unfasten the multitude of little round buttons down the front of her shirtwaist. His big hands were clumsy on the tiny buttons, and with a smile she moved his hands aside and unfastened them herself. He watched her, his eyes and mouth growing heavy with passion as bit by bit she revealed herself to him until she stood clad in only her white cotton chemise and petticoat.

She reached up to untie the ribbon of her chemise, but he stopped her. He ran his fingers along the edge of the garment, the cotton white against her coffee and cream skin. He untied the bow and smoothed the puckers between his forefingers and thumb, loosening the top. The straps slipped down onto her arms, and the material eased lower. It caught on the tips of her breasts, high and pointed, then slid down to her waist.

He sucked in his breath. She was as beautiful as he had ever thought she would be, slender and smooth skinned, with taut, full breasts. Her dark nipples were hard and prominent, urging his touch. But he did not touch her yet. Instead, his hands went to the drawstring at her waist and untied it, then pulled her remaining underclothes from her, revealing all of her to his gaze.

She was long legged, just as he had imagined, her buttocks tight and firm. He reached out his hand to touch her. His hand was dark against her skin as he slid it down from her shoulder over the soft mound of her breast and onto her stomach. Her flesh quivered beneath his touch, and her eyes, fastened on his face, were huge and dark, full of yearning and a touch of fear.

"Micah, I—I've never—"

He smiled slightly, lovingly. "Don't I know that? Don't worry, baby. I be gentle. I take care of you." He leaned over and kissed her on the forehead. His hands smoothed back her hair as he gazed down at her for a moment. Then he kissed her lightly on the lips. He wanted to kiss her much harder; it was difficult to hold back. But he wanted more than that to reassure her that she was safe with him.

She smiled. "I know."

He stepped back and began to undress. He thought Dovie might turn away modestly, but, as usual, she surprised him. She simply stood and watched, and when at last he stood before her naked, she gazed at his large, muscular body with the same sort of hungry awe with which he had viewed her. He was magnificently, undeniably male, and just looking at him she felt breathless and wild. She wanted something that she didn't even know, but she knew that it lay in his power.

Dovie laid her hand upon him, as he had done with her earlier, moving it across the width of his chest. Delightful new sensations sparked through her. Micah closed his eyes, sighing, at the exquisite pleasure of her touch. He let her innocent explorations continue until he thought he might explode, and then his arms went around her tightly, lifting her up and onto the waiting bed. He leaned over her and kissed her, and the heat shimmering in them exploded. And there, in the hot August afternoon, with the breeze from the window drifting over their fevered bodies, he taught her the ways of love.

Luke glanced over at the black man toiling beside him. Micah's fingers sped through the cotton plants, plucking the cotton from its bolls at a record pace, and all the time he hummed under his breath. It was blazing hot, and sweat was running off both of them, but Micah didn't seem to mind— or even notice.

"You're awfully cheerful this morning."

Micah grinned at him. "For a fact."

There was an aura of sexual satisfaction about the man

that was so thick it was almost tangible, and Luke experienced a pang of envy. It seemed a hundred years ago when he had known that kind of peace and energy. He doubted that he'd ever feel it again. But he summoned up a smile because there was a bond between him and the other man, and he didn't want his sourness to tinge Micah's pleasure.

"That's good." Luke straightened from his bent position, flexing stiffened fingers, and pulled the long cotton sack off over his head. He dropped it and walked down the row to the Mason jars of water to take a drink.

Micah joined him. "You know, I done been thinkin'."

"About what?" Luke wiped the sweat from his face with his shirtsleeve and drank another long swallow.

"That forty acres you got on the other side of this place."

"The one in pasture?"

"Yeah. It be good farm land."

"Probably. But it's too much, too far away. I don't have the time to farm it, too."

"You ever think 'bout sharecroppin' the place?"

Luke looked at him, eyes narrowing. "I might. To the right person. Why? You interested?"

"I might be." Suddenly Micah grinned. "I been thinkin' 'bout settlin' down."

"Is that a fact? It wouldn't have anything to do with why you're so goddamned cheerful this morning, would it?" Luke grinned back.

"Yeah. It jus' might."

"Sure. You want to sharecrop that place, it's yours."

Micah's grin broadened. He'd been positive that Luke would not disappoint him. "Thank you."

"Hell, I couldn't ask for a better tenant. Course, we'd have to put up a house for you over there, but there'd be plenty of time for that this winter."

"Yeah."

They started back down the row to their sacks. Luke stretched his back one last time, then looped the long strap of the sack over his head and arm and bent back to work. Micah gazed out across the land as he settled his sack in place. His piece would look like this next summer. Anticipation tightened his chest. For the first time, he wanted to stay somewhere. Wanted to put down roots. Get married.

There was nothing like a sweet woman to make a drifter want to stop moving.

❋ *Chapter 20* ❋

James Banks courted Julia assiduously. She had never experienced anything like it. He called on her formally, bringing flowers and candy and carefully sitting on the front porch in view of all her neighbors. He escorted her and the children to church every Sunday, and Anthea invited them to her house for Sunday dinner. He took her to a church social one Sunday afternoon and to a Chautauqua concert in Greenville another Sunday. His mother came to call on her several times. He even insisted that she attend a party at the Snowdens with him.

Julia was flattered and amazed by the attention James paid her. She loved his visits. He was charming, handsome, and kind. It would take a woman made of sterner stuff than she not to be thrilled by the way he was making it plain to the world that he loved her and wanted to marry her. Every time she saw him, whether at work or socially, she fell a little more in love with him.

But it also made her angry that he was making such a fool of himself over her. People must be talking about him, must be shaking their heads over it and wondering how Dr. Banks could be so foolish as to fall in love with Julia Turner—whom everyone knew had gotten married the first time in a mighty big hurry. She hated for James to lay himself open to gossip this way. It would be even worse if he married her. He couldn't marry her; it was unthinkable. Everyone would talk. Everywhere they went, people would shoot her sly, sidelong glances, eager to see if her stomach gave away their reason for marrying. For the rest of his life people would think badly of James for taking her for a wife.

They'd pity him; they'd wonder why; they'd sigh and shake their heads. *Poor James Banks*, they would say, *he ruined his life when he married her*.

Julia couldn't do that to him. She couldn't be the cause of people pitying him and gossiping about him, maybe even turning away from him. James was too good to realize what he would be letting himself in for. He wouldn't realize what he had done until it was too late. But then, once he understood, surely he would begin to resent her. He might fall out of love with her. He might realize that his love was only passion or a stubborn determination to have what had been denied him years before. That would be the most awful thing in the world: to be married to James and him not love her anymore.

Yet how could she not marry him? How could she resist him when he asked her to? How could she hold out against his persistence or prevail against his arguments? Especially when she wanted so much to yield.

She could think of nothing more wonderful than to be James's wife—to take care of him, to love him, to fall asleep in his arms and wake up beside him, to have his name, to bear his children, to know again the bliss of his lovemaking. Julia could not have dreamed a better life than that, which made it doubly hard to tell him no each time he asked her to marry him. And he continued to ask.

Julia had thought that after awhile James would give up, that he would stop insisting that she marry him and simply take the easy relationship she offered him. She wanted James terribly, and she was certain that he wanted her just as much. It was crazy that he would not come to her bed; he could have her, all of her, without the marriage. Sometimes, sitting a discreet distance apart from each other on the front porch, talking, Julia would see a dark flame leap into James's eyes, and then she knew that he was thinking about making love to her.

Once when he looked at her in that way, she asked in a low urgent voice, "Why won't you come inside with me? The children are at Sarah's sister's house. We could—"

James shook his head once, emphatically. "Please, Julie. Don't torture me."

"I don't want to. You're the one who's keeping yourself from what you want!" she retorted.

"But I'm not the one offering me what I want more than anything in the world—if only I'll betray the woman I love to the gossips of this town. You think that doesn't tear me apart? Looking at you and seeing how beautiful you are, knowing how sweet your lips taste, wanting to taste them again. Knowing that if I said the word, I could have you—and also knowing that if we went into your house and didn't come out for an hour or two, everybody in town tomorrow would be naming you a—" He bit back the word. His expression was thunderous. "I won't do it. I won't have everyone gossiping about you."

"They're gossiping already."

"They'd stop if you would marry me."

"Don't be silly. The tongues would wag even more if you married me."

"Damn it, Julia!" James's eyes flashed, and his words were a hiss. "I love you. I want you for my wife, not an occasional bed partner!"

Tears sprang into Julia's eyes, and she looked down at her lap. "It's not right."

"It is right. It's the only thing that's right!" James stood up. "I have to leave now. If I stay, I'm either going to start yelling at you or pick you up and carry you to bed. And don't look at me like that."

"Like what?"

"You know like what. Like you want me to carry you to bed."

"I do want that."

He gritted his teeth. "What *I* want right now is to rip off every stitch of your clothes."

A flush sprang to Julia's cheeks. She felt the heat all through her. She couldn't speak.

"I'd like to kiss you senseless. I'd like to take you right here on the porch." His eyes were burning, compelling. He turned away abruptly with a low, animal growl of frustration. "Damn it, Julia! How long will you make me wait? You're going to drive me absolutely insane if you keep this up!"

Julia swallowed. She didn't say anything. She couldn't.

James sighed and swung off the porch. She watched him walk away.

Her hands were trembling. She wanted to cry. How long could she hold out against James's persistence? How long could she deny the man she loved?

Luke and Sarah soon knew the gossip about Julia and Dr. Banks. Isolated though they were on the farm, they heard about it at church one Sunday, then again a couple of weeks later when they were in town. Both times a hard, still look came over Luke's face, and Sarah knew that he was seething inside. He hated the idea of his sister's name being linked with James Banks. He was certain that James was trying to take advantage of Julia again.

The last straw was the third time they were told about James and Julia. Stu and Jenny and their children had come out to the Turner farm for Sunday dinner. They had just finished the meal, and the children had run out to play. The two women rose to clean off the table, and Stu settled back in his chair, pulling out his pipe and pouch of tobacco. Luke poured himself another cup of coffee.

"Well," Stu commented cheerfully as he filled the bowl of his pipe, "looks like Jimmy Banks is getting ready to pop the question, doesn't it?"

Luke froze, his hand clenching around the handle of the coffeepot. Sarah sighed inwardly. Why had Stu had to open his mouth about it?

"What?" Luke's voice was deadly quiet.

"Well, the good doctor's head over heels in love with your sister. The whole town's expecting him to ask her to marry him soon."

"That'll be a cold day in hell."

Stu glanced up, surprised by Luke's words and the flat, cold voice in which he said them. "You don't think so?"

"Dr. James Banks," Luke sneered over the name, "would never marry a Turner."

"I wouldn't be too sure of that," Jennifer put in. "Mrs. Gibson told me he's taken Julia to church every Sunday for the past six weeks. And Dorothy Blanton said they went to the Chautauqua in Greenville together. It sounds serious to me.''

''Doesn't anyone in Willow Springs have anything better to do than talk about my sister?''

Jennifer and Stu both stared at him. ''Why, Luke, what's the matter?'' Jennifer asked, amazed. ''Wouldn't you like for Julia to marry Dr. Banks? He seems like an awfully nice—''

''Damn it!'' Luke slammed his hand down on the table, making the crockery clatter. The Harpers' words were like sparks to the dry tinder of his frustrated emotions. ''Don't you understand? He's not going to marry Julia. He'd never marry her.''

''Well, Luke,'' Sarah put in hastily before he got into a fight with her relatives, ''you have to admit that he seems to have honorable intentions.''

''I don't have to admit anything like it,'' he retorted, jumping to his feet. ''He's a scoundrel, and you, at least, should know that.''

''I know what you *think* he is,'' Sarah answered carefully. ''But I'm not sure that—''

''You're saying you don't believe me?'' His voice was thin and sharp as a knife.

Jennifer took an involuntary step back, and her husband rose from his chair. But Sarah faced Luke calmly. ''You know I would never say that. I believe that you think you know what happened, but it's possible to be wrong about a situation, Luke.''

''I'm not wrong about this.'' Each word was short and hard, like little punches, and there was a look of such cold anger on his face that Jennifer couldn't fathom how her sister could stand there and look him in the eye, so unafraid.

But Sarah wasn't afraid of his anger. She would have welcomed an outburst of temper from Luke; any emotion would be better than the remote politeness he'd shown her the past weeks. She was almost eager for the dark anger to break its bounds, to feel his emotions wash over her.

They stood, staring at each other, vibrating with tension and anticipation. Luke wanted to scream at Sarah, to slam his fist down on the table, to grab her by the arms and demand that she agree with him. He wanted to yank her up

tight against his body and kiss her until her opposition
melted.

His fingers curled into a fist. That was the thing. He
wanted to kiss her, to subdue her with his passion. He
wanted her. The flood of his anger was only a hairline away
from desire.

"Goddamn it!" He broke away and walked to the side
door. "I am going to settle this." He grabbed his hat from
the rack beside the door and slammed out.

"What in the world?" Jennifer stared at the screen door,
vibrating on its hinges. She swung back to her sister.
"Sarah? What's the matter? I'm sorry we said anything. I
mean, I thought he'd be pleased."

Sarah shook her head. "Don't worry. It's not anything
you said. He's just . . . upset about something else. This has
been coming on for a long time." She sighed and went to
the kitchen window. She watched as Luke saddled Jo-Jo in
the corral, then mounted and rode out. "I hope he doesn't
do anything foolish."

Jennifer looked at Sarah. It was obvious that things
weren't right between Sarah and Luke. But it was equally
obvious that Sarah wasn't about to tell her what was going
on or ask her for advice. Sarah had always been close-
mouthed, especially when it came to Luke. She wouldn't
say anything that might be construed as criticism of him.

So Jennifer shrugged and dropped the topic. She wasn't
going to pry. She carried in the rest of the dishes from the
table, and as she and Sarah cleaned them, they began to talk
of other things. Neither mentioned the scene again.

Late in the afternoon, Stu and Jennifer gathered their
children into their buggy and left for home. Cal and Emily
stood with Sarah, waving to the other family until they were
out of sight. The three of them started back toward the
house. Sarah rested her hand casually on Cal's shoulders,
and for an instant he leaned into her.

Then he twisted away. "You ain't my mother," he said
sullenly, not looking at her.

Now where had that come from? Sarah wondered. Anytime she thought she was getting close to Cal, he lashed out
at her.

"No, I'm not," she agreed, keeping her voice calm.

"You know, Cal, I'm not trying to take your mother's place in your life. I couldn't. She will always be your mother. You love her, and I understand that. I wouldn't try to make you give that love to me."

Cal kept his head turned away. Sarah made him feel so mixed up. He knew she wasn't trying to take his mother's place. Who would want to be his mother, anyway? The bad thing was, sometimes he imagined that she was his mother. He wished he'd never seen his mother. He wished Sarah would call him "son," as his father sometimes did. He wished—sometimes he wished it so hard it hurt—that Sarah belonged to him as she belonged to Emily. He knew that couldn't happen. He wasn't her son; she wouldn't even want him to be. Her goodness to him was just part of her nature; she was kind to everyone. He wasn't special to her. It was wrong of him to wish that he was and that his real mother didn't exist. It made him feel guilty.

Sarah's hand went out to touch Cal's bright head, but she hesitated and drew it back. Cal didn't like to be touched. "What I would like is to be your friend, though. Couldn't we be friends?"

"I don't need a friend," Cal snarled and ran away from them down to the barn.

Sarah sighed, looking after him. The boy was as difficult to deal with as his father.

Luke rode straight to the Banks house. James himself opened the door at Luke's impatient knock.

"Luke." James's brows rose in surprise, but he said only, "Won't you come in?"

Luke's eyes bored into him. "This isn't a social call."

"Somehow I suspected as much. Why don't we go into my study?"

Luke followed him into the darkly paneled room. James sat in one heavy leather chair and offered Luke another. Luke remained standing.

"I came here to tell you to leave Julie alone." James simply looked at him, saying nothing. "I won't have you playing with her, like you did before."

"I assure you, I am not playing."

"Her name is all over town! There's nobody that isn't talking about you and her."

James frowned. "Something disrespectful? Is anyone daring to say—"

"They're *daring* to say that you're chasing her like a dog with one bone. That you escort her everywhere, that there's hardly a day that you aren't planted on her front porch."

"That's true. You can't blame people for speaking the truth."

"Yeah, and what are they going to say when you don't marry her? What'll they say when you leave her high and dry? Julie will be the mockery of this town. They'll say you got what you wanted from her, so there was no need to marry her. Damn it, Banks, I won't let you lie with her and abandon her again, with the whole town of Willow Springs watching!"

James sprang to his feet, his eyes suddenly blazing. "Damn it, if you weren't Julia's brother, I'd—"

"You'd what?" Luke's eyes glittered. "Get beat up again? Come on, Jimmy, you want to try me?"

"Listen!" James came forward, his body taut with frustration and anger. "You always go off half-cocked, Turner. Have you ever thought of hearing the whole story before you jump in, fists swinging?"

"I don't need to hear the whole story to know that you're the son of a bitch that got my sister pregnant and left her once."

"I didn't."

Luke's lips curled into a sneer. "Sure."

"Goddamn it! I didn't leave her! I won't now! I love her. I want to marry her."

"What?"

"I want to marry Julia. I've asked her to marry me. I've courted her with all the honor, respect, and pomp I know how. I have not compromised her in any way. It's Julia who won't marry me. She won't say yes."

"You're lying."

"Why would I lie? Ask Julia."

"But you walked out on her when she—"

"I did not walk out on her! I wouldn't have, ever. I know

what you think of me; and God knows, I didn't act like much of a gentleman where Julia was concerned. But I loved her. I planned to marry her. She didn't tell me she was pregnant. She just married Will Dobson and left me to find it out from your pa. I never knew she had my child until a few weeks ago. I love her."

Luke stared at James. He didn't want to believe him. He wanted to blame James; he wanted someone to yell at, someone to hit. He needed a release for the wild frustration inside him. But he knew that James was telling the truth. "She didn't tell you."

"No."

It sounded like something Julia would do, taking the blame on herself, asking no one for help. Slowly the anger drained out of Luke. He felt suddenly old and tired. "Christ." Luke took off his hat and ran his hand through his hair. "So I hated you all these years for nothing." He looked at James, puzzled. "Why didn't you tell me?"

"I didn't know what you thought. I never knew she was carrying my child." James sighed and flopped back down in the chair. "I thought she didn't want me anymore. I presumed you hated me for seducing your sister. And I had. I could hardly defend myself against that. Loving a woman doesn't excuse a man from having taken his pleasure at her expense."

"No," Luke agreed in a weary tone. "It doesn't."

For the first time James noticed that Luke didn't look good. He had lost weight, and his face was drawn. He seemed tired, almost ill, but there was something else—an almost haunted expression in his eyes.

"Luke, are you all right?"

"What? Yes, of course."

"You don't look it. Maybe you should let me check you out."

Luke grimaced. "I'm fine. Just tired from the harvest."

"You've lost weight."

"I always do in the summer."

"Mrs. Turner's all right?"

"Yeah. Sarah's fine."

"Is she expecting again? Are you worried about that?"

"No!" Luke flared. James appeared taken aback at his

emphatic answer, so Luke tried to soften it a little. "She's not. She's doing fine."

James's eyes narrowed. He suspected what was wrong with Luke. He should have realized the signs earlier; he'd felt the same ache and frustration often enough the past few months. "You know, there's nothing to keep your wife from getting pregnant again. The premature birth didn't do any permanent damage to her."

"No. She won't."

"You haven't had intercourse with her, have you?"

"That's none of your business."

"Luke, it's all right. I told your wife that you could resume relations in a couple of months."

"She's not getting pregnant again."

"Is this Sarah's decision?"

"Of course not. She'd never deny me anything. She wouldn't do a thing to protect herself."

"Then you're the one who doesn't want to—"

"Damn it!" Luke slammed his fist into the back of the leather chair beside him, his fury and frustration tumbling out. "Of course I want to! How could I not want her? But I almost killed her before. I can't let it happen again. I won't!"

"What do you mean, you almost killed her? Luke, do you think that you somehow caused her to lose the baby?"

"Yes." His eyes were bleak. "I took her, and she was too far along."

"That wasn't the reason, Luke."

"Your father told us it would harm the baby. Harm Sarah."

James sighed. "My father was a good doctor, but he wasn't God. A lot of older doctors think that, but in my opinion intercourse is safe until the last month. No one has shown that it's done any harm to the fetus or the mother. Medicine changes; medical opinions change."

"She lost the baby. She almost died."

"It wasn't because of that. Your wife went into labor too early because the placenta broke free from the wall of the uterus and moved down until it was between the fetus and the cervix. That was why there was so much blood. But that condition is simply something that happens. You didn't cause it, Luke. It would have occurred no matter what you did or didn't do. It was fate."

Luke stared at James. Deep inside him something broke and fell free. He felt suddenly years younger, pounds lighter. Was he really not responsible for Sarah's pain? For the baby's death? It was too good to be true; he wanted too much to trust it.

He ran his hands through his hair. He didn't know what to say or do now. Everything had been turned upside down in the last few minutes. Jimmy, Julia, Sarah's losing their baby. Things he'd been certain of were suddenly false. "I'm sorry. I shouldn't have come here. Julia never told me that you didn't know." He sighed. "I don't know what to say."

"Say you'll give the bride away, if I can ever get Julia to accept me."

"All right." Luke paused. "Why won't she marry you?"

James made a face. "Because she's the stubbornnest woman this side of the Mississippi."

Luke smiled fractionally. "No. The second stubbornnest. I'm married to the first." He turned and walked to the door, then swung back. "Thank you."

"For what?"

"For what you told me. All of it."

"Sure."

Luke left the Banks house and mounted his horse. He rode slowly back to the farm. He felt jumbled up inside. He was enormously relieved. He hadn't caused the baby's death. The heavy guilt that had lived inside him for months could now drain away.

He wasn't a killer. James hadn't appeared revolted or even surprised when Luke admitted that he had made love to Sarah late in her pregnancy. Perhaps he wasn't as bad, as wrong, as he had thought. Maybe tonight when they climbed the stairs to bed, he would follow Sarah into their room. They could sink into the big feather bed where they'd shared such pleasure, and—but no.

He must not let himself get carried away. He hadn't caused her to lose the baby, true enough, but he sure as hell had caused the pregnancy. And that was the real issue. As long as Sarah didn't get pregnant, there would be no risk of the same thing happening, no pain of childbirth, no chance of her dying. It was up to him to make sure it didn't happen. However much James's words might relieve him of his guilt, he still couldn't make love to Sarah.

Julia pushed the file into the folder and stood up, closing the drawer with her foot. She stretched her back, aching from a full day of work, and glanced around the waiting room. It was empty; James was in one of the examination rooms with the last patient. As soon as the man came out, Julia would be able to collect his money, enter it in the ledger, and leave. She was ready. It had been a hot, hard day.

She moved around the room, straightening the furniture, plumping cushions back into shape, arranging her desk neatly. She stopped in front of the small mirror. Wisps of hair had escaped her upswept hairdo and hung in damp strips around her neck. She smoothed them back up and tried to secure them with hairpins. It wasn't an entirely successful effort. She grimaced at her reflection in the mirror and turned away.

Julia didn't know why she was always so concerned with looking good for James. It would be better if she didn't. Maybe then he would abandon this crazy idea of marrying her. It was becoming difficult to work with him, not because he pressured her, but because of the sexual tension between them. The air fairly sizzled with it. She couldn't stand beside him, handing him instruments, without being aware of how close their bodies were, of how little it would take to brush against him and what sparks it would set off if she did. James never touched her at work, but the passion and love were there in his eyes whenever he looked at her.

Julia sighed. She didn't know how much longer this could go on. She rolled down her sleeves and fastened the row of small round buttons along the narrow cuff. There was the sound of a wagon and team stopping in the street outside, and she went to the front window, hoping that it wasn't a late patient arriving.

There were three men in the back of the wagon and a fourth driving it. They all jumped down and went to the back of the wagon. They pulled out two wide wooden planks with a man's body stretched on them, moving slowly and carefully. Julia flung open the door and hurried out onto the steps.

One of the men glanced up at her. "Fetch the doc. We got Bud O'Brien here, and he's busted up pretty bad. Fell off the gin."

Julia flew back into the office, leaving the door open for the men and their burden. "James! James!" She opened the door of the examining room. James was already reaching for the knob on the other side.

"What is it?"

"Some men from the cotton gin. They're carrying in Bud O'Brien; he fell off the gin."

"Good Lord." He glanced back at the man in the room. "Excuse me, Mr. Chandler." He strode toward the front door, calling back over his shoulder., "Julia, get the operating room ready."

Julia did as he requested. The men brought in O'Brien and laid him on the table, and James went to work on him. Both James and Julia knew as soon as they saw the man that it was hopeless, but they worked valiantly nonetheless to save him. Both of O'Brien's legs were broken, but far worse were the massive internal injuries. James did his best to stem the hemorrhaging, but he could not. Less than an hour after O'Brien was brought in, the breath shuddered out of him and he died.

"Damn!" James dropped his instruments into the metal bowl. "Goddamn it!"

"It wasn't your fault, James. No one could have saved him."

"I know." His voice was as weary as his face. "But that doesn't really help."

The undertaker was already there, waiting. The men who had brought O'Brien in had gone straight to him; they had known as well as James and Julia that there was no hope for their coworker. The undertaker removed the body, and Julia cleaned up the room. She washed up at the sink and left the room quickly. It smelled of death.

James was in his office, seated behind the desk. His coat and vest were off and his sleeves rolled up high on his arms.

There was an open bottle of whiskey and a half-full glass before him. His elbows were planted on the desk, and he held his head between his hands, staring down at the desk.

"James?"

He looked up, his dark eyes old and sad. He tried to summon up a smile for her. "Yes?"

"Are you all right?"

He nodded. "I always hate to lose them." He paused and sighed. "Buddy O'Brien and I went to grade school together."

"I'm sorry." Julia's heart ached for him. He was such a good man, so kind.

"He married Frances Brewster. They have some kids." He rubbed his hands across his face. "Christ, Julie, he was only thirty-one, same as me."

Julia came quickly across the room to him, and he reached out and pulled her close, burying his face against her breasts. She encircled him with her arms and laid her cheek against the top of his head. "Oh, James, I know. I know how hard it is for you."

He squeezed her to him tightly, and for a long time they remained like that, drawing comfort from each other. Tenderly Julia stroked James's hair and kissed the top of his head. James didn't want to let her go; she gave him such warmth and strength. Here, like this with her, nothing in the world seemed so bad.

When, at last, he released her, James pulled her down into his lap and sat with his arms around her. Julia cuddled up against him, and they talked while he sipped his whiskey. They talked about all kinds of things—it didn't matter what—until at last the adrenaline and the sadness began to slip away.

"Thank you, Julia."

"For what?"

"For staying here with me. For giving me your comfort." He closed his eyes as though in pain, and his arms tightened around her. "Oh, God, Julie, I love you so much."

"And I love you."

"Not enough."

"What do you mean?"

"You don't love me enough to marry me."

"That's not why—"

"No? Then what is?"

"Oh, James, can't you understand? I've told you. I'm not the kind of person you should marry."

He laid his finger across her lips. "Don't you dare say you aren't good enough. Because you're ten times better than anyone I know, including me."

"I don't know how to act. I'd be an embarrassment to you. You don't think it would matter, but it would. I'd be an embarrassment to your mother. Everyone would gossip about your marrying me. They'd pity you."

"They'd envy me."

"They would not, and you know it. They'd talk about you. They would say I didn't belong, and they would speculate on how I snared you."

"Then you don't love me enough to face the gossip of a few old biddies?"

"It's not that! *You* shouldn't have to face it."

"But don't you see? I don't care about the gossip. I doubt I'll even hear half of it, and the rest I won't pay any attention to. I don't care what other people think. So what if they gossip? Let them. As long as I have you, they can talk themselves hoarse, for all I care."

"You would care, someday."

"When? When I'm ninety? Don't you know me any better than that? Don't you know who I am?"

"Of course I know you. You're the kindest, best—"

He took her face between his hands and held it still, forcing her to look into his eyes. "Do you honestly think I will be hurt by some gossip? That I would be embarrassed because some old ladies don't approve of me or what I've done?"

She gazed at him for a moment. "No."

"Do you think I'm so stupid that I don't know my own mind? So slow that at thirty-one I don't know what I want?"

She wet her lips. She tried to look away, but he wouldn't let her. "No."

"Then let me say it one more time. *I want you.* I don't want a woman who can make polite conversation at the table or who knows how to give a proper party. I don't give a damn if she eats with the wrong spoon, or with a knife, if that's what she likes. I want a woman who knows me, who loves me, who understands what happened tonight and how I felt about it. I want a woman I can share my life with, work, fun, and everything in between. What I need is what you gave me tonight—your understanding and your generous comfort.''

"Any woman could—"

"No. You don't realize how special you are. Not any woman could have done what you did today—stand by my side in that room and face the blood and the death and then have the strength to come in here and comfort me. You're one of a kind, sweetheart. You're the only woman I want. In all my life I've never found another woman to compare with you. I've been so lonely without you, Julie. Please don't tell me I have to spend the rest of my life lonely.''

"Oh, James." Julia's hand went up to his cheek, warm and loving. She had never thought of it this way before, that by not marrying James she was condemning him to a life of loneliness, that perhaps no other woman would suit him as she did. She had been too wrapped up in her own inadequacies and fears to see that she was hurting James. Her hand trembled against his cheek as she realized how willfully she was throwing away their chance at happiness.

"Marry me, Julia. Say you'll marry me."

She gazed at his beloved face. Tears welled in her eyes. "Yes," she said finally. "Yes, I'll marry you."

* Chapter 21 *

James and Julia were married the following Saturday. Both Julia and Anthea exclaimed in horror that it was not proper to have the wedding that soon, but James set his jaw and replied that he didn't intend to wait any longer. He'd waited for Julia far too long as it was. Secretly, he was afraid that if he waited she would somehow get away from him again.

They had the ceremony late in the afternoon in the minister's study, with only their families present. Sarah and Anthea cried, though both declared they were tears of happiness, and after the ceremony they each hugged Julia and all three of the women cried again. James glanced at them a little nervously, wondering what was wrong. Luke chuckled. "Better get used to it. Sarah cries at the strangest times."

"Honestly?" James shrugged, then laughed, too.

Luke shook his hand. "Congratulations."

"Thank you." James looked at him. They were brothers-in-law now. It seemed a strange idea. There was an openness to Luke's face that James had never encountered before. James wondered if they might actually come to like each other in time. Stranger things had happened.

He glanced over at the women. Julia was dabbing at her eyes with a lacy handkerchief. She sensed his gaze and looked up at him, smiling. It warmed James all through. He reached out his hand, and she came to him and took it shyly. James raised her hand to his mouth and kissed it. The plain gold wedding band shone against her fair skin. His wife. It was a little hard to believe. He gripped her hand tightly.

They went back to the house, where Anthea and Lurleen had prepared an elegant wedding supper. The food was sumptuous, but James could hardly eat it. All he could think about was how long it would be before he could have his wife to himself. It was the worst of tortures to have to sit there, talking politely and pretending to enjoy the meal, when he wanted only to be alone with Julia.

Julia, too, had little appetite. In a matter of hours she and James would be on the train to Galveston, locked together in their private compartment, married. At long last they would make love with each other again. Her nerves thrummed with excitement and a hint of fear. What if it wasn't the same? What if James was disappointed, after he'd waited so long for her? She wasn't the young girl he had loved before—what if he found her body old when he saw her naked?

She glanced up at James. He was watching her, his gaze hot and dark. A quiver ran through Julia, and she realized that no matter what the fear in her, her desire for James was even stronger.

He took her hand, lacing his fingers through hers. His hand was large around hers. Julia knew how strong that hand was, how sensitive and skilled. It was suddenly difficult for her to breathe. That hand would explore her body tonight. Julia could feel the blush rising in her cheeks, and she glanced down to conceal it. James's thumb caressed the back of her hand. It moved up to her wrist, tracing the small bony knob there. Her face grew even hotter, and she took a sip from her glass of water.

James watched her drink. Everything Julia did seemed sensual to him—the way her eyelids fluttered almost closed when he touched her hand, the movement of her smooth throat when she drank, the curve of her fingers around the ornately cut crystal. She finished drinking and set down the glass. There was a faint film of water clinging to her upper lip. He couldn't take his eyes from it. Julia's tongue crept out and wiped it away. Desire snaked through him.

Julia wore a dress of pale blue satin the color of her eyes, overlaid with champagne-colored lace, as delicate as cobwebs. The satin bodice was scoop necked and sleeveless, but over it the lace came up high around her throat and down her arms in long, tight sleeves, fastened at the wrist by a row of tiny pearlized buttons. The dress revealed nothing, yet the look of the gossamer lace over the bare skin of her chest, throat, and arms enticed James as the naked flesh of another woman would not have.

His hand slipped up onto her arm. He touched the lace, faintly scratchy against his fingers, and beneath it the softness of her skin. He heard the swift intake of Julia's breath, and that excited him more than anything else. He removed his hand; if he wasn't careful, he would embarrass them both with his obvious arousal.

At last the meal ended, and it was time to catch the train. They said good-bye to Anthea and the children at the house, and Luke and Sarah drove them to the train station. The train was only a few minutes late, but they waited for what seemed like hours before it arrived. James and Julia boarded and found their compartment. They waved a last good-bye out the window to Luke and Sarah, and the train pulled away from the small depot.

Julia had never been aboard a train before, and she looked around her in fascination at the cunning compartment where they would sleep. "It's just like a little room!"

James smiled, watching her. "Mm hmm."

Along one wall was a bed, which the Pullman porter had already made up for the night. Julia swallowed and turned away from it. She went to the window and looked out.

The land was rushing past. How fast it went! She looked back at James. He was still watching her. Julia blushed. "Is there something wrong?"

"No. I enjoy looking at you—especially knowing that I won't have to leave you tonight."

James reached out and pulled down the wide window shade. Julia's heart picked up its beat. He crossed the room and turned the lock on the door. He shrugged out of his suit jacket and hung it on the hook. His eyes never left her as he unfastened his cuff links and set them aside, then removed his vest.

Julia couldn't control her erratic breathing. She was certain that a flush had risen up her neck and face. She couldn't look away; she loved looking at him. Each move he made sent desire sizzling through her. Yet it scared her.

"I was beginning to think this time would never come," James said, undoing the first two buttons of his shirt.

Julia wondered if he would continue to undress before her, but then he stopped. He came across the narrow room to where she stood and stopped so close to her that she had to tilt back her head to see his face. His lids drooped down over eyes so dark they were almost black. His mouth was heavy and sensual. His hands came up to rest on her upper arms. His skin was searing.

"You looked so beautiful tonight. It was all I could do to keep my hands off you."

His fingers slid slowly down her arms, exploring the texture of the lace over skin. When he reached her wrists, he raised her hand and pressed his lips to her palm. His lips were velvety and hot; his breath teased her skin. Julia's hand trembled in his. His mouth moved to the thin skin of her inner wrist, kissing her through the lace. His tongue crept out to trace the pattern of the lace.

"James!" Julia drew in her breath sharply.

"What?" He began to unfasten the row of tiny buttons that stretched halfway up to her elbow.

"I—I don't know. I just—said your name."

He smiled faintly. "I like it when you say my name. I can still remember how you would call me 'Jimmy.' All the different ways."

Julia's breath caught in her throat. She remembered quite clearly how she had whispered his name in the throes of passion—and the low, melting way he had said her name. She saw the same memory in James's eyes. His fingers halted their work on the buttons of her cuff, and for a long moment they simply looked at each other.

James bent his head to hers. Their lips met and clung. His hand came up to cup her neck, sinking into the thick knot of her hair. He kissed her long and deeply, and her mouth opened up eagerly to him. She tasted sweeter than anything he had ever known. Her mouth was warm and welcoming, a hot, dark cave of pleasure. He groaned deep in his throat. It had been so hard the past few weeks to not kiss her or, even worse, to give her only a chaste peck on the cheek. He loved her mouth; he wanted to know every part of it. He wanted to claim it, possess it. He wanted to possess her.

The hunger ran deep in him, a passion unfulfilled for eleven years, so strong that it was both pain and joy. He kissed her again and again, changing the slant of their mouths, working his lips against hers, deepening their kiss. Their tongues tangled and stroked, playing with each other, first slow and languorous, then more and more feverish. James's arms curled around Julia, pressing her into his body, and she strained up against him. Her flesh was soft and yielding to his hardness, and just feeling her in his arms sent a rush of joy through James that was so intense it made him tremble. God, he wanted her. He had done no more than kiss her, both of them still fully clothed, but he felt ready to explode.

James slowly released her and stepped back. Julia gazed up at him questioningly, too awash in her passion to speak.

Her eyes were lambent, her skin glowing, and there was a soft, crushed look to her lips that came from their fierce kisses. She looked like a woman lost in love.

"I love you," he told her huskily. He wished there were better words to express the depth of his passion. "I love you so much."

He touched Julia's face, and his hand moved over her jaw and onto her throat, wrapped in lace. He slid down her chest and cupped her breast. Her nipples hardened, pushing against the soft satin and lace. He wanted to see her, *had* to see her. His hands went to the tiny buttons behind her neck, clumsy in his haste. Julia bent her head to allow him easier access to the buttons, and desire slammed through him at the sweet, trusting vulnerability of her pose. The tiny, slick buttons slipped through his fingers, frustrating him, and he bit back a curse.

Julia giggled, and he smiled, loving the sound of her laughter. "So you think it's funny?" he asked with mock gruffness. "Did you wear this especially to thwart me?"

"No. I have no wish to do that."

James pushed aside the lace that he had parted and bent to kiss the nape of her neck. Her skin was like velvet over the hard bone of her spine. He knew she was strong; he had seen it every day as she worked with him. But she seemed as fragile as a rose petal, as soft as the satin of her dress. He wanted to protect her, cover her, and keep her from all harm. At the same time he ached to rip her clothes from her and push her to the floor, to take her with all the force within him.

"Do you know what you do to me?" he mumbled against her skin. "I'm burning for you. I think I'd kill to have you tonight."

Julia leaned back against him, sighing. His words melted her. James's hands came around to caress her breasts while his lips roamed the back of her neck, sending shivers racing through her. Her nipples strained against the cloth of her dress, seeking his touch, and moisture pooled between her legs. She moaned softly. All her earlier fears and hesitations were gone. She yearned for his touch on her naked skin. She moved against him, rubbing her body up and down.

"Julie! Oh, Julie." James buried his face in her hair, and

his hands pressed her back hard against him, roaming her body.

A shudder took her. "Please. Please. I want to feel you on me."

He tore at her buttons then, popping several free in his haste. Julia worked at the long rows on her cuffs. There had never seemed so many of the little things before. At last James had the dress unfastened past her waist. He untied the drawstrings of her several petticoats and slid them all, dress and petticoats, down her body to pool at her feet.

James stepped back, his eyes on Julia. His breath rasped in his throat. Julia sat down on the edge of the bed and unfastened the buttons of her high-top shoes. James watched her. As she bent over, he had an excellent view of the softly rounded tops of her breasts above the lace-trimmed chemise. Her breasts were milk white and deliciously full. They trembled with the movements of her arms. His fingers itched to reach out and cup them.

Julia pulled off her shoes and reached up under the long, loose legs of her lace-trimmed underdrawers to take off the garters holding up her stockings. She rolled the white stockings down her legs and off her feet. She glanced up. James was watching her every move. She stood up, and her fingers went to the buttons of her chemise. Her chemise, like her underpants, was cream-colored satin edged in lace, a soft, lush garment that invited the touch. The hard buttons of her nipples pressed against the smooth material. James thought of crushing the material in his hands and pulling it aside to reveal her breasts.

Julia knew a flash of uncertainty at the thought of baring her body to James, but the smoldering fire in his eyes made her bold. She unbuttoned her chemise and pulled the garment off. James made an unintelligible noise.

"What?"

"Nothing. Go on. Don't stop."

James undressed as he watched her, his hands moving clumsily over his clothes. Julia pulled the pins from the heavy knot of her hair, and it tumbled down to her waist, a shining waterfall of gold. It barely veiled her breasts in front, parting over the pert thrust of her nipples.

Julia untied the drawstring of her final undergarment. She

could hardly breathe. She felt shy and hungry all at once. She released the underpants and let them fall to the floor.

James gazed at her, entranced, unable to move. Julia was beautiful, small and delicate, yet utterly female. Her figure was more lush than it had been when he knew her before, her hips and breasts more rounded and womanly. She was graceful, with none of the awkwardness of youth. A tremor ran through him.

"You are more lovely than ever."

Julia blushed, pleased and relieved and a little shy before his ardent gaze. "So are you." James was broader and stronger than he had been years ago, the black hair thicker across his chest, his arms more muscled.

He chuckled, and his eyebrows went up. "Beautiful? I think not."

"To me you are."

Heat flooded him at her words. Quickly he stripped off the rest of his clothes and went to her. Julia watched him approach. She had forgotten the full grace and power of his naked male form. His manhood thrust out from among the cluster of dark curls, hard and distended. James stopped inches from her and rested his hands on her shoulders. His hands glided downward over her silken hair until they reached her breasts. He wrapped his hands around her hair and lifted it, revealing the soft white orbs centered by dark rose nipples. He brushed a strand of hair across her nipples, teasing them into hardness. He pushed her hair back so that it fell behind her, exposing the full glory of her breasts. His fingers curved over the luscious globes and cupped them from beneath, lifting them up as though to test their weight. He circled her nipples with his thumbs and watched them tighten at his touch.

He released his breath in a shaky sigh. "I don't know how I lived so long without you."

Carefully he took one nipple between his forefinger and thumb and rolled it, gently squeezing and pulling, delighting in the way it puckered and hardened at his touch. He bent his head and kissed the rosy bud. Sparks showered through Julia's abdomen at the feel of his mouth on her, and moisture dampened her thighs. His tongue slid over her nipple and around it, then softly lashed it until Julia whimpered with pleasure. His mouth widened on her breast, sucking rhythmically.

Julia moaned, and her hands came up to clasp his shoulders, as though to steady herself in a tilting world. Her fingers dug into his flesh at each new shattering sensation. He bent her back over his arm, feasting on her breasts, and his other hand slipped down her body and into the cleft between her legs. His fingers slid into her moist warmth, caressing the slick, hot flesh. Julia's breath caught in her throat, and her fingernails scraped his skin. Wantonly her legs moved apart, inviting his touch. Gently, lovingly, James explored the folds of her femininity, finding the hard little nub that was the center of pleasure and teasing it until she was groaning and twisting in his arms.

Julia breathed his name over and over, her hands running over his back and arms and winding through his hair. James trembled under the force of his longing. Julia's hands on his flesh, the sweet taste of her in his mouth, the feel of her damp, utterly soft womanhood against his fingertips all combined to make him ready to explode with desire. He wanted to explore every inch of her skin with his hands and mouth. He wanted to make her pant and groan and cry out with pleasure. He needed it.

"Julie." He lifted his head and looked down at her. Julia's face was soft and dreamy, focused on nothing but the passion raging through her. Just looking at her sent desire shooting through him. He couldn't wait any longer.

James lifted her into his arms. Julia opened her eyes in hazy questioning. "James? What—"

"I'm taking you to bed." His voice was low and rough with barely restrained hunger.

Her mouth curved sensually. "Good."

He laid her down on the bed and stood for a moment looking at her. Her pale hair was spread out across the sheets, a silken backdrop for her shapely form. Her breasts were plump, the perfect size for a man's hand, and her nipples stood out proudly, dark and swollen from his kisses. James ran his tongue across his lips; he could taste them there. Her waist was slender, her abdomen flat even after children; the knobs of her pelvic bones rose sharply beneath her satiny skin. His eyes roamed lower to the flow of hips into thighs, to the womanly V covered by pale curls. She was beautiful, perfect. He ran a hand down her body, across her breasts and stomach to the soft flesh of her inner thigh, and his fingers tangled in the curls. Julia's eyes closed with pleasure at his touch.

Julia raised her arms to him, and James settled onto the bed beside her. Her hands went to his chest, and James had to bite his lower lip to slow the raging force of his desire. He had to feel her hands on him no matter how close to the edge it pushed him. Her fingers moved across the breadth of his chest, relearning the texture of his skin and the pattern of bone and muscle. She traced the jutting line of his collarbone and slid her fingers down into the prickly black hairs upon his chest. Her forefingers found the small masculine nipples, and James sucked in his breath. Julia glanced up at his face. His features were rigid, his mouth slightly open, and the intensity of his eyes sent a searing heat right through her.

She smiled and lightly moved her fingers back and forth across the nipples. James tightened all over. Shyly Julia placed her mouth on one tiny bud. She had wanted to do that years ago when she had known James, but then she had been too young and apprehensive to try anything he hadn't initiated. When James groaned, his hands clenching into the sheets, she grew bolder. Her tongue played over his nipple, stroking, circling, lashing it with wet heat.

"Oh, God. Julie." He moved quickly then, rolling her onto her back and moving over her. She loved the weight of him on her, loved looking up into his face, burning and taut. Her legs opened to him, and he slid into her. He moved slowly, carefully, despite the effort it cost him, afraid that he might cause her some discomfort.

But there was no discomfort, only the joy of him filling her, the satisfaction of wholeness. James paused, struggling for the control that he almost lost at the exquisite pleasure of her tight sheath gripping him. He began to move, sliding almost out, then all the way in again. He moved slowly, sailing the edge of a dark, wild pleasure. Julia's hands slid down his body to his buttocks, and her hips moved beneath him. James watched her face, taut and rapt, as he stroked, and his movements began to speed up. Their sweat-damp skin clung as his body rubbed over hers. He moved ever faster, his hips pumping. Julia felt each stroke to the depths of her being. Like a knot drawn ever more tightly, her desire heightened, and she strained up against James, seeking the bliss of completion.

He was on fire, every inch of his skin quivering with sensations. Then, at last, the hot surge of utter delight and release came to him, and he groaned, shuddering, as his seed spilled into her. Julia buried her face in his shoulder, holding on to him tightly, and the wave of pleasure took her, too. For one long moment, they were mindless, selfless, bound together in an eternity of love.

He lay upon her, his weight crushing her into the mattress, but when, after a time, he started to roll away, Julia's arms wrapped around him, pressing him to her tightly. James smiled against her skin and kissed her lightly on the shoulder. His arms encircled her, and he rolled onto his back, taking her with him, so that she lay stretched atop him. He couldn't remember ever feeling quite this blissful and at peace. He stroked his hand down her long golden hair.

"I love you, wife," he murmured.

Julia laughed shakily. She thought she could have gotten up and yelled and danced with joy, except she was so wonderfully exhausted she couldn't move. "And I love you, husband. I love you always."

Sarah settled the children in bed, tucking Julia's Bonnie in with Emily and putting Vance with Cal. It was a relief to see Cal accepting the other boy in his room without protest. She had worried that Cal might be difficult to deal with while the other children were with them during Julia's and James's honeymoon. No doubt Bonnie and Vance were a little lost without their mother for the first time, and if Cal had been antagonistic, it would have been an awful situation. But he was chatting with Vance about what he would show him the next day, and Sarah closed the door on them with a smile.

She walked down the stairs to the kitchen just as Luke

stepped in the back door. For a moment they simply looked at each other. The air had been thick with tension between them since the wedding this afternoon. During the ceremony, watching James and Julia pledge their love for each other, Sarah had been swept with a wave of longing for her own marriage. She remembered how happy and in love she and Luke had been, and she had wished desperately that they could recapture what they had had. She had sneaked a glance at Luke and caught him watching her, the same remorse and yearning in his eyes. For an instant there had been the old closeness between them, a sweet remembrance of the commitment and love they shared.

It was still inside them, Sarah knew, blocked by Luke's stubborn insistence on protecting her from himself. He loved and desired her as much as she loved and desired him, yet she was dying of loneliness for him. She had tried to talk to him about it, but Luke had managed to avoid any conversation after the wedding and on the ride home, using the presence of the children as a buffer between them.

But now there was no one else there. There was no way he could hide. Sarah's heart began to hammer in her chest. She was scared that she would fail and ruin what little they had left. But she couldn't continue to live like this!

She drew a shaky breath. "Luke."

"Sarah." His face was closed and cautious. "How are the children?"

"In bed."

"Any problems?"

"No. Cal was fine. Even Bonnie didn't cry."

"Good."

"It was a nice wedding, don't you think?"

"Yes. Julia looked happy."

"I'm sure she is. They've waited a long time to be together."

Luke nodded. He glanced around the room, searching for something else to say.

But Sarah spoke first, forestalling him. "All through the wedding, I kept remembering ours. Do you remember it?"

"Of course." He relaxed into a genuine smile. "I was scared to death."

"Were you? It didn't show. I thought I was the only one who was terrified."

He shook his head. "I remember Stu glowering like he wanted to kill me and Jenny in tears. They hated your marrying me."

"They were concerned for me. They didn't know how happy you would make me, what a good husband and father you would be." She paused. "I want it back, Luke! I'm tired of being alone, of missing you and wanting you and never—" She stopped, fighting back the flood of tears that threatened to overwhelm her.

"Sarah! Oh, God, don't cry." He came to her quickly, and his work-roughened hand smoothed away her tears. "Don't cry. I'm not worth it."

"You are! You're worth far more than my tears!" Her hands came up to his chest, grasping the material of his shirt. "Please. Come back to my bed. Love me again." Sarah blinked away her tears. "What will it take? I'll beg, if that's what you want."

"Sarah, don't! You know that's not what I want."

"Then what? What do you want?"

"You," he replied thickly. "Only you."

Sarah stretched up on tiptoe, offering her mouth to him. "You have that," she whispered.

Her lips brushed his, and a tremor shook Luke. His eyes closed, his face melting into the familiar pattern of passion. His hands came up to her waist, spreading wide, his thumbs brushing the undersides of her breasts. Desire thrummed in him.

It took almost nothing to set him off. He wanted her all the time these days. Luke knew that for a while Sarah had tried to tempt him. She had teased him in hundreds of little ways, taking down her hair in front of him or coming into his room wearing only her nightgown or unbuttoning her blouses farther down than her usual modesty allowed. Sometimes she had simply looked at him in that heavy-lidded way he'd seen so many times before in her, and he knew she wanted him. Even that was enough to ignite the fires in him.

He was beginning to realize that those fires would never be put out. Sarah had stopped the small seductions. She no longer tried to arouse him, but he was still aroused. Sarah didn't have to do anything, say anything, look any way. Just her being there was enough to bring his nerves to sizzling life. He had only to look at her to want her, had only to think about her to know the fierce swell of hunger deep in his abdomen. Luke knew that only age or death would bring an end to his desire for her. Maybe not even that. Sometimes he thought that this must be what hell was: wanting her with every fiber of his being, yet having to stop himself from taking what he wanted.

Today at the wedding Sarah had looked at him with her heart in her eyes, and love and desire for her had filled him. The rest of the day he had been able to think of nothing else but coming to her bed tonight. Now, with her reaching up to kiss him, he was shaken with longing. He could smell her, touch her, taste her—all the things he had been missing for so long. She was like water to a man lost in the desert, and he wanted to drink her in.

For a long moment Luke stood, his entire body rigid, hovering on the brink of giving in to his longings. Then, at last, he jerked away. He strode across the room, crossing his arms across his chest and clamping his hands under his arms, as though to forcibly keep them from wandering where they chose. "God, Sarah! Don't tempt me."

Sarah made a noise of frustration and whirled away, slamming her hand, palm flat, against the door frame. "Damn! Damn! Damn!"

He whirled back and stared at her, amazed by her language. "Sarah!"

She faced him defiantly, chin thrust out. "Oh, I'm sorry. I forgot. A saint doesn't say such things, does she?"

He grimaced. "I never said you were a saint."

"You didn't have to say it," she retorted hotly. "Everything you do shows that that's what you think. Sweet little Sarah. Porcelain doll Sarah. Up-on-a-pedestal Sarah. She doesn't get angry, she doesn't get hungry, she doesn't have low, lustful desires like the rest of humanity. Isn't that right?"

"Of course not."

"Oh? I thought that was how you saw me. You certainly don't see me as a real woman. One who desires her man."

Even her words stirred him. Luke glanced away, struggling for control. "I refuse to endanger you to satisfy my own selfish lust."

"Well, what about *my* selfish lust? Have you ever given a thought to me in all these noble decisions you make?"

"Of course. It's for you."

She laughed bitterly, shaking her head. "Oh, no. Think again. It's for you. What *you* want. What *you* think."

Anger surged through Luke. "Damn it! If I paid attention only to what I wanted, I'd pull you down to the floor and make love to you right here."

"And I'd welcome it! I would have made love to you on the ground by the creek that day, if you'll remember! What do you think I do every night while you're lying in your sanctified single bed? I'm awake in our bed, thinking about you, missing you, remembering the times we made love. The ways."

He swallowed with difficulty. "Stop it."

"I can't sleep. I lie there and think about it until my skin's like fire and I'm throbbing inside."

"Christ, Sarah." A fine sheen of sweat dotted Luke's upper lip. "You're killing me."

"No. *You're* killing me. I'm a flesh and blood woman, not the plaster saint you're determined to make of me. I want you. I want to taste your kisses again. I want to feel you inside me."

Luke groaned and turned away. "Don't."

"Don't what? Don't admit that I have human desires? I know you don't like to hear it. You don't want to see me as I really am. You won't accept that I'm not perfect. That's why you won't make love to me. 'Sweet Sarah' must not feel pain or desire or any other low human emotion. I can't come close to death; I can't labor in childbirth; I can't get angry at the world because my baby died. I must not be allowed to suffer. I must not be allowed to feel pain. I must not be allowed to feel passion or joy. Because, after all, I'm a statue, not a woman. Perfection. Isn't that right?"

"No!" Anger mingled with desire in Luke's gut. He hated what she was saying. He wanted to shake her. He wanted to rip off her clothes and thrust into her. He wanted—oh, God, he wanted. He clenched his fist, trembling with barely restrained fury and lust.

"Oh yes, it is!" Sarah retorted. "I'm not a real person to you. I'm something you've concocted in your mind: the perfect woman. Sweet and good and pretty and never, ever bad, never, ever hurt. If anything bad happens, it has to be your fault, not mine. Because that's the only way I can remain this perfect woman. But I'm not! I'm not! That isn't me! I'm very imperfect. I feel the same heat, hunger, and lust you do. I'm fallible. I have ordinary weaknesses. I'm no better than you are! We're alike inside. Don't you realize that yet? It's part of why we love each other! I want to make love to you; I want to bear your children. And I'm willing to take the responsibility for those things. I'm willing to risk it."

"Well, I'm not! I won't risk your life!"

"It's *my* life! I don't want to be locked into this dry, empty, loveless life for the rest of my years! This is a mockery of a marriage. I'm your wife. I want to be your wife in every way. I want to be at the core of your life, not something you worship!"

"Damn it!" Luke slammed his fist down on the counter, and dishes fell with a clatter. "You *are* the core of my life! That's why I can't bear to lose you. Why can't you understand that? Why do you have to keep fighting me?" He was rigid, the tendons standing out in his neck, muscles bulging under his shirt.

"Because," Sarah's voice was cold and cutting, "I'm not a quitter like you. Because I love you enough for anything. But you don't even love me enough to let me make my own decisions." Sarah whirled and ran out of their kitchen. He heard her feet on the stairs, then the bedroom door slammed behind her.

Her words had sliced through him like a knife. He wanted to grab her and force her to take them back. He wanted to toss her skirts up over her head and take her like a common whore. He wanted to make love to her so slowly and deliciously she whimpered and writhed and begged him to take her. His insides were like hot pitch. She infuriated him. She tormented him. She was the thing he treasured most in the world. How could he love her so much and yet itch to

slap her? How could he go cold as death at the thought of
losing her and yet ache to do what could cause her death?
How could he want her so much and still manage to keep
himself from bedding her? He thought he must explode
from it all.

Luke brought both fists crashing down upon the counter.
He hit it again and again. He felt as wild and furious as he
had when he was young, feverish, and uncontrollable. For
the first time in years he wanted to find someone to beat up,
wanted to feel the pleasure of his fists smacking into flesh
and bone. Instead, he kicked open the door and walked out,
crashing it to behind him. He strode across the yard to the
toolshed and jerked out the ax. He took it to the chopping
stump behind the house, set a log on the stump, and
brought the ax crashing down on it. Like a maniac he
wielded the ax over and over, chopping wood into smither-
eens in the pale moonlight, not stopping until he was
drenched with sweat and dotted with wood chips, his
muscles quivering with exhaustion. Only then was he able
to go up to his bed and sleep.

* Chapter 22 *

Neither Sarah nor Luke was pleasant to live with in the
following days. Though they strove not to take their bad
feelings out on anyone, the air was tense and strained
between them, and their tempers were short. They spent as
little time as possible near each other, and when they were
in the same room, they spoke only when necessary. Sarah
wondered how they could possibly live the rest of their lives
like this. It was obvious that Luke was determined not to
change his mind, and she didn't know how she could rid
herself of her desire and resentment. She cried herself to

sleep almost every night, vacillating between loving Luke and hating him.

James and Julia returned from their honeymoon after two weeks, and Sarah took the children back to their home. Cal went with them, and Micah drove the wagon. Luke stayed at home, saying he had to get some chores done. The truth was he didn't think he could bear to sit next to Sarah on the wagon seat that long. He always felt as if he were about to explode around Sarah. It was easier if he just stayed away from her.

Micah dropped Sarah and the children off at the Bankses' house, and he drove on to the lumberyard to pick up some supplies. Julia greeted the children and Sarah with hugs. She looked happy, content, and prettier than Sarah had ever seen her. Obviously marriage agreed with her.

The children went outside for a few last minutes of play together, and James soon excused himself, leaving the women alone to talk.

"You look happy," Sarah commented.

"I am." A smile lit Julia's face, and her cheeks colored. "It's so wonderful. I never dreamed marriage could be so good, so much fun." She laughed softly. "Now I know what you and Luke have, why you're so happy together."

Sarah smiled stiffly, fighting back the tears that always threatened to come these days. She couldn't spoil Julia's happiness by crying. "I'm glad. You deserve happiness, both of you."

"That's what's marvelous. James is happy, too. I was afraid that after we were married, he would be disappointed in me, but he seems to love me every bit as much. I never would have believed it possible. I'm the luckiest woman alive."

Sarah thought she probably was. She wished that some of Julia's present luck would rub off on her. It was difficult to sit in the presence of Julia's supreme happiness and pretend that things were right with her and Luke, too. As soon as she could gracefully do so, Sarah excused herself and took Emily and Cal to the lumberyard to meet Micah.

Julia watched Sarah and the children walk away, a frown creasing her forehead.

"Doesn't look like the visit was very good," James said

softly, coming up behind her and resting his hand on her shoulder.

Julia jumped, startled. "What?"

"That frown. Something the matter?"

She smiled a little. "You know me too well. I'm worried about Luke and Sarah. All the time we were talking, she seemed so stiff and false, as if she were trying to pretend."

"Pretend what?"

"That everything's all right with them. I know it's not; I can sense it. Sarah's unhappy. I wish I could do something for them."

James bent and kissed the top of her head. She was always kind and generous, wanting to do for others. But he would make sure that things were done for her now. "And what would you do for them, sweetheart?"

"That's just the problem. I don't think there's anything anyone can do. They have to do it themselves." She sighed. "I feel almost guilty, being so happy with you while Luke and Sarah are hurting."

James wrapped his arms around her from behind and squeezed her to him. "Don't you dare feel guilty. I intend to make sure you're happy the rest of your life, and I won't have you feeling guilty the whole time."

"Yes, sir." Julia leaned her head back against his chest. She had never dreamed that she would ever feel this loved, this safe and secure.

James's hands inched down her stomach, pressing her closely against him all the way down. Julia was surprised to feel the insistent hardness of his desire prodding her buttocks, and she let out a little giggle. "Oh!"

"Yes, oh. I was thinking that a Saturday afternoon nap might be in order."

"Really?" Julia twisted to look up into his face, her eyes alight with amusement. "Are you feeling tired, dear?"

"Yes, very tired."

"Then perhaps you should sleep."

"Not I. We."

"But I'm not tired." Her smile grew.

"No? Well, you soon will be, my dear. I promise."

James kissed her hard, then swung her up into his arms. He carried her out of the room and up the stairs.

* * *

Sarah walked with Emily and Cal over to the lumberyard, where they found Micah loading the wagon. Cal pitched in to help Micah, and Sarah swung Emily up into the back of the wagon to ride. She was just starting around the wagon to climb up on the seat when suddenly George Jackson came hurrying across the street and planted himself in front of her. Sarah stopped, startled, then drew herself up and fixed him with her haughtiest stare.

"Excuse me, you're in my way," she said with icy politeness and started to go around him.

Jackson reached out and put a hand on her arm to detain her. Sarah stiffened. Out of the corner of her eye she saw Micah and Cal go still, watching them. Sarah wished that Luke were there.

"Look, Miss McGowan—"

"It's Mrs. Turner."

He ignored her words and smiled at her in a secretive way. Sarah wanted to shudder. He was a thoroughly disgusting man, smelly and dirty, with little pig eyes that saw evil everywhere. She hated to think of Cal's having been under his power all these years. It was a wonder the poor child hadn't had every bit of joy and life squeezed out of him.

"I want to talk to you."

"I have nothing to say to you. Good day."

"I'm giving you an opportunity to get rid of that bastard of your husband's. I figure a lady like you, she don't want that boy in her house. I'm offering to take him off your hands."

Cal edged up beside her, and Sarah felt his hand curl into the folds of her skirts, hanging on. She glanced down at him. His face was white, his eyes huge and scared. He wet his lips anxiously. "Please, don't let him take me."

"Of course not." Sarah looped her arm around Cal's shoulders, pulling him close to her side. She turned her gaze coldly on Jackson. "Cal is Luke's son, and he is very dear to both of us. I wouldn't dream of entrusting any child to your care, let alone one I loved as I love Cal. I suggest you go home and stay away from us. Now, get out of my way."

Jackson's face hardened, his eyes turning into narrow slits

of hatred. "Folks say you're a lady, but I knowed it wasn't true, not with you living with that piece of trash. No one but a slut would let him cover her. You're as evil as he is."

Micah came around the side of the wagon, his fists clenching. The man's words made Micah itch to knock him down, but common sense held him back. No black man could get away with hitting a white one, no matter what the reason.

Jackson looked past Sarah to Micah, and his sneer grew. "Nigger lovers, both of ya. Turner's a devil, and you're his whore."

"Don't you say that to her!" Cal screamed and launched himself at the man, fists and feet flying.

"Cal!" Sarah grabbed at him, but she was too late. Jackson backhanded the boy, splitting his lip, and knocked him into Sarah, sending both of them sprawling on the ground.

With a low growl Micah sprang forward. His huge fist lashed out, catching Jackson squarely on the chin, and Jackson went down in a heap.

"Boy! Mrs. Turner! You all right?" Micah turned and bent over them anxiously.

"Yes. I think so," Sarah gasped. "I—it just knocked the wind out of me a little."

He helped them to their feet. Sarah bent and examined Cal's lip, wiping away the blood with her handkerchief. Micah glanced around, and his blood went cold. Several men stood on the porch of the store, gaping at them. He realized what he'd done. No matter how justifiable his blow was, he was in serious trouble. He turned to Sarah.

"Uh, ma'am . . ."

Sarah looked up at him, then around at the onlookers. "Let's get home, Micah."

"Yes, ma'am."

Sarah grabbed Cal's hand, and they scrambled up into the wagon. Micah leapt up onto the seat and grabbed the reins, calling to the team. They left the town and headed for the farm as fast as he could urge the team to go.

When they turned into the farm, the wagon rattling noisily at its abnormally fast pace, Luke looked up from the corral fence he was repairing. He frowned as he watched the wagon approach.

"Micah? What's the problem?" He started toward them.

Sarah and the children tumbled out of the back of the wagon and came running to him. "Luke! Oh, Luke!"

His heart began to race at the anxiety on Sarah's face, and he automatically opened his arms and pulled her close to him. "What happened? What's the matter?"

"George Jackson stopped us. He wanted to take Cal with him, and I told him no."

"And Micah hit him!" Cal chimed in.

"What?" Luke glanced over at the wagon. Micah had disappeared.

"Jackson insulted me," Sarah explained. "Cal—" She smiled down at the boy. "Cal defended my honor. He jumped in and started hitting Jackson. So Jackson hit Cal."

"And he knocked us both down," Cal put in excitedly. "Then Micah hit him." Cal's face gleamed with excitement. "Boy, he knocked him to kingdom come! You shoulda seen it."

Luke's mouth set grimly. "I would have liked to." He released Sarah and bent down to hug Cal fiercely. "You did right to defend Sarah. I'm proud of you."

Cal beamed up at him.

Luke looked at Sarah. "I suppose others saw this."

"Oh yes. There were several men that came out when they heard the ruckus. It won't go unnoticed."

"He'll have to leave, then."

"Who?" Cal asked, the blood suddenly draining from his face.

"Not you, silly." Sarah laid her arm around his shoulders. "Micah."

"Micah! But why? He was just helpin' Sarah and me."

"It's safer for him."

"Couldn't he stay?" Sarah asked. "If you and I stood up for him?"

Luke sighed and shook his head. "It's better not to take the risk. There'll be people wanting his blood by nightfall, no matter what happened."

"I'll fix him something to take with him to eat, then."

Sarah turned and hurried off toward the house, pulling
Emily with her.

Luke looked after her. Thank God for Sarah. She was
never one to waste time asking questions or dithering
around. She always went unerringly to the practical thing to
do.

He turned to his son. He gazed down at the small face so
similar to his own, and his hand went out to rest on the
bright cap of hair. "We'll never let him take you. You know
that, don't you? You're our son."

Cal nodded. His eyes glistened with tears. "Does she
love me, you think?"

"Sarah?"

"Yeah. I mean, the way she stood up for me and all."

"Yeah. She loves you. You'll never find anyone to love
you better than Sarah." Luke ruffled Cal's hair. "Now go
fetch Jo-Jo from the pasture for me."

"Jo-Jo? Why? Oh." His face dropped. "For Micah to
leave?"

Luke nodded. "It's the only thing, son. Now, get."

Cal took off at a run. Luke went to the hired hand's room
in the barn. As he stepped inside the door, Micah was
turning to come out, a hastily wrapped bundle slung over his
shoulder. They stopped and looked at each other for a
moment.

"You know where you're going?" Luke asked.

Micah shrugged. "Anywhere west of here."

"I wanted to thank you for helping my wife and son. If I
thought we could—"

Micah shook his head decisively. "No. I gotta go."

"I sent Cal down to the pasture for Jo-Jo. You can get
away on him."

"Your horse?" Micah stared. "You mean, take Jo-Jo?"

Luke nodded. He smiled. "What do you think, that I
wouldn't give up a horse in return for your protecting Sarah
and Cal?"

"But I—"

"It's a lot better chance than trying it on foot. You know
that."

Micah hesitated, then said, "Thank you."

"Thank you." Luke held out his hand, and Micah shook it.

Luke wrote out a bill of sale to Micah for Jo-Jo, so that he would have evidence that he owned the quality horse. Cal rode the horse in bareback a few minutes later, and Micah quickly saddled and bridled it. Sarah joined them in the yard, carrying a cloth bag, which she handed to Micah. It was filled with meat, bread, and fruit for his trip. Emily followed her, crying.

"No go. No," Emily wailed to Micah, and his face softened. He bent and scooped the little girl up in his arms. She wrapped her arms around his neck and hung on hard.

"Sorry, sugar. I gotta go. You be good." He set the little girl down. He tipped his hat to Sarah. "Mrs. Turner. Thank you for the food."

Tears sprang into Sarah's eyes. It was so unfair. "I'm the one who's grateful to you."

Micah shook hands again with Luke. He turned and looked at Cal. Cal hesitated for a moment, then ran to him and hugged him as hard as Emily had. "You take care of your sister now, you hear?"

Cal nodded, his throat too clogged with tears to speak. Micah took the reins to the horse and started to mount.

They all turned at the sound of hoofbeats on the road. A horse trotted into the yard, carrying a woman riding bareback. Her hair was a wild mass of tangles, and her skirts were hiked up to her knees as she rode astride. She held the reins awkwardly, and it was obvious that she was unused to riding a horse.

Micah stared. "Dovie!"

She slid off the horse and ran toward them, stumbling in her haste. "Micah! Oh, Micah! You've got to leave! Quick!" She ran straight to him, hardly noticing Luke and Sarah standing beside him. She reached out to grip his arm, panting, her words jerking and tumbling from her mouth. "You have to run. I heard—I heard them talking downtown. They were going for the sheriff. 'Cause of what you did. So I came to warn you. I took one of Dr. Jim's horses."

"I know. I know. Slow down. It's all right. I goin'."

Dovie gazed up at him. Tears gathered in her eyes. All the way out here she had thought of nothing but Micah's safety. But now the awful loss of his leaving shook her. She would never see him again. Never kiss him, never hold him. "Oh, God." She began to cry. "Oh, God, Micah."

She flung her arms around his neck and clung to him. He held her tightly. "I didn't mean for this to happen," he whispered to her. "I done had a different life planned. I sorry, Dovie, love."

Tears streamed down Dovie's face. Micah bent and kissed her hard. "Remember me?"

Dovie nodded, unable to speak. Always. Always. She would never forget him.

He swung away abruptly and mounted Jo-Jo. He lifted his hat in a good-bye gesture. He looked down at Dovie. She gazed back, shaking with tears. She felt as if her heart were being torn out of her. He was leaving, going to that wild country out West where she didn't belong. They would never have the sweet life together that they had dreamed of.

Micah gathered up the reins and touched the horse gently in the sides. He started off at a trot.

"Wait!" Dovie's scream stopped him. Micah twisted in the saddle to look back at her. She began to run, her arms uplifted to him.

Micah wheeled the horse around and bent out of the saddle, his arm stretched out to her. When she reached him, he clamped his arm around her and swung her up into the saddle in front of him. Dovie wrapped her arms around him and buried her face in his chest. They rode out of the yard together.

Less than an hour later, the sheriff rode up to the Turner house and dismounted. Sarah greeted him at the front door. "Why, hello, Sheriff. Come in and sit for a spell. You here to see Luke?"

"Yes, ma'am." Sheriff Bowens stepped inside the door sweeping off his hat. He was an easygoing man who had little crime in his town and was happy to have it remain that way. He had been sheriff for only five years, so he hadn't been the one who had arrested and jailed Luke years before. Though he had heard stories about the incident, Bowens had known Luke Turner only as a well-to-do, model citizen. He liked Turner and, frankly, he disliked having to come out here with trouble in his pocket.

"I'll send Cal out to get Luke. He's in the back pasture. Could I fix you something to drink while you wait? Some iced tea maybe? Or lemonade?"

"Lemonade sounds real good, ma'am."

"All right. I'll bring it right in."

Sarah sent Cal for Luke. He had gone to the back pasture as soon as Micah left, knowing that the sheriff would want to talk to him and hoping to slow him down as much as he could. It took forty-five minutes for Luke to appear. Sheriff Bowens didn't seem to mind. He sat in the rocking chair by the front window, letting the breeze blow over him and sipping his lemonade. Sarah filled his glass again as soon as it was empty.

When Luke arrived, Bowens rose and they shook hands in a friendly manner. Luke smiled. Maybe Micah would have a better chance than he had thought.

"Sheriff. Nice to see you. I hear you had a little trouble in town today."

"Yep. Not the first time George Jackson's been in a squabble." He shrugged. "I understand your hired hand hit him."

"Jackson insulted my wife. He hit my son and knocked him and my wife to the ground." Luke's face turned as hard as flint, the easiness erased. "If I'd been there, I'd have done worse."

"Well, now, that's understandable. But Jackson's all riled up, and so are some other people. They're saying we can't let him get away with hitting a white man. Have to set an example and all. So I reckon I better take Micah in."

"Let me show you where he lives, then."

Luke walked with him to the small room in the barn where Micah had lived. The sheriff seemed unsurprised to find that neither Micah nor his possessions were there.

"Guess I better make sure he's not hiding in the barn," Bowens commented, and Luke showed him through the barn.

They checked the toolshed and stopped by the corral to look at the mare and her colt. They walked back to the front porch, where the sheriff's horse was tied. He glanced at the hoofprints leading out of the yard but made no comment.

"Well, he must have hightailed it. Probably halfway out of the county by now," the sheriff commented.

"Probably."

"You know where he might go?"

"No."

The sheriff nodded. "Guess I'll check around tomorrow in town, though I don't suspect it'll do much good."

"Probably not."

"That Jackson's always a nuisance. Threatened the Jewish peddler last year, you know. I reckoned this would be a wild-goose chase."

He looked sideways at Luke, and a small smile touched his mouth. Luke smiled back.

"He's not going to do anything about it," Luke said, settling back in his chair.

"Are you sure?" Sarah poured him a glass of lemonade and sat down across the table from him.

"It was obvious. I could tell he didn't like Jackson, thought he was a troublemaker. He'll probably ask a few questions down on F Street tomorrow, and that'll be the end of it. He'll say he couldn't find Micah; he's gone and good riddance. Why waste taxpayers' money looking for him?"

"Will Grandpa come back? Is he going to try to take me back again?" Cal stood close to Luke, though not quite touching him, picking at the edge of the table.

"No. We'll never let him have you. In fact, I plan to ride over to his place tomorrow and remind him of that."

"Luke . . ." Fear brushed Sarah. She paused and glanced at Cal, standing so trustingly beside Luke. "Cal, why don't you run upstairs and see what Emily's doing? She's been quiet so long, I suspect she's into something."

"All right." He left the room, and they heard his rapid footsteps on the stairs.

Luke knew Sarah. He looked at her questioningly, waiting for her to tell him what she didn't want to say in front of Cal.

"Are you sure you should go over there?" she began, frowning.

"Of course. Apparently I didn't make myself clear enough the first time with Jackson. So I'm going to make sure he understands what will happen if he bothers you or Cal again. He's already done more harm than I want to see."

"I know, but—I'm not sure it's safe for you to go over there alone."

Luke's eyebrows shot up. "You're saying I ought to be afraid of George Jackson?"

"Yes."

Luke made a noise of disgust. "The day I can't whip a man twice my age . . ."

"Oh Luke, of course you could whip him—fairly, face-to-face. But he's a sneaky, slimy man. I don't trust him. He might ambush you. He might shoot you when you ride into the yard. He doesn't have ordinary scruples; he's convinced himself that God is on his side, so whatever he does is right. He could justify anything by saying it was God's will."

"He's not going to ambush me."

"How do you know?"

"How could he? He won't know when I'm coming or from where. Don't worry. I'll be careful."

"Why take the chance? He knows we aren't going to give up Cal."

"You think I'd let him get by with hitting Cal or insulting you? I ought to horsewhip him. When I think of him daring to say anything to you—"

Sarah smiled a little bitterly. "Does it matter that much to you?"

"Matter! Of course it matters. How could it not?" He stared at her, amazed.

"Sometimes I wonder how you feel about me. I'm not so sure anymore." She knew she should not say it, should not open up the wounds. That's always what they did the only times they talked anymore. It was wrong; it was tearing the fabric of their marriage apart. She knew it. Yet she could not seem to keep from saying the words.

"How can you not be sure?" Luke's gaze carried anger and pain. "You know how I feel about you. I love you. I'll always love you. But I can't risk—"

Sarah jumped up agitatedly. "That's right. You can't risk. One thing I never thought of you, Luke, and that's that you were a coward. That you'd curl up in a hole because of fear."

The skin around Luke's mouth whitened, and for a second Sarah thought he would jump up and start yelling at her. She would have welcomed the release of emotions. Instead he said, in a low, tight voice, "You're right. When it comes to you, I am scared. I'm not like you. I know what it's like to have nothing and no one. I know what it's like to live without love. That makes me want to hold on to what I've got. I'm scared to death of losing you."

Sarah clenched her fists. Her face was tight with frustration and anger. "That's right. You're so damn scared of losing something that you're pushing it away with both hands. I don't want to live like that. I *refuse* to live like that!"

She turned and marched out of the room, leaving Luke staring after her.

After supper Luke returned the Bankses' horse to them, and when he returned he found enough chores around the barn to keep him occupied the rest of the evening. He kept thinking about what Sarah had said to him. He didn't want to think about it, but even though he had escaped her presence, he couldn't escape his thoughts.

She had sounded like she was through with him. He couldn't believe it; a woman like Sarah didn't leave her husband. But what if she stayed with him, and didn't love him anymore? He thought that would be even worse than her leaving—to live with her, see her, be with her every day, all the while knowing that he was nothing to her. That would be an even more excruciating hell than the one he was in now.

He couldn't bear it if things were to be that way between them now. Yet neither could he bear it if Sarah died in childbirth. Much as it hurt to see her unhappy, painful as it was to be around her without sharing her bed, even as hard as it would be to be married to her and not feel her love, nothing could be as bad as watching her die. Knowing that he had killed her.

Luke's thoughts distracted him so that finally he gave up working and sat down on a bale of hay, his head between his hands. He was so lost in thought that he didn't hear the faint noises outside, didn't sense the presence of the three men who entered the barn.

One of the men's arms brushed against a mule collar hanging on a post, and it made a noise. Luke heard it and turned. He saw them: George Jackson, Harvey Cater, and a third man he didn't know. Their eyes were bright with anger and hatred.

Luke's first, burning thought was that Sarah was unprotected in the house, and he jumped to his feet, cursing himself for being so careless. Damn it! He knew the kind of man Jackson was; he should have known how furious he would be that Micah had gotten away. He should have suspected that Jackson would attack him in retaliation. Sarah had even warned him against going to Jackson's place tomorrow, but he had been so sure of his ability to take care of Jackson that he had hardly listened to her.

The three men hesitated, then came forward warily, their eyes on Luke. Luke grabbed the bale on which he had been sitting and flung it at them to buy himself a moment of time. He whirled and grabbed the nearest weapon he could find, a sturdy, sharp-tined rake. He started toward the men, swinging the wickedly clawed tool. They backed up, disconcerted by his going on the attack. Obviously they had expected him to run for the back door of the barn. But Luke's major concern was getting past them to the house to protect Sarah and the children.

He jumped forward, swinging the rake down in a short chopping motion, and two tines of the rake sliced narrow furrows in Cater's arm. Cater howled, and all three men jumped back. Luke followed, swinging the rake in a wide arc. The thick wood handle whistled ominously through the air as he swung it back and forth, pacing the group backward.

Too late, Luke heard fast, light footsteps behind him, and he realized that Jackson had brought a fourth man with him who must have sneaked in through the back. He started to pivot, but just as he did a heavy body hit him from behind, throwing him to the floor.

Luke rolled, tearing away from his assailant and swinging his fist into the other man's jaw even as he moved. The pain in his back where he had been hit hardly registered; Luke's thoughts were entirely on retrieving his weapon. But even as he lunged across the floor for the rake, the other three were upon him. They hauled him to his feet, fists flying. Luke dodged and punched and kicked. He was a good fighter: coolheaded, quick, and fierce. He knocked the breath out of one man, blackened another's eye, and left all of them with bruises they wouldn't soon forget. He even managed for one brief instant to tear away and race out the front of the barn.

But Jackson caught him around the ankle in a diving leap and he crashed to the ground. The other three piled on top of him. There were simply too many of them. They dragged Luke to his feet, one on either side of him, and twisted his arms up behind his back, immobilizing him. George Jackson glared at him, blood running from a cut on his chin and one cheekbone swelling with a dark bruise. Jackson rammed his fist into Luke's stomach.

"Take him back inside, boys. This time we're goin' ta teach this nigger-loving devil a lesson he ain't goin' ta forget."

✳ *Chapter 23* ✳

Sarah changed into her nightgown and sat down at the vanity to brush out her hair. She felt weary and hopeless; it seemed a tremendous effort even to do this simple task. What did it matter if her hair was brushed until it was burnished? Luke would not see it, would not touch it, would not wind it around his hand or bury his face in it. He was gone from her, truly gone from her. Somehow she had to come to live with that fact.

It took a moment for the faint noises outside to penetrate her reverie. She lifted her head and frowned. She heard a distant voice, followed by several thuds. What in the world was Luke doing?

She rose and went to the window to look out. The barn door stood open, light slanting out of it. She saw the flicker of shadows but could discern nothing. Her unease stirred. She leaned out of the window, squinting her eyes to see. Suddenly a form burst out of the barn, running. Luke! Sarah straightened, apprehension slicing through her.

Right behind him came four men. All of them looked wild and rumpled, and one's arm was stained red. One of the men was George Jackson. Sarah sucked in her breath. She was frozen, unable to move, unable to call out.

The men grabbed Luke, pinning his arms behind him, and Jackson hit him. That broke Sarah's trance. She didn't scream; she had enough control not to do that. She must not give away the element of surprise that was on her side. She hurried out into the hall, her voluminous white nightgown billowing out behind her.

"Cal!" Sarah called out his name as she raced down the stairs. By the time she reached the bottom he was at the top of the steps, rubbing his head sleepily.

"What's the matter?"

"Your grandfather's got Luke out there. He has three men, and they're beating Luke up. I'm going out to stop them. You take care of Emily if she wakes up."

Sarah ran into the sitting room and pulled Luke's rifle from the gun rack. Cal ran down the stairs after her. "I'm going with you. Give me a gun."

Sarah didn't hesitate. "You know how to use one?"

"A little."

She pulled down the shotgun and handed it to him, then gave him a handful of shells. "Can you load it?"

"Yeah." He broke the gun and jammed in two shells while they hurried out of the house. Beside him Sarah was loading the repeating rifle and releasing the safety.

"Don't aim for your grandfather, but for one of the other men," she whispered as they trotted across the yard, their

nightclothes ghostly in the darkness. "I'll take care of
Jackson. At close range, that thing you've got will blast
anything, so don't worry about hitting an exact spot."

"I know." Cal's face was grim and pale, all youthfulness
-gone. Sarah knew he would handle it.

Their feet were bare, and they moved without noise,
running lightly across the dirt of the side yard and up to the
barn. As they drew closer, they could hear the sickening
sounds of fists meeting flesh, but Sarah was wise enough
not to rush in. She paused at the open door of the barn,
fixing the position of her opponents in her mind. She and
Cal stood sideways to the others. Two men held Luke while
Jackson stood in front of him, hitting him. The other man
stood to the side, nursing his bleeding arm. Blood trickled
from the corner of Luke's mouth, and the side of his face
was reddened and scraped, a bruise forming on his cheekbone. An anger so fierce that she wanted to rush blindly at
Jackson, swinging, swept Sarah, and it was all she could do
to retain the calm she needed to win.

Jackson drew back his fist to hit Luke again, and Sarah
stepped into the barn. "Stop it!"

Her voice was sharp and hard. The men turned toward
her, gaping in surprise.

"Sarah!" Fear pierced Luke. "Goddamn it, what are you
doing here? Get out!"

Sarah didn't waste a glance for him. Her eyes were on
George Jackson. "You hit him again, and you're a dead
man. Cal, go around behind him and keep your gun on the
others."

Cal did as she directed, carefully avoiding walking between her and her target. He took up his position, the
shotgun level in his thin arms. He looked at the men who
held Luke with a coldness that was eerie for one of his
years. The two men shifted and glanced from him to their
leader and back to Sarah.

"Let go of Luke or I'll shoot Jackson."

Jackson laughed. "A woman and a boy." It had scared
him when she burst in with the gun, but now that he realized
it was only Turner's wife and Cal, he relaxed. "Can't no
woman do nothin' to us. She won't fire that gun."

Jackson started toward her. "You better just put that gun down, and nothin'll happen to ya."

"It's you it'll happen to, if you take another step."

Again Jackson chuckled. He knew that women didn't have the guts or the gumption to fire a gun at a man.

Sarah sighted down the rifle. Jackson continued to walk toward her. She squeezed the trigger.

The noise echoed around the barn. Jackson fell to the floor and lay writhing, clutching his thigh. Blood oozed between his fingers. His companions stared at him, the blood draining from their faces.

"My husband taught me how to shoot. Perhaps you've heard that he's good with a gun." Sarah walked around to stand beside Cal, facing the men who held Luke. She pointed her gun straight at one of the men. "I don't like to kill, so I shot him in the leg. But if you or anyone else does anything except what I tell you, I'll aim for the heart." She paused, her gaze cool. "Now. Release my husband."

Their hands fell from Luke, and they sidled away. "Not too far," Sarah warned. "I believe the sheriff would like to see all of you."

Luke looked at his wife. She stood in her nightgown, soft and feminine, her hair like a dark, silky cape around her. Her hands on the gun were steady, and her eyes were hard as rocks.

Through an aching mouth, Luke began to chuckle. "Damn, Sarah! You're quite a woman."

It didn't take long for Luke and Cal to tie up the men, and Luke loaded them into the wagon. Jackson was moaning piteously, gripping his leg, but Luke merely tied a tourniquet around his thigh to stop the bleeding, fastened his hands, and shoved him into the wagon with the others.

As soon as he was finished and the danger over, Sarah let the rifle slide from her hands to the floor and sat down heavily on a stack of bales. Luke looked over at her. Her face was white as paper, and he could see her shivering even from a distance. He hurried over to her.

"You all right?"

Sarah nodded, but her shivering increased. Luke smiled with pride and affection. You could trust Sarah not to panic in any crisis, but she was too sensitive not to feel it afterward. She had never shot even an animal before, let alone a man. This evening she had been running on sheer nerve.

He lifted her up and put his arms around her. "You're cold. Come on. I'll walk you back to the house."

"What about them?"

Luke swiveled to look at the men trussed up in the wagon. "I don't think they'll go anywhere. Come on, Cal, let's leave them here for a minute to contemplate their future. Then we'll hitch up the team, and I'll take them in to the sheriff."

They walked back to the house together. "You need something warm inside you," Luke told Sarah.

"I'll fix some coffee." Sarah concentrated on the mundane. She was afraid she might begin to sob and shake to bits if she really thought about what had just happened.

Luke set her down at the kitchen table and took out a bottle of whiskey from a high cabinet. He poured a shot for each of them, even a small one for Cal. Luke tossed his down. Cal and Sarah sipped at theirs, making wry faces. Luke smiled and laid his hand on Sarah's head.

He could hardly believe she was safe. When she had entered the barn, it had almost paralyzed him with fear. Even though she was the one holding a gun, all he could think of was the danger she was in.

"Why in the hell did you do that?" he asked in a combination of tenderness and irritation. "You could have gotten yourself killed."

Sarah's head snapped up and she stared at him in disbelief. A little color returned to her cheeks. "They were hurting you! How could you think I wouldn't stop them?"

His hand caressed her cheek, and he smiled down at her. "Are you all right?"

"Of course I'm all right." Sarah took another, healthier swig of her drink. Indignation was beginning to wipe away her shock. "You're the one who's been beaten."

She stood up, her hand going to Luke's face, turning his head this way and that under the light. "I better put something on that cut on your cheek. You're going to have one beauty of a black eye tomorrow, too." She looked at the scrape on his chin.

"I feel fine." There were aches all over his body and face that Luke knew would begin to hurt like hell later, but right now he hardly noticed them. It was far more important to drink in the sight of Sarah's face, filled with tender love and concern. "I have to take Jackson to James to get the bullet out, anyway. I'll let him look at my cut. All right?"

"All right."

Luke sighed. "I better get going before that son of a bitch bleeds to death." He turned to Cal. "You stay here, and look after Sarah and Emily."

Cal nodded. Luke bent down and put his arms around Cal's shoulders. "You acted like a man tonight, protecting Sarah. I'm proud of you."

"I'd a killed him if he'd—" The boy's voice cracked.

"I know you would have. I couldn't ask for a better son." He released the boy and stepped back. "Now, why don't you go up and check on Emily? Make sure she hasn't awakened and gotten scared by the commotion."

Cal nodded and left the room. Luke suspected he would be glad to reach the sleeping tranquillity of Emily's bedroom. Luke turned back to Sarah.

"I'm a little surprised you charged in there tonight. I thought you'd about washed your hands of me. You had a right to."

"How can you say that?" Sarah's eyes were infinitely sad. "Don't you know, even after all this time? I love you. I love you more than anything. Whether you do things I don't want you to or not. Even if you walked away and left me here flat, I'd still love you—and wait for you to come back. You're my life, Luke. You have been for four years, and you will be for the rest of time."

Luke swallowed. He couldn't speak for a moment. Finally he said, "And I love you."

"I know."

He nodded, too full of roiling emotions to express them. "I'll be back soon."

Sarah sat back down at the table. She took another sip of

whiskey. Then she laid her head down on her arms and let herself give way to the shivers.

It was almost one o'clock when Luke returned from town. The light in the kitchen was still on. A small smile touched his lips. Sarah was up waiting for him. He unhitched the wagon and turned the mules loose in the corral, then went inside.

Sarah sat at the kitchen table, her head pillowed on her arms on the table, sound asleep. Luke stopped abruptly, his hand reaching back to keep the screen door from closing with a bang. He stood quietly, watching Sarah. She looked innocent, almost childlike, in the high-collared white cotton gown, with her hair tumbled down around her face and shoulders, softly sleeping.

But he knew full well the lushly feminine body beneath the gown, the sensual woman beneath the innocent appearance. A slow smile curved his lips at the thought. God, he felt good right now, male and strong and sure of his world in a way he hadn't known in months. It was as though the events of this evening had burned away his blindness and shocked him out of the grim grip of fear and guilt. This was his life. This was his woman. This was where he belonged.

Sarah's eyes flickered open as he watched. She glanced up and saw Luke, and she sat up groggily, stretching her cramped muscles. "Hello."

"Hello." Luke continued to watch her.

Sarah went still. There was something in his eyes . . .

Her breath came a little faster in her throat. Anticipation and fear that she was wrong coiled within her. She searched for something to say. But when Luke looked at her like that, there was nothing she could say.

"Luke?" She rose to her feet.

"Yes?" He walked toward her slowly. His eyes were on her, intent and direct, as though nothing else existed in the world. In truth, at that moment, nothing did for him. His blood was pumping hard through his veins, thrumming in his ears.

Sarah waited, her chest rising and falling with each sharp,

short breath. Luke stopped inches away from her. She stared
up into his eyes, her stomach jumping crazily. There was a
deep, compelling hunger in his eyes, and something more—
something she hadn't seen in a long time. A sureness, an
anticipation of satisfaction; the look of a man who not only
wanted her, but also who intended to take her to bed and
ease that desire.

She wet her lips a little nervously. His eyes followed the
movement, the lids drooping sensually. He brushed the back
of his hand down her chest, grazing her breasts with his
knuckles. He watched her nipples tighten in response to his
touch, and his face shifted subtly. Sarah waited, hardly
daring to move lest she break the exquisite intensity of the
moment.

He took her hand in his. "Let's go upstairs."

Sarah nodded without speaking. Luke picked up the
kerosene lamp to light their way, and hand in hand they
climbed the stairs to their bedroom. With every step they
took, the heavy ache in Sarah's abdomen grew. She knew
Luke must feel the faint trembling of her hand in his.

He did, and knowing that his mere touch aroused her so
made his own passion all the more fierce. Months of
unfulfilled desire gathered in him, long night after night of
lying in bed and aching for Sarah.

Luke closed the bedroom door behind them and turned to
face her. He couldn't say anything, but he didn't need to.
Sarah could read in his face how beautiful he found her,
how much he wanted her, how deep his love ran. He linked
his hands in hers and leaned down to kiss her. Their bodies
touched nowhere except their hands and lips, and it was an
exquisite, delightful torment. He kissed her as gently as a
man might kiss a maiden the first time, with restraint and
tenderness, but behind it lay the knowledge of the fierce
passion that had so often roared between them. They knew
each other, body and soul.

Luke's hands clenched on hers. His lips burrowed in.
Sarah's mouth opened, inviting him in, and his tongue
plunged into her. Passion shot through him, as hot, swift,
and encompassing as a grass fire. The sweet anticipation of
pleasure was gone, burned away in an instant, and Luke was
driven by hard need.

Luke dropped her hands and wrapped his arms around her like a vise. He kissed her deeply, his tongue ravaging her mouth, and his body moved into hers as if he sought to shove right through her skin and become part of her. Blindly he walked her back until they slammed into the closed door. His mouth was hungry, undeniable. His body squeezed the breath out of her.

Sarah gloried in it. She had waited so long and wished so much to feel Luke's male strength, his hungry impatience. She pressed back up into him with all her own strength, twining her arms around his neck and digging her fingers into his shoulders. His shirt gathered beneath her restless, seeking fingers, and she pulled and tugged, aching to feel his naked flesh underneath her fingertips once more.

Luke moaned, turning his head to slant their kiss the other way, working his lips over hers. His hands came up to dig into her hair, his fingertips pressing against her scalp, bunching her hair up in great handfuls. He wanted to look at her, touch her, kiss her, all at once and everywhere. His desire was shattering. Uncontrollable.

He pulled away, gulping in great draughts of air. He had to have her now. He could not wait for the sweet exploration of the senses; he was too desperate. He looked at Sarah, struggling to bring himself back under control, to take her with time and care. Then he saw in Sarah's eyes that she wanted to wait no more than he. She desired him with the same fierce immediacy. He chuckled, and there was an exultation in the sound. His eyes holding hers, Luke reached out with both hands and hooked them in the neck of her gown. With a single quick motion he tore down and apart, ripping the front of her gown.

Sarah smiled and shrugged her shoulders to let the gown slide off down her arms. She loved being naked before him. She loved the demand of his gesture.

She walked around Luke to the bed, her hair swaying invitingly across her hips, and he followed, struggling to get out of his own clothing as he went. His boots were kicked off, his coveralls and underwear dropped as he walked. Buttons popped beneath his fingers, and he cursed softly, vividly, at the impediments of material and fastenings.

Sarah chuckled and turned to help him. But her fingers

were as much hindrance as help, for they were easily sidetracked into exploring the hard brown flesh that each unfastening revealed. With his shirt only half unbuttoned and the cuffs still fastened, her hands left the buttons to slide inside his shirt and roam his chest. Her hands went up to the hard shelf of his collarbone and glided across his shoulders. His skin jumped beneath her touch, and she moved forward to press her lips against his chest. He groaned, and she felt the insistent prodding of his manhood against her bare abdomen.

Sarah's hands swept down his arms, shoving down his shirt, but it caught at his wrists, the cuffs still fastened, and pooled around his hips. That was enough for her; it bared his chest and arms to her mouth and hands. But it frustrated Luke, hampering his movements, and with an impatient noise he jerked at the final buttons and sent the shirt sliding to the floor.

He kissed her long and deeply, lifting her into bed as he did so. He slid in beside Sarah and began to kiss her all over, his mouth wild and sweet on her flesh, tasting every bit of the goodness he had denied himself so long. His tongue circled her nipples in loving strokes, turning them hard and thrusting. Softly he blew upon the wet buds and watched them prickle even more. He drew her nipple into the heated cave of his mouth and began to suck gently. Fiery sensations shot down through Sarah into her abdomen, increasing the heat there. Her legs moved restlessly, crossing and uncrossing.

His hand slipped down and touched the softness between her legs. She was hot and slick with the moisture of desire. His fingers trembled. He could wait no longer. He had to come inside her; had to feel her around him. He rolled on top of her, parting her legs. For an instant he paused, the tip of his engorged shaft teasing at her supremely soft flesh. He gazed down into Sarah's eyes, his look searing into her soul, and then, his eyes still locked to hers, he moved into her.

Sarah gasped at the first sweet stretching of her tender flesh, the delicate expansion as he pushed into her with infinite slowness. They felt each inch of pleasurable friction, each sparkling sensation as he opened her to him once more, claiming, filling, surrendering. At last he was buried in her fully, and she was hot and tight around him.

Luke buried his face against her neck. "Oh, my love, my love." His words were barely intelligible. His skin quivered.

He pulled almost out with equal slowness, and Sarah made a noise of protest, moving her hips up so as not to let him go. He thrust back into her, quick and hard, and she whimpered softly at the mind-robbing pleasure. He began to stroke within her, and Sarah dug in her heels, arching up against him, her hips moving frantically. Her world spun wildly, and she was aware of nothing but the unbelievable pleasure and joy building within her. He thrust into her again and again, hard and fast, racing to the ecstasy that danced tantalizingly just out of his reach. Sarah's legs wrapped around him. Her nails scored his back. He was as unaware of the pain as she was of doing it.

The knot inside Sarah grew and tightened with each jolt, and she felt as if she were reaching, reaching, desperate for what she knew would come. Then, at last, it exploded within her. A soft noise escaped her lips, and she stiffened beneath him. The soft pulsation of her inner explosion touched off Luke's own, and he groaned, shuddering under the enormous force of his release.

He collapsed against her, slick with sweat, his skin quivering under the aftershocks of pleasure. "Sarah." She felt his whisper against her skin.

Sarah wrapped her arms around him tightly. "I love you, I love you."

She never wanted him to move from her. This was all she needed in the world. Luke had come home to her.

It was later than usual when Sarah awakened the next morning. She was alone in her bed and for one confused, painful moment, she thought she had dreamed last night. Then she saw Luke standing at the window, leaning against the sill and looking out. She lay for a moment, admiring his lean form.

"Good morning," she said almost shyly.

He turned, his familiar smile lighting his face. Sarah

realized how rarely she had seen that smile the last few months. "Good morning." He strolled back to the bed. "Sleep well?"

There was a knowing quality to his grin that made Sarah blush even as it set up a warmth in her loins. "Very."

Luke sat down on the side of the bed and bent to kiss her. "I love you." He brushed her tangled hair back from her face.

"I know." She smiled up at him and reached up to tenderly touch his bruised face. "Are you all right?"

He shrugged and shook his head. "It's nothing. I've had a lot worse before. It doesn't even make a dent on how happy I am."

"Are you? Really? Are you back for good?"

"For good. And I don't imagine there's any man happier than I am right now."

Sarah swallowed against the lump in her throat. She had a million questions, but she was afraid to question a miracle. Luke saw the curiosity and the hesitation in her eyes, and he smiled.

"You're wondering what happened?" Sarah nodded. "I'm not sure exactly. All of a sudden last night I saw how wrong I'd been." He pulled her into his arms and held her, kissing the top of her head. "What a tiger you are! When you burst into that barn last night, your hair flying, wearing just your nightclothes and carrying that rifle—I was so proud of you, so crazy in love with you. You're right. You don't belong on a pedestal. You're real flesh and blood. Not fragile, not an angel. I thought, that's my Sarah, fierce, loyal, and tough as an old boot sometimes. And I knew I wanted what I had: you as you are, not some ideal, not some statue."

He paused and sighed. "But you scared the hell out of me, too. I could see you getting killed right in front of my eyes. I felt angry and helpless because I couldn't protect you. Afterwards, I realized that no matter what I did, no matter how hard I tried, I couldn't protect you from everything. Something like that could happen, no matter how well I guarded you against myself. I finally understood that your life isn't mine to control. I can't make you stay alive if that's what's fated for you. I could lose you for a hundred

other reasons, and all I'd get from staying away from you is
making whatever time we have together miserable."

"Oh, Luke." Sarah squeezed him tightly, choked with
emotion.

"I thought about it all the way into town and back.
There's danger in your getting pregnant; I could lose you,
and I don't know what I'd do if that happened. But you are
willing to risk it, and it's your decision to make. You're a
fighter, Sarah. You aren't ruled by fear; you meet life
head-on." He chuckled. "I bet if you'd been in the same
situation as Dovie yesterday, you'd have jumped up on that
horse behind me, same as she did."

"Of course I would!" Sarah exclaimed, jerking away to
glare at him indignantly. "How could you think I'd do
anything else?"

"I know. I know. You're the fiercest woman anywhere.
Come back here, lioness." He pulled her back into his
arms. "I used to be like that, ready to face whatever danger
there was. But the past few years, since I've been married
to you, I've gotten scared. I've been so happy that I was
more and more scared of losing it. Since you lost the baby
I've been run by my fear. All I could think about was how I
couldn't stand to lose you. No matter if it made us both
miserable, no matter if it made you hate me, I had to do
anything I could to keep from losing you. But when I finally
realized that I can't control it, I knew I had to put away my
fear. All I can do is face it, no matter what comes, like you
do, and enjoy the good and fight the bad."

Sarah rubbed her cheek against his chest. "I love you so.
I don't ever want to be parted from you again, in any way."

"We won't be. No matter what, we'll be together. I could
die tomorrow, or you could, and we'd still be a part of each
other." He kissed her, and they drew apart, smiling. "You
know, I was standing at the window this morning, thinking
about a long time ago when I finally admitted I loved you.
Then the rain came and saved our crop. And we looked out
and saw a rainbow."

Sarah nodded. "I remember."

"You always believed in that rainbow. But deep down I
didn't. I couldn't. I didn't think I was good enough. That

didn't deserve you. You were too fine for me. I was rough and crude and poor and uneducated."

"Oh, Luke!"

"I felt better about myself than before—because of you. I got to where I thought maybe I was as good as other people. But when you lost the baby and almost died, I knew it was because of me. Because I wasn't worthy of you. I had never really believed in my soul that the good things would remain, that I had really changed. But last night, you said you loved me and would always love me, no matter what. And I thought to myself—Turner, if a woman like Sarah loves you that much, if she believes you're worth something, how can you say that's wrong? A woman like you doesn't give her love to somebody worthless. I realized the rainbow was there for me, too, and it was just me that was keeping me from seeing it."

Tears ran down Sarah's cheeks. She reached up and kissed him all over his face—brief, hard kisses that spoke of her love and determination. "You're the best man in the world, and I love you to death."

She kissed him hard, and their lips opened, tongues meeting and twining. When at last they pulled away, Sarah said breathlessly, "We're going to have a fine life. We have a home and each other and two lovely children and maybe someday more. That's all I'll ever want in life."

Luke kissed her again, pulling her back flat onto the bed. He raised up on his elbow and gazed down at her, his hand trailing over her bare skin. Sarah giggled. "Luke! It's late. What about the children?"

He grinned. "Why, you just said what wonderful kids they are. Cal'll take care of Emily. They'll be all right. Right now you are exactly where you belong."

Sarah smiled up at him and curled her arms around his neck. "You're exactly right."

She pulled him down to her.